PENGUIN BOOKS

THE SERPENT GARDEN

Judith Merkle Riley, the author of *The Master of All Desires*, *The Oracle Glass*, *A Vision of Light*, and *In Pursuit of the Green Lion*, teaches political science at Claremont McKenna College. She lives in Claremont, California.

JUDITH MERKLE RILEY

The Serpent Garden

PENGUIN BOOKS

This is a work of historical fiction.
With the exception of well-known historical personages,
any resemblance to persons living or dead
is purely coincidental.

PENGUIN BOOKS
Published by the Penguin Group
Penguin Books USA Inc., 375 Hudson Street,
New York, New York 10014, U.S.A.
Penguin Books Ltd, 27 Wrights Lane, London W8 5TZ, England
Penguin Books Australia Ltd, Ringwood, Victoria, Australia
Penguin Books Canada Ltd, 10 Alcorn Avenue,
Toronto, Ontario, Canada M4V 3B2
Penguin Books (N.Z.) Ltd, 182–190 Wairau Road,
Auckland 10, New Zealand

Penguin Books Ltd, Registered Offices:
Harmondsworth, Middlesex, England

First published in the United States of America by Viking Penguin,
a division of Penguin Books USA Inc. 1996
Published in Penguin Books 1997

3 5 7 9 10 8 6 4

THE LIBRARY OF CONGRESS HAS CATALOGUED THE HARDCOVER AS FOLLOWS:
Riley, Judith Merkle.
The serpent garden/by Judith Merkle Riley.
p. cm.
ISBN 0-670-86661-X (hc.)
ISBN 0 14 02.5880 9 (pbk.)
I. Title.
PS3568.I3794S47 1996
813'.54—dc20   95–36067

Printed in the United States of America
Set in Adobe Centaur
Designed by Francesca Belanger

In memory of the life and work
of
Anne Trudeau

Acknowledgments

With special thanks to my daughter, Elizabeth Riley, for her thoughtful and insightful review of the manuscript in several stages of production, as well as to my editor, Pam Dorman, for her acute observations and perceptive comments. I would also like to thank Carolyn Carlson for her careful and thoughtful editorial work. I am grateful as well for the support and encouragement of my agent, Jean Naggar, and my family. And to those outposts and guardians of civilization, our libraries, my appreciation and gratitude now and always.

The Serpent Garden

The First Portrait

*Flemish School. ca. 1490/1510. The Wedding at Cana. 13½ ×
12½". Unfinished pen-and-wash drawing. Private collection.*

*This unattributed drawing in the Flemish style appears to be the work of
a follower of Van der Weyden. Note the derivative composition (see plate 32,*
The Wedding Supper*) and the incomplete understanding of human
anatomy, especially in the depiction of the lower limbs of the central figures.*

—*Michaels, P.* Flemish Drawings of the Renaissance

It was in the year 1514 that fate and my sins sent me into the world and thence to the court of the King of France, a very womb of intrigue from which no respectable English widow such as I was might hope to escape unscathed. Little steps lead to the pit, they say, and I must admit I was overfond of nice clothes and the better sort of wine, to say nothing of the great wickedness of making indelicate paintings for the sake of the handsome sound of money chinking in my purse on market day. They led me a long way, my sins, from a life of quiet if rather boring virtue studying drawing and the life of the Virgin in my father's house to the worldly deviousness required of a limner to gentlefolk and paintrix to princes. Ah, that sounds grand, doesn't it? Vanity, yes, that's another sin of yours, Susanna, I say to myself. And that doesn't even count the greater ones. Sloth. Shameless deception. And carnal love. But though I know I should repent, when I think on temptation and where it led me, I find it hard to be sorry.

But I am a painter and the daughter of painters, so I will begin the tale of my transgressions with this sketch that was meant to be for a wedding-portrait, but turned out to be the last drawing I did before I left my father's house behind his coffin. He was a master artificer, my father, brought over the water by old King Henry to repaint the saints in his chapel at Sheen. Being Flemish, which means stubborn and contrary, he taught me his trade just as if he had never left the old country, instead of raising me to English female ways. In this first portrait, I never finished the bridegroom, who has no features but just a splash of wash to show the facial planes and a gown in the Flemish style. I intended to give him the features of my betrothed, Rowland Dallet, Master of the Painter-Stainers' Guild of the City of London. I also intended to make the bride's gown red with a blue underskirt in the finished painting besides putting my own features on her face, but she turned out colorless as well as featureless. And now that I look back on it, I think a stuffed Flemish gown would have done better than Master Dallet for a husband. But then, things would not have happened as they did.

ONE

In the hour past midnight three bobbing lanterns could be seen making slow progress through a dug-up area where a new building was rising in the ruins of the Outer Temple. Two of the men with lanterns were carrying shovels. The third, tall and richly dressed, was guiding an old blind man holding a long, forked dowsing rod. They paused at a pit that revealed a section of the octagonal foundation wall of the ancient tower once called Le Bastelle.

"My lords, I feel the rod dip. There is precious metal there, beneath the earth." Blind Barnabas, the dowser, hesitated.

"It must be down there, Sir Septimus," said the swarthy young man in the leather doublet and muddy boots, "where they're putting in the foundations for the new hall." He held his lantern high to inspect the newly dug pit.

"Well, what are you waiting for, old man?" Ludlow the lawyer, heavily cloaked against the cold, peered over the edge.

"My lords, my payment," the old man quavered. "You promised to take me home once I had found it."

"As indeed we will, once it is dug up." The voice of the blind man's guide was suave. It was no ordinary treasure that could bring Sir Septimus Crouch, magistrate, antiquarian, and master of the conjuration of demons by the method of Honorius out beyond the safety of the City wall after dark. Here, beneath the ruins, lay one of the infernal's most powerful demons of destruction, chained as guardian to a treasure chest by an ancient spell. And both of them soon to be mine, gloated Sir Septimus.

"It's too cold for my old bones. The wind bites through me, standing here. Poor Barnabas has no hood."

"You shall have a hat of rabbit fur after this night's work, that I promise," said Crouch.

"Oh, my lord, a thousand blessings on you. In truth, you are the greatest gentleman that ever lived . . ."

"Enough. Master Dallet, you and Master Ludlow descend and dig there, where the rod points. I'll keep watch up here." Ludlow, the lawyer, cast a bitter look at his patron's face. Ruined and bought, he thought. I have sold my soul. And now I must labor beside this pretty tradesman. Look at him there, that painter, how he sweats, his eyes, how he hates Crouch. What brought him into the diabolist's power?

Pallid and triumphant, seamed with the lines of old vice, Crouch's face loomed above them. Cold green eyes were surmounted by eyebrows overgrown like twin thickets of poisonous weeds. His hair, dark mingled with silver, rose from his head in a smoky mockery of a halo. At the corners of his forehead, two broad, curling white streaks mingled with the dark, shining in the lantern light very like the curling horns of a ram, or perhaps a devil.

"Speed you, Master Dallet, and cease to regret your white hands there. What is beneath will repay your cares a thousandfold. Mistress, wife, tailor, and jeweler satisfied all at a blow. Whatever other venture could extend such promise?"

"Equal shares of everything, remember," said Ludlow, finishing his descent into the pit to join the master painter.

"Three ways, I said, and so it shall be," said Crouch, his voice smooth and reassuring. At the bottom of the pit, he could see only the feeble glimmer of two lanterns, and hear the crunch and clatter of metal digging dirt and stone. You, he thought down into the pit. Awake.

A trickle of life began to flow into the desiccated, captive thing below, and it drank greedily at the thin essence of avarice and hate seeping through the earth. Crouch could sense something dank and feel the presence of an alien mind, tentative and wispy, like the first stirrings of an evil thought. The hair rose on the back of his neck, and his spirit exulted.

"It's solid here," came Ludlow's voice. "It's a pavement."

There is a ring beneath the black stone. The thought came from the depths. Why, thought Sir Septimus, the thing is seeking me out. Excellent.

"Look for the ring beneath the black stone," said Crouch aloud. Ah, my dark friend, he thought, soon you, too, will be my creature.

I am Belphagor the Mighty. I belong to no man.

Nonsense, thought Crouch. He fingered the amulet, engraved with cabalistic signs, once again. *"Onaim, perantes, rasonastos,"* he recited. The words encircled the thing in the chest below with a living, shimmering wall.

You bastard.

But of course. Did you think you were dealing with a fool? Crouch suddenly laughed aloud, so that the blind man started in fear.

Below in the pit, a heavy stone moved with a grating, scraping sound, and the scent of something old and rotted rose from the cavity it revealed. The circle of lantern light shone on a blackened lead coffer, sealed tight with some sort of ancient flux.

"It's an alchemist's seal," said the artist, kneeling to inspect and touch the curious object. "The box is lead. This is no ordinary treasure." There was a scrambling sound as the two men raised the box from the pit.

Master Dallet, kneeling in the mud, was working at the flux sealing the box with his knife. Suddenly there was a hissing sound, and the lantern flickered and was nearly extinguished in a sudden icy wind. "Who's there?" cried the blind man with a start.

Food. I need food. I have slept too long. Belphagor remembered that he had errands, but he had forgotten what they were. Something.

"Where's the gold?" cried the lawyer, scrabbling in the decaying trash in the box, a handful of blackened coins, some old bundles wrapped in rotten silk.

Delicious, thought Belphagor, as he sucked up the rage like hot wine. He was feeling stronger.

"This old cup is silver," said Dallet, scratching the tarnish with his fingernail.

"Their sacramental chalice," said Crouch, taking it from his hand. Crouch smiled as he ran a hand over the obscene figures chased beneath the cup's brim.

Beware. He's stealing it from you. Greed and envy, with a tasty spice of hate, flowed toward him. How easy it was, even after centuries of sleep, to stir men to the evil passions on which he fed. *As clever as ever,* thought Belphagor. *I haven't lost the touch.* The demon felt himself gaining substance, like a fine, acid mist. He stretched.

"That's valuable!" cried the lawyer, rising to seize the cup. Taking advantage of the lawyer's distraction, the painter had lifted a curious, decaying bundle from the box. The wrappings fell away to reveal the jeweled binding of an old book, its silky vellum almost undamaged by mildew.

Keep the book. It is what that old man wants most of all.

"You won't cheat me of this, Sir Septimus," said Rowland Dallet, clutching to him the strange old volume that had lain in the bottom of the chest. "You've taken the cup. I'm keeping the book."

"Equal shares!" cried Ludlow.

"That book is mine! Give it here before you regret it!" As Crouch moved toward him, the painter stepped beyond his grasp. Above them, Belphagor sucked up the confusion and rage like a tonic, growing stronger even as he fed the quarrel. The faint outline of form—limbs, a head—began to be visible as a kind of rolling, boiling smoke. The shimmering wall began to flicker.

"Then have your fair share only, you pander!" cried the painter, and with his heavy knife he slashed through the faded gilding of the calfskin spine of the book, severing it into three pieces. Flinging two into the mud, he held the center portion close to his chest. "I, for one, keep my bargains, unlike you *gentlemen*." The antiquarian's face grew dark with hate.

"The book of mysteries is mine," he said. "Mine by right."

"Then purchase back our shares, if you want it so much. We agreed this time to divide all, and I swear, you'll never cheat me again." Knife in hand, the younger man backed away from his patron, picking up the lantern he had set on the ground.

Kill him, urged the demon.

"I'll kill you for this," said Crouch, putting his hand on the Italian stiletto he always carried.

"Come near me and I'll burn it," cried Dallet, holding it near the lantern. As Crouch paused, horrified, the painter turned and fled into the night.

Lawyer and magistrate together watched the painter's flickering light vanish into the dark. Suddenly the demon's whisper, like a thought, came into Ludlow's mind.

Why settle for just one share?

The lawyer's brain began to hatch a plan. An anonymous letter, he thought. I'll send it to the husband of the painter's mistress. He'll kill them both, and my hands will be clean. And the painter's widow will know nothing of the fragment's value. I'll be able to buy it from her for a song.

Clever man. The demon was beginning to be restored to his old, comfortable, original form, dankly smoky and drifting, swelled with the evil energies he had generated around himself. His lower limbs, furry and greenish, swelled against the shimmering circle that held him, blotting it out here and there.

"My lords, have you forgotten poor old Barnabas's reward? Will you show me home now?" the blind man's voice quavered.

"Your reward?" said Crouch, setting down his lantern and taking his knife from his belt. "Why, of course," he said as he drove the stiletto directly into the old man's heart. At the deed, Belphagor expanded with a burst of energy and the circle around him shattered. Too late Ludlow's cry of horror warned Crouch. Looking skyward, the diabolist knight let out a howl of disappointment as he saw that Belphagor the demon had burst free.

Raging with frustration, the failed demon-master watched as a misshapen form rose higher into the night sky above him, blotting out a patch of stars from his view. The dark thing quivered and paused, as if trying to decide where to go. Then it began to drift toward the walls of the sleeping City, leaving behind only an echo of metallic laughter.

TWO

It was really the fault of the rain. I would never have listened to the temptations of strangers, and foreigners, too, if the rain hadn't been going on so long. Long rain steals away the light and leaves everything gray and possibly mildewed, and you can't get out to church to see who has new shoes or who has recut her bodice in the new French style because they wouldn't even wear them anyway, on account of the weather. So rain had spoiled my mood, and made me crazy for change. Love of novelty and amusement is a bad thing in a woman, for it leads her from duty. Or so says my book, *The Good Wyfe's Book of Manners*, which my mother gave me long ago for the time I would be married and which is as stuffed as a sausage with wise advice as well as excellent recipes for dainty dishes, medicines, and soap. I used to study this book every day, being young, and lacking my dear mother's advice, for I wanted to bring honor to her memory with my fine and praiseworthy housekeeping. Also I thought my husband, Master Rowland Dallet of the Painter-Stainers' Guild of London, would love me better if my cooking would come out. The book assured me that he would. It was just a matter of reading it correctly, which up to that time had eluded me.

Now the day the strangers came was late in March of the Year of Our Lord 1514, and it had been raining five days straight almost like Noah's flood. My husband had been away on business the whole time, and I was just perishing with needing to go out.

"I hate rain, Nan, I do hate it. Here it's supposed to be spring, and it's very near as cold and dark as winter, and there's not a spot of green anywhere outside, and besides that, this poky little room gets duller by the hour."

"You must always remember, you can't have flowers without the rain," said Nan, looking up from her knitting where she sat on the bench by the fire. Nan's face was serious because it nearly always was.

She was so much older, you see, and people who are thin and old and serious like that always pray a lot, because they have renounced the shams of the world for higher thoughts about God and the Devil. Myself, I loved the shams of the world, but I loved Nan, too, who was my nursemaid when I was small and helped with the house, or rather, I should say rooms, now that I had become a married woman. It would not be fair to call her a servant even though I paid her, or, to be really honest, I would have paid her, if my husband had given me more household money.

"But it's dark, Nan. Everything's so gray. And that rattle, rattle, rattle! It's just going to make me lunatic! I need to hear the birds again, and talk to people. Spring! I need spring!" I leaned over my mother's big old brass-bound chest that used to have my wedding linen in it and threw open the shutters with a crash. The wind flew in and the rain spattered straight in my face. Below our front window, the Sign of the Standing Cat clattered and swayed as the rain beat on it. The gutter in the center of Fleet Lane rushed as deep as a river. The brightly painted housefronts shone gray and dismal beneath the sheets of water that tore down from the sky. Not a soul was out. So I leaned out the window and shook my fist and shouted up at the streaming heavens.

"Rain, stop now! I need the sun! I want light!"

"Hush this very instant!" cried Nan, pulling me in by the skirts. "Do you want people to think you've gone insane? You could get wet and ill! Think of the baby. Come in at once and stop shouting!" she pulled the shutters closed with a thump. "Oh, just look at you," she scolded, "you're all wet. What will become of you? I promised your mother I wouldn't let you be foolish. You know I did. Now settle down and have sense, for once. You wouldn't appreciate the sunshine half as much without the rain."

"Yes I would," I grumbled. "I love beautiful things. I don't need to see ugly ones just to like the nice ones better."

"You are entirely too interested in what shows on the surface for your own good," muttered Nan, who had earned the right of criticism not only by long service but by great forbearance on that little matter of wages.

"Master Dallet says that the appearance of things is very important, and that is why he has to take such great care with his clothes. Besides, I should not be seen to burden him when he must give seemly attendance on princes and patrons." My head and shoulders still damp, I wiped off my face on my sleeve and sat down on the bench by the fire. Mending was looking up at me from the basket by my ankles. I gave it an evil stare back.

"I suppose he considers that sufficient reason to spend your dowry at the tailor's and pawn your mother's wedding ring."

"That is the sacrifice that a woman must make to ensure her husband's great success and fortune. A virtuous woman will be repaid with honor a hundredfold for her uncomplaining patience, says my book. And when he brings home a purse of gold and buys me a silk dress, you'll be sorry you ever let a word of complaint pass your lips." I stuck my feet, clad in heavy stockings and homely old clogs, straight out in front of me, not touching the ground, the better to see my homespun skirt, dyed black in mourning and spotted with the gesso that *would* escape my apron, and imagined it transformed into sapphire blue silk, bravely spotted with embroidery. I was certain back then that all this was sure to happen someday, when he attained success because of my labors. And I did labor, more than any other woman, for another woman would not have known his art. I boiled glue for him and I gessoed his tables and made his brushes and ground his paints just as I had learned to do in my father's house. But I never painted anything of my own anymore because it was not proper for a married lady who must live only for her husband's good and not her own selfish pleasures.

"Ah, God, that I should have ever lived to see this day," said Nan, looking down at her knitting and making the needles go faster and faster, clickety click. "Three days already at that godless Mistress Pickering's, heaven give me strength!" Nan always said things like that, especially calling on heaven, because she was always full of worries—most of them imagined. But I would have been very sorry if she quit worrying about death and the devil and doomsday, because that would have meant she was getting sick, and with Mother and Father dead I did not want to lose Nan, because then I would just have had Master Dallet and he didn't talk much.

"Oh, Nan, always so suspicious! He told me himself he is finishing an important portrait of Captain Pickering's old mother, which Mistress Pickering is planning to hang in a place of honor to surprise him when he gets home. I think that's *lovely*. That is exactly like the part where it says that a woman should always plan elegant and thoughtful surprises to bring pleasure to her husband." I threaded my needle as I spoke and took the darning egg from on top of the mending in the basket.

"And I suppose he told you himself that Mistress Pickering was ugly, too."

"Oh, no, he would never say anything to unflattering about a patroness, but he says she has a great deal of trouble getting around on her club foot, and that she must come very close to the portrait to see through her spectacles, and I said I hoped he was gracious to her and he said he would take care to follow my advice. So you see I know she is very plain, although Master Dallet always tries to be tactful about people with money."

Nan sighed as if she were the greatest martyr on earth, which was one of her favorite things to do. It clears the lungs and lightens the digestion, said Goody Forster, who is a very clever midwife and also sells a powder that will make you rich if you burn it at midnight when there is a full moon. I had got some from her, but it hadn't worked yet. And I did need something to pay Nan so she could send money to her brother who was in prison most unjustly and also for the baby, who was very badly in need of a cradle and swaddling bands.

I became very upset thinking about money and jabbed my thumb with the darning needle, leaving a big drop of blood on Master Dallet's brown stocking. But just as I was rubbing it in so it wouldn't show, there was a heavy sound of boots downstairs, which was very surprising, because men in boots did not come to the Sign of the Standing Cat very often. Ordinarily there were just women there, upstairs and down. That is because when Master Dallet got the lease of the house, it was on the condition that Mistress Hull, who is a widow of the Painter-Stainer's Guild, could live in the downstairs room for her lifetime. The lease said we had the use of the kitchen once a week for laundry, and the right to come through the shop on the ground floor and up the stairs at the back of it to our own rooms, which were only two: one for Master Dallet's studio, and one for a bedroom, parlor, dining hall, and everything else all squashed together.

This arrangement made Master Dallet malcontent because he wanted all the space for himself to have a large studio with several apprentices someday, and also because the widow and her gossipy grown-up daughter had the shop filled with very ugly paintings left by the late Master Hull which my husband feared might be taken for his and spoil his custom. Besides that, they had spread out many strange objects they had made to sell, such as knitted women's sleeves and lumpy mittens, which Master Dallet said lowered the tone of the whole establishment.

But the oddest thing about what went on downstairs was that besides women coming to buy pins, mostly it was a lot of monks and other gentlemen of religion who came to the shop. When I asked Mistress Hull why monks wanted pins, she said they came for the devotional paintings left by the late Master Hull. Now that was the greatest mystery of all, I thought, because those paintings never changed. The Christ in Chains was in the same place every day, and that poor, ugly Madonna was dustier all the time, and the Sebastian that had his eyes painted on different levels just squinted away in the corner no matter how many religious gentlemen came and went.

So you see my ears just pricked up when I heard boots clumping instead of slippy-sloppy sandals. That could only mean one thing, and that was the bailiff had come at last to collect our furniture for my husband's debt, and I knew Nan thought so too. Her head popped up and her nose quivered like an old hound that smells danger. Now we could hear the sound of men's voices below, and the voice of the widow's daughter spitefully directing the strangers upward to our rooms. We couldn't hear what they said because that dreadful rain was rattling on the closed shutters. The fire was low and cast little light, leaving the room all dim and gloomy.

"Oh, Nan, I'll hide in back and you just tell them Master Dallet's not home—he left very suddenly for the Continent. A big commission—he'll be able to pay everything he owes."

"Which they'll believe about as much as I do," grumbled Nan. "No, I have every intention of telling them exactly where to find Master Dallet this time." Nan sounded just as spiteful as the widow's daughter, though I wasn't sure why.

But the strangers that Nan showed up the stairs and into the bedroom did not appear to be bill collectors. They paused to peer into the open door to the studio. I watched them look with puzzled eyes at the plaster models of hands and arms, the finely made drawings, and the bright colors on the half-finished portraits of fashionable persons, so handsome and neatly painted compared to the dusty old saints downstairs. They eyed the cupboards and shelves with the boxes and distended bladders containing colors and medium, as if they would be able to judge the quality of work that might come from them.

The floor of the studio was without rushes, scrubbed down to the boards with lye and water weekly by Nan and me, the walls fresh washed with turpentine and chalk, and the whole room spotless. You see, this is how a house must be kept if anyone is going to be making miniatures and illumination, for in fine work the greatest danger is of dust, the second greatest danger being of dampness in the breath, to say nothing of gross coughing and blowing. And Master Dallet was more than just an easel painter who could turn out a neat portrait in stained canvas or a wood tablet. At the tall worktable by the window, he prepared portraits in miniature, an art that my father had made fashionable in England when he first came from Flanders to paint for the king. Master Dallet learned all his cunning in miniatures from father, when he studied with him at our house.

"This is the house of Maître Roland Dolet, the painter?" the taller one asked. The glistening silk and rich velvet of their clothes made a bright splash of color in the somber room. The taller one had on a blue velvet long-sleeved doublet slashed to reveal a flame-colored silk lining, and a linen shirt embroidered in gold thread beneath his heavy, rain-damp cloak, while the shorter, broader one was in green, his long sleeves lined in yellow satin, and his gown edged with marten. Each wore several costly, jeweled rings. Their spurred boots told me that they had not walked. Each had both sword and dagger at his girdle. Foreigners, I thought, from a land of sunny colors, trapped in the gray northern spring. French, by the bold cut of their clothes, and the way they spoke my husband's name, which is really French, though his family made it English long ago. They looked me up and down with arrogant, calculating eyes, and I could feel my face turning hot.

"Yes it is, but my husband is not at home," I answered, and still clutching my sore thumb, I showed them where they could dry their cloaks by the fire.

"Good," said the shorter one in French, "perhaps we can deceive this woman into giving us what the master has refused." Now I must say, that made me angry. It was not just that they were trying to trick me but that they thought me so common that I couldn't understand them. Me, the daughter of Cornelius Maartens, painter of the greatest princes of Europe? Did they imagine I was some simpleminded, uneducated woman? In my father's house, I learned French, Italian, music, and manners, as well as painting. I was silent with rage, and I could tell those Frenchmen took my stare for dumbness. That made me even angrier.

"Madame," said the shorter of the two Frenchmen, "your husband last month had the honor of painting a most excellent portrait of the Princess Mary, sister to His Majesty." Now here was something interesting. That was supposed to be a secret, but of course I had wormed it out of him when he was drunk.

"Yes, he did," I said, "and he tells me it is her to the life."

"We wish to purchase the master drawing," said the first Frenchman.

"My husband never sells his drawings," I said, firmly. A painter's portrait drawings are his stock-in-trade. Suppose the sitter wants a copy for her aunt in Yorkshire? She certainly has no intention of sitting again and may well have shipped off the first portrait to some admirer. So to make the copy, the painter returns to the drawing he made at the sitting, where he has written in all the colors. My father said that in France, where all the gentle families like to have portrait books composed of faces they admire, other artists pay to copy the drawings, but it is just our bad luck that isn't the fashion in England.

"We are prepared to pay handsomely. Surely a woman as young and charming as you would like to set herself off with a gold necklace, or some pearl eardrops." His voice was warm and oozing, like syrup. Ha. Liar. Did he think he was seducing some housemaid? Did he think

I was so silly I knew nothing of the value of the drawing? Now I was just boiling, and I could feel my face getting hot, which I could tell those Frenchmen took for modest blushing, because of their shameless leering.

"New jewelry is exactly what my husband would notice first. Do you want him to think I have a lover?" But when a Frenchman opens his mouth, the Devil listens. Who else could have put the idea in my mind that I had at that very moment? The thought of it just plain took my breath away. It was a large idea, a splendid idea, a lie of most grandly sinful proportions; I'd spare the drawing and take my payment in good English cash. Master Dallet would never know.

"My husband would never give up the drawing, but why not commission another painting?" I asked, just as calm as could be, as if the Devil weren't prompting me.

"It would take too long," answered the tall one, "and we must send it by—" The short one stopped him.

"A copy in miniature could be delivered by tomorrow evening," I answered. "My husband's fee is three pounds." They looked at each other, shocked by the price. Really, I thought to myself, it would dishonor my husband, who only portrays persons of rank, to ask for less.

"Three pounds?" asked the tall Frenchman, rolling a sarcastic eye at me.

"My husband is a Master of the Guild of Painter-Stainers. No one excels him in fineness of work. If you doubt me, go elsewhere and seek another painter. When you see how poorly the work is done, then return here." Nan sucked in her breath at my daring. But I could feel something inside me just like a wild beast stirring, and my boldness just grew and grew because when you let bad seeds that are wrong ideas in you they just grow like those weeds and tares you hear about in church and smother out all the good intentions. The Frenchman looked taken aback, and triumph thrilled through my veins.

"You are sure it could be done?"

"Absolutely," I answered, avoiding Nan's shocked stare.

"We will refuse the miniature if it is not an exact copy of her features," said the shorter man.

"My husband's work is the finest in England," I answered, as they departed, grumbling.

"What on earth possessed you to make a promise like that?" Nan's face was horrified. "You know the master won't be home, and if he is, he'll be in no condition to paint. And a *miniature*, you careless, thoughtless thing! His hands shake when he's been drinking, and he'll have a headache and a foul temper! He'll be furious when he finds out what you've promised. You've ruined his reputation, all with your foolish tongue!"

"I know how to put those three pounds to most virtuous use, Nan. Besides, I need to have that money. I have it all thought out. This way I save my husband from cares and worries exactly the way a thoughtful wife should always do and anticipate his needs and comforts. He won't even be home until after it's done, and we'll have firewood and sausages and linen bands and a cradle for the baby without his ever having troubled the burdens of his mind." Nan looked at me stupefied.

"What are you saying? Susanna, I see your brain turning like a windmill again. Oh, this is trouble. I should never have let you put your head out into the rain."

"Have you forgotten that I am Cornelius Maarten's daughter? Remember my Ascension? Remember my Salvator Mundi, that could be fit in the palm of a man's hand? Even father's friends marveled. I have the same hands as when I was a maid. Look at them! Have they become stupid from scrubbing floors?" I held out my hands. My fingers were all swollen up with pregnancy, and the narrow wedding band cut deep. One palm was all stained with color, and there was blue dye beneath my short-cut fingernails.

Nan pushed a loose strand of gray hair up beneath her cap. All the wrinkles in her face twisted up with worry.

"Wouldn't you like to help your brother?" I said slyly, with the Devil prompting me. "You know Master Dallet said he would help your brother if he could. It would be just as if he did it."

"But, suppose he discovers—?"

"It's really not a bit deceptive, you see. After all, for a whole year now I've burnished his parchments, ground his colors, and even painted in draperies and the embroidery on sleeves. Why, that's practically a whole painting in itself, except for the faces which are what makes it a painting by the famous Rowland Dallet and worth so much. The only difference is that this time, we'll have the money direct in our hands to use the way Master Dallet would have wanted if he'd thought of it. These foreigners will just take it away with them and no one will be the wiser, even him."

"But I promised your parents—"

"Oh, that promise! You're always throwing it up to me! Didn't Master Dallet promise to keep me when my parents arranged my marriage? I'm beginning to come to the conclusion that he deceived them, Nan."

"Oh!" she said, shocked, and crossed herself. "You must never speak ill of the dead. Your mother was a saint. Your father was a man of perfect judgment, perfect! But when a Master of the Guild so condescended to study with him, a foreigner, what could he think but that it was all for love of you? Ah, lord, he was so certain it meant a golden future for you that he couldn't see anything but good in the man."

But painting was in my bones, in my hands, in my eyes. My brain was humming with the plan of the picture, the way I'd lay out the palette. I wanted it again in my hands, the mother of pearl shining beneath my colors, all arranged just so. I wanted the tiny neat brushes, which we limners call pencils, arrayed on the worktable, I wanted to see the shine of color as I first laid it across the tinted ground of the parchment. I looked at his mending, there in the basket by the fire. Suddenly, without knowing why, I hated it. I hated the wrinkles his living had made in it, I hated the smell of his body on it. I grabbed the basket from the bench and upended it into the fire, ugly brown stocking and all, and then stormed into his studio. The gray light of early spring was already failing, but I spread my arms wide, as if I could catch all the light in the world in them. "I'll have *this*," I said, "and may the Devil fly away with you, Master Rowland Dallet." Behind me I could hear Nan scrabbling to rescue that ugly stocking from the fire. My ears were deaf to her agonized wail:

"But I promised your mother to keep you out of *trouble!*"

As I mixed the glue and cut the parchment to prepare the base for the next morning's work, I hummed to myself, "Three pounds, three *pounds* and we shall be *rich*. The froggies will take it *away* and no one will be the wiser." Like that man in the Bible who is so busy counting his granaries or whatever it was that he forgets to repent of his sin and so comes to no good end by being forgetful, I never even stopped to ask myself what two mysterious French gentlemen, who didn't even give their names, wanted with a miniature of the king's sister.

THREE

It was gray dusk. Inside the Green Gate Tavern, they were lighting the rushlights, and the last passers-by could hear drunken singing coming through closed shutters. A man with a gray hood pulled closely around his face hurried past the tavern and on up Lime Street through the melting heaps of dirty snow. Reaching the edge of the city, he stopped before a tall, narrow house crowded in among the crumbling tenements that stood beneath the walls. He looked at the door. Yes, there was a niche above it with an imp carved in stone. It must be the place. But suddenly he could go no farther, his way barred by a beggar who stood barefoot in the slushy mud on the doorstep. The man took in at a glance the beggar's long, patched homespun cloak and pallid face. Behind the intruder, the monkey's-face door knocker gleamed invitingly on the front door of Sebastian Crouch's house.

"Out of my way, fellow. You hinder me," said the man.

"Stay a minute, Master Goldsmith," said the beggar. "Give me a coin and ask for God's blessing." Brazenly, he barred Master Jonas's way.

"Who are you to delay me? I say, make way," said Master Jonas, the goldsmith.

"Go home and finish the bishop's casting," said the beggar. His face was hidden in the shadow of the house's overhanging upper story.

"What business is it of yours? I am meeting someone here. Again, I say, get out of my way." The goldsmith's mind was full of riches and impatient with desire.

"If you go inside, I will abandon you," said the beggar. He was slender and pale. The goldsmith looked down at the strong, white bare feet in the freezing mud.

"Abandon me? Go right ahead, you sturdy, worthless fellow. You should be working for a living, not threatening decent folk in the street."

"Working? Do you think the cunning of your hand comes from you alone? Haven't you seen me standing by your furnace? Haven't you felt my hand guide yours as you poured the metal into the mold? Are you so thankless that still you want to pass through this door?"

"I do indeed, sirrah. I have business with an important man. Get out of my way."

"Very well," said the beggar as he stood away from the door. "I will go from you. There are others who need me more." Relieved, Jonas the Goldsmith pushed his way past the beggar and rapped three times with the monkey's-head door knocker. An elderly servant appeared and ushered the goldsmith into the paneled, oak-beamed hall. Outside, the beggar gazed at the locked door for a moment, then threw off the old cloak and followed them, pushing through the half-timbered wall beside the door as if it were no more solid than smoke. An old woman closing her shutters across the street saw the hem of a rich gown and the tips of a pair of tall, iridescent wings pass into the solid wall and thought she had gone mad.

Several men, Crouch's business partners in this newest venture, were already seated by the fire. Crouch himself presided over all from a cushioned, barrel-backed chair, his feet propped up on a little stool carved like a lying dog, his arms waving confidently as he explained some point of the project at hand.

"Ah, and here is Master Jonas at last. Our company is complete," he announced, as the goldsmith took a seat on the bench by the fire and stripped off his mittens to warm his hands. The fire irons, he noticed, were very curious in form, cast in the shape of two immense, black salamanders, their eyes formed by holes that let the orange flames wink and spark through them. It could only be that their owner was a powerful occultist. "You have seen the drawing, Master Jonas. How soon might it be cast?"

"The question is not how soon, but how much. It will take nearly a pound of gold to make it; a fortune, not even counting the silver and other precious metals."

Crouch turned to address a man in the heavy, Italian gown of a Lombard banker. "You can provide that much?" The man, dark bearded and somber, nodded gravely, yes.

"The thing, what is it? Not a goblet, surely, the upper bowl is too flat. And as for the burnishing, it will cast a strange reflection at the face of the drinker."

"Ah, Master Jonas, not the drinker, the seer. You are now one of our company, and worthy of our confidence. What you will cast is not a mere goblet, but the fabled Mirror of Diocletian, by which this mighty emperor was able to see revealed in its surface all plots and cabals against him, even though they be planned in the depths of the earth or the farthest reaches of the sea. The formula, until now, has been lost to the ages: gold and silver, mingled in exact proportion with certain parts of a black goat and the blood of a virgin." Crouch's eyes lit up, and he rolled these last words on his tongue. "It must be cast with certain—ah—enchantments. Happily, through my knowledge of antiquities, I have discovered the formula anew, concealed in a box of secrets and prophecies guarded by the most puissant demon Belphagor, whose guardian power I overcame with the most terrible commandments of the mighty Honorius. Now I have gathered these gentlemen into my enterprise; this is but the first of the wonders we shall create. We shall command the wealth of princes. We shall see across the world at a glance. We shall fly like eagles. Do you begin to comprehend now the meaning of our oath?"

The somber men about the fire nodded, and Jonas was suddenly seized with terror. What was he, a tradesman, doing in the company of such great gentlemen? If he did this work, he would know too much. What would happen to him? Ah, God, even the beggar at the door knew he should not have entered. But then he thought of the fortune that might await him, his debts, and how with cleverness, he might extricate himself to his advantage. . . .

Invisible on the smoke-blackened rafters above the conspiratorial company, three figures, two barefoot infants with shining eyes and the pale, tousle-headed beggar in the luminous gown, were sitting and listening. Their iridescent wings were neatly folded, and they dangled their toes almost directly over Crouch's head, peering down at the company the way boys who are fishing peer into a shadowy pool to see where the biggest fish is hiding.

"Well, well. So Belphagor's out at last," said the beggar.

"Aren't you going to tell on him?" asked one of the children.

"Who's Belphagor? Pooh! A second-rate demon at best. I haven't time to think about him just now. I'm planning to do that ungrateful goldsmith one last favor."

"What's that?" cried the little creatures, their wings vibrating with excitement.

"I'm going to put my finger on his balance when he weighs out the ingredients; then the mirror won't work properly, and they'll all blame one another, instead of killing him to preserve the secret, which he now understands is exactly their intention."

"Oh, clever, clever! What will the mirror show?"

"Why, their own thoughts right back at themselves. Everything they already think, they'll see and take it for a prophecy. Conceited braggarts. It will do them good," pronounced the beggar with a sniff.

"Then will you tell about Belphagor?"

"We-ell, when I'm done. I think I'll follow the old demon and see what he's up to, first. I need to pay him back for a little trick he played on me back before the Templars stuffed him in that box, and I don't want my fun spoiled. There's time enough to go reporting things to the archangels later." With that, all three of them rose through the ceiling. The men at the fire thought the gusts of air from their beating wings had come down through the chimney.

"By God, Bridget, you grow more beautiful daily!" exclaimed Rowland Dallet, leaning back in his chair and setting his wine cup back among the laden dishes. Mistress Pickering had ordered a nice little supper of chicken cooked with saffron and opened a bottle of Spanish wine for the painter's pleasure. She ordered little Master Pickering, whose round, dark head and large brown eyes had more than a passing resemblance to the painter's, carried off to bed by the nursemaid. Master Dallet had amused the baby and his mother both with his rapid drawings of the bearbaiting he had attended with several gentlemen the previous week. Then she had played the virginals and he had sung in a mellow baritone about the faithlessness of women. Now he returned his attention wholly to the mother of the recently removed infant and to the food on the little candlelit table by the bed. The amplitude of Master Dallet's stomach was already beginning to bear witness to his passion for the table. In time this passion might undermine his dark good looks, and thus his pursuit of other passions, but for now all his passions, as it were, carried equal weight.

"You have no idea what I go through. No man can abide a clinging woman. Whereas *you* are far too lovely to ever cling," he opined, setting down a gnawed leg bone and delicately wiping his fingers. Mistress Pickering loosed her long, black hair, smooth as silk, shaking her head to spread it over her half-bare shoulders like a dark cloak. She half smiled in answer. "Glorious," enthused the painter, admiring the shining blue lights in the flowing dark mass. "You are perfection. Your hair. Your lovely little waist. I want to paint every inch of that delicious skin of yours. Would you prefer to be Venus, rising from the sea foam, or perhaps Delilah the temptress, reclining on a lion?" He held up his hands together, the thumb and fingers forming a hollow square, like a picture frame, to surround the imaginary scene.

"The temptress," answered Bridget Pickering, looking up at him through her long, dark lashes with adoring eyes. It was a bit tricky for her to accomplish this, her most effective little gesture, since she was three inches taller than the painter. But height in a lover was never her first concern. In those proportions that mattered most to her, she had found the painter a perfect specimen. And when you added to this a flattering tongue, a pleasant and frequent offering of gifts, and a random schedule of work that allowed for convenient trysting, it was small wonder that Rowland Dallet was her favorite, if not exclusive, way to beguile the time while her husband was away at sea. She thought, for a brief moment, that she had lost him when he married, but soon enough the *Magdalen* had left port and the painter had arrived once more at her door, not the least chagrined.

"Naughty man," she had said, "what makes you think I will have you back?"

"My damned fine equipment, madame, and your randy eye. Surely you didn't think you could be outmatched by a shaggy little Flemish cow, did you?" And since he had brought her a perfectly stunning bracelet, she'd taken him back in a flash.

"Tell me, how's that virtuous little wife?" she asked, glancing slyly at him as she unpinned her sleeves.

"Fatter than ever. Her face puffs like a bladder. She bleats after me like a sheep. 'When will you be back? Can't you fetch me some oranges? I'm wanting some so.' She irritates me. She positively drives me off. She should study your ways if she wants to be attractive." Mistress Pickering smiled a little, as if she thought any imitation of her to be impossible. Rowland Dallet shrugged a little as if to say, Well, I suppose you're right, and then went on. "Ever since her parents died she's been more of a useless lump than ever." Dallet was seated on the bed now, undoing the points that kept his codpiece and hose snugly fastened together.

"Mmmm," responded Mistress Pickering, "did they leave you anything?"

"Twenty pounds and some ugly foreign furniture, plus a cross-tempered old servant-woman who came with the lot. Oh yes, some cooking pots and a Turkish carpet they brought over the water with them. I suppose I could sell the wretched stuff."

"I've always wanted a Turkish carpet. Is it big?"

"Little. They put it on the table. So now I have a fat Flemish wife, fat Flemish furniture, and a carpet on my table. And all for success in my trade. A devil's bargain. The world in return for marriage to a dowdy woman. Pity me, O goddess."

She sat down beside him on the bed, reached behind her, and unlaced her bodice. As he saw it loosen, he plunged his hand down it, while with the other he pressed her backward. As she felt his weight on her, her mind soared. It was a special kind of triumph, to lead a newly wedded man by the nose like a prize bull. And married to a younger woman than herself. What a fool that woman was to think that a worldly man like Rowland Dallet would be interested in her for any other reason than advancing his trade. She enjoyed imagining the look on the silly sheep's face if she could somehow magically see him there, and see her victorious.

Once, just after the wedding, she'd seen the girl leaving Saint Paul's, on Rowland Dallet's arm. Now Bridget Pickering was envisioning in her mind the plump, almost childish little figure she had seen. What a fool: pink cheeked, round faced, with simple blue eyes, a spattering of ridiculous freckles across a tip-tilted nose, and gingery, unruly hair that crept from beneath her matron's headdress. I've won, she said to the image. The girl's freckled face vanished, and he was in her. The sweet sensation flowed through them both. The warm sweat mingled on their bodies, and his breath was coming in fast, broken gasps when there was the fierce crash of the bedroom door flung back suddenly. There was the heavy sound of men's boots and the howling of women in an outer corridor.

"There she is, the harlot! The whoreson's letter was no lie." Captain Pickering's voice drowned out the frantic cries of her maid. "Damn you! Damn you both to hell!" he shouted. Fear and shock froze her to the bed in the very act. The painter shrieked as he was pulled off her by several sets of work-roughened hands. Before she could struggle away, the captain had grabbed her by the hair and pulled her face to within inches of his. Her eyes widened with horror at the sight of her husband's weatherbeaten, hard-boned face and ferocious blue eyes. "Liar, cheat! You've deceived me for the last time!" he cried. She could hear the thrashing and screaming of her lover as he fought to free himself from her husband's sailors.

"For God's sake, no!" she heard herself shouting as the captain pushed her aside and drew his short sword. Mindlessly, she wept and clawed at his coat, crying over and over again, "No, no!"

Captain Pickering, shaking with rage, plunged his short sword through the painter's naked belly. The painter's face distended in an unearthly cry. Two sailors held down the bleeding body while the captain pulled his sword free and, with a curiously cold precision, cut Rowland Dallet's throat from ear to ear. Blood splattered everywhere. There were pools of it, rivers, oceans. It flowed between the floorboards and spotted the bed curtains. The blood seemed to enrage the furious husband even more. "Whore, whore!" cried the captain, as he battered at her with his bloody fists, then flung her like a bundle of old rags into the slippery puddle at the foot of the bed. But before she lost consciousness, to the very end of her days, Bridget Pickering would swear that she saw a hideous, naked, dark shape leaning over Rowland Dallet's corpse, smiling and picking through it for something with long, scaly fingers, the way a greedy child might pick the silver coin out of a Christmas pudding.

I woke up craving oranges, oranges from Spain. In all my life I've had but one. I'll have oranges, too, I thought, as I popped my feet out of the bed. The rain had washed away the clouds, and new dawn shone pink and inviting through the studio window. Barefoot and in my shift, oblivious to the cold, I used a weasel's tooth to finish burnishing the little circle of parchment which, the previous night, I had glued tight to a base cut from an old playing card and then left to dry. I took out my husband's drawing of the princess. An easy job, I thought, looking at the smooth, pretty face with just a hint of a spoiled pout in the expression.

I set out a row of clean mussel shells to mix the colors in and took six of the best pencils, the narrow little squirrel's-hair brushes I had made for Master Dallet. I ground and mixed the carnation fresh, to get the light, pretty skin tone just right, then coated the parchment and left it to dry. It was all easy; I'd done it a hundred times for him, now the hundred and first was for me. By now I was frozen through, and glad Nan had made up the fire.

Over my clothes, I put on the silk smock my husband used for miniature painting, to protect the tiny image from hairs or lint that might come from clothing, and then I sat at the work table. I had a fierce headache; the parchment circle on the drawing board seemed to move and double itself in front of my eyes. My fingers could hardly bend for the swelling. All at once, I felt empty and cold. It had been more than a year since I'd put a line of my own onto paper. What if my skill had gone? What would I tell those rich Frenchmen? My God, if Master Dallet found out, he might break my bones; he might kill me.

Now I was very frightened; I could feel some shapeless, wicked thing hiding in the corner, making darkness even in the daytime. I could hear a rustling in the chimney and smell something ugly, like old, rotting wood. My skin started to crawl. "You've lost the art," the thing whispered. "Better to kill yourself now, before your husband does it." My chest was all heavy, and I couldn't breathe. It was something, something terrible like an evil presence that was taking away my painting just when I needed it most.

Then I tried to take away my fear with the thought of all that money, and the good things I could do with it which would be entirely for others and so entirely virtuous. I'll just start, and my old skill will come back, I thought. But the dark thing crowded more into the room, and I started weeping even though I was so stubborn as to keep hunting out my drawing things.

But as I laid the big drawing out on the table for copying, I felt the oddest pressure in the air behind me, as if someone curious were watching what I was doing. "Of course you can, Susanna," I heard in my ear. I turned my head suddenly, and caught a flash in the corner of my eye, something that shone, all translucent, and which I can only describe as, well, oddly *feathery*. The light seemed bright and rich in the room, and my heart lost its heaviness. I could feel a calm sort of joy beating through my veins, where sad, heavy blood should have been. Well, I thought, now I'm seeing things as well as having a dreadful headache. Maybe Nan was right and it was all from putting my head out in the rain when she told me not to.

Then all at once the headache faded, as if someone had touched my forehead. The edges of the parchment circle regained their sharpness. A curious heat flooded through me, and I began to sweat. Oh, I thought, I must spare the parchment, so I wiped the fast-flowing drops off my forehead with my sleeve. I was soaking now, and even the silk smock was damp through. My fingers seemed to loosen and felt clever and deft.

With the boldness of a swimmer who dives into an unknown river, I took a deep breath and mixed the first color for the line drawing, carnation with a little thin lake, and laid down the forehead stroke. There it lay, neat and correct. Inwardly, I exulted. As I felt my hands and mind connect in the old way, inwardly, I seemed to hear an odd sound, like the approving rustle of a voice coming from somewhere nearby. All around it, I could hear the faint echo of children's laughter, like a dream or an imagining. The ugly thing, and the smell and evil rustling, had vanished as if the laughter had chased it away.

Lightly I sketched in the features with the pale, rusty color; the proportion pleased me, and I moved on to sketch in the slashed sleeves and jeweled ornaments of the costume. These always give me special joy because I do love good jewelry, and nobody has better jewelry than princesses. "Well done, Susanna," I seemed to hear in my ear. "Go on."

The picture drew me on as I saw it emerge from the parchment. In the shells, I mixed the body colors with water and gum arabic, then laid them on the tiny mother-of-pearl palette with growing sureness. Next came the shading colors, laid on in lines of a single hair's breadth, so minute and close that they appeared solid to the inexpert eye. That is one of the secrets of a perfect miniature, as my father always used to say. Painters in large try to lay on the color in blobs as they would in a big portrait, and so lose the fineness of control that is necessary for a true likeness. They try to turn the form as they would in a large painting, with dark colors, violets, greens, and even black in the receding shadow, and so produce a sinister, dark muddle in place of luminous color. Father's shading tones, which he learned from the illuminators, are rich and bright, only giving the illusion of shadow when seen next to the body color. All these are secrets the English painters have not yet discovered, which is why this work goes to foreigners. Foreigners and Rowland Dallet.

So absorbed was I in the painting that time seemed to vanish. A wide and luminous space opened out around me, where common sounds became muffled. A still chiming, more beautiful than music, filled the edgeless space. Occasional comments of Nan, who would come in to say, "Why, that is very like!" and other words of praise, faded to the meaningless whispering of leaves far away in another world. A perfect pleasure in color occupied my physical being, more pure and perfect than any other kind of pleasure I could imagine. With a curious exactness, my tiny brushes found the precise shade and light to throw the figure from flat into round. At last I was done: in the fading luminosity, I ground the burned ivory for the black of the eye, which is almost a speck, fresh before mixing and applying it, so that it would shine from the picture with a true glance. A background of blue bice, richer than the sky in summer, set off the red hair and fresh, pale face. There were flashes of light caught in every jewel, and the rich gown shone like silk. I looked around, as if I had awakened from a dream. The afternoon was nearly gone. The sensation of watchers in the room seemed to fade. The workroom was again somber, dark, and empty of all presences, either good or evil.

"What is that racket downstairs?" I asked Nan.

"It's that widow quarreling with some customers, no doubt. Don't let it disturb you. The French gentlemen could be back at any moment."

"It's done, Nan, and I like it better than anything Master Dallet ever painted. Listen at the door while I put the portrait in its case; you know I love gossip." There were several plain, round, polished wood cases on hand. For a princess, there should be jewels, I sighed to myself. Well, never mind, if they want jewels, they can have a goldsmith make another case. But suppose they don't come? Then God just hasn't willed it, I thought. I'll keep the picture as a sample of my work. "I'll have to hide it," I said to myself distractedly. After all, Rowland Dallet had sold my Salvator Mundi as a work by a long-dead Burgundian master.

The shouting had grown louder. Then there was a clattering of clogs on the stair, followed by a positively rude banging on the door. Nan flung it open to confront the widow's daughter.

"Mother says she won't have it laid out there. The lease give her right of use, and she just won't have it cluttering up the shop. You have to take it up into your rooms."

"And just what is it you're talking about?" Nan asked her.

"You'll see," she answered, her eyes narrow and her smile malicious. Perhaps a gift, I thought, pushing ahead of Nan down the narrow, spiral stair. Downstairs, two sailors stood beside a long, dark-stained, canvas-wrapped bundle they had laid on the ancient rushes covering the floor. They looked embarrassed as I stooped to uncover the bundle. For a moment my breath stopped. Then I could feel a kind of curious coldness all through my body before I could hear the oddest scream that seemed to come out of me but also from far away. The skin was a bluish gray, and the clotted, open wounds, a deep murrey unlike any I could ever have imagined. . . . The bundle was the corpse of Master Dallet, as dead as a herring.

The taller of the sailors, the one with the black hair and the earring, looked suddenly embarrassed as he stared at my swollen middle, and the wedding ring on my finger.

"Um, an accident in the alley behind Captain Pickering's house," he said.

"Footpads," added the shorter one, with the rusty beard.

"The captain came home from sea unexpectedly," broke in the widow's daughter, with a meaningful look.

"—and found the accident," interjected the shorter sailor. I scarcely heard them, my heart was pounding so. It was all clear to me. This was the terrible punishment for my forwardness and wickedness in daring to paint when I should have been serving my husband better. Now he was dead and we were ruined, all because of me and my selfishness. Who would look after us? Who would help the baby? He might have loved me, if the baby were a son. Now there was nothing. No hope. Tremors went up and down my body, and I felt faint.

"Now look what you've done, and her expecting!" I could hear Nan accusing the sailors. "You've killed her with shock!" The first convulsion threw me at the feet of the corpse, and set the women in the room wailing. I felt heavy hands holding me down, and heard the widow giving orders, "Not there, here—do you want to kill the child as well?" As the seizure passed, the widow, who was kneeling by my side, rolled her eyes heavenward and proclaimed, "Oh, the sorrow! Only a widow can understand another widow's grief!" Groggy as I was, I knew perfectly well that she was savoring the moment with that special pleasure that elderly people get from disasters. "What can a *man* know of women's suffering!" she announced triumphantly. I could hear embarrassed mumbling from the sailors, who backed toward the door, only to find it had been barred by Nan.

"Just see what your captain has done!" she said. "Do you know what great patrons Master Dallet has? He has painted our old King

Harry the Seventh himself, and the new King Harry that is, when he was prince, and many other gentlepersons. Your master will never out-live the scandal of delivering his poor murdered corpse to his pregnant wife and killing her."

"He had a right—" grumbled the short sailor.

"Nan—Nan," I whispered, "I felt something. I think the baby's coming." Nan didn't hear me, but the widow, who could hear a secret through three walls, did.

"Murdering a poor, innocent widow *and* her orphan child—" the widow added, "a scandal to the heavens. All of London will hear. Your master will never escape the justice of God and man," she announced righteously, pointing her finger melodramatically to the heavens. The sailors' eyes darted from side to side. There was no escape through the barricade of women.

"You tell him to come and take care of the orphan he's made, or the world will know," said Nan, still hard against the door.

"Blasted magpies—now look what he's done. I *told* him to get rid of it. Now he has to shut them up," muttered the tall one with the earring.

"A man who does his Christian duty by widows earns only praise," said Nan, firmly righteous.

"Yes, and silent prayer—silent—be sure to tell him that," added the widow, as Nan let them escape through the front door at last. Then she turned to me where I still lay on the floor. "We'll see his burial paid for at least, and perhaps a tidy little purse for us—have you had another pain yet, my poor little dove?"

"I'm sure I felt one—"

"Oh, my, then, it's coming," said the widow, "and much too soon by my count." Oh, that nosy widow. Of course she'd been counting. Old ladies always do, after a wedding date. As she and Nan helped me get up, she announced, "The problem with men, as I see it, is that they never tidy up after themselves. It's the job of women to make sure that they do."

"True enough," agreed Nan, "but we need to help my mistress up-stairs to bed before she has another pain."

"But, Mother," I could hear the widow's daughter wailing behind me, "what about that, uh—Master Dallet?"

"We'll lay him out downstairs. What else? Would you have a corpse in the same room as a woman in labor?"

As I lay down in the bed, Mistress Hull took advantage of the opportunity to peer into every corner of our rooms, which I am sure she had been perishing to do for a long time. "Goodness," she said, "your featherbed is very thin—oh, what's this in the cupboard, only wooden dishes, no pewter?" She took her long, prying nose out of the cupboard and turned to the fireplace, where she lifted the lid on our kettle to spy the quality of the soup inside. Old ladies like that never like to miss anything. "This cooking pot looks old—"

"I had it from my mother."

"I'd have thought he'd have bought you a better one." I could see her skinny old body practically disappearing into my parents' big old armoire. Her voice came out all muffled from among Master Dallet's best suits. "And these clothes—they're all his? Didn't he even buy you a ribbon or two? And here I thought he was a wealthy man, just waiting to take away my poor little rooms. . . ." I pulled the bed quilt over my face, because it was a trial to have to watch all her nosiness and quite bad enough just to hear her rustle, rustle, rustle among all my things. I could hear Nan answering her back, old lady to old lady.

"You've never met a stingier man than Master Dallet. Every penny went for show and nothing for my mistress, that I've looked after ever since she was a little slip of a girl. You have no idea of the wickedness of that man!" Her voice lowered. "Pray for me, Mistress Hull. I—I did a terrible thing. And now I've brought all this misfortune on us, and I daren't tell her." I could barely hear her whisper. "He set her so crazy, with his philandering, and her an innocent that didn't even understand what was happening, that I begged the devil to fly away with him. And now it's happened, and he goes to his grave unshriven, and it's all my fault. . . ."

Suddenly I began to feel better. Maybe it wasn't all the fault of my lies and painting after all. I poked just my eyes out above the bed quilt. The pains seemed to have gone away.

"God forgive me my wicked wish, now we are left in debt and want." Nan's voice was sorrowful as she followed the widow as she went into the studio. "Want? I'm an expert on that," answered

Widow Hull, prying into a packet of pounded serpentine. "Oof, painters! Not much worthwhile here. You'll have to find another painter to buy this, and even so, half of it's junk. Perhaps the guild can arrange to aid you—hasn't he left anything you could sell? Religious paintings? My husband left twelve Christs, but I haven't been able to sell any. God is forgotten in these wicked times. It's Master Hull's Adam and Eves that I sell. And do you know why? It's because they haven't any clothes! Eve in the Garden, Eve tempted by the serpent. Eve braiding her hair, with serpent. Eve being spied on by Adam, with serpent. My husband couldn't deliver enough of them, I tell you. Half the monks in Christendom must own one. Luckily, he left me a good two dozen of them, though not all were finished. Ah, me, when those are gone, I don't know what I'll do for a bit of sausage in my soup."

"Naked pictures? But I've never seen any in the shop." Nan seemed puzzled. I put my head entirely out from under the covers so that I could hear better.

"I keep them behind the Christs, they're that filthy. But people who want them know where to come." I could see Nan trying to distract her and lead her out of the studio, but she kept nosing about, turning over panels, inspecting shelves. Suddenly I heard her cry out, "Oh! What's this I see here on the work table? You can't fool me, I've been a painter's wife too long. Just look at the size of it, and the colors! The features are perfect; she looks as lively as if she could step from the case. And I can see her character from the eyes. That's the test of a true portrait, you know. What a jewel! An emperor would buy that." She stood back from the worktable and put her hands on her hips, inspecting the miniature with her head tilted to one side. "Now that I see his skill, I begin to regret this arrogant Master Dallet," she observed.

"My mistress did that."

"Your mistress? That's a joke. Only a man could paint this well."

"My mistress is the only daughter of the great master Cornelius Maartens."

"Martin? Well perhaps I heard my husband speak of him, and perhaps I didn't. He doesn't sound like a liveryman. I hope he wasn't a foreigner, come to steal good English livings. I tell you, if the guild didn't burn their work, we'd all be living in the gutter."

"Master Maartens was Flemish."

"Oh—well—not that I haven't seen some foreign work that wasn't shoddy. Still, they can't paint a proper coat of arms. It's their strange ways. . . ."

"My mistress was raised a painter from childhood. He taught her all his secrets before he died."

"Now there *is* a strange custom, teaching a daughter to do man's work." The widow seemed disbelieving. She came closer to inspect the painting again. "Just imagine! It would turn her head from duty. How could she ever be a proper wife if she knew a man's trade? No, girls should be raised girls, I say, or soon enough they'd all be wearing trunk hose and short swords, and then where would we be?" She picked up the miniature from the worktable, and her brain was thinking so hard I could almost hear it from the bed in the other room. "Still . . . if she paints like this . . . it's a crime to waste . . . the damage is already done, so why not profit?"

Suddenly I remembered something. I sat up with a start.

"The miniature! Nan, those Frenchmen are coming any time now! We have to hide the body!"

"What Frenchmen?" asked the widow, sensing good gossip.

"The Frenchmen who commissioned that miniature from my husband," I said, sitting up in bed, newly frantic. "If they know he's dead, they won't take it. Nan, we need that money."

"You mean," said the widow, "you're palming off your own work as Master Dallet's?"

"What else?" I answered. "Someone has to find money for this household, and it certainly isn't going to be Master Dallet anymore—not that it ever was."

"My dear," said the widow, with a smile of discovery on her face. "I will help you hide the body on one condition—"

"We can't afford to share the Frenchmen's money," said Nan. "We have to bury him, you know."

"No, I wouldn't think of depriving the poor man of his shroud. What I propose is that your mistress there renew my supply of Adam and Eves—we'll go halves."

A great cloud of worry lifted from me, and I felt suddenly that from now on, fate would look after my every need. "An excellent idea," I said. "Halves it is."

"Ah, blessed be God, who answers prayers in such strange ways," said the widow, as she rolled her eyes heavenward. "Now, dear Mistress Dallet, rest yourself and repair your health, while we go hide that thing downstairs. Praise the Lord it's cold; he won't stink, and we can have him out by tomorrow."

The Second Portrait

Lucas Hornebolt. Princess Mary Tudor. *ca. 1514. 1½-inch diameter. Gouache on vellum. Cherrywood case. Huntington Gallery.*

Attributed to Lucas Hornebolt, this excellent early specimen of the English miniaturist's art portrays Princess Mary Tudor of England (1495?–1533), third daughter of King Henry VII of England and younger sister of Henry VIII. Princess Mary should not be confused with Queen Mary I (Mary Tudor, 1516–1558, "Bloody Mary"), the eldest daughter of Henry VIII and half sister of Queen Elizabeth I. The Tudor strain is clearly visible in the reddish hair and stubborn lower lip of the portrait. This miniature, most likely a copy of a larger portrait, was painted as an engagement gift to King Louis XII of France, dating it sometime in the year 1514. In clarity of jewel-like color and depiction of character in a small space, no school of painting surpasses that of the English miniaturists of the sixteenth and seventeenth centuries.

—The English Miniature, *Exhibition catalog, October 1985*

I have already told you how I came to paint this picture, which is really only a copy and not from life, but it brought me the first money I ever earned with my brush. Faces are my strongest skill, because my father was a taskmaster who never let anything get by, and he made me copy an ugly old skull he had over and over again from all angles until I cried, because he said you can't understand the flesh unless you understand the bone underneath. And my mother shook her head and said girls shouldn't be drawing ugly bones and he was a madman, but here I am so perhaps he wasn't so mad after all. I see a lot in faces. I can see thoughts and hurts and dreamings and sometimes very great evil well concealed. It is a special art to catch these things in the droop of an eyelid, or the way light shines on a cheekbone, and that is what I work at most of all, because I want to get better and better at it.

But the hardest part of a painting is getting the money for it, which never gets any easier no matter how many pictures you make. So many people are tricky and they think the painting is already painted, so too bad, you'll have to take what they offer, or maybe wait, or risk getting nothing, and have to bear the cost of the materials. That is why princely patrons are best, because they are not cheap. Also, always try to get an advance, even from princes.

FOUR

The light had already failed by the time the Frenchmen returned. They were heavily muffled, well armed, and had brought a third man with them, who was incognito in the Italian fashion, in a black velvet mask that covered his entire face beneath his wide, plain hat brim. But the soft leather cuffs of his tall boots were turned back to show red silk linings, and I caught the shine of gold embroidery embellished with seed pearls beneath a brief, inadvertent opening of his black cloak. A man of higher rank than the first two, I thought. Their master. And he must not be known to have been here.

The first two men set down their lanterns on the bedroom table. Apart from the glow of the lanterns, the room was lit only by firelight. Master Dallet always resented money spent on candles because he had plenty of them when he attended his great patrons and why pay extra for such expensive things at home? Now that he was dead, I was beginning to understand that he did not regard his home as a haven of peace from the cares and false snares of the world. The snares of the world were all he had ever wanted and his haven of peace got in the way. It made me very sad because if you cannot trust *The Good Wyfe's Book of Manners*, then what can you trust? Now here I was having strange men in at odd hours and going very far from right things, which shows what happens when you get started on wrong paths. All I could think about was how I intended to be very bold and cover everything up so they couldn't talk down the price.

The red, flickering light from the hearth cast great, black shadows that loomed like giants behind the strange men and seemed very frightening. But I was very firm because right is always on the side of widows who need money.

"Madame Dolet, has it been possible for your husband to finish the painting today?" asked the Frenchman who had first given the commission, the one who spoke better English.

"Yes, he has it finished. He has entrusted me with the sale, since he has been invited across town on an important commission. Would you like to inspect it now?" I answered him in English, the same language in which he had addressed me.

"Curious to leave only a wife here," said the second Frenchman, in French, to the masked man. "It must be a very important commission, indeed. Still, it seems you have not wasted your trip, after all."

"I would have said it was impossible to have it finished this quickly—I won't accept it if the quality is poor," he answered in the same language. Then in heavily accented English, he addressed me: "Show me the portrait." I lit a rushlight in the fire and led them into the studio.

"Here it is, my lord," I said, handing him the closed case. "You may wish to inspect it closer to the fire. I don't want to risk spotting it." I held the sputtering, grease-dipped rush well away from the little case. The lord sat down on the bench by the fire and opened the case. I could hear him take in his breath as the firelight illuminated the little image in the turned wooden case.

"It is a speaking likeness," he said in French. "More exquisite than the original. It shows her exactly as I have seen her, even her character." The man in the mask chuckled knowingly. "Madame can ask for no better." He studied the portrait again. "Still . . . how was this done so quickly? Had she a copy made for a lover? Or perhaps the painter had made another to sell to some interested party. . . ." he seemed to be talking to himself, thinking. I let my face look stupid, as if I did not understand him. The second Frenchman, the shorter one, turned to me and said in English:

"Tell me, did your husband have this already made up?" Oh, dear, who knows what troublesome rumor could come back to haunt us? Why hadn't I thought of that before? It just goes to show how one little deception about a body hidden in the house can lead to all sorts of other things you might never have thought about. And after all, it is really important to look after the honor of your dead husband if you wish to be considered respectable as a widow and not unworthy of concern due to being connected with a wicked person.

"My husband is a man of honor. He would never do such a thing. I told him all about your princely offer last night, and he worked on it all day. It's for the sake of his son that's to be born, you know." Now that he was dead, it was much easier to imagine him as a more considerate husband. "He was overcome with joy when he found I was bearing a child. It was the answer to his prayers, his candles burned before the Virgin at Saint Vedast. Oh, he was a pious man, for all that he put on an easy, affable front for his great clients." Did I imagine that I saw one of them shudder?

But the great lord turned to me and asked, his voice at once stunned and curious, "Did you see him paint it?"

"Oh, yes," I answered. "He sat here all day, quiet as a ghost, just working. I didn't dare disturb him. He didn't even touch his meal. When he was done, he just vanished, without even taking leave. He is so busy these days." At this, even the lord stiffened slightly and seemed to turn pale beneath his mask.

"Tell the woman to tell her husband that this is a masterpiece and well worth the fee he asked," the lord said in French. He nodded at the shorter man, who told me the same thing in English and produced a purse.

"I'll be happy to tell him of your distinguished judgment, my lord. He will be most grateful for your opinion," I answered. Clutching the money and scarcely daring to breathe, I curtseyed, all ungainly, in farewell.

"Tell no one about this painting, or by whom it was purchased," said the short Frenchman with the better English. Was it warning, or fear, or perhaps both, that I heard in his voice?

"Yes, of course, my lord." But as Nan showed them to the door, I stood by the fire, wondering why they had not asked me to tell Master Dallet that he must be silent, too? Their heavy boots creaked on the narrow stair. I could hear the front door bang shut behind them. There was the sound of clatter and company rising from the widow's kitchen downstairs. I thought it must be very amusing company, from the way she was carrying on and giggling and shrieking like some girl instead of a proper old widow who likes disasters.

I was just hiding the money when I heard Nan shushing them at the foot of the stair. "She's in a terrible, terrible way. Prostrate with grief. Poor little lamb, so innocent, to see such dreadful things. Why, the sight of it nearly killed her on the spot." Nan was talking very loudly even for Nan, so I took it as a sign that she was warning me about someone who might be coming up and catching me gloating over money instead of lying in bed like a martyr. So I tucked the money under the straw beneath the featherbed and got into bed and pulled the covers up over my neck so whoever it was wouldn't see that I was really dressed and deceiving him. I felt especially guilty about deceiving and conspiring when I saw that Nan had brought in a holy person who might well see through all my wickedness—that is, a friar, except that he was fat and out of breath and he had been drinking downstairs, so he might not see through anything.

"Master Pickering's confessor, Mistress Dallet," Nan said hastily, so I'd make no mistakes. "Brother Thomas has come on behalf of the captain." I could see him looking around our little rooms, which were all darkish and sort of pitiful without candles because rushlights always look so cheap.

"Oh, Brother Thomas," I said faintly, "please forgive me if I don't rise. I have been ill, and am afraid of losing the child." I really did feel exhausted, and my belly felt all in knots which might have been labor pains but I really didn't know for sure.

"Oh, never, never," he said, looking flustered. "Don't risk the child. You must stay just as you are."

"You are so understanding. Heaven bless you, good friar," I answered, all soft and weak so he'd be sure to know I was ill from grief and be sorry. Brother Thomas looked unsure of what to do. The only bench was by the fire. So he sat on the edge of the bed, looking nervous, as if I might tempt him to sin which was in fact the farthest thing from my mind.

"I cannot even describe Captain Pickering's distress on hearing of your difficulties. Since it was he who first discovered the dreadful accident to your distinguished husband, he takes your own loss almost as if it were his own—" Aha, I thought, you saw the great lords leave and now you are dying to know what they were here for in case they were good friends with designs of vengeance. Well, you should be worried—after all, Captain Pickering didn't just go and murder a nobody. And he had the gall to deliver the corpse that way—with the arrogance of a lord. I imagine he's sorry now.

"How noble of him," I said, making my voice sound ever so weak and frail.

"He consulted with me at length concerning the biblical texts on the assistance of widows—"

"Most devout of him—"

"—and he has sent this purse to assist you and your unborn child in your hour of need."

"How truly charitable of him to take an interest in assisting the unfortunate victims of fate."

"He is a good Christian, unwavering in his duty."

"But, blessed Brother Thomas," I murmured through my pale, bloodless lips, "one thing still causes me great agony. Oh, dear God, is that another pain I feel? Just one thing—"

"What is it, Mistress Dallet?"

"The funeral. I am too weak to make the arrangements. I can't bear the thought of Master Dallet being shamed by a poor funeral. He'll need candles and a coffin—" Brother Thomas looked alarmed. Did you think I'd let you off so easily? You're not throwing a purse to *me* and walking out of here, you hypocrite. "I want a lead-lined one—carved—in good taste—no cheap material. Master Dallet was a distinguished court painter, after all."

"A coffin, well, yes, a coffin."

"You'll need to send notice to the Painter-Stainers' hall, to tell the wardens that he'll be needing the funeral pall. And the procession—he needs more than just the liverymen—a man of his stature must have at least six hired mourners—"

"Surely, one or two—"

"Four. How could you even mention two? Two—so shabby—oh, I feel so grieved, the pain just won't go away. Oh, the pain—it's just shooting through me at the thought of only two mourners."

"Four mourners," he said, sighing.

"I need two lengths of black wool, ten yards each, for mourning dress."

"Mourning dress, yes, I suppose that is needed. Is that all?" His pale blue eyes, buried deep in his round, red face, began to look at me with a strange new sense of appreciation.

"Oh, oh, what is it? Yes? Oh, I feel so weak. Ah, now I remember. A memorial brass—not so large as to be vulgar. My poor, dear husband. How ghastly he looked! He must have an engraved brass at Saint Vedast."

"Understood—" Looking at his face, I couldn't resist.

"With a verse. The finest brasses have verses. Perhaps by you? Some fitting tribute, for the sake of his grieving wife."

"A verse seems excessive. They charge by the letter—"

"A motto, then? Something appropriate."

"Why not 'Ars longa, vita brevis'?" said Brother Thomas, his large red face bland, but his voice ironic.

"And what is that, my dear Brother Thomas? Latin? Is it sufficiently pious? Oh, my goodness, I wouldn't want my pains to start again."

"Indeed. It means that Art lives much longer than our frail, sinful lives." A lot longer than you imagine, I thought, reflecting on Master Dallet's future posthumous career in the religious painting business.

"That would be perfect," I answered. "Master Dallet would be pleased, if he could know."

"I'm sure he would," agreed Friar Thomas, rising from where he sat on the end of the bed.

"Thank you for this visit of consolation, Friar Thomas," I said, in my best fragile-sounding voice.

"Blessings be on you and your house, Mistress Dallet," he said, backing cautiously toward the door, his eyes never wavering from my face. Suddenly he said, "He never understood what he had, did he? A man should put more value on a wife who is as determined as she is shrewd, and as shrewd as she is virtuous. Never fear, Mistress Dallet, I will personally make sure that the inscription is quite elegant enough to uphold your honor."

Really not a bad man, I thought, as I heard him puffing down the stairs. And what an interestingly colored face. Very little massicot and more red lead in the carnation, the first shadings of the features in red, the blue of the eye very pale, a most curious contrast . . .

"Tap, tap!" cried Widow Hull, in place of knocking at the open door. "Come in," I called from the bed, where Nan and I were count-ing the contents of the purse that the holy friar had left behind him. Quickly Nan put away the purse under the straw in the bed next to all that other money, as the widow came in with her candle. "My, you do look awful," she said cheerfully, holding her light up to inspect my fea-tures. Her daughter was behind her, holding a soup tureen, which she set on our table. "I thought you might not be cooking tonight, so we've brought what's left from supper—that is, what I managed to hide from that hungry friar."

"You certainly sound cheerful," said Nan.

"And why shouldn't I be? He scattered money about him like a gentleman. And interesting! Why, he goes every day to Saint Paul's to hear what's new. What a tale he can tell! How the great Wolsey schemes every day to be made a cardinal, and that the queen in France is now dead, and she without a son, and a most marvelous storm that—oh, and they say women are gossips! You should have seen his face when I told him that those were great gentlemen upstairs, who had come to inquire after Master Dallet. Then I showed him how nicely I had laid out Master Dallet in the buttery, with two candles, and very expensive ones, I might add, all to keep his master's wicked secret, and he vowed to have him out of here and buried tomorrow, and I said just as well, even in this cold weather, he won't keep much longer. Oh, yes—a man of the world—What's this? You aren't eat-ing?" I had just turned away the bowl of soup that Nan had offered.

"I don't feel well. Tell me, what are labor pains like?"

"You'll know 'em when you have 'em. That's something no woman has to ask about. Goodness, your eyes look swollen—I thought you'd been crying for the good friar's benefit. Let's see your hand. That's swollen, too—just look at how that ring cuts into the finger! Tell me, do you have headaches?"

"Ever so many. How did you know?"

"Never mind, I know what I know." Nan looked troubled. "Oh, don't carry on so," said the widow to her. "I just want her to look after these talented little hands. Girls shouldn't fill their heads with worries when they're expecting. Now, you must try to eat a bit. Send the tureen down later." But I could hear Nan and the widow whispering at the door.

"It doesn't look good for that child, does it?" said Nan.

"She will be lucky if she loses it now. I know the signs. The infant is poisoning her." The widow's voice sank lower. "I lost my oldest girl that way. Newly wed, newly dead. We buried her in her wedding shift."

"Should I call Goody Forster?"

"It's too late. There's nothing for it."

"Nothing at all?"

"Pray, Mistress Littleton, pray with all your might that that girl comes through safe, or we'll all be on the street." My head was splitting. One foot felt as if it wished to twitch and jump of its own accord. Was that one of the signs? How dreadful, how unfair. Death, you deceiver. Mother had only felt a little fever, and then the sweating sickness came and took her away and father, too, only a week later. Who would have thought it, when only a few months before they had been planning my wedding feast? I could still see Mother in my mind, giving orders to the pastry cooks and serving women in their white aprons who swarmed into our little house, setting down the extra dishes and platters among the drying canvases in father's workroom. And then there was father, his graying hair uncombed, wandering around all grumpy while he surveyed the preparations, for once in his life, useless. Their only comfort was that I was safely wedded to Master Dallet, who said he was rich and promised to take care of me like a queen. And now Death had come again, this time in the form of a baby, making my ankles as thick as tree trunks and my face coarse and swollen in the mirror so that I wouldn't even look beautiful on my bier and make people sorrow at the great tragedy of it all. No fair, no fair, dying ugly.

I didn't want to die. My whole body said it wanted to be alive. I looked into the growing dark and saw a terrible shadow thing, all naked, clammy and cold pressing down on my chest, heavy with wickedness. Then it seemed that it had a very ugly face which peered down into my eyes intently and also long, bony fingers which were very ugly. Even though it was only a vision from fever it seemed very real, and it had greedy little red eyes as if it wanted something I didn't want to give it.

Silently, in my mind, with all the strength my soul owned, I cried out, *Help me.* My eyes seemed to see things all blurry. Through the headache, I could hear the blood in my ears, and a curious rustling sound. There was a flash of light like the glint on armor. Something

strong and fierce had come into the room. The shadow thing boiled
ragefully above me at it, and I swear I could see the bed curtains, which
were pulled back, sway and blow with the hidden tempest. I felt mor-
tally tired, and as my eyes closed to welcome death, something said,
We're here. No, you're not, I answered in my mind. Nobody's left here
but me and Nan and black, shrouded death. Nobody.

"It is here, my lords." The goldsmith had sent away his apprentices for
the day, and his furnace was cold. Rain battered against his closed shutters and trickled through a leak in the ceiling of his workshop. It landed
with a melancholy drop, drop, drop sound in a puddle on the dirt floor.
The Lombard looked about him with a sniff, taking in the shabbiness,
the stiff, old-fashioned models on the workshop table, the calipers and
molds hung on the walls. How backward, how primitive these English
artisans were. In Italy, this man would never be admitted to a mastership. With a flourish, Master Jonas unveiled a cloth-wrapped bundle in
the center of the worktable. Brassy and glittering, it looked very like a
large, flattened goblet on a footed stand. Strange characters were carved
about the rim, and the stand, at the inspiration of the goldsmith, had
been decorated with a pair of shapeless, bloated salamanders.

"Ah," exclaimed the Lombard, impressed by the glossy shine of
the thing.

"Have you looked in it?" asked Crouch, his eyes narrowed with
suspicion.

"Well, only to burnish it. But I did it in secret. No one else in the
household has seen it."

"And just what did you see?" asked Crouch, and the oozing tone
of his voice set the goldsmith's heart suddenly beating hard.

"Why, just my own face. What else is there to see?" The Lombard
looked suddenly at Crouch, his heart alert as he scented treachery.

"Ah, the words. One must know the words," said Crouch, his voice
reassuring. Taking off his gloves, he passed his hands over the flat surface of the remade Mirror of Diocletian. *"Tapas, menahim, orglolas . . ."*
He leaned over the worktable and peered into the mirror. "My face?"
he said softly to himself. "What is this?" With a ferocious look he
turned on the goldsmith. "Did you hold back gold?"

"S-steal your gold? Never, my lord. You yourself saw me weigh it and cast it into the crucible."

"The virgin's blood?" said the Lombard, in his heavy accent, looking at Crouch.

"I assure you, it could have been no other. It was the blood of an eight-year-old girl." The goldsmith's voice broke into the furious recriminations.

"Look, my lords, something moves on the surface." Three velvet-capped heads pressed around the mirror.

"Ah, I was right. He has it," whispered Crouch, as he saw his own worst fear reflected up at him in the magic mirror. "Ludlow, the traitor. He's bought the manuscript from the widow."

But the Lombard's companion saw an entirely different scene moving in the shining yellow metal. As his secret thoughts revealed themselves in the reflection, he shouted, "The whore! With my confessor! And with my own wine!" He tore his gaze from the mirror. "I always knew that wife of mine was no good." He stood up suddenly and put his hand to his sword hilt. "I must be going," he said as he hurried from the room. "This time I mean to catch them at it."

Miraculous, thought the goldsmith, as he watched him go. How fortunate I have memorized the formula. It shows truth to everyone. Why, if I hadn't seen it with my own eyes, reflected in this wonderful mirror, I would have no proof that my apprentices were stealing those eggs from my henhouse. Little wretches. I always knew I couldn't trust them. . . .

Crouch rewrapped the curious object and thrust it under his cloak.

"My payment?" asked the goldsmith.

"Oh, yes, Master Jonas. Come to my house this afternoon and we'll be waiting with it." Crouch and the Lombard cast significant glances at each other, which the goldsmith, his mind aflame with thoughts of the wickedness of his apprentices, never even noticed.

FIVE

That night after my husband's bloody corpse had been brought home, I had a terrible dream, which seemed very real and almost as if I weren't dreaming at all. I woke up in my dream to see that the baby that was inside me was already born. But instead of being small and newborn, the baby was a big ugly boy of about two years old, bony, pale, and with dark, lank hair. He was doubled up in a cradle beside my bedside, and hardly fit, even so, with his strangely long, knobby legs. His huge eyes, shining green like the glowing eyes of owls, fascinated me. Above him, around him, there seemed to hover an evil presence, like a dark shadow.

That big bony changeling whimpered there for food. But what kind? When I tried to go to it, I couldn't move, as if something heavy were preventing me from getting up from the bed. When the strange creature saw that it couldn't draw me to the cradle with the look in its green glowing eyes, it spoke: "Mother," it mewled, "oh, I'm so hungry." But when it opened its mouth, I saw an even row of pointed teeth, shining almost bluish white like sharp little fish teeth. My skin tingled with fear.

"Mother, come," whined the demonic child.

"Don't touch it," said a strange voice.

"But I have to," I answered.

"Let it go. It is evil incarnate." Ah, God, is that what I had been growing inside me all that time? Evil? What was I that I couldn't bear a child like other women have? It couldn't be true. I wanted my child.

"Let it go," said the voice. "Can't you feel the wickedness of it? The force? If you let it, it will suck away your soul." I could feel the evil. It was like a coming thunderstorm, that makes your scalp tingle, and the hair on your arms and legs stand on end. It was pulling me, and I could feel the inferno beyond. Oh, help, help me, I cried in my mind.

"Hold tight. Pull with us, Susanna. You must will it away," said the powerful creature that was holding me tight, pulling me from the abyss. I could hear its heavy wings beating and I suddenly felt that there was more than one of them, as if it had had to call for help from its friends because the black sucking thing was so strong. In the dream, of course, I was very glad to have it, or them, though in real life I would have been more careful about entrusting myself to strangers like that.

"Why?" I cried out in my dream.

"Rowland Dallet, in seeking a treasure, managed to free a being of chaos and destruction. It followed him home. Now it wants an earthly body, and like a cukoo's egg in the nest, it has displaced the child beneath your heart. Do you not understand it will discard you like an empty shell when it is ready to hatch? It counts on your misplaced love to nourish it with your life. We have shown you what it is. And now I say, let it go before it pulls you from my grasp."

"It's my baby and I want it."

"It is none of yours any longer. You must let that creature go," said the voice, which vibrated like the deepest bell in Paul's steeple. For an instant, the room was illuminated in shifting colors, and I saw a towering column of radiant light, streaming up through the roof, miles into the sky. The column was somehow human in form. It had a beautiful face, somber and glorious, and wings that stretched to the heavens. My heart beat hard. But I gathered my courage and spoke again. "If I let him go, what will I have left? I have no money, I have no family. Now I won't even have a baby. I'll have nothing at all."

"Nothing?" came the voice. "No, something. See this." The radiant being moved one hand slowly across the night sky. Where it passed, the black, star-flecked heavens were erased and the blue of a summer noon took its place. Sweeping across the sky was the shimmering arc of a great rainbow. "It's yours, if you can pick it up in your hands," the enigmatic creature said.

"But how? I can't. Nobody can. How can I do it? What if I can't? Stay, stay! Tell me more." But the glowing column had vanished. The room was dark and small. A foul smell and eerie, sulfurous glow surrounded the cradle, which was empty, and stained with black blood.

I woke much later, very weak. Full daylight was in the room, and Nan was peering in my face. "Her eyes, they're open!" she cried. "Look what we have for you, everything you craved. Here is marmalet, made of oranges, just as you said. And a length of linen. And Mistress Hull found a cradle, ready made, for sale. And see here, Brother Thomas has brought you from the captain two lengths of the very finest wool. Just feel it!" She put the wool by my cheek. I turned my head on the pillow. My heart felt cold. Beside my bed stood the evil cradle of the dream. It had not been there the night before.

"How—how did you get all these in only one night?" I asked.

"Oh, dear, it's been more than a night. It's been three nights, and three days, too," said Mistress Hull, who was sitting on the bench, sewing. "And we've watched all the time. You fell into a strange sleep, like death, and couldn't be waked. Sometimes you screamed. Once we had to hold you down, for fear of injury." Nan looked embarrassed, as if she hadn't planned on telling me.

"*Shush.* You know you shouldn't disturb her in this condition," she said to Mistress Hull and gave her that slit-eyed look that can stop runaway horses but didn't stop Mistress Hull, who was even older than Nan and thought that gave her precedence.

"So much has happened," went on Mistress Hull, who is like me in that she doesn't like to be cut off in midstory. "Oh, a world of things. Master Dallet's funeral was as fine as a body could want, and the coffin was very elegant, though it did give off a bad smell, as if it had burst under the pall. But they did him honor, and you, too."

"Not that he deserved it," broke in Nan.

"My husband? Buried? Buried so soon?" For some reason, I felt more bereft than ever. How like Master Dallet to depart in grand ceremony provided at the expense of others and let me have no part in it. At least in death he might have let me have the place of honor I had earned in marriage. I could have walked behind his coffin and people would have respected me. Even dead, that man was a cheat.

"But oh, there were some very elegant people there, very elegant indeed, and strangers. One of them, a distinguished gentleman with two white streaks in his hair, very rich and genial, approached me and said he wished to make arrangements to care for Master Dallet's son, when

he's born in the summer, and raise him in his very own household."
Mistress Hull was bursting with the news.

" 'And what about my mistress?' I asked him," interrupted Nan, eager to show that she was the cleverest and thought of everything, "and he said, 'Oh, I'll take care of her, too. Master Dallet was a very close friend of mine.' But I swear, I've never seen the man before." Nan's words tumbled over Mistress Hull's.

"But he seemed like a very great gentleman. His hat was trimmed with a great jewel and a very fine plume. His eyes were very pale, and he kept looking all about him. I took him for a very brilliant sort of man, too brilliant for me, I must say. I could hear him talking to others, so very high, with things like Latin words just thrown in, the way lawyers and clerks do, so very learned! He wore a robe in mossy-colored velvet, and his hose were silk, real silk. Fine as a king's, they were." Mistress Hull might not know Latin, but she knew price better than a pawnbroker.

"And don't forget the gold chain, very massive, with a strange device on it."

"They told me he was a magistrate, an important magistrate, and a very rich man. Oh, you have no idea how we longed for your eyes to open. And now, you see, there's so much to know." Nan didn't say any more but I am sure she was thinking what occurred to me at that very moment, that there is something entirely suspicious about rich important magistrates who suddenly ask to look after someone's baby, especially when it is not a prince but just an ordinary sort of baby that has not even been kidnapped by Turkish pirates.

"Oh, quiet, quiet. Can't you see we've tired her? How do you feel, my poor little dove? Better now? Surely, you must be better." In answer, I shrieked. The pains were on me, and this time there was no mistaking it. The creature would be born.

"Cat, go and fetch Goody Forster—and don't dawdle," cried Mistress Hull. "Run, now!" And the widow's daughter was off, while Nan stroked my hand and tried to tell me that everything would be all right, and that early babies were often lucky.

"But it won't be, Nan, I saw him in a dream. A boy, with black hair—"

"Hush, now, hush. You must pray to Saint Margaret. Surely she will see it born safely."

"But I don't want it born. I tell you, I saw it. It's a boy. A boy with black hair. And, and—there's something wrong with it."

At midnight, by the light of candles, the midwife brought out the head of the creature, and soon after, held it in her hands. "It's a boy," she said softly. "Born dead. Most likely dead awhile." Goody Forster was a round woman with kindly eyes, and much experience of grief. I lay as limp as a dead eel, but I could hear.

"What—what color hair?" said Nan, her voice low and shocked.

"Black, from what I can see," answered Goody Forster. "And—oh, God, look at the mouth!" Her voice rang with horror.

"Jesus save us," said Nan. "It's got teeth. Pointed ones!"

"God in heaven, I've never seen the like." Mistress Hull's voice was shocked. "Look at them, all fine and small, like fish teeth. Just as well it's dead. What woman would give it suck?"

"Don't let her see it," said Goody Forster. "The sooner it's buried, the better." Even so, I caught a glimpse of the dreadful thing, dead and shriveled up, no bigger than a bald rat, with a head the shape of a ferret's. But it had very nicely made tiny hands even if they did have fingernails just like claws, and as I saw it there, lying with its shriveled afterbirth in a great copper bowl that might have served for its first bath, I could feel tears running down my face with the shock and disappointment. Was there something so secretly vicious in me that this was what I had earned in life? Somewhere, someone was howling like a wolf. *Shh*, I heard them say, and I could feel hands shaking me, so I knew the howling was me.

"I'll get rid of it quietly," said the midwife.

"No, we'll manage," said Mistress Hull, laying some extra money in her hand to keep her quiet. "I don't trust that woman, she's a talker," she whispered to Nan as Goody Forster stumped off downstairs.

"We'll wrap it up tight and have it buried properly, and give out that it was a beauty, slain by its mother's grief, and gone to join its father in heaven. Heaven, ha! It's gone to join him somewhere, but not *there*. If everyone is talking about our story, they might not notice hers." Together they burned the bloody straw of the birth mattress and then went out to bribe the sexton at Saint Vedast's to have it buried in an unmarked grave in the corner of the churchyard. But even dead, that ugly thing went on bringing evil. There was a fire in the church porch that was barely put out in time to save the whole building on the night that the sexton buried it. And it was the last baby that Goody Forster's strong hands ever delivered, because the very next day, she died in an accident when several heavy tiles came loose from a roof and fell on her just as she was passing beneath. Then I knew that I was cursed, because this ghastly work of my inmost self had wrought such monstrous things in the world.

My husband's funeral, with all its pomp, turned out to be a great mistake. Master Dallet, having been buried as he lived, beyond his means, played his final trick on me, in spite of all that I had striven to remake him in my mind as much kinder and more loving. Before the memorial brass was even placed in the wall at Saint Vedast, his creditors determined that he must have been wealthy after all due to the splendor of the arrangements which I had provided and not even got to partake of. I was still bedridden when the first of them arrived, the apothecary from whom he bought his colors. From the remains of the three pounds, I paid him, for he was an honest man and besides he had a sad face and twelve children and a sick wife, he said.

Then came the tavern owners, the whoremasters, and the gamesters, and with each one I discovered more about my dead husband's secret life. By the time the goldsmith came to reclaim the setting of a ring unpaid for, I shouted at him, "Go collect it from his whore, Mistress Pickering!" and Nan added, "You ought to be ashamed, hounding a poor widow who has just lost her only child," as he departed down the stairs. By that time, all the money was gone, including the purse from the guilty captain.

"Oh, dear, oh, dear, they're swarming like flies," said Mistress Hull, who had come to see how I was. "I just saw a notary and a draper go down the stairs. Any more up here?"

"Not just now," I muttered.

"Well, Mistress Littleton, from hard experience I can tell you it's time we hid Mistress Dallet's paints and personal things, or the creditors will have them all. How can she paint for us if there's nothing left?" So the two of them went to work, carrying the lengths of fine black wool, the sewing things, the easels, table, and paints down the stairs. It was a task that suited her, for it allowed her to inspect our household goods even more closely than before.

"What's this chest? It looks terribly heavy. Foreign, isn't it? My, that's nice brasswork."

"It's Flemish. They do things fancier there. Let's try to take it. Get your Cat to help. Maybe if we empty it we can get it down the stairs." So then they had to empty it out and put all my husband's good portrait drawings right on the floor, which seemed something of a sacrilege but not as much of a one as putting my special books, *The Most Esteemed Life of the Holy Virgin and Mother of God* and *The Good Wyfe's Book of Manners*, right there too, even if they were on top of the drawings.

"Now what's this bit of a book here? It hasn't even got any cover," Nan said. I squinted at the thing. It was all wiggly handwriting that no normal person could read even if it were in English, which it wasn't. But it was the highest grade of unborn parchment, and the margins were very wide, just like new, with only the faintest touch of mildew on one corner.

"Oh, Master Dallet would bring home old trash! Good for nothing. Throw it out, Susanna."

"It's very good vellum. He must have got it for that, to scrape it down and reuse it. Father always said that was a stingy trick." Suppose some more Frenchmen came for another picture? This stuff would do very well, and I wouldn't have to pay for it, which can be very expensive if you understand the grades of parchment and don't get cheated. I decided I could just cut up the margins, and maybe with a good heavy undercoat reuse the center for something else, too. "I think I might need it, Nan," I said. "Parchment's high." I cut the last of the binding from the back of it so that the sheets would pack flatter.

"No one could steal the prize from Master Dallet for stinginess, that I'll say," said Nan. "Just bundle it up with the art things, then. It doesn't deserve room in the chest."

Mistress Hull had been staring at the table, thinking, her chin in her hand. "They'll wonder if there's no table and chairs," she said. "We don't want them getting suspicious, now, do we? We'll have to leave them."

"Well, at least take the carpet off it. They won't be looking for it, since Master Dallet made no will and inventory. Besides, it was Mother's."

Of course, Mistress Hull could not refrain from making aesthetic judgements about the half-finished panels my husband had left, which was altogether inappropriate, considering the dreadful stuff her late husband painted. "Goodness!" she exclaimed. "Here's a nasty piece of work. Master Dallet should have done his underpainting in terre verte. My husband swore by it." Well, wouldn't you know it, that explains the green saints, I thought. That old Master Hull didn't have a clue how to give a living flesh tone once he had finished the underpainting. Or perhaps it was his medium, which dulled the colors he mixed with it. I use my father's medium; it was his secret, and he had gotten it in his travels in Italy by bribing the assistant in a great man's atelier. Only Master Dallet and I knew it, and Master Dallet had to marry me to worm the secret out of father. It gives a translucent shine to colors and thins them out so you can build a luminous skin tone through successive veils of color. It was the secret of father's success in stained canvas work and painting in large.

"And who's this dreadful woman with the dragon's eye?"

"The Lord Mayor's wife."

"But it looks finished."

"It *is* finished. She refused to accept it."

"Oh, that's the problem with portraits. Nobody refuses a saint's picture. But a portrait? They take offense and then you never see a penny from your work. My husband said always take part payment in advance on portraits. Claim you must buy materials."

"You can't do that when you deal with great ones. Sometimes, even if they take it, they don't pay."

"Why didn't she like it, except that it tells the truth?"

"She said she had become much more slender since he painted the picture, and she wanted it redone. My husband said he'd be damned if he'd dress up that old sow any further, and there it stands." Mistress Hull inspected the picture up close, then from a distance. She tapped her foot. I was beginning to understand just how Master Hull had made as much of a success as he had, given his very small talent.

"Hmm," she said. "I think this should be your first project. Shrink the old biddy's waist, paint out a couple of chins, and get rid of those frown wrinkles between the eyebrows. Then I'll send my Cat back to the Lord Mayor's house with it and tell her that, before his death, Master Dallet had just finished repairing the picture to give a truer likeness. Then we shall see what we shall see." She tilted her head just like an old hen that spies a fine worm in the beak of a rival. The look in her beady eyes was so funny that for the first time since the horrible birth, I smiled.

"An excellent idea," I said. "Will you be wanting a share?"

"Not on this one," she answered. "I fear by the time the crows are done picking the corpse, you'll be sleeping on the floor. And, after all, what good will you be if you go and get sick?" They finished hiding the necessaries of life, including the best featherbed and the largest of our cooking pots, leaving me to ponder alone in bed on the mysteries of marriage. When my husband lived, I was never allowed a single word as to how he spent his money, and mine as well. But once he was dead, I owed his debts, just as if I'd had the pleasure of the spending myself.

We had only finished hiding things when a bony old lawyer in a fine, fur-lined gown came in with a roll of papers and two workmen. While the workmen carried out the table and the bench and the frying pan, he poked his cold, greedy face everywhere and even prodded under the bed with the staff he carried. "No chests?" he asked. "No plate? No old books?"

"You've come too late," I said. "The carrion crows have picked the corpse clean." I was glad to see him look upset. His lizardy little eyes rolled, and his mouth worked, and his face turned pale.

"He has something that is mine. A book. He . . . borrowed it. It's not here."

"What you see is what there is. Perhaps you should pursue his creditors, who have been parading through this house for the last two days."

"Creditors—yes, it has to be," he muttered. "You two, take down that bed, there. And the cradle, too. It has to be hidden somewhere. Maybe there's a compartment."

"But she's still in it," said one of the workmen.

"But it was my mother's wedding bed," I cried. "My father and mother died in this bed." Even the workmen stood abashed.

"Have you no shame at all?" cried Nan, who had watched the procedures with a face like stone. She helped me from the bed, and as I sat on the floor huddled and weeping by the hearth, they began to dismantle the big old carved bed, dumping the straw out on the floor and carrying away the bed curtains and the second-best featherbed. There it went. The bed where my parents had been happy. The bed I'd been born in. When at last the workman came back and carried off the cradle, I felt a curious lightness, as if I had been freed from some secret curse. The evil had been carried off by the lawyer with the cradle, as proud as could be in his taking of it. I started to laugh hysterically, and I saw the lawyer's workmen turn at the sound and shudder.

There is something liberating about losing everything. First you weep, then you are numb, then you count over the things you have lost and ponder how hard it will all be, and how you will never have any others like those that are gone. Then after that comes a strange lightness. Without the things one has always had, one becomes another person, any person, no person. It is a queer sensation, like being drunk and abandoning yourself. I walked about the empty room in a state of crazed hilarity, my hair wild, my knees weak. I paused to lean on the windowsill. The street, the sky, the trees, the world, all looked different, shimmering with lunatic color. Suddenly I felt capable of anything, no matter how mad.

Someone was knocking at the low door into Septimus Crouch's cellar. "Come in," he called, loath to leave the shining object before him. The reflection of a half dozen candle flames danced in reflection on it. His face was repeated a dozen different distorted ways on its edge, on the salamander base, across the glistening gold surface.

"The door is barred, master," called his servant.

"Oh, yes, just a moment," said Crouch, reluctantly turning toward the door. The cellar of the house in Lime Street Ward was where Crouch performed those experiments that must be done in secret, if scandal were to be avoided. A stone table with suspicious-looking scars and stains stood in the center of the low-vaulted, stone room. There were jugs and boxes on the shelves whose contents did not bear inspection, although the wine barrels that lined one wall were in fact the genuine item. In the very place of honor, at the center of the table, stood the mirror of conspiracy, surrounded by black candles. Hastily, he shrouded it and then threw up the bar of the door. "And how was the goldsmith's funeral?" he asked.

"Very poor, master. But his widow was so grateful for the candles you sent that she kissed my hand." Crouch chuckled.

"No one suspected?"

"Not a soul. The Lombard's poison worked—"

"—exquisitely. As it has, through the irony of fate, worked so splendidly upon the Lombard himself— A joke, Wat, you may laugh."

At the sound of his servant's nervous laughter, Crouch snorted. "Ah, Wat, you are a humorous fellow, aren't you? Well then, take yourself off. Here's a bit of something for a job well done. Fetch me some supper at midnight—a fowl, something light. I don't want heaviness to interfere with my thought processes."

The door rebarred, Crouch turned again to his new passion. With what fascination he surveyed the moving figures! The mirror, already the mirror had proven his truest friend. A sudden suspicion, a fear, that the goldsmith might make use of the secrets he had learned, had sent him to consult the mirror in secret. There, his worst fears had been revealed: the goldsmith could be seen, plain as day, casting another mirror from the mold he swore he had broken. What if everyone had a mirror? How could Crouch remain supreme? His Lombard partner had agreed, and with the most delightful and practiced Italian gesture, swept his ring-laden hand across the wine goblet, then smiled as the goldsmith drank deep of slow-acting poison. The ring, the ring, thought Crouch as he watched. The Lombard has a hollow ring for dispensing poison. Why did I never guess? Who knows what other subtle means of giving death he has? He will not want to share the secret long and I, I have need of the Mirror of Diocletian more than he. . . .

How fortunate the mirror had warned him of the Lombard's treachery; in it he had seen the Lombard laughing with friends at his own funeral. Now he had laughed at the Lombard's, instead.

Until he had gotten possession of the mirror, he had no idea he had so many enemies. Now they stood revealed, all of them. Dangerous, conspiratorial. It was only prudence to remove them. After all, he had great plans. Which one of them had plans of such magnificence, such power? The Lombard was nothing. Someday, kings would rise and fall at Crouch's command; he would rule this world and the next with mighty powers. No one must stand in his way. The mirror, his secret eye on the world, would reveal everything. . . .

The Third Portrait

Portrait of an Unknown Lady. *ca. 1520 National Portrait Gallery. N.P.G.*

This portrait, tentatively identified as one of Lady Burghley in middle age, displays the gradual shift of costume from the late medieval style of the court of Henry VII to the more elaborate court costume of the period of Henry VIII. Note especially the characteristic peaked or gabled headdress of the sitter, ornamented with semiprecious stones, the use of slashing to reveal costly embroidered linen, the quilted stiffening of the undersleeve and the widening of the oversleeve, here so great as to allow the sitter's lap dog to hide within the folds. The anonymous painter has captured with unconscious drollery the identical self-important expression in both the wealthy sitter and her pet.

—Smythe, B. Six Centuries of English Costume

I have skipped quite a bit ahead here to the days long after I became prosperous to show you one of my most successful panel paintings. It did make Lady Guildford weep for joy because she was most excessively fond of that little dog—which died shortly after I painted it from eating pheasant bones that nobody should ever give a dog anyway even if they are scraps. I do believe I caught her to the life, except that I did not put in any wrinkles and I told her the ones that were left were signs of character and appropriate to her dignity.

But the truth is that there was a long time before I got any important patrons. And although I threw myself into my work with all my strength nobody wealthy came to buy, and it was only through the strangest accident in the world that my work later came to the attention of significant patrons such as Lady Guildford. But in that poorer time I had to make an entirely different kind of painting which although they were of a religious nature, appealed to the lower feelings, so I will not show them to you. They were also unclothed, which was why they found so many buyers although not at high prices. And so I did not sign them S.D. Fecit but just left them blank and said someone else must have done them.

To make this picture I stayed at Richmond for a whole month where Lady Guildford was governess of the Princess Mary, whose portrait had started my whole career although she didn't know it. The painting took a long time not because I am slow, but because Lady Guildford was too anxious to spend long at any one sitting on account of her many cares for a huge household and also because she spent a lot of time seeing that handsome gentlemen could not sit alone with the princess, who is very fond of company and good times. But between her sittings I painted several small portraits for the handsome gentlemen who wanted to give them to the princess and the other ladies who were there as companions, and also portraits of ladies who wanted to give them to the gentlemen, and so because they were all very gallant, I left much richer than I came and brought Cat a length of blue wool and Mistress Hull a new cap. I also paid Nan all her back wages, but she spent them on her brother who said he needed them for a business opportunity now that he was out of jail, so she was just as poor as always.

SIX

The very evening after the mysterious strangers left the House of the Standing Cat, at the precise moment that Mistress Hull was standing in the buttery deciding how many candles she could expend upon the corpse she had laid out on the floor, the candles were burning low in the paneled dining hall of the royal palace at Richmond. There the musicians had already been sent away when the conversation at the supper party turned to the supernatural. Mother Guildford's firm stare, which had squelched a newborn discussion of gallantry, softened, for edifying tales of spectral visitations were among her favorites. She smoothed the black silk skirts of her immense, many-petticoated gown and settled her imposing, heavily corseted figure in a more comfortable position on the cushions of her chair. Lackeys filled the heavy silver wine cups again, removing the platters of bones and emptied dishes of stale sauce from the white tablecloth. Mother Guildford's little dog lay at her feet in the rushes, gnawing on a knucklebone.

The princess's ladies turned to each other with wide eyes, and the Duke of Suffolk, a practiced ladies' man, took advantage of the old duenna's brief inattention to cast a burning glance in the direction of the princess. A heavy necklace of pearls and rubies set off her white neck and echoed the colors of her red brocade gown, slashed to reveal heavily gathered, embroidered white silk sleeves. Her heavy red-gold hair, caught in a circlet of gold links decorated with sapphires, flowed freely down her back, for she was still a maiden, and very young. Mary Tudor's face turned pink when she caught Suffolk's look, but her bright eyes flashed in return. Jane Popincourt, her French tutor and lady-in-waiting, began an astonishing tale of the sound of a spinning wheel, which came each night from a wall in a bedchamber she had once had.

"Oh, yes, I remember how very vexed you were that you had no sleep," cried the princess.

"And it was I who ordered masons to tear down the wall. And what do you think they found?" Mistress Jane paused. Mother Guildford cast an expectant eye over the awed company. After a dramatic silence, Mistress Jane continued. "A sealed chamber, with a dusty, unused old spinning wheel, entirely covered with cobwebs. We asked the priest to search the records and found that a woman who spun for the queen had died in that room."

"But pray tell," broke in Suffolk, a bluff, heavyset man, "why should a spirit, freed of earthly cares, carry on work both bothersome and laborious?" Everything about Suffolk looked large and square: his dark brown, square-cut beard, his heavy mane of hair, cut flat below the ears, his neck, his shoulders. Somehow it all reminded most people of an ox—an ox in court clothes, his English-cut dark blue satin doublet and heavy brocade gown extravagantly slashed with crimson seeming to sit uncomfortably on his huge frame. But largeness and roisterous spirits had made him the young king's best friend and partner in high jinks. "No," he went on, "spirits return only when they have a message for the living—or, perchance, a need for vengeance."

"One might ask whether there is a message in the spinning." The young Duc de Longueville, recently captured at the battle of Guinegate, but as free as any gentleman of the court until his ransom should be paid, was impatient to turn the company to his own story. "I believe that when ghosts work, it is always for a purpose. For example, in this very city, someone I know ... very well ... heard of a most extraordinary ghostly manifestation—"

"Oh, tell us!" cried the princess, clapping her hands. Vanity and wine pushed him, at that moment, beyond the bounds of discretion.

"Well, it seems that there was a young painter in the City of London, very handsome, with unique talent in the taking of portraits. He was newly wed to a beautiful wife, to whom he was devoted, and who was expecting their first child—" Longueville was clad in the French fashion, bright and glittering, with his pale blue satin doublet cut well away from his neck to show his beautifully made linen. His flat velvet hat, in dark violet, ornamented with a gold medallion, set off his light brown, shoulder-length curls and narrow features. Half the ladies in the room were in love with him.

"Ah, then it's a love story," exclaimed the princess. Mother Guildford turned a fierce eye, enough to stop a lion in midleap, on de Longueville, but he never hesitated.

"Exactly so," agreed de Longueville cheerfully. "But one with an extraordinary ending. This painter, being newly come to a mastership, had many debts. But through good fortune, a great lord came to him with a princely commission, to create a portrait in small, as a jewel, from a portrait in large." The company leaned forward, and Suffolk set his elbows on the table. The Frenchman did know how to tell a good story.

"The following day, the great lord returned and met outside the door a holy man, going to offer succor to a new-made widow, whose husband had been murdered the night before in a street brawl. It was the artist who had been murdered, the very night that the commission had been given, and his widow, all unknowing, was waiting for him to return."

"Oh, this is so very sad," said Mistress Popincourt. She took an embroidered handkerchief from her wide velvet sleeve. "It is much too sad for a love story." Mother Guildford secretly wiped the corner of her eye with a plump index finger.

"Imagine the nobleman's distress when I—uh, he, found that the jewel could not possibly have been completed. Still, when he entered the artist's studio, the lord found there a masterwork, more perfect than earthly hand could create." The company drew in its breath as one. "'From whence did this perfect jewel come?' the lord asked. And the artist's young wife, still uninformed of her great loss, said that her husband had appeared silently that morning and worked all day without meat or drink, vanishing silently when the work was complete. Little did the wife suspect what the lord knew instantly: that it was the spirit of her dead husband, devoted beyond the grave, that had returned to complete the commission and so provide for her and the infant."

"Astonishing!" cried another gentleman.

"So touching. Oh, in spite of the wickedness of the world, there is still true married love." Mother Guildford wiped away several large tears.

"In the City itself, you say?"

"I wonder who it could have been. Did you say you knew this fellow?"

"I have sworn secrecy for the sake of a lady's honor," said de Longueville, content with the sensation he had made.

"Tell me," teased Jane Popincourt, "the great lord was you, wasn't it?" De Longueville, sated, stretched his naked body back on the pillows of the great bed. Even though the heavy velvet curtains were pulled shut around them, Mistress Jane had discreetly pulled the linen sheet over her in place of a shift. De Longueville smiled impishly and pulled at the sheet.

"Show it to me again," he said.

"Oh, not until you tell," she cried with mock modesty.

"Why, then, I'll tell: it was me," said de Longueville, twitching at the sheet.

"But what woman was it?" asked Mistress Jane, suddenly alarmed and clutching at the sheet with both hands. "Oh, you ingrate! You have another lady!"

"In addition to you, who are everything?" he teased. "Never think it, my sweet little Jeanne." Then, spying the look on her face, he went on more seriously. "It was a commission for another—person—which I carried out. The woman is a great lady, and you will forgive me if I am sworn to protect her reputation." Suddenly, Mistress Jane did not trust his sensual smile, his insinuating voice. Did those dark eyes light up for her alone? She scrutinized his face, trying to read some secret meaning there. She had risked everything, seeing him like this. She had risked her reputation, and her place with the princess, if the word got out. But if he abandoned her, he might well gossip about her. Men, oh, who can trust them? she thought. When can a man ever resist boasting about a conquest? Look at him there, betraying someone else's secret to make a sensation at a dinner party. No, if she didn't want him talking, she would do best to keep him entangled, she thought. She smiled and pulled aside the sheet.

"Beautiful," he said. "You are more lovely than Venus herself." As he rolled on top of her for a second passage at love, she resolved to question his footman, find the widow, and discover whose picture had been painted by the ghost. Distracted by her worry, she found him decidedly less satisfactory than before. But de Longueville, who liked to see his mistresses insecure, rejoiced in her edginess and let passion take his mind from the web of secrets he had so artfully concealed from her. The very least of them was that he was dispatching a portrait in miniature of the king's sister, Mary Tudor, to Louise of Savoy, mother of the heir to the throne of France, at the request of that most formidable and ambitious lady.

Thomas Wolsey, the King's Almoner, member of the King's Council, Bishop of Lincoln and master of military logistics for the recent war in France, was seated in his cabinet at Bridewell when Robert Ashton, one of the secretaries of his privy chamber, along with the priest who was the confessor of Jane Popincourt, were announced. Wolsey was then in the act of conferring with the master cook of his privy kitchen, a personage held in high esteem in a household where food was of the first importance. The master cook was no small person: he was clad in damask satin, with a gold chain about his neck, and he carried himself with the confidence of one who commands two master cooks of the hall kitchen, two clerks of the kitchen, four kitchen grooms, two yeomen of the pantry, a yeoman of the scullery, and a yeoman of the silver scullery, to say nothing of an army of lesser laborers of the kitchen, men, women, and children.

Wolsey's shape illustrated his passion for cuisine, but beneath the effulgent flesh and appearance of health lay a weakness of digestion that must be catered to absolutely. It was the master cook of the privy kitchen's job to keep the internal workings of his master as finely tuned as a well-oiled clock, for as the Wolsey-clock functioned, so prospered the realm. Wolsey had been the secret power that planned England's future since the death of the shrewd, stingy old king who had fathered Henry the Eighth. Under Wolsey's capable management had come all the business neglected by an amusement-loving young king. Whenever there were statutes to consider, treaties to ponder, papers to be inspected before signing, in short, whenever dull work enclosed in a cabinet threatened, the king was only too happy to have

Wolsey stand beside his stirrup and say, "Don't let this matter spoil your day's hunting, Your Majesty. Take your princely pleasure where you will, while I, your humble servant, shoulder the dull duties of the council and dispatch your business entirely according to your will."

So well had Wolsey done that prince's will in the dull matters of business that dull money, dull manors, and dull bishoprics had fallen like ripe fruit into the King's Almoner's busy, if plump, hands. At this time two great projects occupied entire compartments in his multi-compartmented and ever-calculating mind, beyond the project of to-morrow's dinner, which occupied a section that might be called "miscellaneous, recurring." The first project was the search for a manor located near the capital city, but free from its pestilential airs. Wolsey feared illness as only a man with complex and far-reaching plans can. And so he employed tasters, hired physicians, and procured water from faraway sources. The thought that so humble a thing as poisoned air might lay low his grandest schemes offended him; he preferred enemies of rank. He had secured the lease of a place on the river called Hampton Court where his physicians had assured him the air was salubrious; now a part of him was given over to planning a residence worthy of his splendor.

The second project, rather less personal but no less dear to him, involved the complete realignment of the powers of Europe, in England's favor, of course. The centerpiece to this plan was the engineering of an alliance with England's greatest enemy, France, which would offset the power of Spain and the Holy Roman Emperor. But the key to the plan was a woman, or, rather, a flirtatious, lighthearted, spoiled girl of seventeen, Mary Tudor, the king's younger sister. Just as Wolsey had been worrying about how to approach his project, and almost as if God had willed it, the King of France's wife had died. Through secret negotiations (how convenient de Longueville had been!) Wolsey had offered the King of France Henry's newly widowed sister, Margaret, the Queen of Scotland. But the old king had rejected her. The Queen of Scotland, the king had heard, was old and stout, having already reached her twenty-fifth birthday.

Wolsey, like a cat watching a mouse hole, waited while the old king inspected other brides and found them wanting. Quietly, he took the old man's measure; a man trying to recapture his lost youth, speculated the shrewd cleric. He wants beauty, he wants frivolity, he deludes himself into thinking he acts only for an heir. With an almost satiric craft, the King's Almoner had dangled the prize bait in front of him: he had offered to seal an alliance between France and England with the most beautiful and frivolous princess in Europe.

The French king hesitated; Wolsey dispatched by secret courier a life-size portrait of her head in three-quarters view, her lips parted, her eyes shining invitingly beneath long lashes (it had not hurt that the master painter was quite handsome and had a most flattering tongue). It was a picture calculated to set an old man's blood boiling. Wolsey smiled at the remembrance of it. Even his French agent who had received the portrait had expressed his admiration. The most delicate operation, accomplished brilliantly. In what great secrecy he had had to work, to prevent a counterscheme from being hatched against him by the English king's father-in-law, the King of Spain, whose spies were everywhere!

Now, dinner having been planned and all his mind-compartments humming, Wolsey sent off the Master Cook. The King's Almoner was expecting de Longueville shortly, with news from France, he hoped. Instead it was Master Ashton, the newest of his privy secretaries, and a priest whose name he ought to have remembered, but which seemed to escape him at the moment. As his servant and the strange priest were shown in, Wolsey made a point of looking up from some papers with which he appeared to be busy as if to say, Well, be quick about it.

"Your Grace, you have asked me to report any news that pertains to Longueville's activities. I have come to you because I have reason to believe that he is carrying on a separate correspondence with France." Ashton's face was calm as he delivered this news, but in an unconscious gesture, he unrolled the tightened fingers of his left hand with his right. Wolsey noticed it. Ashton might as well have written his nervousness on a sign and hung it about his neck.

Ashton had good reason to be nervous; he was knowingly interrupting the great man at his labors. Being cast into outer darkness was the very least of the penalties that Wolsey imposed on those who annoyed him. And Ashton, in the course of his duties as a confidential agent, errand boy, and letter writer in four languages, had already become well acquainted with the utter ruthlessness that lay beneath the silky surface of Wolsey's ambition. But Ashton, just twenty-five, was new to the bishop's service and had no important family connections. He needed to take risks to rise. Nothing ventured, nothing gained, said Ashton to himself. I can't let Brian Tuke spend all his time wallowing in the bishop's favor. It's Ashton's turn for praise.

What Ashton would have been humiliated to realize was that he had been retained for the sake of an unfortunate gift that endeared him to Wolsey: to anyone with a mind to see, Ashton's honest eyes signaled every thought that went through his head as clearly as if it were written on his forehead. It amused Wolsey to read the continual display of thoughts that passed through Ashton's hazel eyes, and occasionally to give Ashton a prod, or even several, just to watch his face change. The fact that Ashton was intelligent made it even better. Reading Ashton made Wolsey feel older and cleverer, and was always a pleasant thing to do on a rainy afternoon, when reading documents cloyed. For this reason, he tolerated Ashton's youthful brashness, his tendency to be too hasty and too passionate in matters he considered moral, his fits and moods, and the irritating little habits that signaled he had not been trained at court. Besides, the man was useful; he was courageous, he was nosy, he was persistent, and he was eager to rise.

Wolsey cast a long, purposefully shrewd stare at Ashton, taking in at a glance the strapping form, the mobile, intelligent face, the livery dusty with travel and hastily, hopefully, brushed. He measured with a glance Ashton's overeager eyes, in which trepidation and calculation warred with triumphant delight at his own cleverness. Aha, thought Wolsey, whatever he has here, he's planned a counterblow against Master Tuke. It is bound to be interesting. Brian Tuke pleased Wolsey for exactly the qualities Ashton had no hope of possessing: he was smooth, deferential, flattering, and pliant to his master's least wish. Unoriginal and politic, his rise within Wolsey's household was unhindered by the kind of embarrassing incident that Ashton was likely to entangle himself in. He had served longer than Ashton; he did better than Ashton. Ashton resented it, and strove mightily to overtake him. Wolsey enjoyed the rivalry immensely, and every so often did something to overbalance it, first one way, and then another, just to watch the two of them circle each other like fighting dogs in the pit. Another amusement for those dull moments between plans.

The priest, who had let Master Ashton's silver tongue, golden coin, and mention of the mighty bishop's favor worm the secret from him, seemed suddenly to shrivel under Wolsey's cold gaze.

"Surely, de Longueville is too cautious to bring any deep scheme to the confessional. Are you sure it is not some frivolous social correspondence?" Wolsey made his voice icy and was rewarded by the sudden fading of the expression of cocky cleverness in Ashton's eyes.

"It was not he who confessed, but Mistress Popincourt, who was wild with jealousy that he had secretly procured the portrait of another woman," Ashton broke in. Wolsey made his face darkly dubious. Ashton's eyes were filled with a sudden, deeply gratifying, anxiety. "This priest here will bear me out," said Ashton. The priest nodded in affirmation of Ashton's words.

"Another woman? What other woman?" Wolsey's curiosity was piqued, and he let it show. Good, thought Ashton, I've aroused his interest. Now we are safe. The image of Master Tuke's snobbish, irritated glare danced delightfully in Ashton's mind. Next time, Tuke, it will be Ashton who walks behind the bishop, carrying the dispatch case and record books to the council meeting, not Tuke. Wolsey noted the return of the rivalrous glitter to Ashton's eyes, and was silent.

"Hear me out, and perhaps you will draw conclusions similar to mine." Best not to let it out all at once, thought Ashton. Through hard experience abroad, much of it spent observing ruthless men of power, Ashton had become an expert at the timing of telling a good tale. In addition, he could, when sufficiently drunk, mimic the accents and affectations of others in a manner calculated to bring the company into fits of helpless laughter. These were skills of great value to a man who at sixteen had inherited ten pounds and a horse at his father's death, almost as useful as his neat clerk's handwriting, and the gift of languages he had discovered in his brief career as a mercenary abroad.

Wolsey sunk his chin in his hand as he listened. His right eyelid drooped in a way that seemed most sinister to the confessor, who seemed to have lost the power of speech. Ashton paused, and continued. "At a supper at Greenwich, de Longueville was enticed by the guests into telling a ghost story. It seems a certain lord offered a commission to paint a miniature from a stained canvas portrait in large to a certain painter in the city—"

"Yes, yes, go on." Wolsey was impatient with long stories.

"When he returned to collect the miniature, he met a priest outside the house of the artist who had come to inform the artist's wife that her husband had been murdered across town the night before. But to the lord's surprise, the portrait was complete anyway. The wife, unknowing, gave out that in ghostly fashion her husband had returned and finished the work."

"Ghostly fashion indeed," snorted Wolsey. "The man had an apprentice who finished the job and the wife palmed off apprentice work for master's wages."

"That was my thought, too, Your Grace. The French are so excitable, you know. The picture, of course, was reported to be a masterwork of the highest order." Ashton pulled his face into a droll imitation of a French connoisseur of art. Try as he might to be serious, he could not disguise the fact that he loved a good practical joke. This was another quality that had caused Wolsey to retain him, despite his other defects. It made him the perfect agent. Many of Wolsey's finest schemes had the quality of practical jokes on the universe, and it was the unconscious understanding of this that made Robert Ashton able to act at a distance exactly as Wolsey would have done if he were there in person. It was a talent that Wolsey at the same time both valued and despised, as one despises some less elegant part of oneself that should have been left behind when one rose in the world.

"Of course," Wolsey responded. "What else would give so excellent a finish to a story? But go on." Wolsey had become interested in spite of himself. He shifted to a more comfortable position in his big chair. Good, he's settling in, thought Ashton.

"Mistress Popincourt divined through a slip of the tongue that de Longueville was the lord involved, and decided he had another mistress, one he favored more, for when had he ever worn her portrait around his neck? She searched his things, subtly questioned his servants, and found he had indeed had the portrait painted, and paid three pounds for it, too, which made her even more furious. But he did not have the portrait in his possession. The servant would tell no more but only blessed himself to keep the ghost off. Being curious, I made inquiries and found that de Longueville had sent off a pouch containing a small box sewn into an oiled silk cloth to Dover—"

"The portrait."

"Exactly. It was to be entrusted to a French captain who would see it delivered to Louise of Savoy, mother of the Dauphin." The fatal shot. Ashton's face was serene.

"Louise of Savoy! That scheming woman! This French duke plays a double game with me!" Wolsey stood suddenly, furious. "Then the portrait must be—"

"Your Grace, in a moment you will know for certain."

"What do you mean?"

"Your Grace, knowing your mind in these matters, and being your faithful servant in all things, I sent a fast messenger by post and intercepted the ship. My servant bribed the captain's servant and secured the package, on loan, as it were—"

"Brilliant! I forsee a grand future for you, Ashton," Wolsey interrupted. Ashton's eyes lit up.

"—which I have here," Ashton finished. Triumphantly, he produced a leather pouch and placed it among the papers and dispatch cases on Wolsey's immense oak desk. The victorious secretary saw Wolsey's eye glow beneath the sinister, drooping lid; he noted with mixed delight and relief the imperceptible smile and the controlled calm in the bishop's voice as he said:

"My dear Master Ashton, will you be so kind as to show out this excellent priest and to call the clerk of my closet?"

The clerk, a young priest who was an expert at decoding intercepted correspondence, pried loose the seals intact with a practiced hand and delicately cut the threads that held the oiled silk tightly around the box. Inside was a letter folded tight, in cipher, and a plain round case, about two inches in diameter.

"The cipher is a simple one, de Longueville's usual, Your Grace," said the clerk, who had brought his decoding paraphernalia with him. He lit a candle from the fire and delicately applied heat to the letter to bring out any hidden writing, then set to work. In the quiet of the room, the only sound was that of his pen scratching, as Wolsey opened the portrait box with the practiced care of a great connoisseur. But even he was taken aback by the glittering little image that lay inside the turned wood box.

"The Princess Mary, as I surmised," he said. "Louise of Savoy must wish to know the face of her enemy." He turned the box sideways to catch the light at a different angle. Wolsey considered himself an exceptional judge of all that was most exquisite in art and music, as befit a churchman of rank. "This is a copy of the Dallet portrait. But it surpasses the original, a thing most surprising in a copy." He held the picture closer to his good left eye. "And, I judge, it is not by Dallet's hand." He gestured to his code clerk, who understood instantly what he wanted, and handed the bishop his magnifying glass. "See here," said Wolsey, peering through the glass, "the work is finer. See the hatchwork under the jaw? It is almost invisible, the strokes are so finely wrought. This work is not done in England. Or rather, it was not until now. Yes, I imagine we shall find that Dallet had a foreign apprentice—one who surpassed him, and whose name he concealed out of jealousy."

"It is indeed most finely made," said the code clerk, who had finished copying the brief, ciphered letter into plain English and had taken a moment to peer at the miniature painting in his master's hand.

"Master Dallet would not long have retained his crown had he let this apprentice be known. The boy could have set up as his rival even without a mastership," observed Ashton, his intelligent face intently peering over the code clerk's shoulder as he, too, inspected the painting. Secretly, he gloried in the moment of shared connoisseurship. Ha, take that, Tuke. The great man confers with *me* on matters that require a *real* mind.

Wolsey set down the painting and took up the transcribed letter. "Pleasantries," he said, "and not much more. 'The image which accompanies this letter is that which you requested of Princess Mary Tudor, younger sister to the King of England. I can vouch personally for the fact that it is a true portrait in the liveliest detail of her character as well as her features—' Longueville must be in regular correspondence with this woman. The wretch! Now, how can we turn this to our account?" Wolsey tapped an impatient finger on the arm of his great cushioned chair as he thought.

"De Longueville is right about her character. This artist seems to portray the very thoughts of the subject through the features. It is really most extraordinary," said Ashton. He was a good judge of painting, and genuinely impressed and puzzled at such a display of talent from one unknown. Wolsey turned suddenly to him and said,

"And what thoughts do they seem to be? How will that Frenchwoman read this picture? Answer honestly, now." Ashton answered suddenly, with the vigor and bitterness of a passionate soul who has just been jilted and still has the event fresh in his mind.

"She will see a light-headed girl whose thoughts turn on love, jewels, and clothes—a hot-tempered girl without the bitter steadfastness necessary to carry out far-reaching, ambitious plans. In short, a person easily manipulated—"

"—and no match for herself," finished Wolsey. "It is, perhaps, better to let her know this, so she will not try to maneuver against the marriage. We will send it to her by slow courier when the arrangements are nearly complete. Then we will offer prayers that the old king can still get an heir on his new bride—an English heir for the throne of France."

"But if the king dies while the infant is a minor—"

"We must begin laying plans to assure that the English queen is made regent, otherwise—"

"—otherwise Francis of Angoulême becomes regent, and Louise of Savoy the regent's mother. A mother ambitious above all that her son Francis have the throne."

"Precisely. Accidents occur to young children, Ashton. An open window, a sick wet-nurse. Louise will stop at nothing to see her son Francis of Angoulême as king. No, we must always be three steps ahead of her." *We.* The word sounded splendid to Ashton. We. His intelligent eyes watched Wolsey as England's most brilliant strategist reworked the plans in several of his mind-compartments. Already, the King's Almoner calculated, he had obtained the princess's trust. He had no doubt that she would be guided by him. But at such a distance! Wolsey shook his head, regretting that she was so young, so incapable of understanding the forces arrayed against her. If only it had been Margaret! Regretfully, Wolsey closed the portrait case. "I hate to give this up," he said, "but I am consoled for its loss by the thought that I will soon have the unknown master painter in my household service."

The code clerk was already reaffixing the seals on the letter with a careful hand. Wolsey sighed as he saw the oiled silk restitched about the box, exactly as if it had never been intercepted, and the outer seals reattached. "Master Ashton, go find me this painter and bring him to me here at Brideswell," he said. "I can make good use of a man who can depict the soul with a brush." Dismissing his code clerk, he turned his mind to the method by which he would confront de Longueville with his treachery and bring him even deeper into his power.

On the rue de la Harpe, on the left bank of the river that divides the city of Paris and not far from the Hôtel de Cluny, there stands a pleasant old stone house with slate-roofed turrets and tall, narrow windows with blue shutters. Behind its kitchen, with its huge fireplaces and stone ovens, there is an overgrown, walled garden, where herbs grow wild. Its owner, one Maître Bellier, is a doctor of theology who travels extensively on business. But even though he is not currently at home, the neighbors observe that he has been receiving guests this afternoon. The last of them, masked, tall, and imperious, is late. He strides through the hall as if he owns it, descends a narrow stair, and taps a signal on a closed door to the cellars. A man with a candle opens, and then bars the door after them. Behind wine casks, the entrance to a tunnel is concealed, whose dark slippery walls give off the smell of old and fetid water. They plunge unerringly into the dark, descending rapidly along a corridor of smoke-blackened brick until they enter a vaulted underground chamber lit by torches. The floor is slick marble, and at the center of the room, a square pool of black water shines with the orange, reflected glow of the smoking torches. At one end of the pool, a company is seated around a heavy oak table. The thronelike chair at the head of it is empty. This dank and buried ruin is the meeting place of an ancient secret society, the Priory of Sion, mother organization of the Knights Templar, and dedicated, for reasons known only to itself, to the overthrow of the Valois, the ruling house of France.

"Brethren, the Helmsman," announces the man with the candle, and the grave men in black all stand. The tall man throws back his mask, revealing a pair of smoldering, dark eyes set in a narrow, overbred face, tight and bitter with some old resentment. The light picks up the shine of gold embroidery where his black cloak parts. Evidently, in the outer world, he is a man of rank and power. At a sign, the knights of the Priory of Sion sit.

"Brethren," announces the Helmsman, "two grave matters are before us. The first is that the King of France has selected a bride. The prophecy slips from us." A babble of voices responds.

"But is it not the hour? The stars have foretold it."

"Louis the Twelfth hopes to renew the Valois line. As it stands now, he has no direct heir. Only Francis of Angoulême remains between us and the Great Task."

"The restoration of the True Blood to the throne."

"The bride is young, the king is old. Should she bear sons, she will become Queen Regent of France, and her children will push the throne even farther from our grasp."

"We must set her against Francis, and that harpy, his mother, Louise of Savoy. The two camps will destroy each other."

"Carefully, carefully, brethren. We must lay plans. They say the bride is young and foolish. She is the pawn of the churchman who controls the English throne, the bishop Wolsey. He craves an English heir for the throne of France as mightily as we crave no heir at all from the House of Valois. But he will have problems acting at a distance. There is a weakness. . . ."

"We could assassinate Wolsey . . ."

"No easy task. He is guarded and has a man taste every dish from which he eats."

"But it is the second business that is the greater risk," the Helmsman's voice breaks in. "Maître Bellier has written us from London. An agent of this Wolsey has recently purchased several antique coins for the bishop's collection of ancient coins and medallions. These are Merovingian coins, coins of King Dagobert. . . ."

"The True Blood!"

"The London Hoard . . ."

"Exactly. Someone has found it. And if Wolsey's agent, in pursuit of more antiquities, recovers the manuscript that is concealed with it, then our Secret will fall into the hands of the Church—and the Valois." The faces of the men at the table are stiff with horror.

"It must be recovered."

"Exactly. I have sent instructions to our brother Bellier. The manuscript must be recovered, at any cost."

"Louise of Savoy?" spluttered de Longueville. "But of course I maintain correspondence with many of the great families of the kingdom—why should I not correspond with my friends?"

"In the heart of the most delicate and secret of negotiations? Milord de Longueville, your future as well as mine is tied to this great affair."

"Then I beg to remind you, Your Grace, that Louise of Savoy and her son, the Duc d'Angoulême, must be kept as friendly as possible in this matter. The marriage risks snatching a throne from their grasp. The princess will have powerful enemies at court, and it is better that you maintain a connection with them."

"Nonsense. Louis the Twelfth appears old at fifty-two, but he is still sound. And if he dies when I surmise, his new queen will be Queen Mother, and most amenable to our interests."

"I tell you, I have heard that he is ill with grief since his old queen died. He wept on her tomb and swore that he would follow her within the year."

"Pure melodrama. A younger woman will restore him."

"Or kill him, my lord, in which case you will need other friends at the French court."

"Milord of Longueville, you argue for your own convenience." Wolsey feigned an explosion of wrath, then paused, appearing to check himself, shaking his head as if his Christian conscience were battling his lower instincts. Then, brushing a hand across his forehead, he spoke as if weakened by the internal struggle. "But still, I am a forgiving man, and much beholden to you for your private service in this matter. You will be richly rewarded should this marriage be accomplished. But secrecy is essential—the agents of the Holy Roman Empire abound like fleas in this great city. So be careful to spread no news, even inadvertently." It was a magnificent performance, designed at once to terrify the younger man and to give him a sense that he somehow was in control of the older man, that he could understand

him. But it was all illusion. The hidden depths remained unfath-
omable. The sinister, drooping eyelid twitched. The creased mouth
was an emotionless plane.

"But my expenses now—" burst out the young man.

"Ah yes, costumes, masques, worldly pleasures. I hear you were
magnificent at the ball at Richmond. And then," Wolsey added slyly,
"there is the matter of three pounds for a portrait in miniature. Quite
a princely sum. Surely you could have had it for less?" De Longueville
looked taken aback. "My dear young man, never assume I don't know
everything," Wolsey added cosily. "Tell me, they say it was painted by a
ghost. Does that account for the extraordinary fee?" De Longueville,
happy to change the subject, began the narration of the ghost story
that had made him so popular at dinner parties for the last week. And
Wolsey, feigning amazement, marveled inwardly at the gullibility of
the otherwise hardheaded Frenchman.

SEVEN

There was something very discouraging about staring at an old lady with a dragon's eye and trying to think about how to make her more beautiful without making it a lie altogether, but only something of a fib, and how she imagines herself anyway. The studio looked ever so naked, and so did our rooms which were fair pitiful. But still it was better than being on the street or in some charitable institution scrubbing floors or worse for sour-tempered holy people. Now I always secretly had it more in mind to be painting inspirational things like Christ and the Holy Virgin in order to display my virtue. But the dragon lady was the mayor's wife and had money, and we needed another bed to make up for the one that had been taken away. Now here was where imagination came in, and it was just as well as I had such a powerful one because it took a lot to imagine that lady young, but I did it.

First I painted out her chins in shadow with a nice gray violet and made a bit of a shine along a made-up jawline that I copied from the princess, who had a very nice one. Then I shifted the highlight on her nose, which made it much less horsey without actually shortening it—which she might have noticed. Then I put another glaze across the whole face to reduce the wrinkles. By this time I was having a good time because it was really a bit like making an entire new person, and I was losing my sense of shame. Then I decided to make her jewels larger and shinier and put more of a gloss on her silk dress because Dallet never did do jewels right, and his dresses always look as though they came from the same place, just different colors. It was strange; as I worked, I had the feeling of watchers looking over my shoulder, but it didn't seem to bother me; instead, it spurred me on.

By now I was having a very good time, with my sleeves rolled up like a housemaid's and the paint spattered all about the hem of my old skirt, which was much happier not being my best anymore. My nose felt very itchy so I wiped the back of my hand across it so as not to paint it, too, and then I sat back to look at what I had done. It was very good. I'd left the eye, so she'd know herself, but that was about all. The light was almost gone, and I was stiff from sitting on that little stool, so I left the glaze to dry until tomorrow and got up and stretched and peeked out the window and felt good. As I turned back from the window, I heard a little scurrying sound and saw the oddest thing. A little baby's bare pink foot seemed to be vanishing through the wall, but then, it could have been a trick of the failing light.

Nan was down at Widow Hull's talking which gave me time to think. Spring was outside, which includes flowers and birds but also ugly smells because the gutters get warm and stinky, which shows that there is a good and a bad side to everything. Twilight was just trying to push the last of the golden light from the sky. There was loud singing and the sound of some woman laughing coming from the brewhouse across the way, and three men trying to carry a drunk man home but since they were all drunk it wasn't working out very well.

"Hey, look at that woman in the window. She has a blue nose."

"Shut up, you idiot, you're drunk. Now look, you've dropped him."

" 'S blue, I tell you."

I pulled my face in and ran to look in the mirror. A big streak of blue, right across my nose. For a minute I was frightened. He'd see it. He'd tell me I was ugly. He'd hit me for using his things. Then I remembered. He can't. I laughed. Maybe I won't clean it off, I thought, just to prove I can even have a blue nose if I want. But then I put some turpentine on a rag and cleaned it off anyway because it might be harder to get off tomorrow, and suppose I needed to go to the market? So then I sat and thought as I scrubbed up about the good and the bad side, which is like balance and being fair which are all part of the same thing. I mean, on the one side it is bad to be poor and have no furniture, but on the other side it is good to have friends and hope. And now that Master Dallet was not around to give mean looks to Mistress Hull and mock her husband's paintings we could be friends.

"Supper, supper!" Nan called from downstairs, because now we all ate in the kitchen and put together our grocery money to have better things.

"Oh, you stink of turpentine. What's that on your face?" Nan does carry on, but that is because she worries about everything.

"I thought I'd got it all. What's that, a chicken? We must be rich already."

"You need to keep up your strength. Master Hull always needed to keep up his strength when the creation was on him. And besides, you're building back from all that's happened." Mistress Hull was always very considerate about just skipping over mentioning ugly things that could make a person unhappy and possibly mope and not paint. "How's that old lady doing? Have you got her thinned out? I'll show you the Adam and Eves after supper. Maybe there's one you can use as a model."

A light rain had dampened the cobblestones in the courtyard of the Saracen's Head, making them shine, treacherously slippery for the cloaked figure who picked his way gloomily across them to the door of the inn's great public room. Brian Tuke's mood matched the flat gray barely visible above the inn's half-timbered third story. Head down, face sullen, he pushed his way into a corner and sat down, brooding at the disparity between the happy souls he saw drinking and eating before him and his own ever-deepening gloom. The ale was tasteless. It didn't make him drunk fast enough. He had another, and another.

"Hey, brother, why the long face? Has your sweetheart left you?" A garrulous old man sat down beside him.

"Worse," said Tuke, staring bitterly into the goblet. "What do you do when a man wants your place?"

"Why, is he greater than you?"

"Lesser. A nobody. But he finds favor. He's clever, you know. Clever and good-looking and flattering. He plays a slimy trick, and it passes for amusing. Art! He talks about art! Brush strokes and pigments, master this and master that, and what painter has died, so his work goes up in value. Useless stuff! And my master gobbles it up. He listens, he listens. And soon that bastard will have my place, I swear. God, when it was poetry, I learned poetry. When it was music, who was a finer judge than I? I learned it all, just to stay in my master's good graces. What will it be next? Bookbinding? The science of dog breeding? My master amuses himself, and my brain splits."

"You need to make this man a fool. Trip him up."

"So say you. But that's no easy task." Tuke looked up with a sly glance. His speech was slurred. "But I've a secret. I've heard there's a man with powers."

"Powers?" said the old man, looking alarmed.

"I'd agree to anything to get that arrogant bastard out of my way. Not dead, you understand. Then he couldn't see me triumph. A curse, some words . . ."

"Oh, of course, of course," said the man, standing up.

"Why so hasty?" asked Tuke, leaning on the table at the strangest angle and looking up. "Maybe you'd like to meet him. He's coming here. Maybe there's someone you'd like to . . ."

"I don't want to meet no devils out of hell," muttered the old man as he made his getaway. He gave a yelp as he almost ran into Sir Septimus Crouch, who had just entered the public room and had paused to look around.

"Out of my way, sirrah," said Crouch, looking down in disdain at him. The old man took in at a glance the cold green eyes, the strange hornlike streaks of gray in the hair, the perverse and ruined face.

"He's over there," he said, pointing with a finger as he fled.

Now let me tell you in case you think I am vain and boastful that Adam and Eve were the worst trial ever invented to keep a person humble and make her think that scrubbing floors in a charitable institution might not be so bad after all. Master Hull's Adam and Eves were just as green and ugly as his saints, with the exception that the saints were fully clothed and Adam and Eve were as naked as the day they were born, cavorting about the Garden of Eden with a big snake that had an ugly old devil's face on him. They certainly didn't look like religious paintings at all, unless maybe another religion than Christian that I don't know about. Before I saw them, I thought it would just be easy to copy them and the money would come rolling in as a temporary thing before people understood that my true inspirational pictures that I hadn't painted yet were much better.

The minute I saw them, I knew I was in awful trouble because of my showing off and the boasting that I had done secretly to myself, which luckily I hadn't spoken of or it would be worse. You see, Master Hull could not draw human anatomy correctly and his people looked a bit like insects or something. But I couldn't even draw it at all, and his paintings wouldn't do for a model because they were wrong, too. I am very good on faces, because I have studied them a long time, since I was little, and my father showed me many tricks of making the light shine where the bone shows beneath the skin, and also eyes, which need a special secondary highlight that crosses the white if they are to look damp, which they are. I know his secret of painting velvet and jewels real enough to touch as well.

But because I was raised like a lady I learned French and Italian and music, but I did not learn to draw naked bodies which are indecent, and you have to have a nude model anyway, which nice girls shouldn't see. So there I was in a terrible fix because I needed to draw naked people cavorting to make lecherous monks happy but not burst out laughing. I felt a lot like crying, but instead I lied after asking God to forgive me again, and I just said it would be easy to do paintings like that. Then I shut myself in the studio to think and draw and imagine the best way out of this problem, so Mistress Hull could have that sausage she likes so well. Nobody ever bought her knitting anyway and no person can live just on selling pins.

First I started by copying the best of the paintings but Adam came out shaped like a melon with long legs like a spider because I was not sure where they joined on. Eve looked a little better but not much, and the more I looked the more it seemed her bosom was in the wrong place. I rubbed out the bad places and tried again and pretty soon the drawing was just a big black mess and I had charcoal all over my hands and face except where the tears were coming down. Then I felt as if I were smothering and had to put my head out the window to breathe and some awful man who was so drunk he was lying in the gutter in front of the Goat and Jug called out:

"Hey, sweetheart, what've you been doing up there? Cleaning the chimney? *I'll* clean your chimney for you." I was so angry I went and got the chamber pot and heaved its contents out the window at him, but they didn't go far enough so he just lay there and laughed, still dry except for the part that was in the gutter. By this time I was getting very tired of the Goat and Jug and wishing someone would close it down for a bawdy house. Besides, their ale was awful, and we had to go all the way to the Unicorn to get anything good.

Now seeing that man lying in the gutter all stretched out made me think that if he were naked, then I could get the true proportion, which was what was wrong with my drawings. I would have prayed to the Holy Virgin for help in getting a real model, but she would have been embarrassed. Besides, somebody magical and refined like the Virgin could not possibly bear something so smelly and messy as painting. But I love the smell of paint. It makes me happier than anything else.

Thinking about how much I loved painting and how little I loved scrubbing floors, I had a great inspiration. I did have one naked model to get proportions from, and she was right in the room with me—if you see what I mean. It is not that I was so perfect in the body but Eve was not perfect either, so it was all right. So I wedged the stool against the studio door and closed the shutters and took everything off and stood against the whitewashed wall. Then I put the charcoal close beside my body and marked the proportions right on the wall, which was not easy for some of the parts. Then I outlined in between the marks, and it really came out very well. A model for proportions. Now all I had to do was prop up my little mirror to look at myself to do the individual bits. After I had finished one side view and one front view on the wall and measured everything, I was quite surprised because the legs did not join on where I thought at all. Now there was only one-half a problem left, which is that men do not look like women and Master Dallet was never much use in that regard and besides he was dead.

I was so interested in thinking just standing there that I forgot to put my clothes back on, which is really indecent but when I think, I think very hard. It seemed to me that the Adam problem could be solved by concealing all the parts I couldn't draw behind leaves or a tree trunk or something because all the monks are really interested in is

Eve anyway. Then an inspiration for a painting came to me that was very fine, and that is how I had the idea for *Adam and Eve Bathing in the Garden of Eden*, which is the first one I sold. Adam is in the water up to his middle and you only see his back view while he stares at Eve and Eve is lying on a big rock wringing out her long hair and making cow eyes at the viewer who is behind Adam. There is also a large, speckled snake hanging out of a tree and it's got a very lecherous face which seems to be an important part of these pictures. When I got the idea I got very excited and sat down to draw and had nearly a whole rough sketch done when I heard Nan rattling and banging at the door.

"Susanna, what on earth are you doing in there?" she cried.

"I'm drawing Eve!" I shouted back, but then I remembered I was entirely undressed which is not proper and had to stop.

"Why on earth did you bar the door like that?" asked Nan when I opened it for her. I must admit I did look rather funny for my laces were done wrong and my face was still black. "Oh, you look like a chimney sweep!" she cried.

"I had to," I said. "Adam and Eves are a lot more work than I thought. They're awfully indecent, Nan."

"And so you barred the door so no one could see you draw them? You are a funny girl, even if I did raise you myself," she said.

"Nan, did you know the foot is the same length as the forearm?" I asked, my mind still on my wonderful discoveries.

"That's exactly what I mean," she answered.

It turned out that visiting the Lord Mayor's wife was not as easy an idea as it seemed at first, because I had to have my new widow's weeds in that good wool all finished so that the servants would not think I was a beggar and chase me away. So we stayed up half the night cutting and sewing and I designed some nice little touches, such as pleats on the back of the bodice that open into the skirt and some cutwork on the sleeves that brought that plain old black dress beyond the ordinary, though they were not as simple to sew as plain would be. All this work made Cat, who is really Catherine Hull who has no prospects, very angry. She cried and stormed and said she didn't see why she had to help, because it was me that was getting the new dress and I always got everything and never had to help in the kitchen now that I was doing all that stupid painting, and it was no fair. Then her mother said that I was a sorrowful widow, and she said that was no fair, too, because at least I had been married once and she never got anything. And I said she deserved to be married to Master Dallet who was as mean as a snake, anyway. Then Nan said hush and we stayed up all night crying and making up, because it is hard to be women without money, even if you have plans for it later.

All these troubles meant two things, namely it took more days to finish the dress and also Cat got to go to the Lord Mayor's with me to see the sights and her mother told her what to say so she wouldn't make a mistake and spoil everything. She carried the picture because I was a sorrowful widow and supposedly too weak to carry anything, but it was not much trouble because it was not too big, being a table-picture, that is, a picture painted on a wood board, and it matched one the mayor had had done of himself which he liked perfectly well. A lackey in grand livery showed us into the mayor's hall, where we sat on a hard bench and kicked our heels in the straw a long time waiting. Then the mayor's wife came with two ladies attending her, and she was a big haughty lady with as many chins as Master Dallet had painted and a much fiercer eye. I told her all about my husband's last desire to satisfy her above all things in the matter of her portrait, and unwrapped it, and she burst into tears.

"He has captured my true self," she said, wiping away all the dampness and pretending she hadn't cried. "I see I misjudged him. I thought him hard and cynical, but now I understand he was just seeking perfection. What a terrible loss you must feel."

So I wiped at my eyes and said the pain was almost unbearable, but at least he had left objects of beauty like this behind him which was a consolation. All the while I really did feel great sorrow, because I think I could have made a fortune improving rich ladies with bad looks like this one because there are ever so many more of them than pretty ones. Besides it is not their fault they are homely, and every woman should feel pretty once. And looking at pictures of themselves more beautiful and spiritual might soften their dispositions and make them kinder, so it would really be a kind of improvement of the world that one would be doing instead of outright lying.

So we parted with a nice little purse of money, and Cat was walking on air because that lackey who was young and good-looking made eyes at her and pressed her hand as he showed us out, and I felt like dancing because I had done my part very well indeed. When we got home, Mistress Hull and Nan felt like dancing, too. So we all joined hands and did for a while, while Mistress Hull called out the steps.

"Whew," said Mistress Hull, wiping her brow as she sat down. "It's been a long time since I danced. Oh, I used to have such a light foot! But a widow can't be too careful in this wicked world. Did I tell you that the handsomest young man in some lord's livery all hidden beneath a plain black cloak came hunting for Master Dallet's apprentice while you were gone?"

"An apprentice? What did you say?"

"The truth, that he had none."

"And then what happened?"

"He looked at me in the strangest way, and then said he'd get to the bottom of the truth even if I wouldn't help him."

"Then he must have been up to no good. Maybe he's serving someone else who's trying to collect one of Master Dallet's old debts."

"That's what I thought. He had a big hat pulled down over his eyes, as if he were being secretive, and when he thought I wasn't looking, he wandered about pretending to be doing nothing, but looking ever so closely at Master Hull's paintings. And, can you imagine? He rolled his eyes! Such rudeness in the face of sacred works! Young men today are sunk in sin, I tell you. After that he asked about the apprentice. It all sounded very dubious to me, so I told him that I'd suddenly remembered that there was an apprentice long ago, but he'd gone to Antwerp to serve some master whose name I'd forgotten."

"Apprentice, *humpf!*" exclaimed Nan. "It was undoubtedly a trick by someone else who wants money. There's no end to the devices they'll use."

"At least he wasn't from the guild. That would be trouble and a half," said Mistress Hull. "Now, remember, ladies, every painting that comes from this shop was painted by a dead liveryman of the guild."

"Thoughtful of them to leave us so many," I couldn't help remarking.

"Most considerate gentlemen," Mistress Hull said, laughing. "Especially since they are going to buy us a dinner in celebration."

"Not at the Goat and Jug, I hope."

"A low place like that? No, we'll have the best. Those good dead men are going to take us to the Saracen's Head."

I suppose I have made it sound easy about painting *Adam and Eve Bathing in the Garden of Eden*, except for the bodies which I cheated on. But there was another problem about this kind of picture, too. That is, who knows what the Garden of Eden looked like? You cannot make it like England because it should seem faraway and more beautiful than anything on earth because it is Eden. Now I had always been bored with landscapes anyway, and painting Eden is a lot of landscape. Some people do Adam and Eve very large to omit the landscape but I would have to paint bodies better, and not make do with so many leaves and vines because they could not be coming out of nowhere just for my convenience but had to be attached to plants and trees, which gets back to the problem of Eden.

Fortunately, my father was a terrible taskmaster when he was alive and never let anything get by. One of the things he didn't let get by was landscapes, which I hate because they are dull. He had made me copy one of his landscapes that he had done on his travels over and over, for practice in trees and color perspective and also rocks and mountains which are the very dullest of all and nobody should ever have to paint them. He used to say I would thank him someday and now I wished I could. I just took that old landscape because it didn't look like England and loaded it up with flowers and it made a good Eden. I had to fix a few things, for example, the strange tall rocky mountain in the back, behind all the greenery. It had a castle at the top. But since there were no castles in Eden, I just took away the castle and put a golden light on top of the mountain coming out of a cloud as if God were up there. I used that foreign place in all my Adam and Eves, one way or another. It was a kind of joke, especially on Father, who took that landscape very seriously and said if people appreciated landscapes more than portraits of themselves, they would see it was a masterwork.

I had just gotten the landscape done and was putting another glaze on Eve to make her nice and pink when Mistress Hull came up to inspect.

"My, you've been working away up here. Let's see." Eve's hair had come out especially nice, in long, dark ripples, and I do know how to give expression to eyes, even a "come hither" expression which is how I imagine that Mistress Pickering lured my husband to his early but not undeserved doom. There were still a few little problems, but I thought I had covered them over pretty well. "Humpf! That Eve is a hussy! Who would have thought a woman could paint a thing like that! Did you mean for her knees to be that fat? Oh, no, don't look so worried. I know my customers. They all like fat knees. Ha! I could sell a dozen of these! How fortunate you are to be so talented!"

I felt so gratified, I showed her the best of my sketches, and Mistress Hull inspected them with a shrewd commercial gaze which impressed me very much.

"Hmm. *Eve Tempts Adam.* It's nice, that lecherous look you give him while he stares at the apple. But why is he all covered up with vines? That Eve—my, she is generous up top; that's excellent. Oh—my—this one! Ha! You must do several. I'm sure this one will go for double. How did you ever think of it?" Her eye lit up as she spied my sketch for *The Temptation of Eve.* It was altogether my most daring work, which featured my improved ability to draw Eves in such a way that you hardly missed that there was no Adam at all. That is, Eve is lolling back on a grassy bank immorally intertwined with the serpent and a really unregenerate look on her face, and the bitten apple is falling out of her hand which is all limp because she is just so carried away. I'm surprised I thought of it at all, but sometimes these things just come to me and besides, I got all angry thinking of how my late husband was such a snake spending all my dowry money to cut a figure for that dreadful Mistress Pickering that he deceived me about and said she had a club foot.

While I was showing her my drawings Cat came up to snoop around, because she is convinced I just lie at my ease upstairs instead of scouring pots whereas I actually work very very hard except that it is a lot better work than rubbing sand around in a lot of dirty old dishes. Even she was amazed, and when you can amaze a sour unmarried girl who thinks unkindly of everything, that is something.

"Mother, this bathing picture looks just as if a man did it. And it's not too big to hide behind a curtain, the way they do. You can sell that one right away, I think." She looked at it from another angle. "But the colors shine too much. They don't look like father's at all. How are you going to keep the beadle away?"

"Trust your old mother, dearie. These are paintings by Master Dallet representing his secret tendencies that he hid from his wife. It's only natural, considering what they're about, and her so young and newly wed and all. He had them in storage, and a friend returned them all. See that shiny glaze? It looks just like his portraits. It's not his poor widow's fault they're so suggestive—the poor thing has a right to eke out her pension."

Cat gave a wicked laugh. Widow Hull looked again at the bathing picture with her shrewd birdlike eyes, and I took away the sketches because I did not want to see the look on Cat's face if she caught sight of *The Temptation of Eve*.

"It's the medium you use, isn't it?" observed Mistress Hull. "It lets the colors shine through. My husband told me about it once when he was drunk. It's each painter's secret. My husband was always afraid someone would bribe his apprentices and pirate his. But then, along came Browne, and then Hethe, and he tried to pirate *theirs*. Yours is especially fine—it makes the colors shine like the stained glass in Saint Paul's. You're lucky. If you're ever *really* hard up, you can sell the secret of it."

"Who'll buy it from me if the paintings are Master Dallet's?"

"*Hmm*. You're right—oh, what a tangle it all is. It's a pity women can't be Masters."

"I couldn't be one anyway," I said, thinking of Adam's torso, which still resembled a sausage, no matter how many ribs I painted on it.

Spring kept pushing on, with flowering apple trees shining all light and sweet against the rolling gray sky and green blades pushing their way out between the stones of garden walls. I think that painting Eden so much must have drugged my senses, because the idea of color started to take over my mind as if I were drunk. I would just stop sometimes and stare, because I was looking at the exact color of the clouds or the way a mud puddle shines. And all the while I'd be thinking something like what I needed was a good burnt umber, but it costs so high and where can you get the real stuff from Italy and not some fake? Everybody thought I was crazy even in my own house, but really I was just thinking. Nan gave it out that it was the terrible grief, and that made me something of a tragical figure in the neighborhood. Then people would touch their heads with a forefinger as I went by and make clucking sounds, but I hardly had time to enjoy the sensation I made because I was thinking too hard. Also sometimes I forgot to put my clothes on right and once I put my bodice on inside out because I really wasn't noticing, which made people think I really was crazy. Also dogs followed me because they seemed to think I was a sympathetical figure and sort of wandered the way they do.

One day I was coming back from the baker's with a basket of bread on my arm and suddenly I could see the whole street flat as if I were painting it, instead of in depth, with the highlights from the last rain glistening just the way they should be painted on the shiny paving stones where people walk and the dirty mud in the gutter. The half-timbered shops and houses were leaning over the street like friendly ladies having a gossip, and their signs made bright splashes of color like jewelry. People were out, and the burgesses and liverymen in their gaudy colored gowns were picking their way through the ordinary black and russet and dun rabble like fabulous sea monsters in a school of minnows. The shop shutters were up and shopkeepers were leaning out over their counters and some of them even crying their wares into the street when somebody likely came by. It was all very magical and only painting could do it justice, but of course you couldn't sell it because everyone was clothed.

Unfortunately, I was so busy looking that I stopped without noticing in front of that awful Goat and Jug, and the dogs all stopped too and sat down around me because I think they wanted a piece of bread, or at least they smelled it. And then a horrible drunk hairy man dressed like a carpenter came out of that low tavern and bowed and said, "Madame Blue-Nose, may I escort you to your palace where you might renew the charcoal on your face?" I stopped and rubbed my face very suddenly, but turned out to be clean, and all his friends who had put him up to it came out and laughed.

"You should be ashamed to accost a respectable widow like that!" I said, but they laughed again because I was trying to shoo away the dogs who were trying to get my bread. I was furious because he had broken into my seeing, which is even deeper than my thinking. Then all those drunk rowdies laughed and shouted,

"A widow woman better remarry while she's got the chance."

"Especially before people find out her brain's gone soft."

"Soft brain don't matter in a woman, 'long as other things ain't soft."

"Is yer cookin' covered in charcoal, too?" I didn't even look at them to show that rude comments are beneath me. I just stormed off very angry because they had made the street look ordinary again.

But inside the shop at the Sign of the Standing Cat wrinkly old Mistress Hull was just beaming, and then she hugged me, and so did Nan and Cat even before I could put down the bread.

"Good news, wonderful news! We've sold *Eve Bathing!*" cried Nan and Cat.

"To a horrid old grayfriar with a squint visiting from York. Just think! He'd heard about us from so far away!" Mistress Hull was ecstatic. "First he pretended to be looking at a Christ in Chains, but then he asked if we had any female martyrdoms. Ugh! Just imagine! But you should have seen his eyes light up when I showed him *Eve Bathing*. He said it would help him contemplate the wickedness of women in bringing about the Fall of Man. I said, 'Ten shillings, not a penny less.' He said five. I told him it was a masterwork, and since the painter had died, it was bound to increase in value. He said six. I told him these paintings were in the private collections of some of the highest churchmen in England. Finally I sold it for eight, with two needles and a paper of pins thrown in. Now what would an honest friar be wanting with a paper of pins?"

"Well, a *dis*honest friar would be using them to court some married woman with a roving eye," observed Cat.

"It's hard to imagine anyone's eye roving toward *him*," said Nan.

"Eight shillings—and so soon! How's that one with the snake coming?"

"I've only just begun it."

"Well, hurry, hurry, and we'll all be rich." We celebrated that evening with a great big pie that gave me a stomachache that lasted until the next day. But even a stomachache can be inspiring when one is in the painting mood, and that bilious feeling gave me a grand inspiration which made me work with great happiness all day. I mean, since the worst snake I knew was Rowland Dallet, I just decided to put his face on the snake instead of the usual devil's face and I did it all up in green and it was just delicious. Then of course I just got carried away and hunted through his sketches until I found one I was pretty sure was Mistress Pickering, because it didn't have a name on it, just "P." That was certainly sneaky of him, especially after telling me she was deformed and had a terrible birthmark on her face.

Then I gave that Eve Mistress Pickering's goggle-eyed face and it was even funnier, because there she was just wallowing with that grotesque old serpent and clasping it to her bosom though I must say she looked rather plump for a poor crippled lady who was supposed to limp. Limp, ha! The serpent's face which was Rowland Dallet's was leering at her and she really looked carried away, as if it were a handsome man there instead of a big oozing blackish green snake coiled all over her. That bitten apple rolling away I made a nice shiny red, which drew the eye and was the center of the picture.

I worked and worked. Father's landscape never looked better, except that I decided a golden heavenly light on the mountain would not be as good as a thundercloud with some lightning to indicate God's wrath, and that made me feel even better. Sometimes I would stop and wipe the sweat off my forehead and then I really couldn't help laughing, so I did. But it was really very odd; I thought I heard somebody giggling behind me, or maybe two or three somebodies, and I turned very quickly but I couldn't see anything but a sort of flash and hear rustling. There was something else sort of odd, but I must have imagined it. I thought I saw something like a child vanishing in that flash, but I guess it was a dream from working too hard.

"Susanna, Susanna, who's that in there with you?" I could hear Nan's voice calling through the studio door.

"Nobody, come on in. I've got the whole thing down, at least the beginning." Nan came in, and her eyes got really large. "You have to imagine it with the glazes," I said. "This really just gives you a rough idea."

"It's rough all right. What have you gone and done? That's Master

Dallet's face on that serpent, sure as fate. And that woman he's lolling on, that's Mistress Pickering if I ever did see her."

"*You* saw her, Nan? What about that birthmark and that club foot and all those terrible afflictions that big liar said she had? You knew all about how he was sinning and betraying me and you never even let on. That's not very nice, you know."

"Oh," she said, looking sad, "I didn't think you could do anything about it, and if you knew it would have broken your heart, so we all just kept quiet."

"We all? Who all? Everybody in the world knew my husband was a scoundrel and a wastrel and a horrible—horrible, *seducer,* except for me? You are all mean, mean, mean!"

"No we aren't. We just tried to spare you. The world thinks nothing of a man who philanders. It just gives him spice. It's only women that get in trouble. And you—you always take things so *seriously.* That man was a snake, and I never trusted him."

"Then I think I painted him just right," I said.

"That you did," said Nan, and then she looked at the picture some more. "Just look at that brazen woman rolling her eyes," she said, and started to giggle. "And, Lord, the expression you put on that snake's face! What I wouldn't give just to see the look on his face if he were alive to see it! Ha!"

"I sort of thought it said everything right there," I said, feeling pleased.

"Oh, my, oh, my, this is the vulgarest painting I ever did see," she said, "and I don't know whether to laugh or to smack you! For shame!" She put her hands over her face, but I could see her shoulders shake. It seemed to me a very good sign that some low-minded person who did not understand the true meaning of the picture, which was a higher meaning about sin and redemption, would probably pay quite a bit for it. But in spite of what Mistress Hull said about selling a lot of them, I really did not think I could ever copy it over with as much energy as the first time because the inspiration of the moment would never be as great again—if you see what I mean.

EIGHT

It was during the lengthening hours of twilight that two men mounted on mules rode into Lime Street Ward. Here, in a neighborhood where once-fine residences built against the London wall were being converted into tenements, stood the curious, narrow old house of the noted antiquarian, and former knight adventurer, Sir Septimus Crouch. Above the door in a niche stood a strange wooden imp with a toothy grin, and the door knocker was a brass monkey's head from the olden times. The shutters on the upper story were thrown open, but old-fashioned windows of translucent linen proclaimed the location of the master's bedroom and study. Crouch was a believer that evening air, if allowed indoors, carried disease.

The dancing light of a candle could already be seen behind the linen. Sir Septimus was indoors, eagerly studying the muddy fraction of his newly acquired work of ancient wisdom with the aid of an open grimoire. The book, like many from days gone by, was not one, but several useful related volumes collected and copied together for the convenience of the ancient order that had compiled it. Secrets of power, mysteries of the occult, and mystic prophecies were jumbled together in a near-illegible clerical hand.

At first, Crouch had rejoiced in his possession of the first third of the work. Recipes for divination and the casting of invincible swords were here. The secret mirror of the Roman emperors had whetted his appetite for all that followed: verses of prophecy that foretold of the fall of kings and the rise of a new world empire. And who, who would be its emperor? The one with the secrets, of course—ah, damn, this clerk of the pothooks might as well have written in code.... All the while as he read, like a secret itch at the back of his mind, was the irritating thought that the demon Belphagor, whom he had hoped to have chained in his service for the pursuit of this affair, was flying loose somewhere. He'd hoped to catch him when he became entangled in a body, but something must have warned the damned creature, because he'd slipped out of the one Crouch was sure he'd take just before the demon master arrived. How to pursue the secrets of the book without putting himself to undue physical effort? He'd hoped to be flying across the sea in a sieve by now. Ordinary travel was so damp, so uncomfortable. Crouch did not approve of the uncomfortable.

The room around him was cramped and cluttered. The antiquity of the house was proclaimed by its slanting floor. Piles of old charts, maps, strange books, caskets with ancient coins and medallions, and curious goblets, lead daggers, and other implements more suited to the practice of magic than practical use stood helter-skelter on the shelves of an open cupboard, on his worktable, on top of an open armoire, and even under the bed, crowding the chamber pot from its place of honor. Before his manuscript, on his worktable, stood a skull and a beautifully made antique silver drinking cup, decorated with obscene figures.

"Ha, hmm," Sir Septimus said aloud to himself, shifting his huge bulk in his heavy, cushioned chair and pushing his leather-framed spectacles back up his nose. "This is definitely the secret. The holy blood—an object—grants absolute power over all of Christendom and the heathen. It is held somewhere by these people—the Priory of Sion. Never heard of 'em. At some point, given what our Clerk of the Illegible Hand hints at in these first verses of prophecy, they will burst forth to reestablish the true dynasty and create an empire such as has never before been seen on earth. Now do they still exist, or is it an allegorical name of some sort? The Helmsman. Hmm. Commands the Priory in its sacred task through centuries. That's clear enough. If there still is such a fellow. Who could he be? They must have been through several since this book was buried."

Crouch got up and poured himself more heavy, sweet wine from a silver flagon on his table. Morosely he stared into the goblet, swirling the wine. The last of the cask and nothing else like it in London. Well, never mind, he would soon enjoy a better, when he advised kings and supervised the rise and fall of empires with the aid of his mirror and the secrets of the book. Never mind that the mirror showed only the conspiracies of the present, not those of the future. The future was all written here. All he had to do was decipher it—that, and get the other two parts of the book into his hands. The Secret wasn't in his part. Damn! He stood and then began to pace, calling down a thousand curses on that miserable painter, Dallet. He deserved the death he found by Ludlow's subtle ruse. But it has simplified matters, thought Crouch. Now I need only deal with Ludlow and it will all be in my hands again. Wolsey, what was he? Nothing. Crouch would have the power of the book; Crouch would be the power behind the new throne, the greatest Europe had ever seen. Crouch knew. Crouch had studied. The prophetic verses would bring him at last to the place of eminence he deserved. He sat again and drank, then set himself once more to the task of deciphering his fragment, mumbling to himself the while.

"Now here in the beginning, the verses predict the fall of the false kings ... now which ones are they? There are so many, these days.... Let's see, this reference is to the demon that governs the French part of hell, hmm, yes, it must be the Capetian dynasty then ... which is the dynasty of the True Blood then? Every sign says it is later in the book. And this other business, 'the splitting of the oak.' I can't make it out at all, though it appears to be important. I need that middle part of the book, and the end. I hope Dallet's soul is sizzling ..." His fist tightened. At that very moment, the monkey's head clattered on the door below. Crouch listened as the footsteps of his manservant went down to the front door, then hid the fragment of the book beneath a pile of papers.

The stranger who was shown in was tall, gray haired, dignified, and clad in a foreign doctor's gown.

"Maître Bellier, at your service, most esteemed Sieur Crouch." The stranger's eye lit on the obscene cup, and a slight, ironic, smile of recognition played across his features. Crouch's cynical, malignant green eyes did not fail to notice the stranger's expression. Aha, he thought, how curious. My answer has come. And we are well matched.

"An ancient art object, a curiosity I have recently acquired," he said in a falsely genial tone of voice.

"But of course, Sieur Crouch. I understand that perfectly. That cup is an old friend. There are a number of them in Europe, you know." The stranger's face, narrow and intelligent, crinkled up with sly amusement.

"Why, Maître Bellier, I had no idea. Please do be seated and state your business with me. Are you interested in purchasing rarities? I have many curious objects that might interest you, although the cup is not for sale."

"Ah, Sieur Crouch, you have already discovered my purpose. You see, we know that you have stumbled onto the London Hoard."

"The London Hoard?" Crouch raised an eyebrow. "Why, I've never heard of it."

"And you have never heard of the Templars, once masters of great wealth, despoiled of everything by a conspiracy of the King of France and the Pope?"

"I am a student of history, Maître Bellier. I know well they were found guilty of witchcraft and obscene and diabolical practices during the reign of Philip the Fair, when he was King in France." At this answer, the stranger leaned forward toward Crouch, speaking in a new tone of intimacy.

"Ah, my friend, we are men of the world. These were the greatest bankers the world had ever known. Their probity brought them the treasures of the earth for safekeeping—a great temptation to any ruler. You know and I know that they were good Christians—with a few exceptions."

"Exceptions?"

"Why, in any great and ancient organization, there are some who will experiment with ... different practices. In their secrecy, in their isolation, in their pride, there were some that worshiped, in addition to God and Christ, the principle of Generation, embodied in a female deity known to the ancients, and a mighty intervening power between the forces of Heaven and Hell. . . ."

"Baphomet . . ."

"Ah, then you do know. Let us pretend no more. My masters are prepared to buy certain valuable objects from you."

"How do you know I have them?"

"The rare coin you sold to the agent of Wolsey. He sent it for valuation and one of our agents was shown it. Did you know what it is? I think not. It is a coin from the reign of the Merovingian kings of France. From the time of King Dagobert. I assure you, such a coin has no business at all in the Kingdom of England, except as part of the

London Hoard. Of its contents, we are absolutely sure. You see, there are similar hoards elsewhere. In some cities, the Templars were warned by those sympathetic to their cause. Wherever the renegade Templars had time to flee, they hid their chief treasures for the time they would return. The time of the fall of dynasties."

"What is it you want? I do not have everything. It was shared out three ways."

"One thing only. We want the book of mysteries contained in the casket with the treasure."

"The book—ah, the book. Yes, I do remember it. It was not part of my share. . . ." The stranger watched Crouch closely as he puffed.

"My master is prepared to pay well for it, extremely well."

"I might locate it for you. The other one has no idea of its value. But tell me, what was in it?" Crouch's voice was bland.

"Secrets of ancient magic and prophecies of power, as you have doubtlessly already surmised, Monsieur Crouch, since you must have found the text that allowed you to discover the Hoard's hiding place," said the man in the foreign gown. "Prophecies of the Blood which will become master of the known world, of the greatest secret in Christendom."

"Well then, the man who has the book might become the greatest power in Christendom."

"Hardly, Sieur Crouch. You see, we already have a copy of the book, and we are very numerous." Crouch looked at him, his eyes hooded.

"We?" he said. "Why would the Priory of Sion want another?" The brilliant stab in the dark had its effect. Maître Bellier paled, and then replied,

"For the obvious reason, Sieur Crouch. We wish to burn it. We alone are the true guardians of the Secret, and we intend to remain so. Do remember, the man who finds it will be a wealthy man."

"As wealthy as the Helmsman?" Crouch looked at him, his eyes coldly triumphant. I know, his voice said. Be awed by me. Surrender.

"I have no idea," said Maître Bellier. "Let us pass back to what is important. Should you find the manuscript, I do not advise that you keep it. There is a danger—one that not many are prepared to handle."

"A danger? Hardly from a manuscript."

"Certain of the worthy order of whom we speak were great masters of the occult. At every site where they concealed their treasures, they bound a demon of destruction to the box for their revenge. We are in possession of the formula that will return the demon to its own place." Whatever this Priory is, thought Crouch, they are fools, and no diabolists. If they had the ability to bring the demon into their service, they would accomplish their aims much sooner. They were no equals to a man with his years of study of the black arts. He sighed regretfully at the thought of the lost demonic child. Belphagor incarnate, at his mercy, his servant. An occultist's dream. Would the demon, having failed once, attach himself to the woman for a second try? It would be worth looking into.

"A pity, then, it must have gotten away," said Crouch.

"It would be an act of decency to get rid of the thing, but, after all, there are so many demons of destruction loose these days, what is one more?" Maître Bellier shrugged and smiled philosophically. "Sieur Crouch, I thank you for your valuable time. While I am in England, I am staying at the Saracen's Head. Do, please, come to me if you perchance locate that book."

Outside, Maître Bellier's servant was holding both mules. The street had become dark as he had waited, and he had taken advantage of a neighbor woman to light the two torches that he carried with him.

"Eustache," said his master as he mounted his big roan mule, "I believe the man has seen the book. He may even possess it, or part of it, himself. He knows of the Priory. The Helmsman will not be pleased."

"He knows of the Helmsman?"

"But not who or where he is. The man is brilliant, I think, and ruthless. He has learned too much, I am afraid, from our little visit. I want you to watch him, Eustache, and follow him. See to whom he leads us. We must try to get to the book before he does."

"But suppose he has it already?" asked the manservant, handing up one torch, and then deftly mounting his mule while holding the other.

"The secret will do him little good. But there are those to whom he might sell it. The heirs of the Valois. Our enemies in Rome." Bellier's eyes looked distant, and his voice was cold. "If he, or those he leads us to, show signs of traveling abroad, we will have to arrange something."

Upstairs, as Crouch was helped into his nightshirt, his heart was pounding and his mind racing. What a useless busybody that French doctor was. Doubtless, he counted himself clever. But he had given away the secret. The Priory of Sion existed, the Helmsman existed, the prophecies were valid, and their fulfillment imminent. The book was of inestimable value.

For amusement, he calculated first what price a usurper might pay for a book of prophecy that would buoy him up and gather followers to his cause. Then he paused to estimate the price a sitting monarch might pay for knowledge of the future of France. How delightful to approach them with the wisdom of the ages. He envisioned himself holding an auction. Whom would he invite? Wolsey, for the King of England? Henry still has claims in France. Or perhaps the Holy Roman Emperor? A more likely candidate. He has more money, and France is a thorn in his side. But in truth, I wouldn't waste it on them, he thought. Like all rulers, they are too stupid to know what is valuable. Only I would know how to use the book properly. As his mind spun out plots and counterplots, envisioning his rise to the heights of power, the passion to possess the entire manuscript began to grow and gnaw at him. He hardly slept that night.

NINE

I soon found that conducting somebody else's career posthumously was not as easy as I had thought. I had imagined the hardest part would be telling all those lies to customers, but I was wrong. The biggest trouble of all was where do dead men buy their colors? That is, one could only pretend to be on an errand for one's husband so long before the apothecary might say, "Don't I recall your husband was buried in Saint Vedast and has a nice brass in the wall?" So I had to go farther and farther until I had tried out all the apothecaries in London and my feet hurt. And I couldn't send anyone else in the house because they might get cheated. You have to feel and smell and touch and see the color to make sure it's right and you aren't getting something second rate passed off on you.

For a while I could use what I had, but that old Eden scene used up all my greens first. Then I could buy alum anywhere, without anyone suspecting I was making colors at home by mixing that alum with essence of fleur-de-lis and pansies. I could get indigo by pretending I was dyeing a bit of yarn or maybe remaking an old dress that would be better off blue. But when you get to earth of cologne and blue and green bice and verdegris, then people wonder why a painter's widow needs them and the only answer is not very respectable, because they think you've taken up with another painter and are secretly living in sin so that you still get your pension. That was the worst risk of all, because with the gossip that beadle might come around looking for men and find painting instead, which would have been even worse.

After talking it over with Mistress Hull, who is a very shrewd woman, we decided we must take someone into our confidence and pay him a hefty bribe. Luckily I knew just the person. In an alley off Bladder Lane, which is near where where the gold beaters are, there was an apothecary who is an alchemist and not very honest but in an honest sort of way. What I mean is that he would not cheat a person too terribly much but he believed that the law was for other people. That is why my father got on with him because father believed that the law was for other people, too, especially guild laws which were for English painters who couldn't get anything right so they had to shut out their betters. Master Ailwin was very good for alchemical colors such as orpiment and cedar green and white lead, and he could get anything else a person needed, even things for a little bit of sorcery on the side, like dead men's thumbs, but I would never have wanted a thing like that. The only problem with Master Ailwin was that he had too many opinions. So you never got out of his shop in a short time but had to argue, and he did all the talking anyway. Also shady characters went in and out of his place, but that never bothered father. Father always said life was full of shady characters and as long as they want their pictures painted, why give it any attention.

That is why on a fair morning I put on my best black gown, the one in good wool with the little tucks around the skirt and the sleeves cut in the French fashion, and also my French hood, which was very elegant and took Nan with me to pass into the City by Ludgate and find Master Ailwin. The blue sky brought everyone into Fleet Street and there was even music from the engine in the tower on the cistern, which had bells and played hymns. On top of the tower was the image of Saint Christopher and below him were angels and below that the bells. The cistern was hard by Fleet Bridge, where everyone in the world had to pass to enter the City gate. The south side of the street was lined with fair houses built of stone, which had devices on them that were a wonder to see.

Now here is what shows you how important fine dress is in this wicked world. When I wore plain things and was happy working hard, then hairy men from the Goat and Jug rolled their eyes and made sport offering to escort me to my door. But it was quite different when I was up to no good, wearing an excellent gown made with fine black worsted given as a bribe by my late husband's murderer. Then even when everybody was crowding into the gate and there were carts and donkeys loaded with firewood and eggs and fruit, people looked impressed and made way, and important-looking men in merchants' and lawyers' gowns with their iron stares kept lowlier men from brushing up against me accidentally. It did help that Nan shooed away the dogs, because I think my important widow look would have gone away if people knew that animals follow me, which is strange.

Really grand people did not pass by the gate at all but went by water and came up by the steps from the river. They would not have to mix at all except they might be killed passing under London Bridge if they did not get out while the boatmen shoot the rapids beneath the bridge. Then they would get back in, but it was a hard thing to have to mingle with the commons for that little bit of time walking to rejoin the boat on the other side. So I always went by Thames Street to see if there was somebody very splendid getting out so I could admire his clothes, see the parade of his servants, and watch to see if any petitioners come because then sometimes interesting things could happen.

On Thames Street I could hear men in livery shout "Make way, make way for His Grace!" and so I knew somebody important had come up the steps and was being forced to mingle where I could get a good glimpse of him. I was hoping for a lord with gold embroidery but it turned out to be Bishop Wolsey, which the footmen kept announcing just so we wouldn't tread on his hem and that was good, too, because churchmen of rank are allowed to speak directly with God quite often, so it is thrilling just to be near them.

With all that shouting and jostling, the crowd parted, and I could see that in front of the bishop was a crucifer with a big silver cross. Around him and behind him in a long train walked guards and gentlemen ushers and clerks in his livery, as well as several priests in plain robes. There weren't any petitioners, but something even more amusing to see. There was the bishop in especially splendid violet damask, all deep in his holy thoughts about God, and not looking around him at all, but just straight ahead, and following just behind him were two men in livery that I could tell were secretaries by their pen cases. One of them was thin and smooth and rather oily-looking, with pale crinkled eyelids that reminded me of a lizard's. He was carrying a big leather case and looking very puffed up with the importance of it, so I imagined that case was full of important advice and letters for the king at Greenwich.

The second secretary was altogether different, so they made a very comical, mismatched pair. The thin lizard one oozed along, and the other one, who was good-looking and sturdily built, walked straight and strong. He had a profile worth inspecting. A good chin, a nose that arched just a tiny bit where the bone leaves off, nice muscles down the side of the jaw ... His brown curls were cut off below the ear, and where the sun struck them, they shone auburn. Not a bad sort of Adam. A pity ... He turned his head, and I saw dark brows that were not set evenly but one just a bit higher than the other, which gave him a quizzical, humorous, sarcastic kind of look. His eyes were a very nice sort of hazelish brownish green, honest, but not subtle; they seemed to show all his thoughts just as if he'd written them on his forehead. The thoughts I saw there were very amusing. He was looking embarrassed, carrying a very tiny box that I imagined must have the bishop's seal in it. He walked very near the bishop's elbow, and the man with the case looked irritated every time he saw him get too close, as if he wished *he* were close at the bishop's elbow, instead.

"Look at that man, Nan. You can see his thoughts coming right out of his eyes."

"Which man? Oh, that one? I don't see anything different."

"I do. He thinks he looks silly carrying that tiny box. He wishes he had the big one."

"They both look alike to me. Two of a kind. Noses in the air. As arrogant as their master, I'd say."

But the one with the little box just looked to me for all the world as if he were carrying a hen's egg that had gone bad, which he was afraid might break and stink, but still he didn't dare to throw it away. I wonder what's in that box, I thought. Just then the bishop wrinkled up his nose, for the crowd was pressing very close, and then made a little circular waving motion as a signal with his hand. The man with the little box opened it most deferentially, but that sarcastic eyebrow of his spoiled the humbleness of his gesture. Inside the box, it turned out not to be an important seal at all but the bishop's pomander, which he put to his nose. I couldn't help it; I laughed out loud. My Adam cast a sideways glance at me, and I saw his round, hazel eyes flash for just an instant with horrified embarrassment, which made me feel almost sympathetic, so I put my hand over my mouth to cover up the laughing. But that made him turn his face away very quickly, but I could see the back of his neck was turning red, and that amused me even more.

"That man was staring at you, Susanna. I swear."

"Which one, Nan?" I asked, all innocent.

"That liveryman of the bishop's, the one with the tiny box."

But the crowd was closing in tighter on the bishop, who pretended not to notice as his guards moved closer together to split them apart and clear his path. I could see that man take advantage of the disorder to hunt me out in the crowd. His eyes found me measuring him up, depth of chest, width of neck, proportion of leg to torso, and he looked right through me, his face amused. But I just looked right back with a firm and disapproving stare to let him know that it is not right for men to look at respectable widows that way, and he snorted to stop a laugh from coming out.

At the sound, the bishop's eyes darted sideways to make sure the noise wasn't an assassin or something, and his gaze flicked between the two of us as if he saw something amusing, and then it caught mine, which was really extraordinary and something very memorable for me.

Wolsey's face was sunken in fat warped by big worry lines from his many cares, and his eyes were very sharp and fair frightening, the right one with a lid that drooped and twitched, lending him a very sinister expression. His eyes told me he was a worldly intriguer but I could tell all those intrigues wouldn't do him much good, because a man of God should stick to God just as a painter should stick to painting.

But then, just as clear as clear, I saw him reading my face and knew he could see my thoughts as clearly as I could see his. He pursed up his mouth with disapproval, and then looked away. And that's how I knew the great Bishop Wolsey and I were fated to meet someday, because our gazes had locked for one instant on Thames Street and our thoughts had changed places with each other. I could feel my heart pounding and my face, which can be a big betrayer, turning hot. Then the whole parade of them passed by to rejoin their watermen and they were gone, and I put out of my mind the feeling of fatefulness.

In Guthrun's Lane you can see the gold beaters deep inside their shops, pounding gold leaf fine and thin between sheets of parchment. I am good at applying gold leaf, which I did for father, but I had no plans to be doing that again since I had no high custom and my lowlier Adam and Eve work did not need gold leaf. Just at the end was Master Ailwin's shop, which was small and narrow but long in back where he had ovens and glassware with bubbly, smelly stuff and all kinds of jugs and jars and boxes of things you might have needed but mostly didn't. His shutter was up, and I could see someone very large and rich-looking inside buying something. The rich man was in deep conversation with Master Ailwin, who had bushy white eyebrows and hair that grew out of his ears. I could only see the rich man's back, but he was tall and heavy, in a green velvet gown cut like a foreigner's, maybe Italian. He seemed angry because I could see him pounding on the counter with a big, square fist in a black glove. I hoped it wasn't about short weight, because that might have put Master Ailwin out of business and then where would I have been? So I waited outside with Nan and several cats came, which she shooed away, and I didn't go in because I wanted my business to be private since it involved being up to no good.

So I waited on the corner where Bladder Lane is, pretending I wasn't interested in Master Ailwin's apothecary shop at all. Two large dogs had come but Nan hadn't had time to shoo them when that strange man came by, walking fast right out of the door and practically squashing me by almost running into me. His face made my heart stand still. His eyes were pale green and seemed to freeze me through. Above them were strange, bushy eyebrows sprinkled with long gray hairs like insects' antennae that looked as if they belonged on a devil. Just where horns should be growing, his hair had two wide, curling streaks of white that stood up before they mixed with the rest of the dark hair almost as if they really were horns. His face, pale under his square-cut beard, looked as if he stayed up nights doing unspeakable things. His wide, almost lipless mouth gave me a stretched-out smile, but his icy eyes were insane. "I know you," he said. "Aren't you Rowland Dallet's widow?" I wanted to turn and run, but I knew I must not show any weakness. I answered,

"I am, sir, but since I do not know you, our acquaintance will have to wait until we are properly introduced. Good day." I started to pass on, but not in the direction of Master Ailwin's because I did not want him to know where I was going. Nan followed, and also the dogs, who growled. But he moved quite fast and pushed one huge arm in front of me where it blocked my way.

"Why, Mistress Dallet, don't run away so soon. It is so good to see you up and well," he said, pressing his black-gloved hand against the wall so I couldn't pass. Then he leaned so close it seemed to stop my air. I couldn't smell anything but the heavy, rotten scent of him, like something long buried. I didn't want his breath on me. "Did not your late husband ever mention his friend and patron, Sir Septimus Crouch? He was very dear to me; almost like a son. A delightful man, a man of wit, a terrible loss."

"I am afraid he never mentioned your name, sir. Now please let me pass."

"Oh, my, no. Not until I let you know that I am your true friend. For your husband's sake, I stand prepared to look after your interests, to be your protector. Did no one tell you that I offered to make provision for your poor, unfortunate child?" The thought flashed through my mind; could he have known, could he have guessed, what it was? He looked pleased when he spied the horrified look on my face. He smiled, and moved so close that he was only an inch or two from me. I could feel his body heat, but the wall stopped me from backing away farther. "There will come a time when you deny me nothing," he said, his mouth close to my ear and his voice almost at a whisper.

"I think not, sir," I quavered. "I may have to make my own way, but I do not give up my will to strangers on the street." He backed away, his smile mocking.

"Then good day to you, Mistress Dallet," he said, pretending to remember his manners and sweeping off his jeweled hat in a satirical manner. "Next time we speak, I shall make sure we have been properly introduced." He turned, and I could feel my heart pounding with fear as he walked away.

"That will be a cold day in hell," said Nan. We watched him walk down the street and were sure he was gone before we circled back to the apothecary's. But it seemed as if a dark cloud had come over my day.

"Why, it's little Susanna Maartens, I do believe. I'd know those blue eyes anywhere! Come in, come in. What can an old man do for a charming—oh, widow it is. My, that's too bad. Your father set such store by that Master Dalbert, was it? 'A brilliant young man,' he said. Yes, such store. Your esteemed father, an artificer of great niceness and precision, but so opinionated! But that other young man—ever so much better manners than your father—too bad, too bad. Whatever makes you come here by yourself? Would you like a little something to help you catch another man? Or perhaps a money powder—you look perfectly able to catch another man by yourself."

He began to poke around the shelves he had in the front of the shop that were all full of curious boxes and bundles, some with alchemical labels that no one could read. On his counter there was a marble slab for cutting and measuring powders on and a balance for weighing things out. Past the open door into the back of his shop, I could see his apprentice busy sweeping the floor in the long, cluttered room. Dried bats, bunches of plants that looked like weeds, and other curious things were hanging from the ceiling in that back room, and there was a cupboard full of curious glassware.

"But money," Master Ailwin went on, "ah, money—that's something else again. Who can catch money these days without a little help from the other world?" The apprentice looked up and spied me in the front. He pretended to be sweeping closer and closer so he could approach the open door to listen in. Then he leaned on his broom and stared at me. "It's the fault of the currency, you know, which is no good—no good at all, thanks to those criminals at the mint. What currency is good these days? All adulterated, all. Now in the days of the old king, when there were ministers of virtue—" The tip of Master Ailwin's beard was singed-looking, and he had on a ruin of a cap and a leather doublet so stained and old it could have been from King Richard's time. I could hear him getting ready to let loose one of his long discourses. I felt like fleeing.

"I'm in need of some things; colors, mostly. But I need them from someone discreet, like yourself—"

"It's the corruption, you know. Corruption! Bribe taking. The selling of high office. But then what can you expect with the kind of example set by the church, simony—"

"I need to buy verdegris and white lead today, Master Ailwin." The apprentice boy had just started his first growth. He was all bony and knobby and nothing fit together quite right. I noticed he kept staring at me with the oddest look. He had an old, stained apron over his clothes, and his hose were all patched. I thought, what is it that's wrong with me, anyway? Now apprentice boys are following, too.

"Whatever for?" Master Ailwin seemed suddenly suspicious. "Are you keeping house for some other painter? Remember this, my girl, there's a fine line between decency and the gutter. Never cross it. A woman's virtue. It is her crown—"

"I'm painting for myself, Master Ailwin."

"For yourself? Now there's a curiosity. In cuckooland, where the hens crow and the roosters lay, and frogs sing 'hey, ring-a-ding donny,' I suppose the women paint—"

"I'm making good money, and I need a supplier."

"Making good money? Now there *is* cuckooland. Just how do you propose to evade the guild?"

"By buying my colors from you and paying you to keep quiet, that's how," I said, completely exasperated.

"You propose to bribe me to disrupt the proper order of the world?" he asked, tipping his head to one side and scratching beneath his shapeless old felt hat.

"That's what I had in mind."

"Young woman, you should be seethed in oil for that. Do you understand what you are asking from me? In the world of decency, of virtue—"

"In that world, Master Ailwin, any person who needs to should be able to get bread with their own hands. Would you rather I be a beggar? I deserve to earn what I need." I was so irritated, I shouted at him. He looked at me a long time, as if he saw someone new instead of me.

"You are almost one of us," he said. Then he leaned on the counter and looked very closely at my face. "Have you ever read the words written by God?" he asked.

"I have never had that good fortune," I answered.

"It is written in the Bible that in the Christian Church, before its great corruption, all goods were held in common. In common! That means that all riches now held by the great, even the Church itself, have been stolen from the common. *Those* were the old days of virtue, when all men lived by the sweat of their brows—"

"And women—"

"Oh, and women—"

"Painters especially—"

"Why, I suppose painters, if they had them—"

"Of course they had them. And they needed colors."

"We should rise up and take it back. Plant the estates with turnips for all, cut firewood for the cold, trap rabbits for the hungry—"

"And sell paint to women painters. I'm sure that's part of it."

"Why, yes, of course! A small act, but one richly symbolic."

"Exactly. In fact, it would be more symbolic if you sold me those colors at the same price the selfish lords and corrupt liverymen of the guilds paid for them."

"I always gouge them!" he cried. "Less! For Susanna Dillard, I will charge less!"

"It's an important gesture," I said.

"Significant. No more shall the widows go widowless, the orphans orphanless—"

"You've stirred my blood," I said. "I will paint with new vigor, knowing I oppose the corrupt lords of the earth with every brush stroke."

"Every brush a sword," he cried.

"Two ounces of white lead," I cried back again. And, with fire in his eye, he began to weigh out what I needed on his balance.

"What on earth was all that about?" asked Nan, as we left with everything we needed.

"Oh, he's crazy," I answered. "It's all that stuff in the back room he breathes. Mercury fumes, orpiment, God knows what. It rises to the brain. It's gotten worse since I last saw him."

"What about all that property-in-common talk? Why that's positively *indecent*," she said, sniffing. "Heretical, too, I imagine. I mean, lords are lords and common people common because God wills it. If He willed all our goods to be the same, they would be."

"It's all too deep for me," I said. "I'd rather just paint and let other people argue. I'm happier that way. Goodness, I hope he remembers that promise to give us good prices." We had already passed into the main street when we heard someone running and a breathless voice calling us.

"Mistress, mistress!" It was the apprentice boy. Yes, definitely it had happened. Now I was going to be followed by them, too. I was sure of it. He pushed his way past the dogs and spoke to us, still puffing. "Mistress, the master can be sometimes forgetful. His cares, you know, and his work. But if you send a note to the shop, I can make sure what you want is made up correctly and deliver it to you. You'll find it very convenient, I'm sure. Surely, a lady like you should be spared the necessity of going out in foul weather."

"That is most generous of you—ah—"

"Tom, mistress. Tom Whitley, and your servant, mistress."

"Why then, that's just what I'll do," I answered, but as we passed on I saw he stood watching until we had disappeared around a corner.

"Well, goodness, I do believe he's in love with you," said Nan.

"Puppy love," I answered. First dogs and cats. Now apprentice boys. What's next?

"Well, let him down gently," said Nan. "After all, he'll make sure you get good measure as long as his heart's pounding, and if he's angry, he'll be sure you're cheated."

"Oh, don't worry, Nan. There's something about him that reminds me of Felix."

"You mean he can't draw, either?"

"Oh, that, too. But he means so well, and it probably mostly goes awry. Felix was always my favorite, you know. He would have looked after me if he'd lived."

"A lot of things would be different if that were so," said Nan, her mouth all grim as she kicked a stone out of her way in the gutter.

We entered the shop below our rooms to find Mistress Hull deep in the sale of a painting to a broad-shouldered man in muddy boots, a flat, brimmed hat pulled down low, and black cloak. His cloak was splashed with bits of mud, too, and he looked as if he had been traveling far. His back was to us and obscured my view of Mistress Hull and of the picture in front of him. He didn't seem like the usual sort of customer, not being a priest. He was wearing a shortsword. Maybe he's a foreign priest, and they dress like that when they travel, I thought. I watched as he nodded politely every sentence or so to the flow of words from the widow's mouth.

"So appropriate for your private meditations on sin and redemption—" Nod. Obviously a priest. Was she finally selling one of the green Christs?

"The color—the brushwork, too, is unlike the others, surely it is not by the same hand?" His voice sounded curious, but not puzzled. An agreeable voice. Intelligent sounding. It was clear he knew something about painting. And, oh dear, it must be an Adam and Eve he was looking at. I don't need anyone clever looking too closely at my Adam and Eves, I worried.

"My, you are a rare judge of fine painting. No, this is one of the few—the very last—left by the great court painter Rowland Dallet, to his widow. Poor dear, she had been ill with grief, so I have undertaken to sell this along with a few of her other household effects." Oh, clever Mistress Hull, I thought. I should never underestimate her glib tongue. The man nodded. Good, he'll never suspect. "I noticed you looked at the inkhorn as you entered. That's how I knew you were a deep thinker, a man of judgement." I could see the man's hat brim nod again. How odd. There was something familiar about the back of his neck. But there was Mistress Hull's hand right next to the inkhorn. I stiffened. Don't you dare try to throw in an inkhorn with *my* Adam and Eve, I sent the thought to her like an arrow, as if my mind could pierce her brain. Get top price.

"The concept is unusual. The snake ..." The shrewd voice sounded amused.

"Master Dallet was a painter of great distinction."

"I am aware of that. I met the man, you know. It was I who arranged an important commission for him once, on behalf of my master."

"Then, of course, you would understand the *tragedy* of it all." Mistress Hull's voice sank to a dramatic whisper. "To tell you, and only you, the truth, I don't think she knows the value of it. She's set the price too low, in my opinion. But who am I to go against the wishes of such a pious woman in her grief? Selfless she is, absolutely selfless ... it would be a great help to her. . . ."

Nan and I tried to tiptoe quietly behind the stranger to make our escape up the staircase. But a floorboard creaked, and the man turned suddenly. His eyes fixed me to my place. I recognized those eyes right away. Hazel, translucent with thought, and cleverer than I like to see in a man—especially one who spies out my paintings. An odd smile of recognition crossed his face. My heart beat fast. There was no mistaking who it was, standing there looking bulky and out of place in Mistress Hull's narrow, cluttered little shop. It was that man of Wolsey's that I had laughed at. Oh, Susanna, you are in a lot of trouble and had better run fast, I thought. I hurried the last few steps to the stair.

"Stay there, Mistress Dallet," he said, in a commanding voice. I stood, paralyzed, with one foot on the stair. Somehow he seemed larger than I remembered. The way he filled up the little shop suddenly looked quite menacing to me. My breath came hard. I wanted to run away, but my feet wouldn't work.

"Come here, come here. I don't bite," he said, and his voice was suspiciously mild. But still I couldn't move. Silently, he turned the wooden panel he held in his hands so that I could see the painting on it. *The Temptation of Eve*, complete with wallowing snake. He looked at me, his eyes intent, trying to read my confusion. I could feel my own eyes open wide and my knees tremble. The corner of his mouth twitched. Something glittered in the back of those hazel eyes. He had made up his mind about something, and I feared what it was. "Come here," he said, his voice coaxing. "You and I have something to talk about." Unwillingly, I took a step forward. "You've turned quite pale, Mistress Dallet. Do you need to sit down?" I shook my head silently. My stomach hurt and my hands were cold.

"You sent me on quite a wild-goose chase, you know," he went on. "Master Dallet had no apprentice, as I found out the hard way. Now tell me, was that kind?" I couldn't speak a word in answer. He pushed back his flat brimmed hat, and his unruly brown curls popped up like badly trained dogs. He tilted his head and lifted that crooked eyebrow while he looked at me up and down, his eyes quietly calculating. "The look on your face tells me that my conclusions are correct," he said.

"I don't know what you mean," I answered, my voice faint.

"You counted on the ignorance of men, didn't you?" There was a glint of recognition in his gaze. I turned away my face.

"I—I don't know what you mean."

"Just answer me this, Mistress Dallet. Why did you put your husband's face on the serpent?"

The Fourth Portrait

Girl with a Doll. *Artist unknown. 3½"-diameter. Mid-sixteenth century. Victoria and Albert Museum.*

While dolls used in sacred ritual practices have been preserved from earliest times, the very nature of the doll as toy signifies that few will survive the period of childhood intact. This unusual miniature of the English Renaissance, painted with great sensitivity by the unknown artist, depicts a girl of six or seven with her doll, a specimen of the wood "paddle" type with painted features, simply dressed in a straight gown, without arms or sleeves.

—Fig. 142. Caption. N. Boyle.
A Picture History of Toys Through the Ages

This is the first likeness that I took in the service of Bishop Wolsey, which is a portrait of his niece that he set such store by. It was also a test, because children are hardest to do right. You would think that the problem with painting children is that they are so wigglesome you cannot take a likeness, but the real problem is that they don't have much in the way of features except big eyes and foreheads and round cheeks. If you look at a baby's profile all you will see is two half circles on top of each other with hardly even a nose at all, so you should always paint them three-quarters or full on because otherwise it's hopeless. Some painters just give up and paint them like little adults, but they are usually men who don't have children themselves. When you are taking the likeness, if there is any doubt, always paint children to look like the mother's husband, especially since he is usually the one who's paying. I did not start out with this idea, but came to it the hard way.

TEN

"And so you see, Your Grace, the answer to your riddle is found, and the ghost explained. Master Dallet had a clever widow, the daughter of a foreigner, who could herself paint most cunningly in small. When he died suddenly, in debt, she took to paying her way by passing off her work as his."

Wolsey, an immense presence in violet silk and a vast pectoral cross, smiled narrowly, but his eyes never changed. "Most ingenious and persistent of you, Master Ashton," he said to the man who stood before him as he sat in the great cushioned chair in his parlor at Bridewell, in Fleet Street. Wolsey's velvet-slippered feet rested on a low footstool; he was feeling bilious today but had labored on since dawn without rest. At the side of the ambitious prince of the church stood the unctuous Tuke, pleasingly deferential; behind him stood several of his knights retainer. Wolsey regretted the unknown master painter he had lost, but at least this promised to be a pleasant little diversion. A curiosity, like a two-headed calf or a dog that has been taught to count. The retainers shuffled. "The infinite deviousness of women is proven once again," Wolsey observed.

"Yes, Your Grace, that is well put," agreed Master Tuke. Wolsey nodded to him as if in agreement, and Ashton fumed inwardly. That slithery flatterer was trying to steal his credit. But Wolsey was thinking again of the miniature. Perhaps Ashton, in his passion to prove himself clever, had outsmarted himself? Was it a fluke?

"Still, there is a certain sort of industry in such a woman that cannot be dismissed," said Wolsey, nodding in Ashton's direction.

"True, Your Grace." Take that, Tuke, thought Ashton. What do you know of this case? It is me he asks for an opinion.

"You have spoken with her? Is she shrewish and bold? Abnormal? Mannish, perhaps?"

"No, Your Grace, she does not seem exceptional." Wolsey detected the tone of bruised pride in his secretary's voice.

"Except that she managed to deceive you, and it still smarts," Wolsey observed. Tuke snickered.

"I got it out of her at last," said Ashton.

"A woman painter . . ." mused Wolsey. "Clearly a freak of nature. Is the work you purchased her own, or has she deceived you yet again?" Wolsey eyed the wrapped panel beneath his gentleman attendant's arm.

"The character of the painting leads me to believe she is not lying. Tell me, do you remember Rowland Dallet's features?"

"I remember that he appeared to think much of them himself."

"Ah. Then let me show you the painting, Your Grace." Ashton had not misjudged the sensation that would be created when he un-wrapped the panel. At the sight of the vast, pink Eve and the leering, human-faced serpent, Wolsey snorted, and his secretary of the privy cabinet put his hand over his face to hide the smile. Wolsey's knights retainer burst out laughing.

"Now *that* is a portrayal of sin," said the King's Almoner, his voice at once amused and disapproving.

"As you see, she has given the serpent her husband's face," pointed out Master Ashton.

"Hardly a Patient Griselda of a wife, eh, Ashton? I think I under-stand now how the man amassed his debt." Wolsey chuckled. Ashton glanced at Tuke's face, bereft of any chance to say something clever, and felt a sensation of warm contentment flood through him.

"Your Grace, I do believe I have had that woman pointed out to me," said one of the knights retainer, pointing at the painting. "A no-torious wanton. The wife of one Captain Pickering. The features are hers. I'd swear it."

"Pickering? I think I may have met the man. His wife, you say?" answered another of the knights.

"And so the mystery is solved. An adulterous liaison, portrayed by a jealous wife. Hardly a religious frame of mind, I'd say." Wolsey had sunk his chin in his hand while he contemplated the painting again. The color was very fresh, and the portrayal of distance very elegantly done through draftsmanship and color perspective. There was no amateurish look to the handling of the composition, and the greenery around the exuberant pink figure seemed to pulsate with life. Astonishing, thought Wolsey. He turned to look at his secretary. Ashton had managed to make his face bland and deferential, but his eyes were dancing with self-congratulation. "Very clever, very clever indeed, Master Ashton. You are a veritable bloodhound. When I set you to a problem, you pursue it to the end. I won't forget that, I assure you." Ashton bowed in acknowledgment, basking in the great man's approval. "A curious picture," Wolsey went on. "Eden looks a bit craggy, don't you think?"

"It looks like the South of France to me, my lord," answered Ashton, who had traveled far in Wolsey's service.

"Most unflattering. Eden should look like England in summer, in my opinion. Have you brought the painter here?"

"Exactly as you requested, Your Grace. She is waiting in the antechamber."

Behind his pouched eyes, Wolsey's mind was working. He never wasted anything. Now this master painter had disappointed him, being a woman. But then he thought, Women can have their uses, especially if they can be guided. What cleverer, what more innocent and more flattering way to gain a pair of ears than to lend to a gentleman's household a portrait painter to take a likeness? And a woman—she could enter circles where no man could ever gain admittance. It all depends on her character, he mused. I have no use for some unmannerly, self-willed shrew. A docile woman in middle age would be ideal, he thought.

When the door opened and a footman showed in the painter, Wolsey watched her as she crossed the room, adding up the positives and negatives of his plan. She was younger than he thought: good and bad, probably bad. As she knelt and kissed his ring, he observed her closely. Decently dressed in black, proper humility and piety. Good. She will be in awe of my spiritual authority. Then he looked more closely. There was something odd about her. Something waiting to burst out. Was it the stray, gingery curl that had escaped from her plain headdress, or perhaps the green paint that could be spied under the nail of her right index finger? Bursting, definitely bad. The hands were plump, stubby fingered, and agile. Competent-looking. Good. She looked up and he scanned her face with his intimidating, drooped eye-lid gaze. He observed she was woman just past girlhood, with a few childish freckles still sprinkled across her tip-tilted nose, a generous, cheerful-looking mouth. Was she a gossip? That would be bad. But the eyes told the story. Blue, pale lashed, startled-looking. A simpleton. His theory was right. Good. Then he looked more closely. The eyes were observing him back. It was a curious, sympathetic, measuring gaze, skillfully concealed, but one discernible by the canny King's Almoner. Bad. He wanted others measured, not himself. And curiosity in a woman, definitely bad. Altogether a very mixed thing, he thought. Let us see. Let us see.

"Mistress Dallet, have you brought any samples of your work in small?"

"I have, Your Grace," she answered, opening the little wooden coffer she had been carrying. From it she took three plain turned wooden cases, each about two inches across. "These I have done for my own amusement. This first is my good Mistress Littleton—" She handed Wolsey the case, and he opened it with a curiously delicate touch. Everyone present could hear him catch his breath. The brushwork, done with tiny pencils made of squirrels' hair, was minutely fine, the colors glowing and rich. Almost too rich for such a common subject, thought Wolsey, looking at the gray-haired old woman in the plain cap, her pale features set off against a brilliant, sky blue background.

"A servant," he said slowly. Without meaning to, he could feel the empathy coming from the tiny image. The face looked careworn, the eyes kindly. "But more than a servant," he observed. "Honest. Trusted. Careful of your interests—no, self-sacrificing. Someone's old nurse, perhaps. Yours, it seems to me."

"That is exactly who it is, Your Grace," she answered. Wolsey raised an eyebrow and settled his face into his chins. Yes, this was what he wanted. He passed the picture to a knight retainer, who exclaimed over the perfect brushwork but did not see what Wolsey had read there. Character, truth, shining up from two inches of burnished parchment.

"This second one is of Mistress Catherine Hull," said the woman. Wolsey opened the case to see the sharp eyes of a girl in her teens staring out at him. She could have been pretty, with her abundant yellow curls and pink cheeks, but there was something malcontent about the expression.

"This is a young girl whose bitterness poisons her beauty. In a time that should be full of hope, she is without prospects. Tell me, has this young girl a dowry?"

"She has none, Your Grace. Her mother is a widow who keeps a little shop of odds and ends. She has no suitors."

"Is she really as attractive as you portray her?" Something about the picture, perhaps only its intrinsic value as a jewel, made the girl look more important, valuable, and full of interest than she ought to be for one of her station. Curious, what a picture can do, thought Wolsey, as he passed the picture to his privy secretary. Perhaps I should inquire into the girl's reputation and give her a dowry as a charity. Fifteen or twenty pounds would get her another shopkeeper, someone of her own rank.

"Tom Whitley, an apothecary's apprentice," said the painter as she handed him the third case. It was the head and shoulders of a common-looking brown-haired boy holding a rose. Somehow, the painter, in that minute space, had created the illusion of a new, half-grown moustache and mooning eyes. At that moment, the great man missed the younger self that he had long ago left behind and, for a brief instant, regretted the grievous pains of unhatched love. Mistress Lark, fresh and pretty, mopping up the tables in her father's tavern. She had taken a look at his tonsure and laughed. He had plucked a rose from the trellis outside and held it out to her, in the hope that the look in her eyes would change to sympathy when she saw what was written in his face. Avaunt, he said silently to the memory of the strong, pretty girl with her sleeves rolled up. She was a respectable matron now; he had purchased her an important husband when his rising rank had required that he divest himself of her. Hadn't he treated her honorably? Hadn't he behaved honorably by their children, raising them as his own niece and nephew? Wasn't this what God, and his own vaulting ambition, demanded? He looked again at the compact, buxom little woman in black who had brought these feelings back to him. She seemed unconscious of what she had done. Astonishing. A true freak of nature.

"You should paint only in small. I find these works superior to—that—" He gestured to the oil panel. She blushed.

"I prefer to work in small," she said. "The colors are water based, and more cleanly. The oil paints give a headache if the room be not well aired."

Yes, a freak. Entirely unaware of what she was doing. That was the only possible explanation. Wolsey had once seen a strange child, which drooled and never spoke except to recite the Psalms, which it did perfectly. The creature was presented to him as a kind of holy fool, having been taken by its keepers on the rounds of fairs for several years. He seem to recall it had died, once confined beneath a roof and properly fed. God made freaks to remind us He was capable of anything He wished. Wolsey watched the agile, round little fingers closing the cases. The deft competence of her hands unnerved him. An unwanted thought came to him: Suppose women might express themselves with as much ability as men if they were given the same training that men had? Ridiculous. He pushed the idea away with mental explanations. In some strange, instinctive way, this God-created freak had probably absorbed her skill from watching her husband. That had to be the answer.

"In my judgment, Mistress Dallet, your work in small is the equal of the best foreign work in my collection." Wolsey's courtiers, quick to support their master's views, nodded and muttered assent. The painter looked around that circle of strange men and the immense, gaudy figure enthroned at the center and caught the look in their eyes. Now I know what a dancing bear feels like, she thought. Suddenly, she wanted to flee. But one cannot hide from the summons of the powerful, so she stood her ground, miserable at the thought that she had brought this all on herself. How could I have ever wished this? she thought. I should have stayed home and been content. Fear flashed through the startled-looking, wide blue eyes. No one saw it but Wolsey. Aha, he thought. I have her.

"I wish to retain you in my service, as paintrix, at fifteen pounds a year. You will attend my wishes here, and in my absence, Master Tuke will instruct you." A curiosity for his collection, like a chiming clock. But this time, more than a curiosity. Remembering the poor freak, he reminded himself he would have to be delicate, to preserve the gift he wished to make use of. "I will expect you to be always attended by a respectable woman of your own choosing," he added, taking pains to look avuncular. She saw the look and managed to stifle her sudden panic.

"I am honored to accept, Your Grace," she answered, her heart pounding.

The entire interview had taken scarcely a quarter of an hour. Wolsey, who organized wars and masques with the same driving efficiency, paused only briefly in thought before turning again to the endless parade of business that made up his working days. A painter who could depict likeness was a valuable asset to any prince. One who could do likeness in miniature was even more admired, a source of honor for the patron, who could show favor by offering precious trinkets depicting the sovereign, depicting himself. But a painter who could depict character in the span of a man's hand was a treasure useful beyond belief to a diplomat who must assess motives at a thousand miles of distance. And this one a simpleton, too, Wolsey mused. *That can have its uses. But I'll have to give her a keeper. I don't want her wandering off or getting purloined by some other prince.*

Wolsey cast a glance about the room at his retainers. Whom could he spare? His eye caught sight of Ashton, still glowering at the spot where the paintrix had been standing, his big hands hanging at the sides of his bulky frame like a pair of hams hung up to dry. His resentful eyes and sulky profile, at once offended and infuriated, told the whole story. *Hmm.* She's already injured his pride in some way, thought Wolsey. *Excellent.* He smiled almost paternally at his most troublesome secretary. *After every little triumph, Ashton always needed to be set down hard, to keep his pride from growing overweening. First the pomander. Now the paintrix. It would be perfect.*

"Master Ashton," he said, "I'd like you to keep an eye on that woman." Wolsey's look was bland and avuncular as he admired the way Ashton's eyes rolled sideways in his head with ill-suppressed horror. "When I dispatch her on assignment, I want you to make the arrangements for her travel." A muscle twitched on the side of Ashton's jaw. His neck was growing red. *Better and better.* "And, of course, I will hold you responsible if she is lured away from our service." Ashton stared at him, and his jaw dropped. *How unpolitic,* thought Wolsey.

"But ... but ...." Ashton began. Tuke smirked. "I'd ... I'd have to follow her everywhere, like ..." Like a lapdog, his eyes seemed to say. How could you? The wounded look. Outstanding, thought Wolsey.

"She'll need instruction, I'm sure, in proper court etiquette ..." Wolsey could not refrain from driving home the knife and giving it a turn or two.

"I'm not a governess ... um, I mean, Your Grace, I'm not *fit* ..."

"It's a *very* important assignment," announced Wolsey firmly. From behind him, Wolsey heard Master Tuke's faint snicker. He's next, thought the bishop. I think I'll give Master Warren the dispatch case next time. "Master Ashton," he said, "I wish you to order two gold cases made. I intend to try her out with portraits of my niece and nephew." Yes, nothing less than gold for his daughter, Dorothy, and his son, little Thomas Winter, whom he would make a prince of the Church in his turn. After all, hadn't the Pope had a son? And Wolsey had every intention of becoming the first English Pope.

For all the problems there were with being a dead man painter, there were even more with being a live woman painter and it started getting uncomfortable right away. Almost the same day, that man of Wolsey's, who was all full of himself from discovering my secret, came snooping up to the studio and looked about at everything as if he didn't approve of it. Then he shifted from one foot to another and said he would assist and instruct me so that I would understand the etiquette of great houses better, which he thought was very subtle.

This little condescension irritated me worse than a whole mattressful of fleas. Ordinarily I would have just thanked him for all his concern to get rid of him, but I was in my own studio and it made my tongue freer. So I looked at him and said, "I suppose every dancing bear needs a keeper." He just stood there, looking large and out of place in my little room, as well as humiliated, among all those round pink Eves, and I could see an odd look flash through his eyes, a look as if we understood each other. "Does he always send you on jobs like this?" I asked.

"It is a privilege to be the humble servant of a man so great and noble," he said.

"That's exactly what I think," I answered.

"These things will have to go," he said, waving his hand around him.

"I know," I answered. "They aren't very respectable. Good women shouldn't be seeing them."

"Let alone painting them," he said. "What gave you the idea, anyway?"

"Oh, the painter downstairs used to do them before he died. So when Mistress Hull said she needed some more, I obliged."

"So you were actually two dead painters."

"I guess so," I said, sighing regretfully.

"You should be ashamed," he said.

"I would be, but I hadn't time for it. It's not easy, trying to make a living, you know. Everybody says good Christians should care for widows and orphans, but I guess they just overlooked me—and I'm both."

"I'm aware of that," he said and looked away. And I knew he wouldn't be saying more, even though there was more inside. I couldn't help wondering what it was. But I thought I might know because the edges of his ears turned red in a way that would have been almost endearing except that he was promising to be such an interfering burden in my life.

Gusts of rain blew down Seacole Lane, rattling the house signs and rushing in noisy torrents from the leaden-faced downspouts at the corners of the steep tile roofs. Beneath the overhanging second stories of the houses, a slight man wrapped in a heavy black cloak and hood made his way toward the Saracen's Head. Hurriedly, he pounded up the outside staircase in the courtyard to a little room under the eaves and threw open the door without knocking.

Maître Bellier sat at a table lit by the feeble light and warmed by the even-feebler heat cast by a charcoal brazier that stood on a tripod in the corner. He was wearing a heavy, fur-lined robe and hat with earflaps. On the table before him lay a series of curious antique medallions, which he was inspecting with the aid of a glass. The room filled with the smell of wet wool as Eustache threw off his long black cloak.

"Well?" said Maître Bellier. "What is the news?"

"I began by making inquiries. This man Crouch is a well-known occultist, given, they say, to the most dangerous practices of diabolism and necromancy."

"*Hmm.* Interesting, but not unexpected, given the nature of the manuscript he was in search of." Bellier's face was calm, as he inspected the agitated servant who stood before him.

"More to the point, last winter he engaged a dowser called Blind Barnabas, who lived with his widowed daughter, a midwife, in Chicken Lane, to assist him in finding a treasure. Two gentlemen went with him, but Blind Barnabas never came home. He was found with his throat cut the next day, outside the walls, at a building site in the ruins of the Old Temple."

"Aha, Eustache, our lost treasure. A determined man, this Crouch." Bellier looked quietly amused.

"Some time later, a roof tile fell mysteriously on this Goodwife Forster, the daughter, and killed her. But not before she had told everything she knew to her gossips, one of whom is called Mistress West, the wife of the proprietor of a sordid tavern in Fleet Lane called, *hmm,* the Goat and Bottle, I believe." Eustache rubbed his hands together to warm them at the brazier.

"The two outsiders who knew of his discovery conveniently dead, eh? He might as well have written us a letter saying that he has our book. His tale of sharing it was an invention." Bellier was now listening intently, his chin sunk in his hand as he thought.

"No, wait, I think not. Two men accompanied him on that midnight expedition from which Blind Barnabas did not return. One was some sort of painter, whom the tavern keeper's wife knew by sight, since he lived across from her establishment; the other was a lawyer, she thought, but she didn't know his name. There was a great scandal in the neighborhood when the painter's corpse, as full of holes as a dovecote, was delivered to his widow by a man who claimed he had been beset by robbers. Shortly thereafter, the lawyer appeared and searched the house, taking away all the furniture, leaving the painter's widow bereft and lunatic."

"A charming trio of adventurers," said Maître Bellier, and an infinitesimal, pale smile crossed his face.

"But wait—a little while after that, the occultist Crouch came and made inquiries, offering to assist the widow, but when he found that the lawyer had taken away everything in the house, he was beside himself with rage."

"Aha. Then we must find this lawyer. He is the one who has what we want. He obviously got hold of the manuscript when he took possession of the painter's goods." Bellier tapped his fingers on the table impatiently. Eustache was so often slow to perceive the obvious.

"That is what I thought, but hear what I have just heard this past hour and you may come to another conclusion. The widow of the painter, the lunatic, has been given a position and pension by Bishop Wolsey, the King's Almoner and closest advisor, who had, before this time, no previous connection with this family. They were all abuzz with it at the tavern. No one can understand how it happened. They say she must have become his mistress. She has new dresses; her debts are paid; she has bought new furniture . . ."

"Mon dieu," whispered Maître Bellier, turning linen white. "This could only happen if she had provided him with something of great value . . ."

"Or it could be to buy her silence."

"If that is so, then our worst nightmare is fulfilled. The Church is on the trail of the Secret. Our mortal enemy . . . We are all dead men when this news reaches Rome . . ." Bellier stood, bracing himself by placing his hands on the table. They were trembling. To be burned alive for heresy was a fearful fate.

"Master, you must examine all the possibilities logically . . ."

"Yes, logic, logic . . ." muttered Maître Bellier, now pacing the room, his eyes desperate. "We must see whether the lawyer experiences a similar turn of fortune. Do we have anyone in Wolsey's household?"

"No, but we can warn our agent in Rome to watch this Wolsey's correspondence . . ."

"Good, good. But wait—the King's Almoner is an ambitious, worldly man, they say." Bellier's face looked suddenly hopeful. "What good would our Secret do him in Rome? None! No, he will serve his king before his Pope. There is a good chance he will keep the Secret to himself, if he has it, and bide his time . . ." Bellier paused, looking back at where his servant was still trying to warm himself. He was nearly wet through, and shivering. "I want you to discover, Eustache, how much this woman has revealed. Or if, pray God, it is only a carnal relation that brings her this good fortune. Follow her. We must know. In the meantime, I myself will make subtle inquiry about this lawyer. I will pretend to have legal business, perhaps a land title, yes ... we may have to end by silencing them all. If it is not too late ..."

Ashton sat alone at a narrow scribe's desk in the antechamber to Bishop Wolsey's cabinet, his even-featured, pale profile intent on the papers before him. With an oddly precise motion, the quill in his big hand traced across the pages, recopying and then translating annotated drafts of the King's Almoner's latest letter to France. A few coals glowed in the grate, and dismal gray light shone through the narrow window onto the page. He paused and with one hand brushed his unruly dark curls back from his forehead. The flickering firelight caught on his intent face. He frowned, bringing his brows together almost across his nose. His whole face managed to look truculent and grief stricken all at once.

Spring, cold and damp, had made his heart melancholy. Once again, it was Master Tuke who had followed Wolsey to the council, but for once Ashton hadn't minded. He wanted to be alone, to hide his confusion. It was the very season two years past when Mistress Lucas had sent the letter breaking their engagement in favor of a betrothal to a wealthy older neighbor. Putting down his pen, he saw the whole scene again in his mind; still yellow with fever, his future shattered by an Italian crossbow bolt, he had stood in front of her father's door, to find it barred against him. There on the steps, with the birds singing, he had read the cutting words, penned in simple girl's handwriting.

"I did not know my own heart well enough," she said, but then she had listed his faults, so many faults! He could see her father's hand in that list. He had called him a "little man of no estate." He ground his teeth with the memory of the insult. His left hand began to draw inward, his fingers folded in, half paralyzed, as it had been before his recovery. Unconsciously, he unfolded them with his right hand, pushing them straight again. He had willed his hand well again, willed it with pure rage, and the determination to be avenged. Ha! He wished he could show them now the rewards open to the servant of a great man like the bishop. How poorly they had calculated, that ambitious chit and her father. They had made one mistake. A man of intellect can go anywhere. Too bad a humble country esquire wasn't worthy of being received at the great bishop's court. He felt aching and feverish, as if the surgeon had cut away the bolt a second time. Damp weather, he ruminated. The damp brings it back.

But something interrupted his annual season of bitter musing. He kept seeing in his mind a freckled face with a smudge of green paint right across the bridge of the nose, and hearing a droll little voice explaining the truths of life out of a book of manners. Just as he had fixated his rage on his memory of the narrow features and neat blonde braids of Mistress Lucas, he could hear someone saying, "I suppose every dancing bear needs a keeper," and found himself looking down at an oddly sympathetic pair of blue eyes and a buxom little figure tightly laced into solemn black. A curious pain seemed to radiate from his heart. Food poisoning, he thought. It often begins like this. He tried to recall what he had eaten. He hadn't eaten anything. Not for a day and a half. It must be a different illness. But not food poisoning, after all. Something more dangerous, perhaps. Well, never mind. Maybe a fatal disease was the best way for everything to end, after all. There wasn't even anyone to feel sorry for him. . . .

She wasn't neat and well kept, he thought, remembering the random drops of white he'd spotted at the hem of her second-best dress. I can tell at a glance that she's wilful and spoiled. And a widow, too. She's no innocent. Then he found himself wondering what lay beneath that dress and hated himself for falling into the lures of an undoubtedly practiced temptress. She probably put the paint there on purpose to draw my eye to her ankle, he thought. A deceiver. She is no better than the rest. If anything, worse. A *practiced* deceiver. At least Mistress Lucas had never deceived anyone before, and you could blame a good bit of it on her greedy parents. But the paintrix was entirely different. A bad character, a liar, a schemer, a climber, and filthy minded, too. First she deceived everyone with that ghost story. Then she and that woman sent me packing, looking for an apprentice that didn't exist. And just look at how she painted those lurid Adam and Eves and passed them off as the work of a dead man!

But in spite of himself, somewhere inside, a fountain of amusement began to flow. Not one, but two dead men! How did she ever keep it straight? Beneath those innocent-looking blue eyes, her mind must be whirling like the gears in a windmill. She certainly wasn't *dull* ... Roughly, he pinched off the new feeling. A widow without substance or family—not respectable, not worthy. But wait? Aren't you playing the hypocrite, using the arguments old Master Lucas used against you? No, it couldn't be. The facts showed that this woman was just another of the same kind, a user, a shrew with a false, designing front. Only bolder and cleverer than the last one. Again his mind fastened on her, this time on the memory of agile, short-fingered little hands, so neat and careful, but with blue under the nail of the forefinger. And hadn't he seen a bit of curly, reddish hair escaping from her gabled headdress? That proved it. The woman was trouble; people with that color hair always are.

Again he picked up the quill and began to write. The smooth, diplomatic phrases soothed his mind. But still something ached and bothered him inside. A touch of fever coming on, he said firmly to himself.

"Master Robert Ashton?" At the sound of the voice, Ashton looked up and saw someone he had dealt with before, a lesser magistrate in one of the courts over which Wolsey presided, who from time to time showed up to cultivate the great man's favor with a rare coin or ancient medallion for his collection. Quickly, he sprinkled sand across his work, dried it, and put it away in a drawer before he looked up and answered.

"Good day, Sir Septimus. May I be of assistance? What brings you here?"

"Ah, Master Ashton, busy, busy as usual. What admirable devotion to duty!" Crouch's eyes had an oddly malicious glitter. "I have found a little oddity or two that might interest the bishop. I would be most grateful if you would bring it to his attention that I have a rare Byzantine medallion to offer for sale. The profile is exceptionally well preserved. The next audience—could you assure me a place?" Ashton nodded silently. "Ah, delightful. I knew I could count on you. But, Master Ashton, why so grim and silent? I hear your latest assignment is delicious. Looking after a randy widow, what could be a more pleasing task for a young man like yourself? Have you got under her skirts yet?" Ashton drew his mouth into a disapproving line. Another simpleton, thought Crouch. He has betrayed himself. He wants her. And I have him.

"Word of my disgrace seems to get around quickly these days," Ashton said. Crouch smiled. And now, a double purpose. Dig out a bit of information and plant the poison. He will come running to me with his confidences, and in the end, I will discover to whom she has sold it through him.

"Ah, my boy, gossip travels on wings. But all will soon be mended. It's really just a backhanded recognition of your talent. There will be more and better to come after this, I am sure, knowing the Bishop as well as I do ..."

Ashton looked up at him, pleased and almost grateful at the praise.

"But tell me, since you have dealings with her now, has the widow offered any little rarities for sale? Say, an old manuscript or some other antique treasure? I am always on the lookout for things of that sort."

"She doesn't seem like a collector. Her rooms are very bare." Interesting, thought Crouch. Does she know its value, so she has it hidden, or has Ludlow got his hands on it?

"Ah, but her husband was. He possessed a number of rare treasures. Enough to keep a widow comfortably, if she could free herself from him before he poured it away on other women."

"What do you mean?" asked Ashton, and Crouch smiled knowingly, leaning close to the young man's troubled face.

"Why, dear boy, we are men of the world. How does a clever, vengeful woman get rid of a husband who troubles her? She sends an anonymous letter to the husband of his mistress, and the next day, the husband's murdered body is found in the street." With pleasure, Crouch watched Ashton turn pale. Well, well, he was falling in love with her, he thought. How fortunate I got here in time. Proximity would have done its work, and the manuscript would have been beyond my grasp. Young men, so predictable, so inflammable, so simple. A few more little confidences, and I will own him, too. "You seem upset. Live as long as I have, Master Ashton, and you will see that there is no end to the deceptions practiced by women. Look at history! The evils of the world have been brought about by temptresses: Eve, Helen, Messalina. Beautiful forms hide evil hearts." Pleased with the effect he'd caused, he watched Ashton shudder. "Don't blame yourself, my boy," he added, his voice oozing confidence. "We have all been shipwrecked by the Siren call at one time or another. It is a grief no man escapes. It is through pain that the Lord would instruct us."

"I've been blind. It was right in front of me all the time. And I thought I was so perceptive," Ashton whispered, almost to himself. He looked as if something had cracked inside. His shoulders slumped, and he bowed his head, turning it away so Crouch could not see his face. Crouch beamed and put his arm around the crushed younger man.

"Don't be ashamed to weep, my young friend. It is women who bring us to this pass. Remember, you always have a friend in me." Crouch was a man who delighted in creating human wreckage. But this job was so simple it almost failed to please him. What was a single man? The destruction of a family was better, and to bring down a dynasty a worthy challenge. Yes, I'll soon have the rest of that book back, he thought with satisfaction as he summoned a page at the front door to call his servant and fetch his mule.

Within the week I went to Bridewell to attend my new patron like all his other courtiers. The good part was that it was not so very far from our house, so I did not have to get up early in the cold, and also that they had very good food in the bishop's kitchen. What with all the comings and goings on estate business, church business, and the king's business, the house was always abuzz with visitors and knights and foreigners and priests and musicians and servants going to and fro carrying things. So I just fit right in as one more novelty except that people came to annoy me by staring as I worked and also some big hunting hounds with brass-studded collars started following me about because that's how it was with me and dogs.

My first portraits were a kind of test because I think they still weren't sure it was really I who did the paintings I had showed the bishop. Everybody came to inspect the things I brought out from my box that Nan carried, even Master Ashton, looking all pale, with dull, red-rimmed eyes, as if he were coming down with the ague. Well, you crowd, just watch this bear dance, I thought. You're going to see something.

But the surprise was that Mistress Dorothy and Master Thomas Winter were children, and it made me very impressed to see that the

bishop was such a good Christian as to give such kindly care to two orphans even to having their portraits taken, which is far more than the
Bible says, I am sure. I began with Mistress Dorothy because she was
quieter and less fidgety, and I did want to make a good impression.
Then all those nosy liverymen and knights and priests goggled while
Nan helped me put on my silk smock and exclaimed over the tininess
of my brushes and my strokes as if they had never seen a miniature
taken. But I just painted on without paying them any attention and
didn't even notice the time pass.

"Aren't you done yet?" I could hear Master Ashton's voice behind
me as I was rinsing out my brushes. His ague had certainly made him
surly. Maybe I'd been mistaken in what I had thought I'd seen in him.
His eyes weren't full of interesting hidden thoughts any more. They
were dull and hard. His face seemed like a mask.

"Work is not done until the tools are put away," I said, which is
what my father always said when I wanted to leave things and play.

"I hear you put away things very well indeed." His voice sounded
bitter. Well, Susanna, I thought, once again you let yourself be misled
by a pair of interesting eyes. You just imagined you saw a light glinting
in them, because you wanted to.

"Good brushes are a lot of work to make. I don't want them
spoiled for no reason at all."

"You made them?" His voice softened, curious. Watch yourself,
Susanna. Quit imagining. I found myself looking at his big hands. Like
bear paws.

"Of course. They aren't found on the lawn after a heavy rain, like
mushrooms, you know." Words put a wall between us. Bears can be
dangerous, after all.

"They seem well done . . . practiced."

"Of course. I made my father's brushes. I made all my husband's
brushes, too. I suppose that's why he married me. It saved the cost of
an apprentice." He shuddered, though I didn't know why. Since darkness was falling, he escorted me and Nan home, but he didn't say a
word, even when he left us at our own front doorstep, under the sign of
the Standing Cat.

Master Thomas I did another day, and he turned out very well,
too, although he had a spoiled look to him that I wasn't able to hide

without losing the likeness. When I brought the two miniatures to the bishop, he stared at them a long time and then harrumphed and said they were well done, and no less than he'd expected. As Master Ashton brought me away from my audience, he looked more annoyed than usual, and at last, when we had left the house at Brideswell by the side door, he broke the long silence that had lasted for days, and said, "You are a bold hussy. You are lucky you got away with it this time."

"I don't know what you mean," I said, stepping over the gutter ahead of him.

"You know you gave them both the bishop's features," he said, catching up with me in one big stride.

"I paint what I see, no more, no less," I said. "Besides, he's their uncle. Why shouldn't there be a strong resemblance? It's only natural."

"Oh, right," Ashton agreed in a sarcastic voice. "You think you can get away with anything, don't you? Either you are an idiot or the slyest, most willful woman in the world."

"I think maybe I am a painter and you are too sly for your own good, whatever you are trying to say," I said, and he was silent all the way to my door.

But on giving the strange conversation thought, I supposed that perhaps I deserved suspicion about my paintings because of already having been two dead people, which is rather deceptive and would tend to give a person a bad reputation. But all those snoopers and watchers that had been there while I painted those children went about with the word that I was a prodigy and a freak and then there were twice as many watchers when I took my next likenesses for the bishop, and they prodded each other to get a good view, and other rude things. They also spoke about me as if I weren't even there, saying such things as, "She hasn't very slender fingers, I'm surprised she can make it so tiny," or "What's she doing there? I say there's entirely too much blue," or worse, "Damned fine bosom, eh? What's she doing painting? It's like teaching a good hunting mare to jig." It must be boring, waiting around as a courtier, I think, if all you have to do is goggle at novelties to pass the time. Of course, sometimes Wolsey went hunting with the king or attended him when he was far from London, and then those courtiers and petitioners and hangers-on just swarmed after him like a hiveful of bees after the queen, and I had peace and quiet.

But with the great man's patronage, I soon became fashionable, with a parade of notables waiting to be "done" by me. Partly it was that they wanted to flatter Wolsey, by asking for my services, and partly it was that Wolsey flattered them by asking for their portraits "for my collection of notable persons of the age," as he would say to them, in that confidential, insinuating way that he had. Soon it was known that one of Wolsey's pleasures was inspecting his growing collection of miniatures, medals, and ancient coins with portrait heads. Then everybody ambitious craved most fiercely to be in the drawer with Nero and Charlemagne, and I was beseiged at home and when I attended my lord bishop's court.

All this should have made me rich, but of course, great people take everything on credit and pay when they wish, and so far I had only gotten a very small advance from Master Tuke and had to beg for it because materials aren't free. It was a lucky thing I had all that excellent parchment all ready to cut, and the margins started disappearing from the pages of that old piece of book which my stingy husband had saved.

"You do well," said Master Tuke one day, as he repeated the great man's orders to me. I could tell I was in favor with the bishop because of how agreeable he was to me. The bishop was very clever about paintings, and I knew that Tuke was taking instruction on art appreciation from a liveryman of the guild in order the better to flatter his master. I heard it was a bit of a waste, because he was color-blind, but that was just gossip.

"See here," said Master Tuke, "they say the best flattery is imitation." He held out a framed miniature to me, a shoddy piece of work with muddy shadows and a face resembling a turtle more than a human should. Master Tuke's face was impassive, but I could tell he was waiting with some amusement to hear what I would say.

"Only competent imitation flatters," I said. "Look at those eyes; they're not even on the same level. Whoever painted it must have been drunk."

"The masters of the guild are claiming that foreign work is cheap and shoddy. What would you say to that?"

"Why, that I am English born. Did a master do that? I think he needs a lesson or two, before he ventures into painting in small."

"They fear the importation of more foreign artists for the new craze, so they venture into the business themselves, even though they have no jurisdiction."

"And no skill, either," I said rather sharply, but then tried to redeem myself by saying, "I am grateful to have a patron of such distinguished taste that he can see bad work at a glance."

Tuke laughed. "He wanted to know what you would say when you saw it. And I judged correctly, for you are no bad judge of a painting, even if you are a woman." Before I even had time to be offended, he went on, "And who do you imagine the portrait to be?"

"By the B there, and by the hat, which I have seen before, I judge it to be Sir Thomas Boleyn, but not by the features."

"Right again, and most puffed up he was when he showed it to me."

"Master Tuke, what manner of man would show off such a work?"

"Why, Mistress Dallet, has no one yet told you that the bishop makes a game of showing your work to the visitors in his cabinet? He finds someone unsuspecting and says, 'What manner of painter do you think did this?' And then the visitor says, 'Why, surely he is a cunning worker, no doubt from overseas.' And then my lord bishop says, 'Ha! You are deceived! It was painted right here in London, and by a woman, too!' Ah, then they are embarrassed, and shuffle and say, 'A woman? By Our Lady, I would never have supposed it so.' And my lord answers, 'Find me a man who paints like this, and I will make him great.' Then he laughs up his sleeve at what they do unearth, for they are no judges."

My next sitter was the king's boon companion, Charles Brandon, the king's Master of the Horse who had been made Duke of Suffolk and who was famous for being married to different rich ladies, which shows that the hand of fate was moving very mysteriously but luckily to my benefit. It turned out he would be very important to me later, but indirectly and not in a way I'd ever imagined. However, I did not understand that it was the hand of fate at the time and instead was very annoyed. The duke came to pay court to Wolsey for assistance in some financial matter, then when he had inspected the collection in the cabinet he demanded that I take his likeness on the spot.

"Paint my glance fiery," he demanded, settling his huge bulk into the chair.

"My lord, I always paint what I see, and I assure you, your natural glance is very fiery," I answered. But it was no easy thing painting a man who looks first out the window, grunts and readjusts himself, stroking his beard, then admires his shoes, and then glances at a maid-servant while he makes odd noises to draw a hound closer.

"Your Grace, can you return your face to this side again? Yes, that way. First turn the whole head toward the window, then return only the eyes toward me."

"You're not done yet? How long do you take, anyway? Lady Bourchier assured me you were swift."

"It takes more time to capture the fiery eye of a warrior than the mild eye of a lady," I answered, because I was becoming more like a slippery courtier every day from being exposed to their bad examples, which are nothing like the models of discreet conversations recommended in *The Good Wyfe's Book of Manners*. That contented him, so he settled back into the chair with a lot of snorting sounds.

It was not until I was packing away my things and Suffolk was inspecting the near-finished miniature that I saw among the watchers a man who made the hair go up on the back of my neck. I knew him even at a distance by the streaks of white that swirled up in his hair like two curly goat's horns and by the cold glitter of his eyes, which seemed to fill up the room. He was conferring with Master Ashton as if they were the dearest of old friends. He darted his eyes at me with a triumphant look, as if to say, See my power. Then he leaned forward toward Master Ashton familiarly, almost intimately, whispering something to him, and Ashton looked back at him most trustingly, as if he were drinking in every word. My heart started beating so loudly that I hardly heard Suffolk's farewell in my ear. That ghastly man that even dogs didn't like, accompanied by Master Ashton, was approaching me.

"Mistress Dallet, here is a collector of rare art who has heard much of you and wishes to make your acquaintance," said Master Ashton. "He tells me he knew your late husband well." Once again, I found myself staring into that pair of pale, calculating eyes. I scarcely heard as we were introduced. "... Sir Septimus Crouch ... has pro-

cured several curious and ancient coins for the bishop's collection. . . ."
The words just seemed to flow past my ears.

"A tragic, tragic accident. How glad I was to hear that you were
prospering." I felt my skin crawl at the sound of his voice. Ashton
seemed perfectly unaware of the man's repulsiveness. In fact, they acted
like the best friends in the world, as if they had shared some secret.
That's how men are, I guess. Cozy. They never see anything.

"Rarities? How lovely, lovely," I stammered.

"Rarities indeed, though not as rare as a paintrix of your *virtue*,
Mistress Dallet," and I didn't like his tone.

"Sir Septimus, you are too modest. Nothing like them has been
seen in England before. First French coins of an antiquity greater than
Charlemagne himself. And now, a Byzantine medallion in an almost
perfect state of preservation. His lordship will be delighted. Only an
authentic coin of King Arthur could please him more."

"It will be a rare accident, indeed, that unearths such a treasure—
though a treasure chiefly to men of learning and wit, such as the great
Bishop Wolsey. Only the highest minds are interested in my curiosities.
Your late husband, I believe, Mistress Dallet, was also a collector of curiosities. Should you find anything of this sort among his possessions,
say, an ancient casting or a bit of old manuscript, remember I would be
delighted to purchase it from you at a fair value." He fixed me with his
cold, repellent eyes in a way that didn't seem delighted at all.

"My late husband's creditors took away everything," I managed to
croak out. Ashton's eyes narrowed, and the muscles on his jaw tightened.

"Such a pity," said Septimus Crouch.

"Pity, indeed, that she could not reap more benefit from a well-
sent letter," muttered Ashton, and I noticed Crouch glancing at him to
quiet him.

"A pity that works of the soul should fall into the hands of the
soulless. Perhaps I should seek out these creditors. With whom should
I speak?"

"The whoremasters, the tavern keepers, dicers, drinkers, and tai-
lors of London. Try also a lawyer called Ludlow, who took away even
the baby's cradle." Hearing this, Crouch's eyes narrowed. But Ashton
looked surprised and puzzled.

"Master Dallet's son was born dead from the shock," I said. Master Ashton took a half step forward, but Crouch spoke suddenly, interrupting and taking his elbow.

"But Mistress Dallet, you have wrested triumph from tragedy. I have great hopes of becoming better acquainted with you and your exquisite likenesses." His voice was warm and oozy. He stepped closer to Master Ashton, as if he owned him somehow, partially blocking my view of him. It made Master Ashton seem, suddenly, corrupt, as if some of the repellent qualities of Sir Septimus had rubbed off on him. His intelligent eyes that used to shine and speak seemed flat and deadened, and his even features cold, marble without soul.

As I fled the room, I noticed that the hounds were already gone.

The Fifth Portrait

Louise de Savoie, Duchesse d'Angoulême. *Engraving from a lost original.*

Married at the age of twelve to Charles d'Angoulême, a great-grandson of Charles V, Louise of Savoy was widowed at nineteen. From that day on, she devoted her whole life to the career and fortunes of her son, whom she never doubted would one day be King of France. This nineteenth-century engraving is an authentic copy taken from an original miniature held in a private collection, dated 1514, that regretably vanished during the Paris Commune.

—*Frontispiece.* Journal de Louise de Savoye

In my travels I have painted many ladies but none so fierce as Madame Louise of Savoy, whose likeness I took in the wintertime in the Palace of Les Tournelles in Paris, when I was at the court of the King of France. Madame Louise was short and pale, with metallic black eyes that could see right through a person, especially if he was what she called "of low condition," which included everybody but French princes of the blood. That is how it is with poor relations; they get even more snobbish than the rich ones because they haven't anything else to go on. I used my palest carnation for her complexion, and what with her black widow's gown it looked as if I hadn't bothered to use color at all, but I do believe I captured her grim, suspicious look very well, and everybody told me it looked like the portrait of a saint, so I got much credit.

Everyone said Madame Louise was clever, because she read books, but I think she was one of those people who get one idea stuck in their heads and that makes them cleverer than they are because they don't waste time on other things. The problem was that Madame Louise's one idea was the same one several other ladies also had, which made them hate her as much as she hated them. That idea was that she would be mother of a king. Now in my experience there's no one more ruthless and cunning than a mother who is advancing her child at the expense of somebody else's child. And all the while these ladies are tearing at one another more fiercely than Turks, they claim they are martyrs who only live for the good of others. Never cross one of them.

ELEVEN

Louise of Savoy received the messenger from Paris in the spacious antechamber of her bedroom in the Château of Blois. The luminous sun reached through the tall windows, dappling the bright tapestry on the wall behind her with patterns of light. Outside, below the walls of the château, the lazy green of the Loire meandered between glistening sandy banks. The cries of the boatmen on the river, of washerwomen on the shore, the sounds of the village at the castle's feet carried upward in the warm air, reaching her ear as a vague buzz of prosperity and content.

"Ah, the messenger from Longueville," said the mother of the heir apparent to the tall, graceful young woman beside her, as she spied the little packet sewed in oiled skin in the hand of the dusty-booted messenger who knelt before her. "He has certainly taken his time in answering me."

"My lady, the ship was delayed by the weather," said the messenger. "The English weather, you know, the Channel . . ."

"I suppose, then, we are fortunate that it has been so lovely here," she answered. "Rise, and my ladies in waiting will see to your refreshment while you wait for my reply." As her attendants escorted him out, the young knight thought how like a nun Louise of Savoy looked. It was hard for him to imagine that this austere little woman in black might once have been beautiful. Her pale, even features were tense with watchfulness and dedication. It was clear that everything he had heard was true. She was not a woman to be wooed to the sound of a lute. A life without luxury and an early widowhood had left her with a single passion: to see her only son, her Caesar, mount the throne of France.

"Stay, Marguerite," she said to her daughter, as the young woman seemed to accept her dismissal with the others. "I want your assistance in this." Marguerite, married to the Duc d'Alençon, had been away in

Normandy, but the funeral of old Queen Anne, Louise's great rival, had gathered the family in one place again. As Marguerite turned back, a stray shaft of sun caught her luxuriant chestnut hair, only half hidden by her headdress, and her mother delighted briefly in the color. It was the same shade as that possessed by her younger brother, Louise's glorious hope, her Francis. Francis, though only a first cousin once removed of the king, was the last direct male heir of the Valois, now that the king had failed to produce a son. And all this time, Louise had planned and schemed. Louise had raised Marguerite as her most faithful ally in her great cause, and now that her most trusted friends seemed to turn like weathervanes to the new wind blowing from Paris, she had new need of her daughter's fresh intelligence, of the renewed strength she could draw from Marguerite's unwavering loyalty.

Ah, bitter, bitter, thought Louise, to have waited so long, to have the throne within grasp, and now have it come to this. The past winter, her old enemy Queen Anne had died, her infant son preceding her. This removed the last obstacle to the marriage of the queen's deformed daughter Claude, heiress of the Duchy of Brittany, to Francis. By May, Louise had finally been able to force the marriage. Now as Duke of Brittany, only Francis could unite the lands that properly belonged to France. She had gathered her whole family here at the king's seat in Blois, to press her intrigues on behalf of her son. Francis must rule. Aloud she said, "The old king still dreams of a son; he has begun negotiations with the English again." The English, hereditary enemies of France, who had just withdrawn their conquering armies after the humiliating rout in which her son had barely escaped capture.

"The English, and not the Spanish, Mother?"

"The Pope has forbidden the alliance with the daughter of King Ferdinand. But the English king then offered his sister, widow of the King of Scots, who is of a likely age, and not barren, as a token of peace. Then my agents told me he considers the Englishwoman too old and too fat. Ah, I breathed again! No Englishwoman should sit on the throne of France. The obscenity! Does he not understand God's will in this matter? His first wife was barren; his son by the heiress of Brittany has died. It is our François who is willed by God to sit upon the throne. But now the English king has written again offering his youngest sister to tempt King Louis. I swear, that English king is too young and inexperienced to have thought of this; he would never have had the wit if someone wiser were not advising him. Longueville has told me of this Wolsey, this devious priest, who whispers at his shoulder. The woman, they say, is young and healthy, sure to outlive the king. The question: Is she too ugly to please him as her sister was? The subtle priest plots to make an Englishwoman Queen Regent of France, I swear. This shall never happen, not while I have breath in my body. Open this for me, Marguerite, and you shall help me judge whether or not the king will accept this offer."

Marguerite snipped the threads with a little silver penknife that lay on her mother's desk. She held out the letter for her mother, but her intelligent eyes lit with curiosity at the round, sealed case that accompanied the writing. Two years older than her brother, she was devoted to his cause and person. Like him, well educated, amber eyed and witty, she had turned to the enjoyment and patronage of the arts to console herself for the boredom of a mismatched marriage. The little case promised amusement.

"This letter, useless," pronounced the mother. "A shallow description that could fit a hundred girls, and a silly ghost story. At least he has sent a copy of the portrait that has gone to the king. That Longueville is a superstitious fool. Useless. Hopeless. I want to know the dowry, the conditions. Is this the woman that will sit on the throne of France?"

But Marguerite's eyes had lit up at the sight of the tiny painting revealed when she opened the little case. "Mother, look at this. It is a match for Fouquet. Why, the brush strokes are invisible!" Handing the letter to her daughter, Louise took the little portrait case in her hand. Involuntarily, she drew in her breath. The golden French sun made the colors glow with new warmth. The ropes of pearls, the jewels had a radiant luster. The princess's red-gold hair shone like silk; her skin seemed as soft and luminous as if alive; her eyes glinted with boldness, with youth, as she stared out into the face of the bitter, watchful older woman.

At the sign of the neat red head and sparkling eyes, Louise's own eyes had narrowed. "This is the one," she said. "He will not be able to resist. The treaty with the English is as good as signed. He will imagine she can restore his lost springtime. Ah, God, what cursed illusion is it that makes old men think they can still sire sons! And the eyes—look at that, Marguerite. What do you make of the eyes?"

"Flirtatious, Mother, and spoiled. This princess has never been a moment without her slightest desire being granted. You must take care, Mother, that she does not provide the king with an heir by some gentleman of the court."

"You are right, Daughter. I had not thought of that until I spied this picture. I imagined he was being offered some milk-fed pious little thing more suited to an old man. This creature is too clever, too head-strong. Her father was a ruthless usurper, after all. Never forget, it is in the blood."

"But you must also take into account that her father was old and shrewd, and died in bed."

"All the worse. This one is at least young. It is best to catch them unhatched."

"What will you do, Mother?"

"I will begin by planting a rumor at court that she has had a lover in England. This will make the old king jealous and watchful. That, at least, will keep her from making a false heir with a more vigorous sire."

"Write Longueville and ask if there are any men whom she seems to favor, then you can let that be known as well."

"I needn't bother. The king will send his own spies. He will ap-point his own guardians. In fear of a cuckold's horns, he will raise a wall of steel around her."

Marguerite laughed. In a flash, it was all visible to her. A jealous old man, frantic with rumors, desperately trying to prove himself young, trying to satisfy a demanding girl. "Why, Mother, he'll exhaust himself!" she exclaimed.

"Exactly," said Louise, with a thin-lipped smile. "That English princess is too spoiled, too inconsistent of purpose for the task those foreigners have set her. She has not the force of will to be Queen Re-gent of France." Marguerite's shrewd gaze flicked from the miniature to her mother's indomitable face. A kitten and a lioness. There was no match.

"So, Mistress Susanna, you have been traveling again. What brings you to grace our humble establishment after flying so high?" The white hairs growing out of Master Ailwin's ears seemed to have gotten even longer in my absence, and he was altogether more eccentric-looking than ever, if that is possible. He bumbled around humming something to himself. "I suppose you're too grand now to use orpiment made in my poor little establishment. Send to France, send to Italy! I remember a time you were grateful and paid a little something on the side. Now I'm not sure I have the time for you." He started to weigh out earth of cologne, then forgot he was about and began to put it away again.

"Master Ailwin, just because I was invited to Richmond to paint doesn't mean I don't have to come home and buy colors just the same as ever. That Lady Guildford used up everything I had! First she liked her picture so much in small, she had to have it in large. Is it my fault I have a gift for flattering old ladies? It was all wearisome, and the food wasn't even good. Besides, grand houses wear me out. They treat me just like an oversized chest that is an inconvenience. 'Oh, yes, put the paintrix there—no, perhaps over here.' That's how it is for someone who's just a servant and not a great lady. I'm lucky to get a decent corner for me and Nan where silly ladies won't go pawing through my things and getting their greasy fingers on the carnations so the paint won't stick."

"So now they cover you in flowers. Laurel wreaths. You have become spoiled."

"Carnations, Master, those are the parchments ready made for painting," said Tom, who had come to listen in.

"I knew that," snapped Master Ailwin.

"Master, if you allow Mistress Dallet to accompany me into the back room, I can find what she wants and weigh it out and save you the inconvenience."

"Inconvenience? You rogue, you were supposed to tidy up! The society meets here tonight, and I see things heaped everywhere back there, and not a bench to sit on!"

"Why then, I'll go back right away," he said, gesturing me to accompany him, while Master Ailwin began to rearrange things on the shelf, fretting and fuming all the while about youth and their disrespect in these wicked times.

"Mistress, you must forgive him. He's having another one of his spells," said Tom, and I did feel sorry for the poor boy who was so faithful and caring for such a grouchy old master, even if he did sometimes make cow eyes when he delivered things.

"Of course I do," I said, looking about the room. "How on earth do you find what you want here?"

"Every time he puts something back, it's in another place," said the apprentice, "so I just follow him about and replace what I can. Sometimes even I can't find it. Let's see, it's green bice you're wanting?"

"Oh, say, what are these things lying here?" Amid a jumble of old glassware and half-filled containers on a worktable lay several old parchments covered with queer figures, an open book with diagrams in it, and several antique coins.

"Interesting, aren't these? They're very old." He picked up a medallion of some dead foreign king. "We have a regular customer who collects odd old coins; he has a standing order with us to save anything like this for him to see first."

"Not a tall, heavy man with a square-cut beard and white streaks in his hair up here?" I asked, gesturing to the corners of my forehead. Just thinking about the man troubled me.

"Oh, you must mean Sir Septimus Crouch. No, this one's a thin old French fellow with a lined face and gray hair. Now he's piecing together a rare manuscript. If anybody comes in with fragments, we're to tell him. Odd that you mention Sir Septimus. He's doing the same thing. It must be all the fashion these days, not that I keep up with fashion. We don't like Sir Septimus much—he's a slimy dealer. But we have our ways of getting even. See here? To him we sell these forgeries as antiques."

"These parchments? But they look old."

"If they're not old to begin with, they look old when we're done with them. Treasure maps, alchemical allegories for finding the Stone. People bring things in for the master to decode, and if they're worthless, he buys them and doctors them up. Crouch is such a believer, he'll buy anything. We even sold him a map to the lost treasure of the Templars. But look here—" The boy dug under the trash and brought out a wooden panel painting, brown with age, or at least aged-looking varnish. Even in its new disguise, I recognized it at once. One of my *Eve*

Bathings, complete with leafy Adam and glowing mountaintop in Eden. In the front of the shop, a bell tinkled, and the growl of conversation could be heard in the background.

"We got it from a tavern keeper who kept it for payment of some monk's bill. Isn't it perfect? The old boy will love it. And if he doesn't take it, the Frenchman will."

"I thought you only cheated Sir Septimus."

"Well, after all, a Frenchman's a Frenchman, isn't he?"

"What is it, exactly?" I asked, feigning innocence, which was not easy, seeing the wreckage of my nice glazes.

"Well," he said in a learned, pompous voice that sounded exactly like Master Ailwin when he is showing off, "this is an allegory of the Holy Grail, painted by the dead French master Jean Fouquet. See? Here are Adam and Eve, representing Original Sin, and there is the redemption, waiting on the mountaintop, bathed in golden light."

"But how do you know it's about the Grail?"

"It's the mountain, mistress. All students of the occult know that mountain, even without the fortress on top. Why, Master Ailwin has a woodcut of the very place. It's Montségur, the heretic Cathar fortress. There has always been a tale that they had smuggled the Grail from the Holy Land and kept it hidden there. But once the Cathars had all been killed by the Inquisition, no one could find the hiding place. Whoever finds the Grail can rule all Christendom, they say. Or if it's an unbeliever, he can destroy it. We do a great business in Grail secrets. This one will be splendid. See how the vines and the serpent appear to make letters? P, S. Those are occult symbols. So's this thing here, and the way Adam's turned around so you can't see his front. It's all a code. I tell you, this stuff is nearly as good as the Stone, or invisibility ointment."

"Invisibility ointment? How can you sell that? The minute people aren't invisible, they'll come back and get you."

"Oh, no. You have to purify yourself with just the right rituals, and say a very complicated formula perfectly, without hesitation. They always hesitate. So—no invisibility. Sometimes Master says there's a curse on anyone who doesn't say all those words perfectly. So then they're sure to hesitate. One little stammer, and zip! Then they're cursed and have to come buy an exorcism manual. That reminds me, we need some new ones printed up. You don't know a good cheap printer, do you? I have to make all Master's arrangements these days, and our old printer's been arrested."

"Why don't you just have them copied?"

"Then they'd be more costly, and you know the Master. He says it is unjust to keep all these secrets only for the rich."

"But they're false secrets, Tom. You just said so. Wouldn't he think it better to cheat the rich than to cheat the poor?"

"Well, it's those meetings of the society. They keep him all roused up. And these days, he can't keep more than one idea in his mind. 'All for the poor,' he says, 'we must end this damned injustice.'"

"The society? What society is that?"

"Oh, Mistress Susanna, I shouldn't tell. But I know by your kind blue eyes that you won't think them wicked. It's the Society of the True Religionists. They meet to debate the Testament, to determine the date and manner of the Second Coming. But mostly, they argue about the nature of heaven. Does it have ale, as well as milk and honey, what sort of music is played, is dancing allowed, if you've been married more than once, do you get to live with all your wives, that sort of thing. You mustn't tell on them. Even though it's heresy, it's a harmless sort, and keeps them occupied."

"Well, I certainly wouldn't want to meet my husband in the after-life. I hope he's properly sealed in hell."

"Oh, sweet Mistress Dallet, he must have been wicked indeed to ever be cruel to *you*.... Oh, my, there's trouble in front." The sound of shouting and stamping came to us through the open door. "Mistress Dallet, I've finished with your packets. There's the back door, so you needn't cross through this quarrel. I need to help Master. Oh, why can't God give him his sense back again?" He slipped the money I gave him into the cashbox, picked up a heavy iron bar, and rushed off to the front to assist Master Ailwin.

"Cheated! I've been cheated!" came the howl from the front. I crept closer and hid behind a stack of kegs. Who was cheated? I could see the sleeve of a legal gown gesturing wildly. A lawyer cheated? Good, it served him right. I peered out. Oh, it served him more than right. It was that horrible lawyer, Master Ludlow, who had come and taken away mother's bed. But his usually pale face was quite crimson now. "These verses of prophecy don't tell me where it's located?"

"No, Master Ludlow, for you have only the end of the book. These are mighty prophecies of the distant future. The fall of the Kings of France will destroy the Kings of the Earth, a great emperor will arise who conquers both Christian and heathen lands alike, then he falls into chaos—this must mean the end of the House of Valois is at hand, brought by the Finder of the Secret. . . ."

"Oh, a curse upon all scribes and clerks! Why couldn't they have put the secret at the end of the book? Who cares about the fall of kings? Of course kings will fall to the holder of the secret! Now I understand it all! It's the secret that damned Crouch is after. And it's in the middle of the book! Why should he rule the world when it can be me? He has the center, the Devil take him! He got to the dead man's house first!"

"Come, come, now, Master Ludlow, there are other ways to the secret. We have just purchased from a foreign dealer in curiosities a rare allegorical painting by the famous dead French master Fouquet. . . ."

I had heard quite enough. I tiptoed out by the back way and into the alley. I had waited far too long, and twilight, and with it danger, was sinking over the city streets. Setting my face straight ahead, I hurried into the street toward home. Behind me I heard footsteps. They sounded as if they were following me from the alley. Terrified, I glanced behind me.

"Mistress, mistress, wait." Puffing, the apprentice caught up with me. He was still holding his heavy iron bar, and his knife was at his belt. "I'll escort you home," he said. "You've been delayed too long. The streets are full of . . ." Suddenly, he pulled at my sleeve to stop me. The lawyer was hurrying down the street, his face furious. In the cool violet light, a figure stepped from beneath the overhang of a tall house. We could not make out the features, but that was unnecessary. The large, menacing shape was eerily familiar.

"I've been waiting for you, Ludlow. You know I can't forgive a man who cheats on an agreement. Do you have it with you?" I knew the voice. Who was it? I searched my mind.

"I have no idea what you mean."

"The manuscript. You have brought it to Ailwin." Now I recognized who was speaking. It was Septimus Crouch there in the twilight. "What else would bring you here?" he said. "It was you who sent the letter to the captain. You arrived at the painter's house first and seized his possessions. . . ." With a rising horror, I realized what I was hearing. It could only be Captain Pickering that he meant. It could only be my house that held the secret. I thought I could hear something fluttering in the alley, like an immense trapped moth, and felt a coldness, as if some evil being were present. No, it couldn't be. It must be my heart beating.

"I don't know what you mean. I was acting for a client, that's all. . . ." The lawyer seemed to flick his head from side to side, as if hunting for the sound.

"You have it, Ludlow. You have it here. Both parts. The mirror showed me that you had it. It showed you conspiring against me for my part. Do you understand what a fool you are? You can no longer deceive me; no one can, while I own the mirror. And now you will give me the parts you have stolen from me." In the violet, summer-scented air above, I could hear a suppressed, high-pitched squeak of excitement, like the cry of a bat. Some evil, gloating thing seemed perched above us on the rainspout.

"I haven't got them. I swear it. It's the center you want. I haven't got it. My part's useless, useless, I swear. . . ."

"Feel this, Ludlow? It's eight inches of Spanish steel pricking your liver. If you do not want to be skewered with it, come into this alley, where the passers-by will not disturb our little conversation." I could feel Tom's arm pressing me against the wall of the shop, into the shadow, as the lawyer entered the fast-darkening alley, the menacing figure of Septimus Crouch close with him, embracing his neck as if in friendship.

"I haven't the center, Sir Septimus. I—I couldn't get it. Here— take my portion—gratis, free. In—in token of our friendship." The lawyer reached beneath his robe and held out some sort of bundle to the antiquarian.

"In token of your oath to me, I now own your—soul—" There was a ghastly cry, and the lawyer fell to the ground. Smiling, the antiquarian leaned over the groaning body and felt through his clothes with his gloved hands. Then the strange, heavy eyebrows drew together, and the pallid, lined face grew distorted. "Gone! Not here! You lying whoreson, where did you hide it? At home?" He shook the dying man, and a sort of gurgling sound came from him; black blood oozed from the corner of his mouth. "I swear, I'll find it, if I have to go to the ends of the earth." Swiftly, he cut the lawyer's purse from his belt, and then stepped quietly from the alley and vanished from view. Deep purple rimmed the edge of the sky now, and the first stars had come out. How odd, how terrible, to be bleeding to death on a sweet summer's night. Was this how the curse had ended? Had it been my fault, somehow? What would happen to me now?

"Master Ludlow, Master Ludlow." Tom was leaning over the body. "Lie quiet, now, and we'll carry you into the shop."

"I am killed, boy. It's my corpse you'll carry. Seven years . . . it has been . . . since I pledged my soul. And now . . . the contract is up. Beware the demon master, boy . . . don't be lured . . . by false promises of wealth . . . ah, God, I am damned. . . ." The gurgling breath had faded away to nothing. The tall, close-set houses had blocked the last of the twilight from the alley, and we were thrown into absolute darkness. But there, in the stillness of fear, I thought I heard the soft "huff, puff" of a heavy man's breathing.

"Assassinated by street ruffians, you say, Eustache?" Maître Bellier smiled as he put down the cup his servant had offered, then took up the lark's wing delicately between thumb and forefinger. "Ah, this is excellent," he said, crunching it down, bones and all.

"The sauce, master, or the assassination?"

"Both, of course. Our hostess has developed a sure touch, since you have instructed her. It is the garlic, I think. Or possibly the rosemary. Delicate, but fearless. And the Sieur Crouch has now collected the entire manuscript for us, proving in so doing that it was not sent to Rome." Before him on the table was propped a curious painting. It depicted a most lascivious Eve, being spied upon by the serpent as she bathed. It was brown with age.

"Master, I suspect he does not have it, or at least all of it, if it was in fact divided," said Eustache, pouring more wine into the silver goblet. "I have been watching his house. Almost immediately after the, ah, accident, he went to Maître Ludlow's rooms, under the pretext that he must recover some books he had lent to him. He searched frantically, then left, his face desperate, and hurried off somewhere. That leaves the third person."

"The widow? Then it is already in the hands of Wolsey, you may be assured of it."

"It may not be."

"But her sudden fortune . . ."

"Master, I have investigated. The widow has been engaged as a paintrix. She makes portraits."

"A likely story. Have you seen one?"

"I have not, but I have been told they are very good. I suspect she has entered into a secret partnership with a foreigner who paints for her."

"Or an arrangement has been made to give her the appearance of a legitimate trade while she serves his secret vice ... The bishop is a canny man. Or one of his servants is. No, it must be he, not some lesser priest. Who else would go to such trouble to cover his tracks?" Bellier finished the wine in the goblet, then wiped the tips of his fingers on the napkin his servant handed him. "Eustache, what you have brought me here is a puzzle. What do you see in this picture?"

"They told me it was very old. I saw immediately it must be concealed. An allegory of the Secret, to anyone who can read it, exposed to the public! See, here? The arrangement of the apples in groups of three? The stone, and the shape of the cloud? Here are the initials *P, S,* Priory of Sion, worked into the picture, and here is the portrait of our sacred mountain, a depiction of the Original Sin at the beginning of time, which God answered with our Secret and the destiny of the world."

"No, look closer at the color. It is new, smoked up by those charlatans in Guthrun's Lane." With a hand, he quelled Eustache's expression of indignation. "It was doubtless intended for another customer, when you demanded they sell it to you. Eustache, your following of Sieur Crouch has led you to more than you even know." He smiled ironically, then continued. "I have seen a copy of this very painting kept behind a curtain in Maître Montrose's rooms. He is ignorant of its meaning. Someone is taunting us, I believe. Someone who knows the Secret." He reached out with his dinner knife, and scraped lightly across a corner of the painting, then rubbed it with his thumb. The fresh color, still slightly smoke stained, emerged. "Yes. New, you see? Very new. You can even smell the pigment still." Eustache picked up the picture and ran it under his nose.

"Yes. New. Who would know the Secret here? Who would paint such a picture, but the widow's secret lover?" Bellier's servant shifted from one foot to another, his face a study in worry.

"A lover, we imagine, who has gone through her things, has seen the value of the manuscript, and kept the Secret for himself, to sell in his own good time. You must watch her more closely. We need to find this man," said Maître Bellier, taking back the picture and propping it before him again. "This mockery—he has gone too far, do you understand?" Eustache nodded.

"Some fruit and cheese, master?"

"Ugh, this English fruit. What is there?"

"Cherries, but still a bit unripe, I think."

"At least their cheese is reasonably worthwhile," he said, using his knife to remove the rind from the slice his servant proffered. "Would I could say the same for their climate."

"This lover, he hides himself well."

"Of course. It is a conspiracy. Look for a man who has traveled, who has been to Montségur. I rely on you, my bloodhound, to discover his identity."

"I think, perhaps, this Crouch will lead us to him."

"A possibility, a possibility. I begin to breathe easier. Rome and the Valois must continue to dwell in the darkness of ignorance." With growing good cheer, Maître Bellier cut himself another slice from the second-rate, but reasonably acceptable English cheese. It had become almost delicious.

TWELVE

Murder is never easy, but the afterwards part is harder yet. What with telling the authorities about finding a body, and having it taken away by holy monks who devote themselves to things like that, it got very late. And the later it got, the more worried I got. We couldn't tell that we knew who did it because Sir Septimus was a very important man, and then he would know we knew and something bad could happen to us. But maybe, if we didn't tell, he wouldn't suspect we'd seen. But then, maybe again if he knew we'd seen but didn't tell, he might leave us alone for now. So the only person we told was Master Ailwin, because we needed a plan, and it is always wiser to have an older person of experience guide you when you are in trouble. Master Ailwin looked into the air a bit and then said never tell the authorities anything because it Fed Power, and all Earthly Power was due to vanish soon, so it shouldn't be fed. Not bad for a man whose brains have been floating as loose as an unmoored boat for a long time. Then all those fellows from the society came for their meeting, and they were a fair raggedy pitiful lot who looked up to Master Ailwin as a Great Philosopher because he was even odder than any of them. But then they all discussed our problem, and it did us good in the end.

First the society all grumbled and said this murder had spoiled their evening, and after that someone said they could discuss the Evil of Earthly Power as a change from heaven, and then someone else said they thought Sir Septimus might have seen us, from what I said, and so we were in great danger. So after that, they had a bit to drink, and shouted and scuffled and debated about what to do. The result was they decided that Tom should hide at my place because I was protected by Wolsey and that they should all escort us home because it was very dark out and no moon. So they all lit torches and surrounded us and marched through the street singing a drinking song that didn't have very much religion in it at all. People opened their shutters and shouted and threw out their chamber pots and also old shoes and rotten fruit just to be annoying, but the watch didn't bother us because there were too many.

"What's this?" cried Mistress Hull.

And Nan said, "Never again, no never, shall I let you out alone like that. We thought you'd been killed!"

"Come in, come in. Who are all these fellows with the torches?" asked Mistress Hull.

"Good Christian men, come to escort Mistress Dalbert home in safety," announced Master Ailwin, and Mistress Hull looked very impressed at a man who had so many friends and such an excellent long white beard in the bargain.

"My, who did you say that thoughtful man was, Susanna? Master Ailwin?" Mistress Hull said as she closed the door with a thump behind us and barred it tight. "I do like a man with pale blue eyes like that. I can tell they're full of thought."

"That they are," I agreed.

"And is Tom staying for supper again this time?"

"He'll be staying over. We saw a man murdered, and he needs to hide here, until we can think of a better place."

"My, that's splendid, to have a man about the house," she said, and Tom began to look more pleased with himself, and less downcast.

"And now, you'll tell us all where you've been, while we eat."

"In a bit, Nan, but first I have to put my things away upstairs." I took a rushlight upstairs into the darkened studio, but as I put my new colors on the shelf, the shadows felt all dark and heavy on me, and I had the sense that something evil was in the room. It was just like the feeling I had had in the alley when Master Ludlow was killed. Oh my dear Lord, I thought, I am very much in need of help even if I haven't done much to deserve it lately. There was a sort of metallic grating sound I didn't like and a smell of something rotten. I was very sure of it then. Somebody or something very nasty was in the room. I could feel my knees tremble, and I put my hand on my heart to keep it from beating so hard. The rushlight flickered and went out, and the blackness rushed in around me.

There was an eerie, silent howling sound in my ears that made my blood freeze with fear. The black was thick and heavy and made the hair rise up on my neck, my arms, my head. Then something strange, like wind that was not wind, was swirling in the room. It was pale glowing stuff, like light, swirling and mingling with the fearful dark, mixing and pounding like silent ocean waves, as if there were some secret struggle going on. I was so terrified I couldn't move, and hardly even dared breathe. I clutched the dead rushlight to me. Then all at once, as if nothing had happened, the blackness became ordinary dark. I looked down and saw that the flame of my rushlight had burst up again, as if it had been only hidden, or as if something invisible had rekindled it. I thought then that I heard an odd sound. Feathery and rustling, like when I was painting the picture for the Frenchmen. Then there was a laugh a little like chimes, very sweet, in the distance. Somehow, my voice came back to me. "Who's there?" I cried, turning around.

"Don't worry," said a charming voice, "nothing I can't take care of." Something, or someone, was standing in the corner of the studio, furled in a dark cloak. My hands trembling, I held up the rushlight and saw in its flickering orange circle the prettiest face I have ever seen. I couldn't tell if it was a man or a woman.

"How did you get in? Did you follow me?"

"Oh, I've been following you awhile. But I think you need me just now. *It* has followed you home, so I thought I'd drop by."

"What is *it?*"

"Oh, it will just worry you to think about. Chaotic spirits exist to make trouble, that's all. Now if you don't mind, I'll just follow you downstairs to make sure you get there."

"What do you mean?" I said, frightened.

"Oh, it might trip you and catch your skirts on fire. It's rather puffed up with the trouble it has made just lately, and it knows I favor you. Come, I'll hold your elbow as we go down."

"But the stair is too narrow for two."

"I don't need the stair," said the lovely thing as it came closer. It had great brown curls that seemed somehow translucent, and I could see a bit of a handsome gown beneath the plain cloak. But the poor thing was hunchbacked. Behind its head was a huge, quivering mass, hidden beneath the heavy cloak. It was barefoot, too, and its pale feet looked too tender for our splintery floorboards. But as I went down the narrow spiral stair, holding the rushlight in one hand and the book under the other arm, I could feel something very strong holding me, and my feet felt unusually sure, even though the stairs are very worn and slippery in places.

"Who's this?" cried Mistress Hull. "How did he get into your rooms? I swear I let no one up today. Well, knowing *your* friends, I suppose he'll want supper, too." The visitor's face crinkled up in the most amused smile, as if he couldn't imagine anything funnier than Mistress Hull.

"I'm Hadriel," he or maybe she said, as if that explained everything.

"Well, Master Hadriel—or is it your Christian name? Surely not, it doesn't sound very Christian to me—I mean, not to insult, but, well— you're invited to supper, if you want any—well, you know, I mean, not to sound stingy—that is, if you're hungry, you're welcome—" Hadriel laughed to see Mistress Hull so flustered, and the sound made the shadows vanish from the corners of the room.

"I'd love supper," he said—or was he a she? I still couldn't tell. And a name like that, well, it wasn't a proper baptismal name so you couldn't tell from the name either. At any rate, Mistress Hull had no doubts, so Master Hadriel it would be. He followed me into the kitchen, looking amused, then stood by the wide stone fireplace, inspecting the cooking pot that hung bubbling there as if he had never really seen anything like it before. Everyone was sitting in the kitchen, where it was cozy and agreeable and fine smelling.

"Who's that?" asked Tom, with a suspicious, jealous-sounding voice. I could hear a fluttering sound, like a bat caught in the chimney. A sort of heaviness seemed to be oozing into the room. Hadriel took up the poker and leaned over the boiling pot, clattering the poker in the chimney.

"Master Hadriel, who's come to dinner," announced Mistress Hull. "But what *are* you doing there, Master Hadriel?"

"I hear you up there, Belphagor," said Hadriel, speaking into the chimney. "Begone." The fluttering ceased, and Hadriel beamed at Mistress Hull. "You had a little something stuck in your chimney, but I've chased it out. Now, how's that supper coming?"

"All done and waiting for you. Wash your hands and we'll set out the bowls. Oh, where's the bread knife?" As Nan began to bustle, I turned to see Hadriel sitting on the kitchen bench wiping the soot off his fingers onto his old homespun cloak. His pale, almost translucent feet were crossed one over the other, while the loveliest little smile played across his face.

"The things I do. There are those who say I'd fare better if I didn't get my hands dirty."

"If anything's worth doing, it usually dirties your hands. Look at me and my painting. I couldn't be happy being a lady with clean hands." As I brought him the basin and ewer, Hadriel looked at me and smiled again. "It's more than your hands, Susanna. How did you get that bit of ochre on your ear?"

"Oh!" I said, and clapped my hand to my ear. Hadriel laughed.

"Let's see, two more dishes . . ."

"Oh, since there's company, let's have the wine, here. . . ." Suddenly, everyone felt light and joyful. It had to do with Hadriel laughing. We all laughed, too, for no reason. Dishes clattered and the wine went around, and Cat had a giggling fit that ended in hiccups with her mother slapping her on the back.

"Hold your breath, Mistress Cat," suggested Tom.

"Count to ten," said Nan.

"Try sipping water through a cloth," said Hadriel. "I've been told it's infallible." His face had gotten pinker from eating and drinking, which really was a mercy, since he looked much too pale for health.

"Yes, yes, try the guest's remedy!" everyone cried, and after several tries, Cat managed to drink through a dish towel.

"All gone," she spluttered, her face still red, and we all laughed and passed the wine around again. Master Hadriel was looking definitely tipsy, even though he had hardly drunk anything. Mistress Hull splashed some more wine in his cup.

"Oh, not a drop more, dear Mistress Hull, I simply can't," he said. "Wine goes straight to my head, I have it so rarely."

"Then have a bit more to eat, Hadriel, dear," said Mistress Hull, who had had quite a bit to drink herself.

"Sweetheart," he answered, tilting dangerously to one side, "I can hardly touch a bite. I usually don't eat or drink." Was I imagining it, or was the hump on his back quivering?

"Your mother should have looked after you better—you're far too thin. Not eat or drink! And what ever possessed her to give you a name like that? Now George is a nice name, or maybe Michael—but Hadriel?"

"Well, actually, it was my father's idea," said Hadriel, all pink.

"Well, doesn't that account for it!" said Mistress Hull. "Men! I'd say you look much more like a Michael to me."

"Oh, no, he's much bigger. Definitely bigger," said Hadriel, pouring himself more wine.

"So tell me why a nice boy like you was hiding up in Susanna's rooms. Really! You could have come in by the door and at least greeted us properly!"

"Wasn't hiding—come fairly often. Itsh her art, you see. My job ... helping out ... smallish ... but I do like a nice painting. The Adamsh ... what a joke! I haven't had a proper laugh for shimply *ages*. And she's got herself a peck of ... trouble ... yesh. Shushanna, dear girl, you need looking after ... there was something ... something I was going to do. Influensh shomeone. Prince of the Church. Which one, now? Oh, yesh, the fat one at Brideshwell. You have no idea the trouble the Church givsh ush. What was it? Oh yesh, must go. . . ." Hadriel staggered slightly as he got up.

"Going so soon? You can't go out at night. Why, you could be set upon by thieves!" Mistress Hull looked alarmed.

" 'S never bothered me. Nothing to shteal . . ." Hadriel was making his way to the kitchen door, steadying himself on the wall as he went.

"I simply can't allow you to go out like that!" The old lady was firm.

"Like that? What you mean . . . ?"

"Just look at your feet! You haven't any shoes!"

"Whatsh wrong with no shoes? I never wear 'em," Hadriel said.

"Why, you'll hurt your feet out there in the dark! Cat, go into my room in the big chest where I keep your father's things, and bring that pair of shoes I've been saving."

"Mother! Father's things?"

"Cat, my dear little Catkin, I've been saving too long. Keeping his shoes won't bring him back to me, and this poor boy's mother hasn't given him any." Then she flung herself on Hadriel and wept on his shoulder. "God should have given me a son like you! Poor, dear boy, so lovely, and nothing to eat and no mother, either! Just — sniff — think of me as a second mother. . . ." Hadriel looked terribly embarrassed, all red in the face as he was, and then he gave her an awkward pat.

"Sho shorry," he said softly. "Haven't got any of the big bleshings— blessings . . . jusht little ones . . . the artsh, you know, not much . . ."

The shoes looked strangely clumsy on his delicate feet, and as I watched him struggle with the laces, it was clear he'd never worn a pair in his life, which was odd, considering how fine and pale his feet were. I thought about that awhile, and then I thought about the way he kept his cloak on inside the house, and the way he helped me down the stairs. There was only one conclusion I could come to. As he stumbled out into the dark, I was sure of it.

"Look, that Master Hadriel's left a quill from his pen case. Oh, why have you opened the shutters?" I could hear Nan's voice behind me. But I was leaning on the sill and didn't turn. And my eye was following the zig-zagging, radiant flight of a tipsy angel making his way up into the night sky.

So powerful was the king's wrath that the heavy oak paneling on the walls seemed to quake at the sound of his voice.

"I tell you, he has betrayed me! And he has betrayed you, too, sister. Do not deceive yourself." Henry the Eighth, clad in blue silk slashed with gold tissue and reembroidered with gold thread and pearls, strode about the room with his rolling, powerful gait like an enraged bull. Still young, he was tall and athletic, his muscular frame not yet gone to fat, though there was promise of it for the future. His red-blond hair fell in damp disorder about his ears; his clean-shaven face was bright red with fury. Veins stood out on his thick-muscled neck. His eyes were slits of rage.

"But did he not say he was too ill to receive me, and have I not written him and called him husband, and has he not sent me jewels to show his favor?" The anger terrified Mary Tudor, who had for so many years been her brother's favorite, his plaything, his pampered and adored baby sister. No one had joined more joyfully in his masques, sung to his accompaniment on the virginals, greeted and amused his friends. Now, suddenly, this terrible storm. Her lord and brother had come to tell her that her marriage, arranged in childhood, was no longer valid.

"His aunt, that wily witch who governs the Netherlands, persuaded him to it, to keep me soft until the blow was struck. A secret treaty they signed behind my back! The emperor has played me false since the beginning. I tell you, sister, you are no longer betrothed to that miserable creature. Prince Charles of Castile may find another bride!"

"But—but my jewels, my trousseau in the Flemish style, my plate . . . and was the marriage not consummated by proxy? He did kiss me, I do recall. I fear the sin of it." Mary's eyes glanced from side to side, like a trapped doe. She wrung her hands. Frantically, she thought of excuses. No one must ever guess why.

"The plate will suit the King of France better, and so will you, my sister. The King of France is a great prince in all his strength and maturity, not a miserable stripling. You will be Queen of France, and he will dote on you. Wolsey, explain again to my recalcitrant sister that this marriage was not truly consummated, and therefore does not exist."

"Consider, my lady, that not only do you owe your king and brother obedience in all things, but that his wisdom in matters pertaining to the Church is excelled by no one in this land. The Pope himself has commended your brother's faith and wisdom. Now by all the understanding of those wise in these matters, this consummation was no true consummation, in that a kiss is hardly sufficient, even with the giving of the ring. It is to your marriage *de praesenti* that the witnesses swore, the consummation to be completed when you and he were of age. I tell you with all the authority granted to me by the Holy Church that your marriage was in name only and therefore no true marriage. True marriage requires true consummation, witnessed in the marriage bed. So you see? Even the Holy Church says you are free to obey your lord's will. You are most blessed and fortunate to become queen of so great a realm as France due to the great care and concern of that most noble prince, your brother." Wolsey's voice was oily and subservient. From the corner of his left eye he watched the red color fade from Henry's neck. Women, Wolsey's tone of voice seemed to say, they are hopeless in understanding. One must tempt them with toys and not try their minds over much.

King Henry watched his younger sister look at her lap and pick at the embroidery on her dress. Over and over, she rolled a little seed pearl between her fingers. Wolsey is right, thought Henry. Again he spoke, and this time his voice was softer.

"Mary, Mary, you shall be a great queen and the mother of kings. You shall wear the jewels of France; there are none more famous or beautiful in the whole world. A great prince pines with love for you, while that sickly boy will not live to grow up, without a doubt. Think of your great happiness and obey one who is wiser than you."

"It is my pleasure to obey you in all things, my lord," said Princess Mary in a low voice, still not looking up. King Henry took the gesture for humility. He could not see her eyes. "But—but is not the King of France old, and a cripple?" Mary spoke softly, hesitantly, as if she were ignorant and possibly misinformed. As sly and willful as her brother, she knew she must play the role of a simpleton if she were to get the one promise she wanted most.

"A cripple?" Henry laughed. "Never, sweet sister. True, he is in the autumn of his life, but virile still. All the better for you to enchant him."

"Brother, may I ask from you one favor? Then I shall wed the King of France most readily and do your bidding always when I am queen in France."

"And what is that? What is in my power to grant you?" asked Henry, the storm past and content to see such rapid acquiescence in his strong-willed sister.

"If—if the King of France should die, may I then choose whom I wish to be my husband?"

Henry was taken aback. Unheard of. But deluded by his own word-painting of a masterful king in his autumn years only, and secretly reserving the right to change his mind for reasons of state, which was only proper in a king, he answered his sister:

"Yes, if that is what pleases you."

"What pleases me will always please you," she said so meekly that her brother did not hear the double edge in her words. Clapping his hands, he called:

"Ho, Wolsey, bring the paper you have prepared. You must practice this speech, sister, until you are letter-perfect. Then tomorrow, we
will hold the formal audience in which you renounce this false and malicious prince Charles." There was a rustling as the formidable Wolsey
brought out a roll of papers from beneath his outer gown. There were
documents to sign and a florid speech for Mary to deliver renouncing
her marriage vows. Wolsey had outdone himself. As he read the speech
aloud, King Henry smiled and nodded. The fault was Charles's; he had
let evil counsel and malicious gossip turn him against her. Having
breached faith with her, he had so humiliated her that she now dis-
claimed any wifely affection for him. The contract was null and void.
Of her own volition entirely, she now severed the nuptial yoke. Mary's
face changed from sullen to amazed as she listened to the words she
was expected to deliver.

"You must end, of course, by petitioning the king for forgiveness
and declare that in all things you are most ready to obey his good pleasure. Now, shall I repeat it slowly, while you speak it after me?" asked
Wolsey, assessing Henry's reaction from the corner of his eyes. The
king's face was a study in contentment.

"Well done, well done, Wolsey. You have served me well in this affair."

"Your Majesty, my sole endeavor in life is to serve you exactly as
you would serve yourself, had you the time for these small details."
Wolsey had prepared the speech and the documents the week previous,
never doubting that it would be a simple matter to bring this weak
woman to the service of his vast plans.

Bright summer light shone through the narrow, diamond-shaped panes
in Bishop Wolsey's cabinet. Outside in his orchard, birds competed in
song while gardeners propped up the heaviest of the fruit-laden
branches. Inside, Wolsey had been working since dawn with Masters
Tuke and Warren checking lists. The greatest diplomatic *coup* of his
career must not be allowed to founder on a single misplaced detail. Now Wolsey had two weddings to plan for: one by proxy in England, and one in France, graced by the greatest lords and ladies of the
land. English horses, English soldiers, English pavilions for the wed-

ding tourney, everything from carriages for the dowry plate to chamber pots must be listed and accounted for. An army of secretaries and clerks prepared the lists for his inspection. Fourteen ships were requisitioned for their transport.

"Plate, yes. The great saltcellar, *hmm*, serving dishes, candlesticks, all here. And let's see—two carriages, ten mares to pull each at tenpence a day apiece . . . Tuke, have you the list of maids of honor to accompany the princess?"

"Here, Your Grace." Fluidly, with a pleasing graceful gesture, he produced the list. Warren looked irritated.

Wolsey put the list atop the lists of plate, horses, linens, and bed hangings and scrutinized it closely with his good eye. "What is this? You must strike her; her father is not of enough significance. And here . . . What is Mistress Popincourt doing on the list?"

"The princess has specifically requested her. And you said to favor ladies who spoke good, clear French. Such ones are not as easy to find as you think—"

"The King of France has sent me a letter. Jane Popincourt, he hears, has a light reputation. Rumor has it that she gave her favors to de Longueville before his return from France. He says he would sooner see her burned than serve his queen."

"He mentioned her by name?"

"By name. And there are others. His espionage service works overtime, it seems. *Hmm*—I see here Mary Boleyn, Sir Thomas's daughter. She, too, is mentioned. Strike her. Has Sir Thomas answered my request yet about the other girl? Her French, I am told, is excellent, and the Regent of the Netherlands has had her well tutored in courtly manners."

"He has written Margaret of Austria to release her from her position as *fille d'honneur* at the court of the Netherlands and she is presently on her way to Greenwich."

"How old is she, did you say?"

"Fourteen, my lord."

"Not too young, then. And a virgin, doubtless. Yes, Anne Boleyn. She goes. Now, about the white palfreys, let's see . . . harness, yes, here it is. Master of the Horse . . ." Wolsey gestured to the stack of paper. "Which of this is going on the *Great Elizabeth?*"

"The ladies of honor, the plate, the musicians—"

"Are they all women? The King of France will have no men."

"All but the musicians of the chapel and the trumpeters. The paintrix goes, too, with her serving woman and a boy to grind her colors. . . ."

"Strike the boy. Who does she think she is, with such a retinue? The Queen of Persia? What on earth gave me the idea of sending her, anyway? I was sure I had decided not to. Then it just came to me in the night, the wisdom of the plan. A sort of voice in the dark. Now, the bed hangings . . . What is that commotion? I told you I was busy, Ashton." Wolsey's other privy secretary, in somber gray, had entered the cabinet as silent as a shadow.

"My lord, I bring a letter that has just come from Rome. From Sylvester de Giglis, at the Papal Court." Ashton's eyes seemed sunken, and his face was pale. Why did I ever think him amusing? thought Wolsey.

"From Rome? Why didn't you say? What says de Giglis about my cardinal's hat? Does that wretch, Bainbridge, still block my way?"

"My lord, I know not. The letter will tell."

Wolsey undid the seals and read the letter in silence. Then, after a while, he spoke. "The Cardinal of York is dead in Rome," he said slowly.

"Your Grace, what a felicitous coincidence," observed Ashton. Wolsey didn't like his tone.

"Not entirely felicitous, though indeed a coincidence," observed Wolsey blandly. "Bainbridge was poisoned by his chaplain. An Italian fellow, I believe. And you know what they are." As he spoke, Wolsey looked long at Ashton's silent, drawn face. Just how much did he know?

"Thank you, Ashton. You may go," he said, briefly enjoying, in the old way, how Ashton's eyes flicked resentfully sideways to Tuke's self-satisfied face. An ungracious fellow, thought Wolsey. Skillful, useful, but still unaware of his proper station. Tuke's right, for once. I think I'll send him off for a while. Give him something even he can't do. Then he'll realize that all depends on my grace and favor, not his own accomplishment. He needs much more humility if he is to be shaped to my needs.

"Your Grace, will you be attending the king tomorrow? It would be well to take the opportunity to press for the See of York." Tuke's unctuous voice broke the long silence.

"Why, Tuke, what an excellent idea—the notion had not entirely escaped me. My lord of York. An excellent title. And York House—a most convenient residence, though it wants a bit of redecorating. Oh, yes. And send for the paintrix. No, not through Ashton this time. Tell her it's confidential. Before she goes, I wish a portrait of myself in profile—the better side. In crimson."

THIRTEEN

"What did the boy want, Susanna?" asked Mistress Hull as Nan and I crossed through her crowded little storefront on the way to the street. The spring had passed into summer, and my fortunes had risen very nearly as fast as my patron's, who became ever greater with each passing month. Mistress Hull was knitting busily in a chair beneath the display of green saints, and Cat and Tom were seated on the long bench at the back of the room. Cat was engaged in winding wool into a ball from a skein held on Tom's outstretched hands. He rolled his eyes at me as we passed, in a look of utter boredom and irritation.

"He wants me to attend the archbishop at York House, for another portrait. What's that you're knitting there? It looks pretty."

"It's the first of a pair of knitted sleeves. I had an inspiration, the night after that Master Hadriel left, that if I took two colors like this and alternated the stitching—so—I could make a pattern just like slashing. Very fashionable, don't you think?" I looked closer. Mistress Hull's stitches had never been as smooth.

"Why, those are very clever. Everyone will want some."

"I tell you, I've been just ablaze lately. I even dream about knitting. I've an idea about alternating rows that will make a pattern just like tiny drops. I can hardly wait to see how it turns out. I tell you, I haven't been so happy since I lost dear Master Hull. Though of course nothing will ever take his place . . . still, what was that dye you mentioned, Tom, that Master Ailwin can compound? I think I shall take to dyeing my own yarn to get the colors just right. My mind is full of visions, and I can't rest until I see them in real life, before my eyes. I tell you, it's an inspiration from God."

"Visions of *knitting?* Mother, that is humiliating. God is interested in higher things, I'm certain."

"Nonsense. His eye is on the sparrow and His eye is on knitting, too. I'm sure if I could search in the Bible like a priest, I'd find the place. His eye is on surly girls, as well. Why haven't you finished that ball of blue wool yet? I'll be needing it next." We hurried out the door without looking backward. Across the street, I thought I saw a skinny little man in a black cloak vanish into the doorway.

"Nan, did you see that man? I swear I've seen him before."

"At the Goat and Jug? He's probably just in love with you, like that man who lay in the gutter. You're rising in the world, Susanna, if your admirers can stand on their own two feet."

"I think I saw him someplace else, but I don't remember where. It makes me nervous."

"Nonsense. It's the weather making you nervous. Even horses get nervous in this kind of weather."

The day was cloudy, damp, and close, with the smell of a storm in the air. A curious, sultry wind made the trees rustle. We went by the Strand into Westminster with a crowd of guardsmen, archers, gowned clerks and lawyers on mules. Sure enough, there was a young man in a green gown and high boots having trouble with the mare he was riding. As he struggled to pull her in, a woman with a basket scurried to get out of the way.

Behind us was a boy driving pigs. The stifling smell of them hovered over us on the wind. Something heavy seemed to be oppressing me. At Charing Cross we paused, and I looked all about us. I thought I saw that same man slipping along in the crowd, but there are so many people with black cloaks, I couldn't be sure. To the south on the right were the tilt yards, and we could hear even there the clatter of noblemen practicing fighting at the Barriers. On the left were the great tenements and wealthy houses that gave way to the walls, gates, and towers of the archbishop's great palace, York House. I could feel the hairs rising on the back of my neck. Yes, it had been the same one. I was sure we were being followed.

"Oh, what dreadful air! I'm sure there's a storm coming, and as far as I'm concerned, it will be a relief." Nan tugged at her headdress with one hand, while with the other she held the case with my paints. A sudden gust tugged at my skirts. I stopped and pulled at them, turning suddenly. There seemed to be an ugly muttering in the air above us. Could it be distant thunder? The gray clouds were moving swiftly now.

Behind us, I thought I saw the figure in black vanish into an open doorway. Was it that ghastly murderer, Septimus Crouch? Who was it, trying to find me alone?

"Nan," I whispered. "I swear I saw him—that man. He's following us. Suppose it's a hired bravo from that murdering lord?" Nan looked suddenly horrified. We were near the gatehouse to the great courtyard of York House now. He won't bother us inside, I thought. There are servants everywhere. There are guards at the gate. I began to run, frantic with blind panic. Nan followed, as best she could, the heavy case bumping and rattling as she ran. The first drops of rain had begun to fall. Warm rain, not yet enough to clean the air. We were nearly there now; the gatehouse loomed before us. I put my head down and ran toward it. But, unseeing, I had bumped into someone. A man's heavy arms grabbed me. I regained my footing and tried to pull away, screaming. The man in black had caught me.

"Quiet, be quiet there. Look before you scream. Would you have the guards on me?" He put his hand over my mouth, and I could feel him pulling me through the little wicket gate.

"Susanna, you goose, it's Master Ashton. He's in front of you, not behind you. Shut your mouth and open your eyes." I did open my eyes and found myself looking directly into the angry, confused ones of Robert Ashton, Wolsey's secretary. His arms were still tight about me to keep me from struggling, and I realized with some embarrassment that I had kicked him in the shins. I could feel my face turning hot.

"And what new mischief have you done, that you flee as if the Devil himself were chasing you?" I could tell he regretted his shin.

"There's a man—all in—black," I managed to croak out. "He's following me. I—I thought you were he."

"I saw no man in black," he said. "Mistress Dallet, could it be that at last your conscience pursues you?" He paused a long time and looked very odd indeed. "Search your heart. Have you not ... been a part of a man's betrayal to his death?"

"Death? You know? I saw him do murder in secret. A—a great lord—" Suddenly I realized Robert Ashton would never believe me. Crouch was his friend, a gentleman, received in Wolsey's house. Who would believe a woman nobody? And telling would betray me to Crouch. What could he do, an important man like that? Have someone else arrested for the crime? Tom? Master Ailwin? Ashton's face seemed to collapse and sink inward.

"He was right," he whispered, though I didn't understand why. "You are quick to invent a story," he said, his eyes bitter and sorrowful. "Clever. I always knew you were clever." He shook his head. "And what makes you think, Mistress Dallet, that a great lord who had done murder would bother to follow you around? A great lord would send his retainers to wait for you at your door, or perhaps have you arrested on some false charge." As he spoke, he seemed slumped, as if he had taken on a great load. Now, straightening himself up, as if determined to show nothing, he accompanied us up the steps and through the winding corridors and public chambers of the archbishop's great palace. What was wrong with the man? "No, admit now that you lie, in the name of your own salvation." He still had my arm. I looked up at him, puzzled. He waited for my answer, then turned away. "God, twice a fool," he muttered to himself. Then he turned again to me and said, "Yes. Here we are. Past the antechamber, there, where you see the workmen hanging the tapestries, is his new cabinet. He's waiting for you." He pushed me through the arch into the antechamber and vanished like a shadow.

Oddly enough, I found Wolsey by himself. Even Master Tuke, the lapdog, wasn't there. But outside the open door, I thought I heard footsteps, as if some man were lingering outside, trying to listen in. Wolsey was seated in a heavy oak chair, all carved and cushioned like a throne. After I had kissed his ring, he told me to send Nan away into the outer chamber and ask her to leave the door closed but for six inches, so people would know he was occupied. Oh dear, I thought. This is a dreadful proposition that he is going to make. And I don't dare refuse him.

"Mistress Dallet, I want you to vow on this holy book here that you will never reveal what has transpired in this chamber." Now I was really frightened. Suppose he changed his mind someday about how well I could hold my tongue and decided I could hold it better in the bottom of a dungeon?

"I'll swear, Your Grace. I'll beg that God will strike me dead if I utter a word." The oath was not short, and by the end of it I was thoroughly frightened.

"Now," said the Archbishop of York, leaning forward in terrifying intimacy and smiling in a way that made me almost certain what he wanted was dishonorable, "now, I want to have you paint a portrait of me, for my own private closet. No one is to know it exists. It is for myself alone."

Oh, dear, I thought. As if Adam weren't enough. I was sure he wouldn't be satisfied with vines or a large lake of water. Well, at least it isn't an indecent proposal.

"Do you see this material, the weight, the shine of it? Can you paint it?" Wolsey had taken out a sample of crimson silk, glimmering with light, approximately two hands' breadth in size.

"Yes, Your Grace."

"I want you to paint me in profile—the good side, the left, wearing a gown cut as the one I have now, but in this color." A flood of relief went through me. I can paint anybody dressed.

"Of course I could do that. But why profile?"

"My right eye—I would not have you paint that."

"If I may beg your pardon, Your Grace, if I can paint you in a gown you are not wearing, I can paint your right eye as fair as your left. Three quarters is very distinguished. It is the new fashion in portraits. Profiles look antique."

"I doubt that you can paint this in three quarters. This is what I wish upon my head. The same color as the gown." Now it was all clear. He had brought from his desk drawer an old medallion bearing the profile of some ancient cardinal. It was a cardinal's hat he wanted painted on his head. In the privacy of his winter nights, he would stare at this picture to gather his ambitions like troops to scale a city wall. He would be cardinal, no matter what.

"Then you wish it like the medallion?"

"Exactly like it." I began to set out my colors. "I am a busy man," he said, "I want it done quickly."

"I'll begin it here and finish it in the studio," I said.

"I don't want you taking it to the studio. Who goes to your studio? I hear travelers make a stop there to see the wonders, these days, exactly as they pay a visit to see Paul's jacks beat the hour in the steeple clock. No, you'll stay here until it's finished, where no one can see you." Outside the window, there was a rattle of thunder and the sound of battering rain, as if a sluice gate had been opened. I hurried to close the window. Suddenly I was frightened.

"I will need candles, Your Grace, if the clouds make it darker. I can finish before nightfall . . . I think . . ."

"If the rain has stopped, I'll send you home with an escort. If not, you can remain here with your maidservant until it is finished," he said, folding his hands in his lap and settling his chins while I sketched in the profile on the carnation.

"Hold your head so . . . yes, that's the most becoming," I said, trying to stop him from moving.

"You will need to be packing soon, anyway," he said.

"Your Grace, what do you mean?"

"Why? Didn't Tuke or Ashton tell you? I've made arrangements for you to travel to France with the Princess Mary's wedding party. You are to paint a pair of commemorative miniatures for His Majesty and divers portraits of the court of France for my private collection. I have made you a list. Ashton has it. Have you seen the portrait in large of the King of France that Perréal has made? No? Well, we English must show them that we are not backward in the arts. No, not at all. Even our women paint better than Perréal. Are you sure you didn't see the portrait when you were at Greenwich?"

"Your Grace, I have not yet had the honor of seeing the paintings at Greenwich."

"Oh—well, then, it must be arranged, it must be arranged, so you will be able to compare them with those of the King of France when you are there. The King of England has asked me what paintings in the new style the King of France possesses. He would have greater ones. Masterpieces. England must not be backward in paintings. You will subtly inquire, so that no one will know, and you will send me an inventory. My agents fail me in this. They write, 'a fine great nativity,' but not how great, or in what style, or even who has painted it. Yes. That you will send me. Then our king will have a bigger one, in better style, hanging more favorably. Then, casually, you understand, casually, I will accompany the French envoys on a stroll in the gallery, past the paintings. And when they say, 'What a provincial, piquant charm this little nativity has. Have you nothing by Leonardo?' I will know they lie, lie!"

As I painted, I began to wonder about the negotiations with

France. Clearly, arranging to marry off a princess was more complicated than I imagined.

"You look downcast. Why do you not rejoice at this honor?" asked the great man.

"Your Grace, it is my pleasure to obey you in all things, but I was thinking what I would do if some French courtier said my paintings had piquant provincial charm."

The mighty Wolsey chuckled. "I have imagined that myself," he said. "Let me see the sketch." Silently, I held up to him the portrait of his secret desire. "Very good," he said, nodding. I stayed the night, and by the light of the next morning, in a secret chamber, finished the glimmering red and jewels of the secret portrait.

"I have been ordered to escort you home." I looked up quickly from the basin of water in which I was scrubbing up my brushes and the little mother-of-pearl palette. Robert Ashton stood in the doorway, looking disheveled. There were dark circles under his eyes, and he stared at me with a long, haunted look.

"And what makes you think I want escorting? Especially by a man who has clearly been up all night drinking and even now can scarcely stand? Go back to bed until you can enjoy the day again."

"And I suppose you enjoy it all too well. Why did I never guess? Why did he do this to me? To rub my nose in the dirt? Did he see what I felt? Did it double his pleasure, to use me as his pander? And you, it is the morning of your triumph. No wonder you have risen in favor. You have perfected the ability to seem what you are not. Your husband vanishes conveniently when you know his secrets. Then with your pictures, you worm your way into great men's houses. How clean, how hypocritical! And when you have pandered to their filthy lusts, they can pretend the payment is for a painting or two. All on the account books, as openly as the cost of a chapel singer or a side of beef. I could never have believed it if I had not seen with my own eyes. You make me sick." He had come into the room now and stood directly in front of me. His shirt was undone at the neck and I could see a bit of his collarbone, and the place where the tendons of the neck join. Adam betrayed, after the apple. Blaming the snake, blaming the apple, blaming Eve, but never blaming himself. An interesting new composition, very realistic. But monks wouldn't buy it. Definitely not the sort of thing a man would want to own. Nan looked alarmed.

"I hope you are not saying what I think you are."

"I am saying that and more. Do you think I don't know with whom you were closeted yesterday? For an hour and a half? The man who takes anything he wants. How perfectly matched with the woman who will stop at nothing."

"What were you doing? Snooping outside the door? Then you will know that Nan was with me, and you should be ashamed for thinking to blacken a widow's reputation." Nan nodded vigorously in agreement with me.

"Don't worry about your reputation," he said, his voice bitter. "You stand too well with my master now for me to dare breathe a word. But I know this, too. He made your serving woman wait outside."

"And left the door to the inner chamber open."

"Open by six inches only. What a virtuous six inches! How much can be done in a chamber behind six hypocritical inches!"

"And what was your interest in these six inches? That they were too small for your prying nose? Or was Master Tuke lurking behind you to keep you from daring to spy?"

At the mention of the slippery and politic Tuke, he turned so crimson I thought he might explode. I've hit it square on at the first try, I thought. Master Tuke has been taken into confidence, and he has not. And Wolsey is rubbing it in by asking him to see me home.

"What bad sprite has made you so surly and suspicious? You go beyond yourself, Master Ashton. If you were more humble and took more care to please, you would advance more in favor, as Master Tuke does," I said, just to annoy him further. I was rewarded by seeing him wince.

"Jezebel," he hissed, as he followed us from the room. Silently, he followed us through the muddy streets. When we reached the Sign of the Standing Cat, he turned and left without a word. Nan and I stood and watched him go, his hose wrinkled, his hat askew, and his walk angry. Gone. Too bad. He really would have made a good-looking Adam.

"What ever possessed a great man like the archbishop to have such an obnoxious person about him?" asked Nan.

"They say he does well on foreign assignments," I answered. Suddenly, my heart froze with horror. His crazy suspicions were one thing, but what if he went around talking about them? He could spread rumors and ruin my custom along with my reputation. Everything I'd done, all my work, my hard-earned living, could be spoiled in a moment with a few ugly, careless words. That's what he'd do. He'd ruin me.

"As a diplomat?" snorted Nan. "Clearly foreigners are less demanding about manners than we English."

The Sixth Portrait

Jean Clouet. Marguerite of Navarre. *4½ × 3½ cm. Gouache on vellum. Ca. 1520? Gold frame, encircled with diamonds. Obverse: arms of d'Alençon. Louvre.*

This early portrait of the future Queen of Navarre and celebrated authoress of the Heptameron *and* Miroir de l'âme pécheresse *depicts her sometime in her early twenties, during her first marriage to the Duc d'Alençon. The exquisite workmanship and characteristic use of the sky blue background are derived from the French school of manuscript illumination, which, developed in the masterful hands of Clouet, influenced the works of Holbein, predating the so-called "English school" of miniature painting by at least two decades.*

—*R. Dupré.* Histoire de la peinture française

The Duchess Marguerite had a very long nose, although her brother's was longer. But I think she was the cleverer of the two, and it is too bad she was not born the boy, given that she had more sense. Their mother, Louise of Savoy, only had an ordinary nose, so I think the noses as well as the brains must have come from their father, who was long dead so I couldn't see whether my idea was true. But they say he not only collected books but had his own illuminator, which is what made Marguerite such a good judge of painting and so quick to like my works in small. I painted her in three-quarters view in the new style, and I think I got the eyes just right though I must admit to shortening the nose just the tiniest bit because it was too long for the fashion.

But my greatest problem with the painting was that it was nearly stolen by that arrogant bully, Duke Francis's friend Bonnivet, who thinks he is such a great lover and handsome stallion, which irritates me terribly because even if he is a lord, he is not what I count handsome. He came into my studio while I was working, pretending to be "just visiting" with that big show-off Fleurange and maybe thinking about having his portrait done, and then he "accidentally" picked up the duchess's portrait to look at. It was about to disappear when I just as accidentally snatched it back, which is a big offense to a lord, and said, "Thank you for praising my work so when it is only half done, but I am sure Duchess Marguerite will let me make a copy for you." He looked totally shocked, and Fleurange put back his head and roared with laughter, which meant I was safe. But it also meant Bonnivet had wicked desires for the duchess, so I was not at all surprised when I heard a very long time later that he hid in her bedroom and tried to force her and she took several bruises fighting him off before her servants could come. Even so, he was too important for anyone to do anything, and besides, it was all considered just good sport. I'm sure his friends just cuffed him on the arm and made fun of him for not being able to finish the job. That is how it is with those lords, and you have to know it if you want to get on at court.

FOURTEEN

A light rain had fallen the previous night, and the damp had brought the cranes to the rolling meadows beyond the Loire to feed in the hours after dawn. The old King of France, unable to resist the auspicious signs, had ordered out his falconers, huntsmen, and harriers while the light was still rosy. The hunting of four-footed beasts, with noisy horns, baying hounds, and feats of strength, bored him. But falconry was a science; it required a perfect knowledge of beasts, of birds, and of men. Silence and strategy were more important than boastful prowess. Too frail to sit a horse, he was borne, gaunt and gray faced, in a litter carried by two quiet bay jennets to the damp, green meadows beyond the Château de Blois. On his wrist was his favorite gerfalcon, and riding beside his litter were his old councilors, dressed in the dark, earth-toned hunting clothes that kept the birds they stalked from startling and taking flight. A dozen falconers rode at a distance, and the masters of the harriers walked beyond, their shaggy gray hounds quiet beside them. Yet another party of mounted falconers circled beyond the feeding cranes. The crane, sharp beaked, much larger than the falcon, was the noblest prey. The most difficult art was to hunt them with a cast, that is, several trained birds attacking the crane at the same time in the air.

An old crane ruffled its feathers and took flight. At a signal from the king, two falcons were loosed, to which he added his own. With shrill cries, they flew at their prey. Perfect, thought the king, it will be perfect. The crane slashed at the first falcon with its sharp beak; the second, and then the third joined in the attack. But behind him, the king heard the clatter of hooves and the whinny of a badly trained horse. Loud voices drifted to him in the wind, and laughter. The young lords of the court, careless, unconscientious. The noise had startled the feeding cranes. Their great wings flapped and they rose into the air to join their battling comrade. With high, keening cries they flew at the falcons, bombarding them, battering them. The king's mouth closed in a tight line of rage, and his complexion grew grayer at the sight. How dare those careless oafs destroy the cast! It was rare that cranes could be alarmed like this. It was the rattle of harness and voices that had aroused the birds to their danger and spoiled the kill. Already, sensible of what they had done, the younger men had brought their horses to a walk. The king did not even need to look to see who it was. Their voices had told him. François of Angoulême and his friends Bonnivet and Fleurange. Noisy, troublesome, brash.

But like a general on the field, the king must look to the battle at hand. "The hounds," he said, and as the struggling crane fell to earth, still slashing, with two falcons perched on top of it, the harriers, freed at his orders, seized it by the feet. But his own falcon had fallen, wounded. His best, his dearest. The king's chief falconer rode to it at a gallop. Could she live? The king's face, usually so somber, was frozen with a rage that he allowed to show itself only in his eyes. The escaping cranes were already blobs of white against the pale blue morning sky.

"Your Majesty, a terrible pity . . ." said the Comte de Guise, leaning toward the infuriated king.

"That gross infant," the king hissed between his teeth. "For the sake of France, there must be another heir."

Once again they were together, brother and sister, almost like the old days before her marriage to the Duc d'Alençon had taken her away to isolation in Normandy. The family had gathered at Blois at the beginning of the summer to celebrate the long-awaited wedding of Francis to Claude of France, eldest daughter of the king and his second queen, Anne of Brittany. It was the penultimate step toward the supreme power, but one bitterly contested. Unlike the kingdom of France, the vast lands of Brittany could be inherited through the female line. The king had wed Anne, his brother's widow, to maintain the territorial integrity of France. But the threat of the marriage of her daughters, the heiresses of Brittany, abroad led the Parlement to beg that Claude be betrothed to Francis, her cousin, the male heir to the throne. The old queen was furious. She knew that to place the fate of her frail, deformed daughter in the hands of this brilliant, careless, and ambitious family would doom her. She loathed the tenacious, scheming Louise of Savoy, and until death struck her down, she prevented the marriage. Now that she was in her grave, everything she had once feared had come about: her beloved child, deformed and sweet tempered, had fallen deeply in love with a husband who considered her only a convenience. Once again, Louise had triumphed. Her son was now Duke of Brittany. Quietly, Louise informed her son that if he ever allowed the younger daughter, Renée, to wed, he would lose half of Brittany to her future husband. Francis resolved that his infant sister-in-law, should he become king, would never be allowed to marry.

"I have taken your knight, my lord," announced Marguerite, her eyes still fixed on the ebony-and-ivory chessboard. Her chestnut hair was nearly entirely hidden under her peaked matron's headdress and black velvet hood. Two of her favorite little white lapdogs lay at her feet. Francis, at twenty still slender and clean shaven, looked up. Their faces were nearly identical, with long noses, shrewd, intelligent eyes, and a glint of humor about their mobile, narrow mouths. Louise had spared nothing on their education, and their accomplishments, since childhood, had been near legendary. Already, Marguerite, accomplished with her pen and bored in exile from the court, was collecting stories for a book of naughty, humorous tales; her brother wrote poetry and pursued women in his leisure hours. Their fates had taken them on different paths, but they understood each other perfectly.

"Then my rook will avenge me," answered Francis, making the move. He was clad in pale lavender satin, and on his head was a flat, brimmed hat of crimson velvet. Already it was twilight, and a servant came to light the candles in the long gallery. The great tapestries undulated with a stray summer breeze that came through the open windows, and the candles flickered and smoked in the newly raised chandeliers. At the end of the gallery, one of Claude's ladies of honor was playing the virginals, while another sang. Claude's needle passed up and down through an embroidery hoop that contained an altar cloth. At sixteen, she was swollen as if by a strange disorder, hugely fat, her face round and puffy. A rich gown in pale blue satin only emphasized her pallor and desperate plainness. Every so often, she raised her eyes from the cloth to cast adoring eyes at the marvelously handsome, dashing man to whom she had been wed. How far from her he sat, and how engrossed he was, talking with his tall, elegant sister. Francis was playing chess, a game that she could never hope to master. How clever he looked, sitting there, engrossed in things that were beyond her. If only he would turn and look her way!

"I knew you would do that. Check," said Marguerite.

"Is this just? You won last time. I should win this time. After all, I am the dauphin." Francis evaded Marguerite's queen, but he knew the respite was only temporary.

"You know if I let you win every time, you would have no sport," answered Marguerite. "Check and mate."

"Bah, chess is boring tonight. Call your ladies to dance for me, and I will give a prize to the fairest, like Paris."

"Paris caused a great deal more trouble than he thought with his prizes. And you, my lord, must be more circumspect. The king looks to replace you."

"Ridiculous. An impossibility. He's far too old."

"What if his blood were stirred by the English princess?"

"She would have to be a miracle to raise life in that old hulk."

"She's not bad, brother. And you must quit playing and lay plans. If she bears a child, you must be sure to be made regent. An English Queen Regent would destroy France. You need to go to court. Speak to the old ones, de Guise and La Tremoïlle and the others who bore you. Flatter them. Show yourself wise and mature." Francis had paled. The throne, so close, could be snatched away. He, the lone male heir of the Valois, the only son, his mother's adored Caesar. In his vast self-confidence, he had never thought it possible.

"Who has spoken of this? Has mother concurred in this plan?"

"It was she who thought of it. But I warn you, you must go to her and act as if it had come over you as your own idea. She frets so, these days, that I am worried for her health. The king thwarts her at every turn. He rages at the orders she gives the cooks, the laundry maids. Only he shall command in his own house, he says. Have you not seen how bitter, how resentful he looks when he spies her among the ladies of the court, or even you, these days? Show mother that you are changed, serious. It will relieve her. She loves you above all things and lives only for your happiness."

"It won't happen. It can't," said Francis, shaking his head.

"It could happen easily, and you must not let things go by until it is too late," she said. "The negotiations are far advanced, and encouraged by his closest advisors. They, too, despise you. They have whetted his appetite and encouraged him in this fantasy." Francis shook his head in disbelief.

"A child heir? France would be torn apart. Brittany would be separated from the crown. Unless—would they wed this infant heir to Renée? Shameless—divide my inheritance? Then Bourbon would be as great as I.... Yet, no, no—it makes sense. Until the infant's majority, they would need a puppet regent. A foreign queen, a weakling who could be ruled. In a regency, those old men would prolong their power, cost France what it may." Even Francis, whose young mind never lit on one subject for very long, began to see the path of destruction that hung on an old man's whim.

"Just see this," said his sister, "and you will understand all. Only don't tell mother I showed you." From a reticule at her waist, she took out a tiny, round wooden box and laid it in the middle of the chessboard. Artfully, she blocked the view from the others in the gallery by her body. "There is the most curious story about this painting. De Longueville said it was painted in London by a ghost." As his sister launched into the story, Francis undid the lid of the box and stared for a long time at the fresh, willful face. A great beauty, not a deformed, fat little woman such as he had been saddled with for the sake of having Brittany. Suddenly he was filled with anxiety. Anxiety for the bold-faced heirs this woman could put between him and the throne. And in the midst of anxiety, something else. Desire.

The Great Banquet Hall at Greenwich was hung with arras of gold, laced with an embroidered frieze emblazoning the royal arms of France and England. It was already mid-August, and the bright sun of midsummer glinted on gold and silk, steel and cloth of gold, as the gaudy assemblage of English lords, foreign dignitaries, and Papal envoys waited for the arrival of the bridal party. Wolsey was there, resplendent, beaming, along with Norfolk, Dorset, Buckingham, Suffolk, and the principal earls of the realm. A huge lace collar and a massive gold chain set off Suffolk's broad bull neck. His complexion was reddish from the indoor heat. Sweat ran from beneath his rich, jeweled and plumed hat, gluing his dark hair to his temples. His gait, as he mingled with the crowd, was the rolling strut of a man who enjoys the highest favor. His face was a study in self-satisfaction. For his part in the wedding negotiations, the French king had awarded him a pension of 875 *livres tournois* a year, an extraordinarily handsome sum for a man of "petite famille" who had risen on the King of England's friendship alone.

Wolsey's French pension was three times Suffolk's, but for him it was only pocket change. Even at a celebration, he was full of business. With one of his mind-compartments, he was taking note of who talked to whom in the crowded hall. Aha, said this part of his brain, I know who is missing. The Spanish ambassador. He seethes with envy; a sign of our triumph. Simultaneously, with another mind-compartment, he was calculating how soon the backing of the Pope would get him his cardinalate. Very soon, very soon, it whispered. You have bribed everyone so handsomely. Go cautiously, go cleverly, Thomas Wolsey, and you will be the first English Pope. In one of the lesser mind-compartments, he was deciding whether he should spend King Louis's money on redecorating Hampton Court or save it for York House. So much to do, so little time to do it in. Perhaps I need a larger staff, this brain-compartment was thinking.

At last the royal party arrived. King Henry the Eighth and Queen Catherine of Aragon led the bridal party. Mary, stiff in her immense bridal gown, accompanied by her ladies, immediately preceded the delegation that represented the French king. Two ministers sent for the peace conference that had preceded the wedding walked in state; the French general, Thomas Boyer, and the President of Normandy, John de Silva. But most resplendent of all was Louis d'Orléans, Duc de Longueville, who glittered in a heavily jeweled velvet gown as the proxy of the French king. The Archbishop of Canterbury opened the ceremony, speaking in Latin. As the long Latin speeches rolled on, the Princess Mary, her face pale beneath her shining red-gold hair, cast her eyes first on the glorious embroidery of the archbishop's vestments, then wider, hiding her gaze beneath her lowered lashes. Her heart was pounding, and her knees shaking. It was the greatest day of her young life. She would be queen in France. In her mind, she reviewed the many honors and advantages Wolsey had recited to her. She must be careful, careful, not to make an unlucky slip in speech as she let de Longueville take her hand for the espousal *per verba de praesenti*. Her French must be perfect. How she had practiced for this moment!

Precisely, slowly, she repeated her wedding vows in French. She could feel the hundreds of eyes on the back of her neck. They were watching her face, her gown, her hands. They see that I am beautiful, she thought. De Longueville put the gold ring upon the fourth finger of her right hand, and then kissed her. Almost, almost complete, she exulted secretly, and not a slip in her French so far! Then her ladies took her from the hall and changed her into a magnificent nightgown for the public consummation. Her breath came short; she could feel her heart battering at her ribs as they brought her to the immense, ceremonial bed. Already, the priests had finished sprinkling and blessing the place where she would lie. De Longueville stood beside it, waiting. He had removed his gown; beneath it were a bright red doublet and hose. Carefully, her ladies helped her up into the tapestry-draped bed. De Longueville stripped one leg to the thigh and lay down beside her.

Mary, propped up by richly decorated pillows, lay as stiff as a statue, gazing out into the crowd of dignitaries that filled the room. More speeches in Latin droned above her. She could see those nearby straining for a better look. A tall, heavy man's head, dark haired beneath a green-velvet, egret-plumed hat, showed above the crowd. Suffolk, glittering with gold and success. Everything a man should be. Bold, brave, randy, young. And English. And she was going to a foreign old man's bed, for the sake of jewels, for the sake of clothes, for the sake of power her brother craved but she cared nothing for. Unknown to any in the room, this bull of a man, whose eye was kindled by any woman of wealth, had, in the months before her engagement, sent her a letter, whose violent misspellings, once decoded, spoke of love. And she had answered it. Hidden away, she had a marvelous, tiny portrait of him, his face most admirably fierce and warlike, that he had sent to her. But the king's sharp gaze had caused Suffolk to flee. Still, she thought, wasn't he her brother's closest friend? What could a dried-up old man know of love? Her eyes lit, for a brief moment, and Suffolk studiously looked away, his face vaguely alarmed, as if he didn't understand. How dare he not understand! Would it always be this way, when she was queen in France? Her youth and beauty poured away in empty ceremony, and no man ever again daring to speak to her of love?

But then her mind flitted to her French wedding jewels. Grander than Queen Catherine's they would be, Wolsey swore it. There would be gowns, and dances, and masques. She was very fond of these things, of dancing, of playing, of being admired in company. Surely this would sweeten the burden of being an old man's bride. And couldn't a widow do as she wanted, especially if she were a queen? Wolsey had said it, and he must know. Queen. The word had a good sound to it. Queen of France.

The droning in Latin had ceased. As the crowd waited, the French lord touched his leg to her body in symbol of sexual relations. A ripple of approval traversed the crowd, necks craned, and Suffolk's face disappeared. The archbishop declared the marriage consummated. The princess's ladies dressed her again, this time in a checkered gown of purple satin and cloth of gold, and the entire party, dukes, lords, and delegates, processed to the palace chapel to hear mass. De Longueville walked with King Henry, whose satin clothes shone with gold and appliquéd jewels. Mary now walked with Queen Catherine, their heads covered with identical caps of cloth of gold.

The hundreds of dishes at the wedding banquet passed by Mary in a kind of daze. Compliments and gallantries swirled around her, leaving her feeling dizzy with gratification and the sense that from now on, all her days would be like this. She would be the center, the queen. To the music of the flute and harp, the dancing began. Henry excelled at dancing, and stripping off his gown, he and Buckingham danced in doublet and hose with such enthusiasm that it infected the entire company. The center, Mary thought. I am the center. It is for me he dances. My brother, the king, celebrates for me. All thought of Suffolk flew from her head. I shall be queen, she thought, and all things will come to me. I will forever be the center. Men will worship me. Women will envy me. Forever. The thought dazzled her.

"So, Master Tuke, report to me everything that transpired at the reception of the Sieur de Marigny." Once again Wolsey was in bed, trapped

by his old recurring illness, a bloody flux of the bowels. Pale and flac-
cid, his great bulk propped up by pillows in his canopied bed in
Brideswell, he was annotating reports on a lap desk propped on his
commodious stomach. About him on the coverlet was stacked correspondence from all over Europe. Tuke, usually repelled by illness, was
quivering all over with the glory of such intimacy with the great man.
Closer even than Ashton. Greater trust, greater honor. It almost overcame his revulsion at the unpleasant smell.

"Your Grace, the Sieur de Marigny brought with him on a white
horse two coffers of plate, seals, devices, and jewelry. Most unctuous
he was, bowing and scraping in the French fashion before the princess,
offering compliments to the bride. The jewels were magnificent. I have
the inventory here. . . ." Tuke handed a scrap of paper to his master,
who nodded.

"The valuations, Master Tuke. How came you by them?"

"The king had the jewelers from 'the Row' waiting to set a price
on them as soon as the coffers were taken from the chamber. But even
he was astonished by this big one, here, the 'Mirror of Naples.' The
jeweled diamond is as large as a man's finger, and the pearl beneath it
the size of a pigeon's egg."

"Clearly, Master Tuke, the King of France knows how to astonish.
And Marigny's mission?"

"He is sent to attend the princess and instruct her in the etiquette
of the French court."

"And how did you find him?"

"He is a great lord, of impeccable politeness, but he looks about
him with a glance like an eagle."

"Or a duenna. Old men, old men, Tuke. There's no one more jealous. Pass me that barley water there, Tuke, I am so dry, and feel a weakness passing through me." Brian Tuke felt genuinely alarmed, for
Wolsey's complexion had turned suddenly ashy. From the great silver
pitcher at the bedside table he poured out the barley water.

"Your Grace, the physician . . ."

"Spare me that man yet a moment, Master Tuke. I swear he does
nothing that does not aggravate my condition. See there? The small
bottle? Put it closer so I can reach it when I need it." Tuke's whole ca-

reer passed before his eyes in a spasm of fear; suppose, after all his efforts, Wolsey were to die here, at this moment, his bowels bleeding
away his life? Ah, God, how unfair, how cruel! But if he recovered, for
this service, what advancement ... His eyes full of concern, he
arranged the pillows behind Wolsey's head, then held the cup while his
master sipped it, eyes closed.

"Ah, God, I thank you, Master Tuke." Wolsey opened his eyes to
spy his servant's distressed face. With a sly smile, he whispered, "So,
Tuke, I believe you consider I merit a more discreet illness. What say you
to a thorn in the side?" Amused, he watched the warring emotions in
Tuke's face: shock at the heretical comparison to the apostle, desire to
flatter by agreeing, and puzzlement as to whether it was all a joke or not.

"Your Grace ..." began the shocked privy secretary, but then he
heard Wolsey's snort of laughter. To be agreeable, he laughed, too,
though nervously.

"So, Master Tuke, through all your report, I have sensed a certain irritation. What else happened to you this day? Was de Marigny offensive?"

"De Marigny? Oh, no, Your Grace, he is the soul of courtesy. A
true gentleman, though French. It is that—that ghastly, that, that ...
Master Perréal he brought with him. After the reception I was entrapped, entrapped, I tell you!"

"Perréal, the King of France's painter?"

"That very Perréal. De Marigny brought him. A small, wiry, dark
fellow with the most offensive little smile. He pretends he cannot understand French that is not spoken with a Parisian accent. 'Oh?' he
says, cupping his hand behind his ear, when the pronunciation of
some word offends him. And then he smiles that little smile as the person who has spoken tries again and again to mend the flaw. I tell you, I
wanted to strangle him...."

"I take it, Master Tuke, it was your French he found objectionable."

"Mine, and others', Your Grace. He is to design the princess's
wardrobe and paint a wedding portrait of her to match the great ugly
one of the King of France that he brought to us. Knowing that I
would report to you, His Majesty sent me, as well as one of his gentlemen of the chamber, to take him to meet with the princess's ladies of
honor to inspect her dresses. The entire afternoon, hearing that horri-

ble man comment on the cut of her undersleeves and the placement of the points for her trains. 'Oh, how old-fashioned. A queen of France cannot be seen in a bodice of such a provincial cut. What is this décolletage? How unbearable, it is cut in the Flemish style.' As far as I know, he knows all too much about ladies' clothing. It's not decent, I tell you. And then there was the gallery. . . ."

"Ah, you had to show him the gallery as well?"

"He wanted to see the king's paintings. The man was insupportable. 'How charming, in an old-fashioned way. So northern, so provincial. This nativity, it's fading already? Ah, yes, I see, the glazes are poor. Who did you say painted this? Hethe? He does not understand the art of stained canvas. What a pity you English do not have a truly great city of art such as Tours. The Italians do wonderful things these days. Haven't you anything by Leonardo?' I though there'd never be an end to it."

"Ah, Master Tuke, I see you are ripe for revenge." Tuke bit his lip and bowed his head. "I think we will show this portrait painter our private collection. Tell the truth, Tuke. Who is the most irritating man you know?"

"Him, Your Grace. He raises irritation to new heights."

"But before that—be truthful, now." Brian Tuke was silent. "Come, come now. Wouldn't you have answered, 'Ashton,' if this French fellow had not carried off the palm?" Tuke's lizardy eyelids blinked with alarm. "I see I am right," observed Wolsey.

"He follows me, he thinks of a thousand little things to prove himself superior to me that he thinks I do not notice. Your Grace, I would rather spend time in a barrelful of fleas than in his company." Wolsey chuckled. Even in his illness, the daily drama of their rivalry did not fail to amuse; it was the true flattery, since it centered on who would bask first in his greatness. It kept them both in line and assured that he would always hear of the doings of one from the lips of the other. It was one of the many little tricks of power that Wolsey had mastered in this rapid rise. Men, they were easy. It was women he did not understand. But it is our good fortune that God had ordained that women must do as they are told, Wolsey thought as he pondered the issue briefly.

"I'm thinking the Frenchman could use a bath of fleas, and the bath of fleas might benefit from a Frenchman." Tuke glanced quickly at the archbishop's face, uncertain how to respond. "What say you, Master Tuke, to having Ashton conduct Perréal through my collection?"

"An excellent idea, Your Grace," said the privy secretary, with a bland smile. Wolsey looked at his face and burst out laughing.

"Ah, I see. This 'York House' is undergoing redecoration. His Grace, the mighty Bishop Wolsey should have a single man of taste overseeing the renovation. The Italian style—that is the style to be most admired. This rather primitive arras here, I take it, is to be replaced."

"The hangings in this room are entirely new," said Ashton, suppressing a powerful impulse to shake Maître Perréal until his teeth rattled.

"Yes, the northern style. So angular, so dated. Here, you see, the cornices lack fluidity of line. That charming grace of the Italian—a cornucopia, or perhaps a cherub, would look well over that window. Ah, but it must be the austere taste of a man of the church—still, in Rome . . ."

"Rome should no more be in London than London in Rome," growled Ashton. His accent had a Norman twang. Perréal listened politely but every so often allowed his nostrils to twitch as Ashton spoke, as if there were the smell of something slightly putrid in the room.

"Profound," replied Perréal. "Simple, yet profound. It might be engraved over the lintel here." He waved a hand at a doorway that lacked cherubs. Ashton caught something in the word. A trick of the *r*s. He smelled revenge.

"Master Perréal," he said, in a voice of feigned admiration, "you are so very knowledgeable about the new styles. Tell me, when did you study in Italy?"

"Italy? Why, the Italian style is known everywhere . . ."

Ashton sighed heavily, with false regret. "Except here, where we are so far, so very far. How fortunate you are to have studied in Tours. I imagine Italian artists find it so much easier to travel there. How unfortunate we lack such a great center of refinement. . . ." Ashton watched Perréal's face stiffen. It was his *r*s that still retained a bit of the Tourangeau. "The bishop's collection is through this doorway," added

Ashton, unctuously. "You'll find the paneling in the cabinet a charming example of the northern style. Very simple, with that austere angularity so suited to a prince of the Church. Did you know that Lord Wolsey wears a hair shirt?" Perréal cast a look of pure hatred at his guide.

Above the shoulder-high wainscoting, the walls of the cabinet had been richly gilded and painted with a religious scene: the presentation of the infant Jesus at the temple. The figures were angular, the brightly painted and decorated draperies symmetrical, in the old style. The background, a temple not unlike the Tower with a gilded dome set upon it in place of a crenellated battlement, was depicted in a stylized fashion, entirely without perspective. Ashton watched Perréal's face. It was a study in concealed disdain. Good, thought Ashton, my strategy is working.

"And what master painted this?" asked the French artist.

"Master Brown, of the Painter-Stainers' Guild."

Paintings hung on the paneling, each protected from the dust by a damask curtain. Religious scenes for contemplation, portraits of long-dead churchmen and patrons, the usual furnishings of an archbishop's cabinet. Many were obviously the product of some long-gone studio, the faces flat and ill fitted to the ready-painted bodies, costume detail and elaborate gilding used to mask the defects of composition.

"Lord Wolsey, I take it, is not a connoisseur."

"Oh, these he inherited from his predecessor. They have mostly historical importance." Ashton was nonchalant.

"This one in the corner. Why do you neglect it?" Perréal lifted the curtain. Ashton smiled to himself as he heard the Frenchman suck in his breath. *The Temptation of Eve,* with rich layers of color shining through semitransparent glazes, so fresh and prettily modeled that you thought it would be possible to reach right into the depths of it. In the foreground, a vast, pink Eve, surrounded by a flowery Eden; in the background, a familiar-looking mountain, being struck by the lightning of God's wrath. Ashton, his hands behind his back, inspected both the Frenchman and the painting at the same time. Suddenly, something struck him. Eve's hands. Short fingered and plump, oddly familiar. Had she used her own as a model? The face, of course, was not hers. But had she used the rest of herself, too? The bosom for example, and what about that dimple at the knee? The blood began to prickle in his veins. Susanna, that shameless wretch . . .

"Fascinating," said the French painter, and then, with a malicious smirk, he could not help adding: "But of course I have recently, in this very city, been shown one almost exactly like this, painted with dark varnish and blackened with candle smoke, being passed off as a work by our great Fouquet." Smiling, he watched the muscles of his guide's jaw clench. "It seems to me that this false Fouquet must have returned from the grave to paint the scene anew. *Hmm.* The use of glazes is excellent. The depiction of form—precise, but more literal than graceful. There is no true art here. I would say this man is Flemish. Flemish with an Italian master. I hope your archbishop did not pay too much for the work."

"It was given to him," snapped Ashton, turning to a great locked chest that stood upon heavy, carved legs. "The archbishop's collection is here. He has several rare coins he would like you to identify and value. He also has a collection of portraits in miniature in the new style."

Ashton watched while Perréal made oddly birdlike humming sounds, turning various medallions and coins over and over in his hands. "This one," he said, "is the profile of the emperor Nero. The inscription is worn off yours, but we have several like it at Les Tournelles. These—Aha! They are Merovingian. The time of King Dagobert. Where were they found? Here? How very curious." So busy was he inspecting the Frenchman that he never looked up when a familiar figure spoke in English from the open doorway.

"Why, Ashton, how good to run into you here. How goes it with the frog painter?" Brian Tuke, unable to resist, had come to spy out Ashton's discomfiture. Ashton glared his beaming, slippery rival. "Ah, look," Tuke observed, "he's opened the first of the Dallets." Together, they watched the supercilious Frenchman's eyebrows rise in amazement. Differences temporarily put aside in the interests of national rivalry, the two Englishmen looked at each other and grinned.

"Who did this?" demanded the French artist.

"Just a simple provincial style," said Tuke.

"Yes, the English style," added Ashton. "Admit it is naively amusing." Caught up in his baiting of the irritating Frenchman, he had forgotten how infuriated he was at this new evidence of Susanna's trickery. A smoked-up antique, indeed. How much had she managed to trick Perréal out of? Was she incapable of shame? All over town, she must have left deceptions like this just waiting to be unveiled. Still, there was a certain appropriateness in setting the sly little paintrix on the French, just as you'd set a ferret on a weasel. The French deserved her.

"This style was developed in France. Our Fouquet . . ."

"The French style is confined to manuscript illustration," observed Ashton. "I say, have you ever noticed, Master Tuke, how all those French manuscript portraits look alike?"

"Odd, I have remarked on it, Master Ashton. They all look like fishes," answered Tuke.

"It is hardly original to separate the portrait from the manuscript page," spluttered the Frenchman.

"The technique is new, too. Would you like to have a glass to inspect the shading? The strokes are quite invisible to the unaided eye." Ashton beamed maliciously at the little Frenchman as Tuke produced a magnifying glass for him. What a pity I can't introduce him to Mistress Dallet, Ashton thought. She'd make short work of him. Briefly, he imagined her attending Perréal's funeral, all in black, dabbing at her eyes, having artfully arranged his death. So charming, so deadly. And yet his heart pounded when he thought of her. She's trapped me, he thought. How did she trap me? Sir Septimus says she is like Messalina. Did Messalina paint portraits of her unclad body to entangle a man's mind into thinking of nothing else? Her gestures, her comings and goings, her wily schemes had become engraved on his mind. Even away from her, he found himself imagining, What would she say about this? What would she do if this or that happened? And now these Eves. They were all over the City. Would he hunt them out, comparing each with the next, to see if his sudden suspicion was correct? Was it some kind of curse or enchantment that she had had cast that drew him, despite all that he knew of her depravity, to want only to be closer to her? He found himself mulling over random things he overheard her say. He craved to know the secret details of her life, even as he told himself thousands of times he wanted nothing to do with her. Women. Crouch was right. Remember the danger.

"The background," added Tuke helpfully, noting the Frenchman's rising emotions. "The blue is quite original. It is a secret process. Don't you find it sets off the skin tones well?"

But what had upset the Frenchman was not the idea of the paintings, or even their technique, dazzling as it was. The secret of the serene sky blue he intended to discover at home in his alchemical laboratory. No, what had upset him most was the depiction of the faces. There was a trick to the lift of a brow, to the light in the pupil of the eye, that proclaimed the unknown master of *The Temptation of Eve* to be also the author of the exquisite little portraits he had just lifted from the drawer.

Perréal, artist, sculptor, and alchemist, was more than a mere designer of royal weddings and funerals. He was also a member of the Priory of Sion, that international web of alchemists, artists, builders, mystics, cavaliers, and romantics that had existed since the time of the Crusades: the Priory of Sion, severed from the Knights Templar at the Splitting of the Oak. The Templars had been destroyed, but the Priory remained, brooding over its great Secret and leaving conspiratorial messages in code across the face of Europe: stones like grave markers covered with secret carvings, secret signs and code words depicted in acrostics, poems, paintings, maps, and cryptic prophetic verse.

Now, as he stared at the picture, Perréal shuddered at the coded secrets revealed as clearly as if they had been printed in prose. He saw the sacred mountain, the home of the Secret, before the Redemption. He saw a mound, like a tomb, he saw patterns in the greenery, patterns he might have missed had he not recognized the mountain itself, bathed in unearthly light. It was all true. Maître Bellier was right. There was an outsider who had discovered what had been concealed for so long by the ancient secret society. And Wolsey knew him. Why had Wolsey asked his servant to lead him to this particular picture? Was it a secret sign? Did Wolsey wish to threaten, or was it a sign he wished to negotiate? This prince of the Church had obtained the Secret. Was he keeping it for his own power, or was the Priory betrayed? He must find out more, the Helmsman must be informed, and Wolsey and his agents must be dealt with.

"Does the man who painted these live in London?"

"No *man* painted them," said Tuke, grinning at Ashton as they saw the Frenchman turn pale.

"The Devil . . ." whispered the artist. "What powers . . . ?"

"He said," announced Ashton, "that a man didn't do them." The Frenchman looked up, puzzled, at their cheerful faces.

"No man? If it was no man, then . . ."

". . . it was a woman." The Englishmen burst out laughing at the Frenchman's confusion. Furious, the artist pulled himself up to his full height.

"You brought me here only to mock my art," he said.

"Us? Oh, never," said Ashton.

"How could you ever think us so ungracious?" said Tuke. "You? The greatest master in France? Our master is full of gratitude that you could identify his ancient treasures. See here, he has sent this purse to show his appreciation."

"Purse? Is my honor to be purchased with money?"

"Oh, such a thing could not be imagined," said Ashford. "Our master wanted you to see his collection so that you could offer advice on what he should do to make it more complete."

"Yes, it requires the most subtle artistic judgment."

"We wouldn't want to think it might overburden you." Bit by bit, they mollified the furious Frenchman with flattery. His raging subsided into spluttering, and eventually the spluttering gave way to rational speech.

"There is only one question that perplexes me," he said, his face returned to its normal state of disdain. "You say these Merovingian coins were found here in England. I am tremendously interested in rarities of this sort. Tell me, was anything else found with them? Jewels, a rare coffer, or perhaps an antique manuscript?"

"That, I would not know. The archbishop collects only coins and medallions. But you might inquire of Sir Septimus Crouch, the antiquarian who offered the coins for sale," answered Brian Tuke, his voice dripping with false helpfulness. "He resides right here in London, in Lime Street Ward, beneath the City wall. I would suggest consulting with him as soon as possible." Behind Perréal's back, where only Ashton could see, Tuke made a shooing motion with the back of his hand.

Ashton was annoyed that even this hidden insult to a man he couldn't stand was performed with a graceful, aristocratic languor that he could never hope to achieve. Lizard, thought Ashton. The English lizard and the French weasel. They deserve each other, too.

"Ah, the Sieur Crouch. That explains everything," said Perréal. How odd, thought the French alchemist. Bellier hadn't mentioned Crouch. Maybe he needed to be told.

"Everything?" asked Ashton, puzzled.

"But, Maître Ashton, he is well known. He is an advanced disciple of the Grand Grimoire and of the method of Honorius."

Ashton's face turned pale.

"Oh," said Tuke, "didn't you know about Crouch? Quite the dia-bolist, they say. But I don't imagine it's got him anywhere. If he could really call the Devil, then he'd be rich, wouldn't he?" Tuke smirked as he noticed Ashton's brief, involuntary shudder.

FIFTEEN

Once again Robert Ashton stood in the cluttered little shop front of the Standing Cat, surrounding by squinting, lopsided green saints in various stages of gory martyrdom. He was not in livery but in his old gray doublet and baggy-kneed hose, looking as crumpled and disarrayed as if he had slept in them. His face was pale; his thick, curly hair stood out at several different odd angles from his head, and his eyes were sunken and haunted with the nightmares that had stolen his sleep. Crouch, turning into a demon with bloody fangs; Susanna, turning into a succubus; horror and desire and a man's accusing, bloody corpse in a winding sheet, all mixed together in a ghastly brew. He was almost relieved when he was told to go to the house of the Standing Cat and give her the date of departure; I'll see her for what she is and free myself, he muttered to himself as he pulled the latch on the door beneath the house sign.

Mistress Hull scarcely looked up from her knitting at the bulky form that stooped to enter the low doorway.

"You can't go up; she doesn't want to see you."

"I've a message for her. About the sailing. She has to be ready."

"Then leave it here. She's sick. I'll take it up later."

"It's to be given to her personally."

"Then come back and give it to her later. She can't be disturbed." The needles never stopped moving as she looped the yarn first this way and then that, across her index finger, as the complex pettern crept across her needles and then spilled into her lap. The cat, offended by something in Ashton's demeanor, suddenly unrolled itself from her feet, got up, and stalked away, its tail held straight up in the air. Even the cat insults me here, thought Ashton. I won't be put off by this collection of viragos anymore.

"I have orders," he said, "and I haven't time to wait." He put a foot on the narrow spiral staircase to the upper rooms.

"You have time enough to wait around trying to peer into rooms where you had no business," announced Mistress Hull, without looking up and without losing a stitch. Ashton, one foot still on the stair, turned back to glare resentfully at the old lady. "—And time enough to insult Mistress Dallet's reputation." He hunched his broad back slightly, as if bracing against a high wind. His face was bleak and angry. "—And no time at all for the man in black."

"I won't be used," he said, turning and stumping up the staircase. Above, the door was open, and he could see right into the little room that was the parlor, bedroom and hall all in one. He knocked on the open door.

"You can't come in; she's sick and doesn't want to see anyone. Especially you," a voice said, and Nan appeared from the studio to slam the door. But she was too late.

"Sick indeed. I see no one in bed," he said, pushing into the room.

"You've done enough; go away," said Nan, standing directly in front of him. He could see past her into the studio. Susanna was sitting at her easel, working on a panel portrait two hands' breadth in height. The smell of oil and solvent came to him, all acrid, and he felt his eyes burn. "Go away, I say, it's indecent for you to see her like this." Ashton stood rooted to the spot, staring. Susanna's hair was unbound and flowing down her back like a waterfall; a circle of reddish ringlets clung about her face, all damp with sweat. Though it was midday, she was still in her long, white nightdress. It was speckled and dotted with flecks of color, wringing wet, and clinging to her body. Her face was flushed, sweat pouring down her temples, dripping down her cheeks and the sides of her nose, and sticking in droplets on her upper lip. Her eyes were glittering with the heat and craziness of fever. In her left hand was her palette; with the brush in her right she was laying highlights onto her subject's hair.

Ashton couldn't help noticing that even groggy with fever, her hand never lost its steadiness. Flick, flick, went the brush, and the portrait's hair went from a flat shapeless mass to waving and light filled, almost as if you could see each individual hair suddenly lie there, shining. The painting had an unusual brightness, the eyes striking and bold, as if the fever had spoken to the picture. In all that he had pictured to himself of her secret life of extravagance, murderous conspiracy, and unbridled love affairs, he had never imagined her like this. A light burned from within like a flame, her face was intent on her work, her body pink, round, and inviting wherever the wet nightgown stuck to it. She glowed, passionate, for things he barely understood. This was beauty beyond artifice, uncaring, and none of it for him. He looked, and looked again; she was entirely unconscious of the impression she made. That was the most devastating thing of all. He wanted her to turn; he wanted her to smile; he wanted her to include him in that tiny universe between her eyes and the easel. He was shattered with new knowledge. He had never wanted anybody more in his whole life.

"Quick, Nan, bar the door. The man in black is coming," she said, never looking up. "I have to finish. I have to finish before he takes me away. Will I be dead then, Nan? You must have Mistress Hull deliver the portrait and get the money for you both. I can't leave you without money." At the sound of her voice, he thought his heart would stop. But this was not the kind of speaking he wanted to hear.

"I, um, Archbishop Wolsey has ordered that you be ready in four days' time. Friday. Packed. One box only . . ." He was horrified and humiliated to discover this ghastly weakness in himself. Dark, raw, unholy desire. He started to back toward the open front door.

"See what you've done? This is what you've done to my darling. Now get out, Master Ashton, and don't come back unless you're invited," said Nan.

"I didn't . . . ," he started to say. But Susanna had put down her brushes.

"The man in black has come. I told you, Nan. I told you he'd be here." She stood and turned, staring at Ashton. "Ah, he's big. Bigger than I thought. His face looks like Master Ashton's. Master Ashton has ruined me, Nan. How will the archbishop have me paint if there are evil rumors? He'll send me away, and the guild will burn my paintings." The pupils of her eyes were huge and black. She seemed, to Ashton, to be looking over his shoulder at something. "Go away," she said. "Not yet; I haven't time." She took a step, then staggered. Nan tried to hold her up, but she was not strong enough to keep her upright.

"Be of some use, you great oaf," Nan said fiercely to Ashton, who stood paralyzed on the threshold. "We have to get her to bed. She's been like this for two days, vomiting and painting, and it's all your fault for the evil things you've said. Help me." His eyes shocked and wild, Ashton found himself shaking as he stepped back into the room and took the damp, disheveled figure in his arms. As he leaned over to put her in bed, he had to pry loose her hands, which had clutched tightly to his half-buttoned doublet. Her eyes bright and lunatic with fever, she stared intently at his face.

"Mother," she said, "you've come." Her face relaxed and her eyes closed. At that moment, Ashton felt all twisted inside, as if he didn't know which of them was whom, what was good or evil, real or unreal. As Nan pulled up the covers, he turned away and fled downstairs. His face burning with shame, he didn't even pause to hear Mistress Hull call after him, "Well, I hope you're happy *now*."

"Nan, I'm thirsty. You've let me sleep too long." The shutter was up and the room dark, but I could see afternoon sun creeping through a crack.

"You had a fever. We brought it down with cold compresses. You've been sleeping." Nan woke up from where she was dozing, sitting on the bench. But she looked confused and waspish all at once, I suppose from being up too much. I felt very guilty. I always get a fever when I work too hard, and it worries her. But what should I do? Quit working? Then who would buy the groceries?

"It was just a work fever, Nan, not a real one. Too many commissions. Lots of people would pray to have such a fever. Why are you so quiet? Has something happened? Oh, I've slept too long! And Mistress Ferrers's portrait not done yet! What day must we leave for the sailing? God, I wish we weren't going. I know it's an honor, and will make my fortune, but foreigners, Nan! Sometimes I think I would rather be painting Adam and Eves again." I sat up in bed. There was something I was trying to remember. Something had happened that was important, but I couldn't get it to stay in my mind. When I would get close to it, it would just fly away again.

"The portrait's done and sent off already. You've just forgotten, that's all." Nan was dipping water from the basin into a cup and looking sullen.

"Oh, *there's* my nightgown, right here on the stool. Why, it's got paint spots on it! Can't I keep *anything* without spots?" I held up my nightgown to inspect it. Too bad. Well, maybe I could take the spots out with turpentine tomorrow.

"Was I painting in it again?" Suddenly, as I was putting it on, I felt as weak as a snail.

"Again." I hadn't seen Nan so cross in ages. As I drank the water she'd given me, she opened the shutter, and warm light, dancing with dust motes, came in at the window. I noticed the whitewash peeling on the sill as the summer smells flooded in from the street.

"That's so odd; I don't remember a thing. It's done, did you say? Did anything else happen? Something happened. Did someone come?"

"We leave day after tomorrow. You're absolutely forbidden to get up until then. No painting. I don't want you even cleaning a single brush."

How strange I felt, the way one often does after a fever. Curiously light, noticing everything so precisely. The exact color of a blue-green fly that buzzed by the bedpost. The way the light flecked across the uneven grain of the table. And I could hear the sound of birds so clearly through the open, unglazed window.

"Now I remember. Nan, I had the strangest dream; it just came and went." Nan looked up suspiciously. "I dreamed that I was going to be with Mother and Father again. But I didn't want to go to heaven; it really wasn't very nice. Father was busy shouting and blaming me for skimping on the underpainting and laying on the color in one sitting. He shouted at me that painting *alla prima* is for bunglers and I was just wasting good materials, and I shouted right back at him it was just a new way I was trying out and he said new ways were for Italians. Oh, he was angry! So I said too bad, I wasn't staying anymore and I was going back, because I had some other new ideas I wanted to try out. Are you sure I finished that painting?"

"Yes you did. Mistress Hull carried it off. She said it was very fine."

"Then I had an awful dream, all mixed in with the first one. The man in black came for me. He was all bones. But Master Ashton came and chased him away with a big broom. He just swept him out the door."

"Ridiculous. That man sweep? He's too grand to do you such a favor. He thinks of no one but himself."

"Still, it seemed very real. Almost as if he were here. Are you sure he wasn't here?"

"No, never," she said, folding her arms. "Dreams can be liars. Remember, not one brush, not one drop of turpentine. I don't want you putting so much as a foot on the floor." I must have looked strange. Nan seemed suddenly concerned. "Does your head hurt?" she said, worried. "Do you want to read in that book of yours?" But for once, I didn't want to read. I could feel something odd inside, something small, like a speck or a seed, but I didn't know what it might grow into, and that left me troubled, with something I could not name turning over and over in my mind. I could hear a goose honking outside in the street, the clatter of horses, and the sound of children playing. I'll soon be gone from here, I thought. Maybe this feeling will be gone, too.

The fever had spent itself, but not Nan's worry, which spilled over onto everything. At last she decided that her worries were a sign that she was doomed to a watery grave.

"We leave tomorrow, and I can feel it in my bones," she confided to Mistress Hull, who had come with a potful of soup she believed to be especially strengthening.

"You haven't finished, dear, how can you make a long trip unless you get rid of that pallor? You must be rosy by tomorrow, so you can become rich, painting for foreign princes."

"How will I stand before God at the Resurrection, if the fishes have eaten my body and carried it away?" Nan interrupted. Nan was so fussy about finding her body at the Resurrection that she even gave her cut-off hair and nails a burial. Myself, I think it's God's business to find all the parts, not mine, so I just burn those things so witches won't get them. Also, everyone knows it is very bad luck if birds make a nest using your brushed-out hair, so you need to be careful not to leave it around. Mistress Hull looked very irritated at having her dreams of glory broken by Nan's gloom. She took away the soup dish I'd just finished and fixed her birdlike eyes on Nan.

"Nonsense," she said. "I just had my horoscope drawn, and it's not in the stars."

"Our lives in your stars?" Now Nan looked irritated.

"Of course. I'm to get rich and happy, and my Cat well married, all because of the intervention of influential friends—that's you, because I haven't any others."

"Your stars are false. I burned the hair last night, and that's a sure sign."

"You burned *my* hair last night? When did I say you could?" Now I was irritated, too. Nan has no right to go fortune-telling with my hair without asking first. Everyone knows if a lock of your hair doesn't flare up when you put it on the fire, you're doomed to death by drowning.

"It didn't blaze up?" asked Mistress Hull, looking worried.

"It didn't flare up much," announced Nan, gloomily triumphant. Mistress Hull nodded knowingly.

"Not *much*," she repeated. "Ha!"

"I plan to be shriven before we sail," said Nan, in a tone full of doom.

"If you cared about your friends, you'd make a vow to Saint Christopher's relics and come home safe. That's what I'd say." Mistress Hull nodded righteously.

"Care about your friends!" Nan stood up in such a rage she nearly overturned the bench beside the table. "Well, I like *that!* We're doomed to die a watery death, and our *friend* isn't even sorry!" Now I popped my feet out of bed, because they weren't noticing me anymore.

"Watery death, indeed! You just want it because you'd rather see us weeping than prosperous! Selfish, I call it! See if *I* pay for any funeral mass for *you!*" Mistress Hull grabbed up her pot and flounced out the door, giving it a hard slam.

"That dreadful old witch! Get dressed at once, Susanna. We're going to Saint Sepulchre's. Stars, she says! I'll show her! Is that silver shilling of mine still hidden in the sewing box? I'll put the biggest candle of all in front of that relic! And it won't do a speckle of good! I'll show *her* who knows more about doom!" It was late afternoon by the time we left the house, and as we set off up Fleet Lane, I couldn't get rid of the feeling that eyes were watching us.

Saint Sepulchre's is not far and very fair and large, being rebuilt by a rich man in my father's time. It has a tower with a great bell that rings the night before executions and sits right next to the Saracen's Head. Of course I had my usual problem, and by the time we were near the inn, dogs were following, ugly spotted ones and a poor yellow hound with only one ear. Nan stopped to shoo them, and I was admiring a woman with a dashing green velvet hat being helped from her horse in the courtyard, when there was the sound of a shutter opening above us. Then I looked up and it slammed all of a sudden. The dogs wouldn't go away at all but sat all around my feet with their tongues hanging out, and then clustered up so close around me as I walked that I very nearly tripped over them. But we shut them out of the church, which was very dim and cool and dusty, and I was glad to be rid of them.

Nan reconsidered buying a candle, and I could tell she thought they were too high; so we decided we would just pray at the relics in the north chapel, and promise a candle if the saint got us back safely. The afternoon light was all yellowy and dim in patches between the columns in the nave, and the altar was lost in shadow. Racks of candles flickered and smoked before painted wooden saints in their niches. Here and there were chantry priests going about their business, businessmen from the parish, bent on asking favors from heaven, as well as a lady all in silk with her maid come to visit a tomb. The chapel seemed deserted except for the dark, musty carvings, and the most dismal triptych at the altar. There was a Descent from the Cross, with Christ dripping in blood to hide the fact the man had painted Him with bony legs like a grasshopper and facial bones all wrong. Also you couldn't tell the men from the women except that some were wearing turbans to show that it was far away in the Holy Land, and the Roman soldiers were wearing French armor, which I suppose the painter thought was exotic. I found it hard to have religious thoughts in front of that painting. But I also did not feel so bad about all those vines I'd painted on Adam when I saw that trick with the blood.

There was just a bit of dim, colored glow about the window, so you couldn't really see the thigh bone and the piece of hair shirt in the saint's reliquary at all, even though it had a little crystal panel to let people peek in. Besides, it was set too far up for me to see properly, in a niche high on the wall with a lot of dusty woodwork carved with ugly faces and plantlike things under it. Over it was the saint, carved in wood and painted very gaily, with his gown all tucked up for wading, and with Baby Jesus on his shoulder. There was a bank of candles lit in front of the statue that gave off the rich, heavy odor of melting beeswax. Above them, twinkling in the reflected light of the candles, little ships and hearts in silver were hanging up around the reliquary as thank offerings. I was just feeling embarrassed that Nan was being so stingy with the saint when I thought I saw a shape in darker black standing quietly in the black shadows behind the screen that stood on the far side of the chapel altar.

"*Pssst*, Nan, do you see somebody there?" I whispered, pulling on her sleeve.

"Why of course she does," said a man's voice. The shadow moved and became visible. I could see a stray bit of light catch pale green eyes that seemed to glow in the dark. Above them, two coils of white rose from his forehead like ram's horns. There was the sound of a boot on the hard tile floor and the soft whisper of his velvet robe as he stepped toward us out of the shadows. "I, ah, discerned you might pay a visit to the saint on the eve of your journey. And I craved, for the sake of your husband, whom I loved like a son, to give you some assistance to help you meet the demands of foreign travel. And, too, I can offer you a letter of introduction. . . ."

"Bishop Wolsey has arranged everything for my convenience," I answered, my mouth almost too dry to speak.

"Ah, Bishop Wolsey. Tell me, has he given you a letter to deliver?"

"I don't need letters of introduction. I'll be serving the princess."

"No message? How strange. Not even a painting delivered by your hand?"

"Why would he entrust me, a woman, with letters? I go to paint two wedding miniatures. I am sorry, I must be going." I dodged away from him, but he was too fast. In a few long strides, he had caught up to me. He grabbed me by the shoulder and whirled me around, pressing me back into the screen. The agreeable mask dropped and I could see lunacy glittering in the eyes.

"Don't lie to me. I have means to see secret truths. The mirror showed you plotting; I saw you in your chamber making secret conversation with a man in a dark cloak. Ha! You're surprised? Never underestimate my powers. And now I tell you, the secrets your husband stole from me—you traded them to Wolsey and carry them now to France. Who would ever suspect a woman? But ever since you gave the bishop your favors, he . . ."

"I did *not*," I said, trying to push his hand away.

"How *dare* you!" said Nan, who is ordinarily very quiet around gentlefolk.

"Ashton has betrayed you," said Crouch. "Don't you understand? Ashton is mine." He leaned closer. I couldn't move. I turned my face away from Crouch's to keep his foul breath from me. My bones felt liquid with revulsion.

"Sieur Crouch, how well met, and how unexpected. Surely I do not interrupt some important business?" A foreign voice, even and polite, spoke from beside the columns just outside the chapel entrance. A strange man, with a narrow, intelligent face, was standing there in the nave behind Sir Septimus just like a guardian angel. Crouch took his hand off me and turned to meet him.

"Bellier," I heard him say.

"I have long yearned to meet the famous paintrix, Sieur Crouch, and when I saw her pass beneath the window of my little lodging, I hurried forth, only to find that you seem to have taken up collecting miniatures ahead of me. Perhaps you could introduce us?" Crouch stood there, too furious to speak. "No? Please accept my apologies for being so abrupt, Madame Dolet, but I am Maître Bellier, theologian, traveler, and collector of rare works, at your service. I have in my possession an exquisite allegory of yours, *Adam and Eve in the Garden of Eden*, which I would love to discuss with you sometime at your leisure." He bowed grandly, which seemed to enrage Crouch even further.

"So it's you who have it, Bellier. That explains your gloating image. I saw your evil eye glinting in the gold. Is it you who has the dark cloak? By coming here you have revealed your secret. How dare you think you can come so as to gloat at me? Do you know my powers?" At the word *powers* Bellier sniffed and smiled condescendingly. Though Crouch was taller and wider and more threatening than the strange man, it warmed my heart to see how this Master Bellier seemed to stop him dead with his piercing glance and cynical, knowing smile. There was a weakness in Crouch; he was vulnerable to someone. The sudden paralysis of will that Crouch had caused in me began to fade. "But you do not yet have all of it, remember that," Crouch said to the foreigner. I would have been pleased to see him so angry and so rattled, except that his anger also contained something very frighteningly insane, which made my hair want to stand on end. And what was this "it" that he didn't have all of? What was stirring his mind to ever-greater madness? While the two of them faced each other, I began to slither sideways as silently as possible. Nan saw what I was doing, and tiptoed to the chapel entrance. Crouch put a hand on his dagger, but Bellier just tipped back his head and smiled, and I could see the hilt of a short sword protruding from an opening in his foreign robe. I took another few steps.

"Ah, Sieur Crouch, I see Madame Dolet is anxious to return home before evening. I am afraid I must take leave of you to accompany her on her way. I wouldn't want her to be struck by a *falling tile.*" I couldn't understand a thing that he meant, but it seemed to strike Sir Septimus very hard and make his eyes blaze with rage. He didn't take a step as Master Bellier took my arm as if I were some great lady and led me out into the nave, with Nan following behind.

The late-afternoon shadows were long as we stepped out of the great arched doorway of the church. The dogs had tired of waiting, I guess, and were gone. As we passed the open courtyard gateway of the Saracen's Head, I could see that a merchant, his mules, and several drivers were crowded inside, and hear the cries and commotion of ostlers and stable boys running to their assistance.

"I am afraid, Madame Dolet, that the Sieur Crouch is quite evil," said Master Bellier, in an agreeable voice as we passed the corner of Saint George's Lane.

"I already know that," I answered.

"You would. A painter of such mastery could not miss the signs in his face. The crosses on the line of Mars ... and he has grown quite frantic of late.... Now, about that charming allegory of Eden that you created, tell me about the symbolism. We do not, for example, see Adam's face, and he is entirely covered with vines...." I was silent with humiliation. That is how bad business and a sinful past come to trap a person just as she is on the eve of truly remarkable success and re-spectability. It was just like the moral tale in chapter the fourth of *The Good Wyfe's Book of Manners* only worse because it was happening to me. If Crouch hadn't been following me with evil designs in his heart I would have run away from that foreigner with his earnest, probing questions, but instead I just answered with only one word at a time, which wasn't very polite.

"Why are you so quiet, Madame Dolet? Is there some secret you wish to impart. Your delightful art ... Tell me, what significance has the mountain?" Gingerly, he led me around a pile of entrails and kitchen garbage in the street, keeping me under the overhang of the houses as we passed into Fleet Lane.

"I copied it," I said.

"Copied it?"

"From another painter." We were almost at my door.

"Ah, *another* painter, yes," he said, in a strange voice. "One living here?" I couldn't bear to tell him. Suppose my father who was already so mad at me up in heaven that he said I was worse than an Italian heard him?

"No," I said.

"So charming, so modest," said Maître Bellier. "Do you ever travel? I often do. I maintain my principal residence in Paris, though it has been ill kept since I became a widower." Mistress Hull had the shop shutter down for air, and you could see right into where Saint Simon with the squinty eyes and misplaced navel reigned in glory over his corner of ghastly painted saints. Again, Maître Bellier smiled his amused, cynical smile, and I knew right away he was an excellent judge of art.

"The House of the Standing Cat. Your house, I believe? We shall have to speak again, Madame Dolet. I know it is fated." He looked deep into my eyes. Now he was white haired and rather too old for me, but you know how foreigners are. And he really did have an interesting sort of face, with excellent, if somewhat narrow bones beneath the skin. "My admiration for you will lead our destinies to intertwine," he said in a deep, meaningful way. But I was all stiff and pink with embarrassment, because I was sure it was my Adam and Eves that had stirred him up. I hoped he would go away quickly and not make a scene. Luckily he was a gentleman and went away after kissing my fingertips, which I wiped off.

"Well, *there* was a gentleman," said Nan. "Here we've never seen him before, and he pops up and does you a service just when you needed it. I do believe he's interested in you."

"He just likes paintings, Nan. You shouldn't mistake him."

"No, I can tell. He's interested in more than paintings. Otherwise he wouldn't have mentioned that he's a widower and doesn't always live in an inn. I wonder what that house he mentioned is like? He seems well-off, too. Did you see his gold chain? And that ring with the curious design? The ruby was the largest I've ever seen. And here we are going to France. Think about it, Susanna. You might do well."

"I thought we were doomed, Nan."

"Oh, that was before we visited the saint. Now, you see, he's listened, and this strange gentleman is a Sign."

"Another Sign? Well, at least you think this one's favorable. There's only one thing I don't understand."

"And what's that, my treasure?"

"Just how did he know where we live?"

Master Ashton came the next morning before dawn with the horses and stood outside the door while I tied up my box, even though I asked him in. He just looked away down the stairs as if he were thinking and kept opening and shutting the fingers on his left hand with his right, in some odd sort of absentminded gesture. I noticed he held his left elbow close to his side, as if it were stiff. His hair, too, was new combed, all dampened in a valiant attempt to make it lie flat beneath his hat, and his face fresh shaven and quite pink with recent fierce scrubbing. He was wearing his good livery, a foolish thing for a long trip. I noticed his eyes followed my every move.

"What's that?" he said, eyeing my easel, all folded up next to my box and tied with twine.

"It's not a box, so it doesn't count. It's my easel. The archbishop can't expect me to paint without one, you know."

"You should get another there."

"They don't grow on trees, even in France. And this one I had made especially for my work." He growled, but he had to agree, even though he didn't like it.

"And what's in this thing," he asked as he shouldered my box, "lead shot?"

"Only a few little things. Just what I need to get by. Nan said I should have been allowed two boxes—one for necessaries, and one for paints."

"Nobody gets two boxes. Only gentry," he said, tramping down the tightly coiled staircase, the box on his right shoulder. It was packed so tightly it didn't even rattle: two pairs of stockings, an underskirt, and my nightdress padded the tightly rolled bundles of knives, burnishing tools, brushes, chalks, and dried pigments. Weighing it down were my muller and slab for grinding colors and a heavily sealed bottle of sepia. Finally, squashed in flat on the bottom of the little chest, there were my books and sheets of good-quality paper, several plain, turned wooden cases, and the last of my parchment, including that good old piece with the writing, which was now shrunken and full of holes where I had cut away bits for use.

Outside, his servant was waiting holding the horses, an old brown mare and a big, rawboned roan gelding, with pillions behind the saddles, and a swaybacked packhorse from Wolsey's stable with another bundle and a seaman's chest strapped to the packsaddle.

"Oh," I said, looking at the packhorse's burden, "are you coming, too?" Pink light was beginning to stain the sky and paint the fronts of the half-timbered houses with a soft, rosy gold.

"I've been sent to France on other work. Exiled, really. Probably thanks to that weasel, Tuke." He paused in thought and drew his mouth into a grim line. Then he looked at me a long time. "Don't think I'm going to be trailing you about anymore. Seeing you to the fleet is the last of this job." He turned abruptly and handed up my easel and my box to his man, who loaded them onto the packsaddle. Nan handed him her bundle, and he strapped everything down tightly. There was a mounting block before the Goat and Jug, and there he led the big roan to boost me up behind. It had a wicked eye, I thought. For once, all was silent behind the latched shutters of the tavern. I'll miss you, street, I thought. I'll even miss the Goat and Jug. Ashton had gathered up the reins, and the horse shifted under us. Mistress Hull and Cat stood in the doorway, weeping—Mistress Hull with missing us and Cat with annoyance that she could not go see the court of France herself.

"Good-bye and Godspeed, Tom," cried Mistress Hull, embracing him. "I won't be recognizing you when you come back, all full grown and filled out." Ashton turned suddenly in the saddle.

"What do you mean? He's not going," he said.

"Not going?" I answered. "But he must—you promised. . . ."

"You're not the Queen of Persia, Mistress Dallet, and you have no need of such a train of followers. One maidservant is all you are allowed." He looked at the figures in our doorway, almost puzzled to see the shock in their expressions. "Didn't they send word?" he asked.

"Never," I said, clutching the cantle of his saddle and addressing his back. "You know he has to go. I told you why."

"That tall story about an assassin?" he said scornfully, looking again at Tom's stricken face. The boy had come to stand at his stirrup. "Is it true?" Ashton asked. His voice had softened, and he sounded puzzled.

"Yes," said the boy.

"And for that you left your master?"

"It was his plan, sir. I know the man saw me. Later he came to my master's, asking after me. My master told him I had died of the pestilence."

"What do you know of grinding colors?"

"Mistress Susanna uses such little that . . ."

"In short, you know nothing at all, and she has no earthly need for you." He shook his head, with the strangest look of commiseration. "Still, it could be true, why else . . . ?" he said to himself. Then he undid the purse at his belt and leaned out of the saddle to press a few coins into Tom's hand. "Here," he said, "I'm sorry, but the bishop himself approved the list. Go find yourself another master. A woman painter's apprentice? It suits a boy ill. Find an upstanding man who can raise you to a proper trade." At these last words I bit my lips hard to keep the rage from coming out. All in a moment, he'd belittled me, my trade, and thrown away Tom the way you'd drown a litter of kittens, doubtless telling himself it was all for the best and he was an unusually thoughtful fellow. Men! They think they are the gods of creation and capable of passing judgment on anything. As the horses clop-clopped out of Fleet Lane, I writhed with the thought of having to sit as close as a pair of lovers all the way to Dover.

"Quit moving so, I feel the saddle shift," he said, leaning over to feel the girth. We had come nearly even with the cistern, on our way back to Bridewell, to join the rest of the bishop's party that was going to join the wedding fleet.

"I'm not moving at all," I said.

"It's loose. The old windbag puffed himself up. Let go a moment." I let go of Ashton's waist and he took a foot out of the stirrup and pushed it back to get at the girth to tighten it. "*Aha.* He feels me pull it up and puffs again. A sign of my latest fall from favor, to be given the most spoiled nag in the stable." He grunted, leaning down again to check the girth. At that very moment something shot between us, over his bent back. There was a hollow sounding *"thunk"* as the missile embedded itself in one of the timbers of the overhanging second story of the house near us.

"My God!" I cried. "What was that?"

"Get out of here, before he reloads!" cried Ashton to his servant, but the sound of the bolt and the alarm in our voices startled our horse, which threw its head up and scrambled sideways. "Damned screw!" he said, trying to bring the roan's head in and put his foot back in the stirrup at the same time. There was a vicious hiss as something passed directly in front of us; the horse rose beneath me, and Ashton's broad back came straight at my nose. The houses swam crazily around my head as the horse reared and in almost the same moment I found myself hitting the street hard. Lying there limp and still feeling my bones, I saw the horse rear again, as Ashton, one foot still out of the stirrup, held his seat, still cursing. Shutters were flung open.

"Get that nag out of here! Can't you even ride?" a man's voice shouted. But he could ride; I'd never seen a better man worse mounted. The crazy horse filled the street like an explosion, and he was still on it, sweat rolling down his face, his jaw grim, his eyes determined.

"Close the shutters; someone is shooting!" he cried. Perversely, at his cry, all the rest of the shutters on the street opened, and filled with nightcapped faces. All in an instant, I thought I saw, from where I lay in the street, still staring groggily upward, a movement among the bells in the tower over the cistern.

At that very moment the loosened saddle rolled beneath the horse's belly, pulling the whole harness with it, and I heard Ashton fall to the ground with a crash. There was a scuffle, the clatter of horse-shoes on stone, and the rattle and jingle of loose tack, and I saw that one foot was still entangled in the stirrup. Steel-clad hooves danced perilously close to his head as he struggled to pull his foot loose. Curs-ing, he lost his grip and was thrown back flat into the road, still held by his foot. The horse, eyes rolling, bucked once and began to head away in big strides, Ashton still struggling and entangled. If the roan took it into its head to run, Ashton would be dragged to death over the stones. I could see him trying to protect his head with his arms. There were shouts of alarm from the windows. I pulled myself up and ran, limping, for the horse's head, but as it saw me run, it tossed its head away and moved faster. Its evil yellow eye glared at me, and it showed me the big, ugly green-flecked teeth in its foaming, open mouth.

By this time, Ashton's man had turned back and dismounted, leav-ing Nan holding the pack mule, but he was not close enough to reach us in time. I snatched at a dangling rein, and pulled hard. The horse whirled about, dragging Ashton's struggling body in an arc across the stones and through the muck in the gutter at the center of the street. His entrapped foot was near my hand. Dropping the rein, I heaved at the stirrup with both hands, forcing his foot loose. The horse, half bucking and half running, the saddle dragging and rattling beneath its belly, ran off down the street, accompanied by a chorus of guffaws out of the open windows. Ashton lay in the street, not moving, blood run-ning down his dirt-stained face. His eyes were open.

"Headed straight for the stable," he whispered. "I'll never live this down."

"Is anything broken?" I asked.

"My reputation. My best coat. My pride. Maybe my head. I swear Tuke bribed someone to set me up with that old screw. He can't ride a baby's pet donkey, and now I can't show my face at the stable. Jesus ... my back ..." He winced as he tried to move his legs. "It's just as well I'm headed for France, if I can ever get up. I can hide my shame there until this is forgotten. If ever."

"Look there, I can see a bolt in the timber. Someone was trying to kill you. If you hadn't bent over at that very moment, it would have been in you, I swear."

"They'll think I just produced the bold so strengthen my story. It's impossible to worm out of being the butt of a practical joke. Especially one of Tuke's, that smooth, smiling son of a bitch."

"I can tell them it wasn't made up. Nan and your man can, too."

"They are servants. And as for you, they'll say you're just amorous. Ashton . . . goes courting. A joke . . . for every stable boy and page in London . . ." He groaned and tried to sit up. "God, my head," he said.

"You see how easy it is to break a reputation," I said, but he was too busy thinking about himself and sitting there and checking his bruises to listen.

"Master, are you hurt? Take the other horse." His man's grizzled face was full of concern as he knelt down close to help him.

"No, Will, I'll walk. I wish to wallow in my degradation. Go ahead of us and get the surgeon. My head's cracked." Still lying there, he wiped the blood from his eyes with the back of his hand, then inspected it. "And I'm cut," he said, as if taking inventory. Slowly, painfully, he got up out of the gutter. He was standing now, wiping off his clothes and looking glumly up at the faces that lined the open windows. There was the sound of laughter as he bent down to pick up his hat from the street.

"There's an elegant cavalier," said a voice.

"A fine way to impress a lady," added another.

"What did he say they were doing? Shooting? A likely story." Silently, Robert Ashton plucked the bolt from the timber above his head and stuck it in his belt.

"But, Master Ashton, the man who shot?"

"I'm sure he's long gone. There're too many witnesses now. The people here would set up the hue and cry, and he'd be caught."

"I'll walk with you," I said. "It's not so far, and it will work the bruises out." He didn't say a thing. His pores oozed humiliation.

"Stupid. Stupid. I should have checked sooner. But no. I had to be off. Taking you. Stupid. Women." He shook his head.

"Women? Why do you say women? Are we at fault somehow? Men are crazy, I say. How can you be more upset about your horse returning with a loose saddle than about a man shooting a crossbow out of a tower at you?"

"Not *a* crossbow. The bastard must have had two. How else could he have reloaded so quickly? No. He wasn't shooting to hit me." Suddenly I had a horrible thought.

"Suppose he was shooting to hit me?" I asked.

"You? Whatever for? No, if he wanted to hit anyone, it was me. If I wanted to conjure up a conspiracy, I'd say it was someone who knew of my business abroad. But no, I swear it was some fellow Tuke hired, to give me a scare, and maybe make the horse shy in the hopes I'd not checked the girth, which I hadn't. No, he knew me, how it's been for me. . . . Whoever did this knew me too well to be anyone but Tuke. . . . He figured I'd be rattled this morning, I might not check. Who else but Tuke?" He was limping along, his head straight ahead, not even looking at me as he spoke. Sometimes he shook it as if an invisible argument was going on in his mind. He seemed almost as if he were talking to himself.

"Rattled? By what? Why that?"

"Why do you think?" he said, avoiding my eyes, then hunching his shoulders and setting his head down. We had come to the gate of the stable yard now. It was lined with ragamuffins, all laughing and pointing. He glanced up at the crowd ahead of him with damaged eyes but set his head back down again, as if facing a high wind, and walked straight forward, looking at no one. Knights and priests, already mounted for the journey, tipped back their heads and guffawed at the sight of Robert Ashton, once arrogant and officious in the wearing of his master's rank, now filthy and bedraggled, trailing a spoiled, runaway horse home on foot. Even better, he was escorting the stuck-up freak, the lady paintrix, equally bedraggled and brought low. My good dress, I thought, brushing off a bit of dirt I'd missed on one elbow. I limped as I followed behind him. I ached everywhere. It wouldn't make the trip to Dover any better. A fine joke. It it was a joke.

Nan had gotten there first and brought us wet towels, and the bishop's barber-surgeon put a bandage on Master Ashton's head, right there in the stable yard. Then there was a sudden, pregnant, silence, as a stable boy with a sarcastic smile led the very same horse, resaddled, up the to the mounting block. Ashton heaved a sigh, lifted up the stirrup and felt the girth. It was tight. The big, bony roan had made himself as round as a barrel. Under the eyes of the whole party, Ashton led the horse a few steps. The horse heaved a sigh, too, an even heavier one than Ashton's, as it deflated its puffed-up belly. With a wickedly fast movement, before the horse could change its mind, Ashton tightened the girth. There was a titter from an elderly chaplain, then a suppressed snort from a clerk who stood under the stable arch, his arms folded. Then it broke loose. Gentleman and priests, scribes and stableboys, they all laughed. The ruder ones even slapped their legs. Ashton stared straight at the ground under the horse's belly. The back of his neck was crimson. He didn't say a word for miles.

Our little party of the bishop's servants, at every turning of the way, was joined by other parties as streams join a great river. Every lord of the realm, it seemed, had demanded the honor of escorting the princess and her suite to the ships, so in order to displease none, all were going, each with a more magnificent train than the next. As we crossed London Bridge into Southwark, among the bustle of mounted knights, liveried servants, pages with banners, and ornamented litters, I saw a familiar little figure dodge behind an abbot on a silver-harnessed mule. Tom was following us.

The weather was blustery, and the sky slate gray and threatening rain as we rode on toward Dover. The road was thick with riders in glittering armor, pennants flying, with servants, with clerks and attendants, lords on fine gennets and ladies on palfreys and in litters, that stretched in a train so long I could hardly see the beginning of it winding away in the distance ahead of us. At the head of the procession were royal guards and the king and princess riding together, the pregnant queen beside them in her litter. This I know because I heard it, but not because I saw it. Everyone of importance was there: the greatest lords of the realm dressed in gold chains and rich gowns especially made for the occasion. Four hundred knights and barons, two hundred gentlemen and esquires, and a thousand palfreys clattered through the fall mud beneath the leaden sky. Over a hundred wagons filled with great ladies moved ponderously along the road.

Behind this grandeur trudged servants, musicians, secretaries, and footmen. Mounted stablemen led heavy horses, gift palfreys, and amblers. Guards surrounded carts loaded with pavilions, with the gowns and jewels of the trousseau, with the dowry plate. In the midst of his lesser rabble, Nan and I made our way on horseback, mounted behind Ashton and his servant, our packhorse trailing behind.

Fearful of falling, sore and bruised and still washed out from the fever, I clung to his waist, feeling how he moved with the shifting motion behind us. What an irony, I thought. If I didn't know him, this would be exciting, sitting behind a strange man like this. But with all that's gone on, it's only an agony I wish were over. His back was still bad, I could tell. Or maybe his ribs. When I held too tightly, I could hear his breath come hard, but he wouldn't make a sound. As the hours passed, my head dropped until it was resting on his shoulder blades. He still smelled of dust, and of the gutter, and of something else, strong scented, a man-smell that I had never smelled on Rowland Dallet, who favored perfume, like a dandy. Mile after mile, I could feel the misery rolling off him in silent waves.

"Master Ashton, how much longer?" We could hear the cries and whips of the drovers. Around us were a ragtag bunch of servants, some on horseback, some on foot. We didn't ride near the others, because the roan had a nasty habit of trying to bite strange horses. It had a big, rough gait like a cart horse, which ate up the miles and left every joint aching. I suppose that's why it hadn't been sold. It did travel. When I die and go to purgatory, it will be on that horse. I hated its big yellow teeth and malignant little eyes, and stiff, ugly mane like a row of bristly hairbrushes. Its coat stank, and its sweat stained my skirts. Master Ashton rode it with an extraheavy bit and a riding crop that could slice a mail coat.

No answer.

"Master Ashton, can't we rest?"

No answer. The flat, gray September sky stretched overhead, endless and heavy. Beside us, behind us, and ahead of us, the wedding escort crept on through the mud. We could hear the screech of seagulls in the distance.

"We can't stop. We must keep up."

"What are you thinking? Speak to me. You don't speak even when we dismount. Will speaks to Nan. See over there? He tells a joke, and they both laugh. I still think about that fall. I could have been killed.

You could have been killed. Say something and stop my mind from turning."

"I'm not your jester, even if the archbishop's entire household now sees me as one."

"Someone tried to kill you, and failed, and that's all you think of?"

"Someone tried to humiliate me, and succeeded. That's what I think of." Now we could smell the ocean—a rich, salty smell like a barrelful of mussels.

"Where is the ocean? I can't see it."

"We're nowhere near yet. You're not supposed to see it. The wind just brings the smell of it." From pure fatigue and soreness and irritation as well as the last of the fever, I could feel tears coming up, though I didn't make a sound.

"What are you doing?" he said. "You're soaking down the back of my neck."

"I'm tired, I hurt, and I fell off a horse, and I wish I were home in bed," I answered. There was a long pause.

"I suppose I should have thanked you," he said.

"I didn't want you dragged," I said.

"There's more dignity in being carried home on a litter than limping home covered with horse dung," he said.

"You wouldn't know unless you tried it the other way," I answered.

"I have," he said. "That time the bolt hit home." And then he was quiet again for a long time. The ocean smell was stronger now, blown on a stiff wind, and seagulls circled overhead beneath the low, gray sky. On the hills ahead of us was the great castle that guards the cliffs above the docks. Nearly there. But then the first heavy drops fell on my face.

"Damn, rain," he growled. Ahead of us, horsemen began to hurry, urging their mounts to a stiff trot. "We are so far behind that every corner of the castle and every great house nearby as well will be stuffed full. I swear, even lords' servants will go bedless tonight."

"Surely, the great Wolsey's liverymen . . ."

"Will be last in line. Have you seen the number of lords gathered here? We'll have to fend for ourselves. If we cut away from the road now, we may yet get a place at an inn by the docks that I know. Hold on, we'll have to make better speed." Now was when I regretted my cozy rooms all the more; indeed, they seemed cozier and cozier to me as we left the parade of toiling servants and soldiers on the muddy road and trotted bumpety, bump across the open fields with the pack horse trailing behind on a lead rope, its head and neck stretched out as it pulled to try to slow us down. I should have stayed with the Adam and Eves, I thought. If only I hadn't gone and put Rowland Dallet's face on the serpent. Everything was all his fault. Rowland Dallet, Rowland Dallet, what else will you be doing to me? All because of him, I was bumping along in the rain with sore bones and wishing I'd offered up something much more impressive to Saint Christopher when I'd had the chance.

But then the wind got stronger and the rain heavier and by the time we were in the city so was everyone else, and all looking for shelter, too, and the White Horse was all full, and so were the Castle and the Lion and we were soaked through and shivering. Finally Master Ashton found a low tavern at the Sign of the Mermaid, which was full of sailors lying drunk on benches shouting and singing before the fire and other persons who appeared to have no daily occupation.

A one-eyed man in a dirty apron told him there was room for our horses in his stable but we would have to pay double for feed because of the princess and all, and feed was very dear these days. Then he winked the only eye he had and said he had a bed, too, the very last in town, and that would be double, as well. Master Ashton's ears grew very red, and I could feel my face getting all hot, so I turned it away. Then he stamped on the floor and cracked that dangerous riding crop on his boot, and said if there was only one bed fit, then he would sleep on a bench before the fire like all those sailors. But then he changed his mind when he found out there were two beds in the room and the big one was already full of six gentlemen travelers. Also the one-eyed man said the second bed would really hold five and it would cost extra for him not to sell the last place in it, because he was only a poor man and had so many expenses. I might have laughed at Master Ashton once, the way his face twitched with disgust and his eyes rolled, but I didn't have the heart for it just then.

We ate supper in the tavern sitting on our boxes so they wouldn't be stolen, but Nan seemed to do all the talking, and I could see Master Ashton's eyes were sunken in; his face was turning grayish and blood had soaked through the bandage around his head. When we were finally dried out, Master Ashton's man went to sleep with Bishop Wolsey's horses so they would not vanish in the night or turn into different horses with lame feet, and we stumped upstairs with a single rushlight that Master Ashton held up ahead of us. In the narrow, slant-roofed attic room with the beds, one of the gentleman travelers was already in bed asleep, fully clothed, with his boots on. Another was drunk and pissing in the fire, and his friends were commenting on how much wine he held. The room was smelly with mildew and stale beer and unwashed men, and I could feel things crawling on my ankles.

"Oh, this nasty bed. I swear the linen's never been washed. And what's this? Ugh! It's full of bedbugs!" Nan was very disgusted and began to shake out the linen and bedding in the largish bed we had rented. I could see the bedbugs all scuttle away into the cracks.

"Hey, you woman, don't shake those bedbugs out here!"

"Yes, every man to his own bedbugs!"

The rain was battering on the closed shutters harder than ever. I couldn't imagine how anyone could sail for France in this awful weather.

"There's a lucky man. Two women for himself, and none for us. Share, you wretch." Master Ashton put his hand on his knife, but he swayed slightly. They took it for drink. I was glad he was sturdy-looking.

"You'll answer to the King's Almoner if these women do not depart safely for France in the morning." His speech was harsh and unsteady.

"Oho, Bishop Wolsey's doxy, eh?" Now that made me just furious, because it is disgusting when a gentleman, even a drunken one of small family, cannot tell a respectable widow from a woman of ill fame. All that anger pushed away my fatigue and made my tongue sharp.

"God will punish you for your wicked speech," I said firmly. "I am paintrix to the bishop's household, and I go to France to paint the queen and gentlefolk so that men here can know their faces. I come with my respectable woman, here, that my lord of York appointed especially to attend me, and if it were not so very crowded in this town we would be in a much more elegant establishment, and you would not be worthy even to see my work, which is not for vulgar people with no taste, but only for great gentlemen and princes." Master Ashton's eyes flicked sideways at me, and I could tell he was surprised that I could be so firm. But I know how to deal with drunken rogues because of living across from the Goat and Jug for so long.

Then those drunken fellows drew back and pretended to make their eyes wide with awe. "Oh, my, listen to this. A paintrix! Who ever heard of such a thing?" "*She* speaks only to princes. Should we bow?"

But I am used to having to prove myself, which is why I brought so many things that were not clothes in my box.

"If you are respectful, I will show you. Which of you has a sweetheart or a mother who would be pleased to have the image of his face?" That set them a-quarreling and joking, and while they were distracted, Nan opened my box and handed me paper cut the size of a man's palm, and I untied my little easel and unfolded it and stood it on its four little legs. When I saw them stare at it, I knew I had them, tired as I was. At last they managed to push one of their number forward, the youngest, and I seated him by the fire, wet my pencil, and began to draw in plain sepia.

As the likeness began to merge from the fluid black lines, I could hear the rowdies grow quiet and feel them pushing and crowding to watch. "Your face," I said to my sitter, who was perched on his trunk. "Don't turn it that way or you'll spoil the picture." He struggled to keep his eyes from blinking. Master Ashton had seated himself beside me on the bench. I could feel his eyes watching my hands and hear his breathing grow still, as if swallowed up in the watching. When the likeness was taken, they all crowded around the fellow to see and compare and after that were much more orderly, since they each secretly hoped to coax another drawing out of me before we departed. Master Ashton, his head supported on his hands, just looked dully from them to me and back again, as if there were something he couldn't understand. What was it he was thinking of me?

Still, all those rowdy gentlemen started to joke again when Nan put the bolster down the center of the bed, and then, with a firm look on her face, got in on one side of the bolster, fully clothed, and Master Ashford sat all slumped down on the other, also still fully clothed, and started wiping off his boots.

"Master Ashton, you sleep in your boots?" I asked from where I sat on the far side of Nan, taking off my muddy shoes.

"I don't need them walking away in the night," he said. "See how the others are doing? This is not Bridewell."

"But what about your spurs?"

"I'm wrapping them in my cloak, here, as I suggest you do with your shoes, if you wish to wear them tomorrow." So I rolled up my things in my cloak also, to make a pillow the way he did, since the bolster was being used for another purpose. But with Nan and the bolster in the middle, that left me with the edge of the bed, which is the coldest, since the covers never seem to reach far enough. My worries made me stay awake that night, staring at the ceiling and listening to the bedbugs drop from it back into the bed. Plop. Plop. Scratch and scratch. I could hear Robert Ashton groaning and crying out in his sleep and the other men turning and scratching vermin all night, while Nan snored like a trumpet, whiz, *wheeze*, whiz, *wheeze*. I had mixed up thoughts that gave me troubles, such as, suppose they laugh at me in France the way those knights and clerks laughed in the stable yard. Suppose I get a ghastly disease? Suppose I never see home again? Too late I regretted the smallness of the candle we had offered, and that only on account, too, which might be construed by the saint as rather cheap. There I was, all alone in the dark, even though there were people crowded all around me in that smelly, bug-ridden room. This is not how people are supposed to set out to make their fortunes. I wasn't so sure I hadn't dreamed it all. The saint must have been annoyed with only the promise of a cheap candle.

"It *was* rather cheap, but so like you, Susanna," said a charming voice in the dark, or perhaps in a dream I was having.

"Hadriel, you're back!" I think I said or dreamed. There in the damp, dark cool stood a quiet shape, with a soft, glowing face and the funniest, knowing smile. "Stay with me; I'm frightened here," I said.

"Oh, I can't do that," he answered. "I'm so busy inspiring people. Now here, now there. Such a job! I haven't half gotten through my list." I thought I saw him hold up a roll of pale vellum. He opened it partway, and I saw it was crammed with thousands of names, written very small, all in gold. "Just look at all these!" he said, pointing to the letters with a pale finger. "Italians, French, Flemish, and everything in between, and not a woman on it. All over the place! I tell you, I spend most of my time traveling these days." He stretched his wings, first one, then the other, the way a cat stretches its legs. Then he ruffled the feathers on them with a soft, *brrrr* sound. "Now tell me," he said, "how do they expect me to have a bit of time for my own ideas? But I just *had* to stop by anyway. You *are* one of my favorites, you know, list or not."

"But, Hadriel, I've never done these things before. There's no one to show me the way. I'm in the wrong place. You know I'm supposed to stay home and be married and cook, except that Master Dallet spoiled it all."

"Show you the way? You *are* funny, Susanna. Here I've gone and broken all the rules for you, and you want me to just stand about being a signpost in the bargain! Honestly! Now that was a very nice little face you did today. And watching you use it to put them all in their place like that; why, it was worth coming just for the entertainment of it! You know, it was all getting so *ordinary* before I ran into you. Susanna, can you believe how *dull* the archangels would have the world if they could? Now, listen to me: just you look closely, and the way will show you itself." He started to fade.

"Stay, just stay another minute," I begged.

"Oh, my dear, if you only knew how many visitations I have to make tonight. Simply *impossible!* They really ought to give me more assistance. Busy, busy, busy. It's just a *whirl!* And you have to take *time* to do things right. You'd think they'd understand that. Really, pottery, gold and silversmithing, jewelry, sculpture, stained glass, and painting, too! The organization's so old-fashioned! But do they listen to me? Oh, no. What does Hadriel count? Hadriel's only the one who does the job. What does Hadriel know? Surely nothing worthwhile. Susanna, darling, if you could even *begin* to understand all that I had to put up with, you'd feel sorry for me. . . ." The room was empty. But my heart felt easy, and the warmth Hadriel had left in the dark seemed to settle on the sleeping figures like a blessing.

Now here is the problem we woke up and found in the morning. No one could sail for France after all until the weather was better, which looked as though it might not be for weeks. That whole castle and city and every manor house roundabout were all crammed full of people who had come to escort the princess to her ships for the honor of it and also to rub shoulders with anybody important whom they might meet. So it started out like a celebration, except that it rained, which spoiled it. Nobody could leave before the king, because he is king, and the king was going to sail out to sea in his very favorite ship, which is named after himself, to accompany his sister partway. But he couldn't sail, so they couldn't leave, it was too wet to go out, everyone was bored, and even cards and dice weren't enough.

Then Milord of Suffolk discovered that I was there, and since he was a simpleminded fellow with an eye for the ladies, he decided that it would be amusing, since they were all gathered up together there, to have a series of drawings made of the "great beauties of the court." He put the idea to the king, who regretted greatly that his own court painters were not there to execute the idea. But then he was convinced by Suffolk and even helped to select the ladies himself. So that is how I got a bed in the castle after all, squashed in with three ladies' maids and an embroiderer, which Nan said was beneath me, but I was glad of the close company of respectable folk. I was also kept plentifully busy in the week that followed, both with painting and with kneeling. For the King passed through the upper apartments of the tower right often, they being on his way from his chamber to the gate, and whenever the king passed through and his eye lit on a person, then that person must kneel, right in the middle of everything until his sovereign would raise him up. But it was all very fine and thrilling, and I had the honor of having the king himself view my drawings and pronounce them "very like."

I was in the upper apartments, all surrounded by chattering ladies pointing out the corrections and improvements they wanted in their drawings, when I noticed Master Ashton's man, Will, standing beyond the open door of the antechamber, his hat in hand, motioning silently for me to come. Having promised the ladies everything, they at last dismissed me and I tied my drawings into the portfolio and fled toward the door.

Outside, the rain that had battered at the apartment windows for days had turned into a heavy ocean mist, obscuring such light as had managed to make its way into the castle apartments. The feeble illumination dulled the colors of the arras and the stiff, silk dresses of the ladies. Even the smoldering oak logs in the great fireplace scarcely took away the dank. Not a day fit to go out, even if it *has* quit raining, I thought. As I passed the door, Will pulled at my sleeve, and Nan turned to stare at him with a disapproving look.

"What is it?" I asked. He was muddy and disheveled. The gray was showing in his beard.

"Mistress Dallet, you must come. You have to come!" Will burst out. "He has work, he has messages, he has errands, and all he does is lie before the fire, dead drunk! He's scarce moved to get up and piss for the last three days. He won't eat, and he won't say a word, except sometimes, 'Damn Tuke,' or 'Devil take them all.' Sometimes he says your name, and spits." At that, I felt insulted.

"Well, what am I to do about it?"

"Come and take the spell you've laid off him." I could feel my mouth purse up. Spell, indeed. Not that I haven't been tempted by money powders and lucky pieces, but I would never do something like a spell, which is really very wicked and, besides, *The Good Wyfe's Book of Manners* says that women who resort to spells come to no good end. That is probably what happened to Goody Forster, who had the tiles fall on her head.

"Nonsense. It's his head. Change the bandage."

"No, it's not his head or his ribs either, though they're right properly cracked. It's a spell, and you know it. He talks like a man bewitched. All nonsense. Your name, over and over. He says he sees you standing there in the corner, like a succubus, dressed only in your nightgown, holding a paintbrush as if it were a dagger. Admit you've done this to him! And he drinks as if quenching a fire. Why did you do it? Haven't you had vengeance enough? I beg you, mistress, free him before he pulls down the archbishop's business and us with it."

"I don't do spells, Will. I paint."

"I swear, I'll never tell. I keep secrets. I keep his. I told Tuke he was up and busy. But if he doesn't get up off his back, he's ruined. Have mercy, just this once, mistress. I beg you, for the services he's given you, come and take it off."

"Just this once?" sniffed Nan, as we followed him down the muddy trail to the town beneath the castle. "Well, I like *that!* Who does he think we are? And if we *could* place spells, why would we bother with him, anyway? I can think of dozens better."

"Nan, what's wrong with you? You're acting so odd."

"It's just a trick to get you close. And after all he's done to you. He has designs, that's what. I can tell. Now that genteel Frenchman, that Master Bella-whatchamit, he's a good one. He's got a house. What has that Ashton got? He can't support you."

"Why, Nan, I do believe you're jealous! I'd never abandon you, Nan. Don't even think it."

"Still, a house is better," Nan grumbled. Above and behind us, the castle walls loomed, scarcely visible in the mist. Water glistened on the stones of the road, and drifting swirls of mist hid the buildings below. Beyond us, we could hear the roar of the unquiet ocean.

The town below the castle was filled with the sound of horses and the clatter of carts being unloaded at the docks. Not all the ships of the fleet had arrived yet, due to the weather, but the crates and barrels of the dowry were being hoisted aboard those that were there. The streets were full of people on errands, goodwives with baskets, drovers, cattle and swine, and pack animals laden with food and goods to keep the crowded town well fed. There was a kind of nervousness in the misty air. When would the great enterprise be undertaken? Would the rest of the fleet arrive safely? The dank, cloud-filled skies did not bode well for the wedding fleet.

Slipping unnoticed from the back door of a squalid tavern, a short man in a black cloak hurried through the mist, turned into an alley, and climbed the outside staircase behind a tailor's establishment, vanishing into a door up beneath the eaves. Inside, Bellier, dressed in traveling clothes, paced back and forth in that part of the room where the slant of the eves permitted standing. Behind him on the unmade bed stood a packed trunk and an open coffer of papers.

"Ah, Eustache, is it done? We must be going. I have passage for us both with the tide tomorrow. It must be of great importance that we are ordered back so soon." He paused to shake his head slowly. "Still, I hate leaving loose ends behind me. The Sieur Crouch ... at least the man of the scheming Wolsey will not be leaving."

"I doubled the dose this time. It should finish things within the hour."

"But did you see him take it?"

"No, but he will. Even his servant thinks he is drunk."

"A sad end to a promising career, Eustache. Drinking oneself to death in a low tavern. There is a moral to this story: avoid low company." Bellier shook his finger at Eustache like a schoolmaster. He then took up a list of names from the coffer. Several were crossed off with ink. With a little piece of chalk he marked out "Robert Ashton, servant to Archbishop Wolsey." Beneath it was written "Mistress Dallet, wife of Rowland Dallet, deceased, above." "I wonder," mused Bellier. "What about her? How much might he have told her?"

"You wish her poisoned, too, master?"

"How ungallant. The Priory, to go about eliminating women? No, Eustache. Perhaps I shall go courting. If she knows something, well— that's regrettable. But if she doesn't, just think ... a court painter. Imagine an unknowing set of eyes and ears for the Priory in the heart of the Valois. A valuable connection, don't you think? At first, I was disgusted. So very English, this vulgar life, those awful paintings of Eden. Then, as I thought it over, I began to see the uses. Besides, she is not unattractive."

Susanna pulled her heavy cloak tightly around her and turned up her nose as she and Nan pushed into the tavern's dank, warm front room behind their guide. Firelight danced across the long trestle tables and benches. It caught on the pewter cups and lit the dulled faces of the drunken, roistering sailors who sprawled across the tables, on the benches, and even in the mucky heaps of stale rushes on the floor. There was the smell of cheap ale, of cabbage, and of salt pork cooking, and the sound of quarreling from a game of dice in one corner. Several mongrel dogs lay beneath the tables gnawing on scraps, and an old yellow bitch dog with two rows of huge, freckled, pink teats lay by the fireside with her tongue hanging out.

"Ho, a woman!" came the cry.

"Who have you come for, mistress? Come for me. Hey, let's see what's beneath those skirts! A widow, and a young one. Who misses a piece off a sliced loaf? Ho, sweetheart, you've come to the right place...." A babble of drunken voices greeted their entrance. A drunk on the floor made a grab for Susanna's hem, and she stamped smartly on his hand, leaving him howling.

Ashton was lying on a bench before the fire, flat as a worm, his points undone, and one shoe off. One arm trailed down beside him to the hearth, a full pewter cup of dark wine sat on the stones beside his limp hand. His eyes were sunken in black circles, his face was flushed, and the bandage on his head was filthy and peeling. At the sound of the howl, he turned his dulled eyes to the door, and saw several Susannas, all overlapping, advancing on him, elbowing sailors out of the way.

"See what you've done?" he heard Will say. "Take the spell off him, mistress, or he's not long for this world." Three Susannas leaned over him and peered suspiciously into his face.

"He's been drinking," the Susannas said. As they leaned over him, three beautiful pink bosoms peeped out of three tightly laced black bodices. The color, he thought. It's exact. I'm right. Every one of those pink Eves is she. Then the three became one. One Susanna, with fog-damp curls escaping from her headdress.

"Eve . . ." he said. "Eve tempting Adam, Eve bathing, Eve combing her hair."

"You see? He's insane. You've made him that way." Susanna was looking at Ashton suspiciously.

"You have a dimple at the base of your spine," said Ashton. "They're all you, from the neck down." Susanna turned bright red from the roots of her hair all the way down to the top of the décolletage that Ashton was inspecting.

"You—you lecher!" she exclaimed. "You're drunk! You called me here to insult me! Just look at that filthy stuff! You should be ashamed!" With a single indignant gesture, she scooped up the pewter wine goblet and poured its contents melodramatically on the hearth. The blackish crimson splattered on her hem, on Nan's, and on the old bitch dog, who opened her eyes. Drops hissed in the fire, and a spreading puddle formed at her feet.

"Women!" came a cry from across the room. "They never let a man have any fun."

The pupils of Ashton's eyes were unnaturally huge, even for the ill-lit, smoky room. Susanna could hear his heart pounding. The bitch hound roused her wrinkled old body from the hearth and began to lap at the puddle.

"Get up," she said, pulling at his arms. "Will, go get a bucket of water. We're going to douse him. Then we'll make him eat. You want a spell lifted? Well, this is how it's done." He groaned, then fell back again. His eyes began to wander.

"There're two of you again. No, three. Will you paint three Eves? I thought there was only one. . . ."

"Susanna," Nan's voice was urgent. "Look at the dog." The dog had fallen on the hearth in convulsions.

"That's not wine—it's poison," said Susanna. Shocked, the three of them watched the dog shudder and stiffen in the ashes, oblivious to the sparks that lit on her yellow coat.

"You bastards, you've poisoned my master!" Will cried. "Who did this? I swear, I'll have the law on you!"

"You must get a purge immediately," cried Nan. But Will had already run out the door in search of an apothecary.

"The man in black," whispered Ashton, his pupils huge. "I'm seeing him. He's small, with a white, wrinkled face, and little black eyes like raisins. Now I'm seeing a devil, all green and naked, sitting up there on the rafters in the smoke. My dreams are floating in the room like colored clouds." Susanna shook him frantically. "Don't close your eyes, Master Ashton. Open them, open, I say! You're not dreaming. The man in black's real. You've been poisoned by him, I swear."

"Poison," he said, his voice weak. "I thought it was . . . an evil spell."

"Cast by my mistress. *Hmph.* Men! When have they ever believed any but the worst about a woman?" Nan said with a sniff, surveying the scene.

"Belladonna," said the physician, when the purging was done and he had inspected the contents of the bowl to his satisfaction. His severe, dark gown rustled as he stepped into the great fireplace and touched the dead dog with his toe. It lay there as stiff as a poker, covered with ashes, before the fire irons. "Enough for ten dogs in that cup, I'd imagine. It sets up a thirst. In a place like this, everyone would assume he was drinking himself to death, the way the others all are. I imagine someone decided the lower doses were not killing him fast enough, so they made this last cup much stronger. The eyes tell the story. The pupils. And the hallucinations. Who is this man, anyway?" Master Ashton, feverish and disheveled, lay on the bench, his eyes huge and staring, a fine tremor shaking his arms and legs.

"A secretary of Archbishop Wolsey's privy cabinet," answered Susanna, her face twisted with worry.

"*Hmph.* No surprise there. Probably carrying messages. There's always intrigue where the great ones gather. He'll live. I want him carried from this house. You're his man? Are his things upstairs? Go fetch them. You two—yes, you, you stout oafs with the earrings. I'll want you to carry him. Of all the dens in this town, this is the worst. Landlord, I see you skulking there. If there is any talk of a bill, I'll report you. You deserve to have this place burned down around your ears."

As the two sailors slung him up between them, the physician turned to Susanna. "Just as well there's someone with sense around here. Whatever possessed you to pour away the cup? Never mind. I'll have him up and about in a few days. Once the poison's gone, it's gone. Wolsey, did you say? I hope his gratitude takes the form of something metallic. Clerical blessings are skimpy sustenance."

But Susanna was trembling all over. The next morning, news came that the *Great Elizabeth* had been lost on her way to rendezvous with the wedding fleet at Dover. The king would not sail on the *Great Harry* after all but return home, and the princess set out on her wedding journey without his escort. Evil omens, they increase, thought Susanna. We should have bought the candle, even if it was too expensive. She could not purge her heart of the feeling that the wedding fleet was doomed.

"What think you of the new Flemish style of trunk hose, Master Arnold?" Crouch was standing on a low wooden dais in the center of a small, paneled room in the most fashionable tailor's establishment in all of London. Fog swirled against the narrow, diamond-paned windows, but the chill had been taken off the room by a handsome brazier that stood smoking in one corner. At Crouch's feet knelt the master tailor himself, his mouth full of pins, setting the hem of a nearly finished brocade gown at a dignified knee length.

"Ump," said the tailor, then, transferring the pins from his mouth to the pincushion, answered at greater length. "My lord, the largeness of the padding is to set more in fashion the spindly shanks of the Flemish gentlemen. Good Englishmen's legs, being always more handsome, are better set off with moderate padding at a shorter length, and more elegant slashing. His Majesty has lately ordered a most regal pair of trunk hose in cream-colored silk, with slashings in crimson, embroidered around in gold. They are none so wide and long as the Flemish, or, God forbid, the Germans which are most uncouthly huge, for His Majesty shows the handsomest leg of all. I would say, do as His Majesty does, for his is the finest judgment. Here, my lord, you will see that the murrey and silver sets you off marvelously well." An apprentice removed the pincushion and handed his master a burnished silver mirror to hold before Sir Septimus for his approval.

Handsome still, he thought. Septimus, you bravo, you are a handsome figure of a man. Fuller than in youth, but fullness lends gravity. The silver that streaked his square-cut, dark beard harmonized elegantly with the silver embroidery at his collar. The great, curling streaks of white rose in the dark hair that stood up from the corners of his brow pleased him, with their hint of the diabolical. You are a splendid-looking fellow, he said to himself. But at the very moment of the thought, the sound of a sarcastic laugh seemed to split the mirror. Crouch started back with shock, but the tailor never moved. Had he heard the raucous, smoky laugh? He couldn't have.

"Crouch, you are one vain old bastard," came a malicious voice from the mirror, and Crouch, to his horror, saw his own reflection gradually fade and a new set of features begin to take its place.

"No, no don't move it," he said to the impatient tailor. "I'm still looking." Quelling his rising panic, Crouch sent out a silent thought. *Who are you?*

You know me. A ghastly green face, with a huge nose full of bristly hairs, tiny red eyes, and a mouth full of pointed teeth began to form up in the mirror. Watching Crouch's face gradually change from horror to covetousness, the face in the mirror laughed again. *You seek me here, you seek me there, you've been hunting everywhere.*

My lost demon, thought Crouch. But how do I imprison him in

the mirror here, in the middle of a fashionable shop, without my grimoires, my black candles? He knows it. He taunts me.

I mock you for a mortal fool. Do you hear me laughing? I have just collected the soul of your goldsmith. One by one your servants vanish.

You want to be mine, too. Crouch turned a soothing, caressing thought on the demon. *You wouldn't be here to taunt me if you didn't crave it.*

And now you try to seduce me like a women, eh, Crouch? Ha! You have to offer me something better than that.

I swear, I'll catch you.

As you'll catch the Helmsman? At this, Crouch's wide, sagging mouth compressed into a thin line of fury. *I saw your trick, Crouch. You told Wolsey the conspirators of the Priory menaced his precious treaty, and he sent his man Ashton to find the Helmsman.*

Ashton will return to me first, and I will know all.

No he won't. Say good-bye to your scheme. Ashton is no longer yours. Sir Septimus's heavy, hairy eyebrows lifted. When had a man ever escaped him, once his claws were deep into his soul? Rageful pride seized him. Impossible, he thought.

You're losing your touch, Crouch. Ashton belongs to that busybody round-faced widow now.

"Never!" shouted Sir Septimus into the mirror.

"My lord, is it the set of the collar that displeases you?"

"Oh—oh, that. Yes, it's too wide. Entirely too wide. Perhaps it needs to stand up more. Stiffening. That's what it wants." Crouch sounded rattled. The mirror once again reflected only his own face. But in his mind, he could still hear the infernal spirit's rusty laugh. Rising fury stained his face. No demon will mock *me,* he thought. I will destroy Ashton.

"Is next week soon enough?" With concern, the tailor saw Crouch's face redden and the veins stand out, blue and throbbing, on his neck.

"Oh, yes, by all means. Next week. Sooner, if possible." The terrified tailor ushered Sir Septimus out of his cutting room with a thousand bows, collapsing onto a bench once the door was safely shut behind him.

❧❦

At last the weather broke, and the fresh breeze blew apart the gray clouds in the sky. I made myself cheerful by wishing it and delivered to Suffolk the nine fine drawings in ink and wash that he had ordered for his master and companion, the king. Thanks to the purse he gave me, I was able to do my duty for Tom, who had made himself so useful to me with carrying and minding my things. I paid a hefty bribe to the mate on the *Jesus of Lübeck* to smuggle him over among the horse boys and counted myself very clever that he should escape the great dangers we had seen so handily. Besides, I really could use a boy to help me, and I'd a thousand times it would rather be Tom than some sly foreign creature who would try to steal my secrets.

By the time the news came that we were to sail with the tide at four in the morning, I had arranged for everything to my satisfaction except for Master Ashton, about whom I had heard nothing even though I had sent two messages by Tom to him but had gotten no answer. Tom said he didn't want to answer, which struck me as very ungrateful of Master Ashton, considering that I had in a way saved his life, even though I hadn't told Tom the story of it.

So it was that we went down to the docks by starlight, in the hour after midnight, in the company of the attendants of the maids of honor. The great fleet had been loading all night, by the light of torches. For plate could sit in the hold until the weather broke, but living creatures could not. Squealing palfreys were lowered into the hold in slings, while servants, attendants, and lesser fry staggered laden up the gangplanks. Flame glittered and danced in the black water as little boats ferried back and forth to the fourteen great ships, bringing late soldiers and sailors clad in green and white, the King's colors, from the shore out to the ships that were standing in the harbor. Huddled on our baggage among the clatter and shouting, we were waiting our turn to be loaded from the dock, when I saw Ashton pushing his way past the crowds of navvies and torch bearers to meet us. He was dressed in his dark traveling clothes and plain, flat hat, so different from the brightly dressed household officers who were traveling on the princess's ship. Even in the ruddy glow of the torches, he seemed wan and pale. Silently, he escorted me and Nan to the gangplank. Laden footmen, household officers with last-minute instructions, and musicians who carried their shrouded instruments on their backs were struggling past us up onto the immense ship. I saw the princess's chaplain and priests on the deck above. The flickering torchlight caught the gilding and carving on her forecastle as it loomed high above us. *Henri, Grace à Dieu.* Above it, the towering sails and their web of rope faded into the endless dark. The greatest of the great king's fleet. Ashton's face was somber and shadowed in the dark beyond the torches.

"Well, I suppose this is farewell," he said.

"I suppose it is," I said, "though I am glad to see you well again." He looked puzzled.

"I thought . . . you were too disgusted to inquire after me."

"You think me that rude? I sent Tom twice to ask after your health."

"Twice? I only saw him once. I sent a message to you, and he returned to say you never wanted to see me again. I thought it only right, after . . . after all that has happened." I could see him folding and unfolding his left hand in that curious gesture.

"He told you that? He told me that you didn't want to answer my message. I thought it very rude and ungrateful of you. Possibly ruder than you are."

"That little devil. If I catch him, I'll strangle him. To show me no gentleman in front of you . . ." Something about him seemed so right and natural now. The dulled look had gone from his eyes, his emotions were quick, strong, and honest, not warped and strange as they had been in the bishop's palace. It was as if a spell had been lifted. I couldn't help thinking how well made he was. The facial bones were very good, a nice proportion of bone to muscle . . .

"They've put us on the lower deck, with the cannons," I said, a bit quickly, to cover my thoughts. "I doubt we'll see anything, but I'm going to try to stay on the main deck."

"You'll be in the way. They won't let you," he said.

"That's what you say. You're just jealous I'm going to the King of France's court and you're not."

"But I am," he answered. "I have orders from the archbishop."

"To escort us, then?"

"No. I have a few . . . errands. I don't know . . . if we'll meet again over the water. I came . . . to give advice." I looked at him, puzzled. "Don't stray from the princess's suite. Don't be cozened by the French, no matter what they offer. Take always a good English escort with you. You often run errands for the gentlefolk you paint. Don't carry any letters for any-one, especially ... Norfolk and his suite." He had lowered his voice with these last words.

"Is something wrong?"

"No, nothing ... but ... there are those who do not like the treaty, for it advances my master and yours at the expense of others, both in France and in our own king's favor." Silently, I stared at his face. I could tell he regretted he had told me even that much. I nodded, trying to look very clever and wise, as if I understood it all. Politics are not for me. They tend to be nasty and dangerous, and lead to the execu-tioner's block. Painters should stay away from politics.

"Will you sail with us, then?"

"No, on the *Lübeck*," he said, and his eyes were distant. Oh, dear, I thought, suddenly guilt stricken. I hope Tom stays well out of the way.

"I am sorry for what Tom did. I think ..."

"... that he is as desperately entangled by you as I am," said Robert Ashton, his voice low.

"Entangled?" I said, looking up at him, my eyes opening wide.

"Enmeshed, tied, captured. I see you ... day and night. There was a time I prayed to be freed, but it only grows stronger, and I have given in...." I could feel something warm, something desperate, coming off him like a scent. Something I had never felt before from any man. It called me and pulled me even though I didn't want it to. I came closer. I could feel his warm breath on my face, and his hazel eyes, all dark in the torchlight, became somehow transparent, showing me the depths of him. Something was burning there, something close to madness, that made my skin prickle and my mind melt as if drunk. What woman could see such forbidden things and ever hope to free herself again? I turned my face upward and suddenly felt his lips on mine, his warm, heavy-scented embrace around me. Something like molten silver shot through all the nerves in my body, hot, powerful, full of white light. My skin felt detached from my body, alive and crackling. Every hair on it felt as if it were standing up. My mind melted away. Never in my life had I dreamed that such a transformation were possible in my own, plain, earthly being. It was he, he had done it, and the forbidden stuff was shared between us now, like some pagan curse.

"Doomed," he whispered. "I'll see you again if I have to walk through the gates of hell itself ..." I was terrified at what I had felt in me. I stepped away to stare at him, my eyes wide with shock. Can a man do that to a woman? Is that what it's about, those songs and stories? Why him, why me? Why disgrace and death and loss? I looked up and saw that great patches of black were once again eating up the stars above. The wind was cold. "May God attend us all," he said, turning on his heel and leaving abruptly.

"Well," sniffed Nan. "There goes the strangest, rudest man I ever did see. Twice you have saved his life and not a word of thanks. But he steals a kiss like a ruffian. The man's no gentleman ... I swear, he's not for you." Her voice sounded distant, and I felt the strangest floating sensation. When I looked down, I realized I was shaking all over.

Together we mounted the swaying gangplank and managed to stay on deck long enough to see the king himself bring his sister to the waterside and kiss her farewell beneath the smoking torches before the trumpeters welcomed her on board.

High up in the rigging of the *Henri Grace à Dieu* sat a lovely, translucent figure in a blowing gown of dappled colors and the ugliest shoes imaginable. Invisible to the ordinary human eye, Hadriel stretched his iridescent wings to the blue sky and joyfully let the brisk, cool ocean wind ruffle the feathers on them. The sails of the *Great Harry* had been painted with lions and the Tudor rose, and her linen pennants, over a hundred feet long each, had been replaced by ones of embroidered silk. Far below the joyful angel's seat, the deck of the galleon heaved crazily on the swells. Around the ship, white sails spread and pennants flying, the wedding fleet dotted the gray, whitecapped ocean like goslings following their mother. Hadriel was so pleased with the sight that he began to sing, but no one beneath him could hear it. A curious sound of the wind in the rigging, they thought.

Gray clouds began to gather in the sky, and Hadriel stopped his singing and looked up, annoyed, when a drop of rain fell on his nose. Impatiently, he shook his curly head at the dark clouds, and they blew on, then gathered again. This time, he pointed firmly at them with his slender, pale hand, and again the wind parted them. The sailors below looked impatiently at the sky, and the admiral of the flagship, still wearing his green-and-white damask dress livery in honor of his royal passenger, gave orders that sent them scurrying. The clouds, now black, began to gather anew, and there was a distant rumble of thunder.

"Stop this at once," called Hadriel, furling his wings and looking irritated. "Belphagor, I know you're there. Do you think I haven't noticed you following me? Quit blowing up these clouds. You have been absolutely *insufferable* since those fools let you out of the box."

"Get your ridiculous little nose out of my business," growled a surly voice. "Go flutter home, you hymn-singing flatterer. You're not wanted here." A greenish, smoky figure was forming up, crouching on the yardarm below Hadriel's perch: Belphagor the demon, red eyed, long nosed, and sagging of stomach.

"Nice outfit, Belphagor. That little furry thing sets off the green. But don't you think the shade's a little *passé?* I mean, that sort of bilious mustardy tone. A sort of a lettuce-y color would be much more becoming."

"That's my goat tail, you imbecile. You know I don't wear clothes. I come in this color. We're not vain like you celestial folk. Besides, you can hardly talk, wearing those ugly things on your feet." Hadriel stretched out his feet and wiggled them, gazing admiringly at his shoes.

"They were a *gift*, Belphagor. Ten thousand years, and nobody's ever given me a gift before. I give, I give, but I don't get. I like them. Anybody ever give you anything?"

"You infant. I get offerings all the time."

"Offerings to get you to do something. Not gifts for no reason at all. And pretty tawdry your offerings are, too. What was it you couldn't resist last time? The corpse of a black rooster, I seem to recall. You got yourself locked up by those renegade Templars for it. Cheap, Belphagor, you sold yourself cheap. Now these nice shoes—"

"It was so a gift. It was a gift because ... because ... because they only asked me to do what I'd do anyway. So it didn't count."

"Sow destruction and vengeance, you mean? That takes a mind, Belphagor, and when I last looked, I didn't notice you had much of a one."

"I do so. I'm sowing destruction and vengeance right now. I'm going to sink all these ships. I hate weddings. Nobody ever invited me."

"And what would you do if they did?"

"Sow destruction and vengeance."

"Exactly. Which is why they never invite you, you nit." When Belphagor was concentrating on his conversation, the wind abated. Startled, he looked around him and saw the gray clouds part and realized he had been deceived. Turning his fiery eyes on the sky, he revived the tearing wind and gathered the storm clouds anew. Swelling slightly, he raised himself up from his seat high into the air and let the first drops of rain spatter against the swirling, smoky green of his half-manifested body. Then he turned his long nose over his shoulder to gloat at Hadriel, who was still in the rigging, sitting below him now.

"You'll be sorry you said that when I sink all these ships and that silly, round-faced girl you've been following. Glub, glub, glub. Horses, carriages, soldiers, plate, silk dresses, princess and all. Down to the bottom. Then the French king can't be wed, and I've sowed my vengeance, and I'm freed. Ha! You see how clever I am?" The wind was blowing fiercely now, and the fleet had scattered over the surface of the dark waves. The rain began to fall in sheets from the blackened sky. Topheavy with its wet sails and high, gilded, and carved superstructure, the ship heeled over, shaking Hadriel from his perch. Unfurling his great wings, he lifted into the swirling air. The demon laughed. "You see? Even you abandon them, you flyweight, no-account, feather ball!"

Furious, the rain streaming down his face and hair, Hadriel grasped the mainmast of the ship and pushed it upright again. The sound of his great wings beating was lost in the rush of the wind. The demon, older and stronger, grasped the mast from the other side, pushed it back, and then sat on it, squatting like a vast carrion crow. With the weight of his corrupt centuries, he bore down on the struggling angel. The leaping waves were perilously close to the gun ports now. A woman's shriek could be heard. Inside the ship were the desperate sounds of men manning the pumps, trying hopelessly to stop the sea.

"Why?" cried Hadriel, the rain streaking his face like tears. "Why this ship?" The mast dipped lower. Any farther, and the gray water would flood through the gunports, swamping the ship.

"I told you," gloated the demon. "It has the princess. It has your little pet. You spoiled my first plan. I was going to be born and walk the earth like a human, making trouble. You spoiled my birth. So now I have my liberty a new way. And my vengeance on you. See where I am? Above you, Hadriel. I spit on you." A bolt of lightning struck near them, illuminating Hadriel's pale features with a strange flash of greenish light.

"Vengeance on me you'll have, but not your liberty, you tortoise brain." Hadriel spoke swiftly, mockingly, trying to divert Belphagor's attention. The demon's hairy eyebrows raised. The thunder rolled.

"But of course I will. And it's a small price for a chicken." Belphagor looked smug.

"Recall the words of the spell the Templars put on you. It wasn't vengeance on the King of France, it was vengeance on the King of France and his house. Besides, you have the wrong king. It's King Philippe you want, and he's dead. But you won't be free until you've got vengeance on his whole family. Ha! You've been locked up a long time, Belphagor. There's probably hundreds of them by now." Lightning zigzagged past them, its crooked fingers lighting the black waters beneath.

"You don't expect me to count them all, do you? They're all alike. Besides, there're so many." Again, there was a crash of thunder.

"A spell's a spell. You're finished, Belphagor. No more vacations. No more visits to your cousins in hell. And as I recall, Satrinah is very annoyed that you haven't been to visit her lately." The fierce effort of talking and keeping the ship afloat was telling on Hadriel. For the first time in his ten thousand years, sweat mingled with the rain on his face, and his great wings beat slower. As the deck of the ship tilted farther, the hungry waves leaped to meet it. Around them both, demon and angel, the evil winds were whistling. Below them, a sailor fell overboard with a cry and was drowned.

"Satrinah?" Belphagor looked alarmed. "But what will I tell her?"

"Tell her you're too stupid to find your way out of a spell, and see what happens," answered Hadriel, his breath coming in gasps.

"But . . . but . . . his *house?* I'd have to become a genealogist. They breed like rats, these humans. Who can keep track of them?" It seemed to Hadriel that the demon's weight was lightening. The ship began to right itself.

"Start studying. No visits until you figure it out." The rain was beginning to lessen, and the sound of thunder became distant again.

"I can't read, Hadriel. You have to help me." The waves began to subside.

"Help you? Whatever for? I'm the angel of art, not the angel of helping demons. Besides, you called me a feather ball. No, it's your job, Belphagor."

"But how will I begin? How can I do it?"

"Give up on these ships, Belphagor. You have to make a trip to Paris. Maybe a nice tour down the Loire, and a visit to some monasteries—French heraldry, it's difficult, you know. All those quarterings." The rolling clouds were beginning to separate. The ships were spread all over the channel now, only three others within sight of the flagship. Beyond them, the dim gray line on the horizon grew taller and formed itself into the dappled outline of rocky cliffs. France, and safety. The galleons pitched hideously on the choppy seas, the still-gusting winds driving them farther from their destination. The admiral ran his signal flag up the masthead to gather his ships to him, and from ship to ship, across the deadly gray ocean, the sound of trumpets calling into the emptiness reverberated and was lost.

There was no view at all from a gun deck except of cannons being lashed down and everyone being sick as the ship rolled. The passengers were all weeping and praying, and even the horses below in the hold were making a horrible noise. There were five hundred people squashed onto that ship, and hardly anyplace to hold on, so when the ship tipped first one way and then the other, Nan and I were bumped around considerably. Then the ship slid so far we could see water coming in at the holes where the guns are supposed to go out, which I am sure was not the way things were intended to be. Then I prayed very hard and recounted all my sins and said I was very sorry, but in the middle of it I thought of Robert Ashford and that kiss which surely must have been a sin and I couldn't keep my mind on being sorry, so I tried to pray for him, too. But it was hard not to be selfish in my praying because I kept thinking about how very awful it would be to drown in that tiny dark space with all those people clawing and grabbing and trying to open the hatches, which had been shut tight somehow, I think to keep the water out.

But then we heard a sort of grinding sound and a lot of curses, and the ship stopped moving, and the gunners said we had run aground. The ship was sort of tilted, but at least it was not moving around and making everyone sick anymore. Then I heard a lot of rattling and clattering above, and also footsteps and voices, and so Nan and I peeked out of one of those little holes for the cannon and sure enough, they were lowering the boats to take the princess and her escort to the beach. First they sent her knights out, but the waves were very high and they had to row very hard in those little boats to get them there, and they had to leap out and wade to the shore anyway. Then they took her and her ladies and Mother Guildford, who were quite a few, and a big wave came and splashed all over them. Then they all had to wade to the beach through that cold water, except for the princess, because one of her knights carried her through the water to the beach.

"Well, I imagine *that* will be worth something," said Nan, who is cynical about chivalry and says if you think about anything, it all boils down to money.

"Nan, he is devoted. My book has told me all about how it is a gentleman's pleasure to serve his lady honorably in such ways."

"You and that book," growled Nan. "You live in a cloud. What will you do when it rains?"

"It's rained quite a lot that I can see, Nan, and my cloud's still here. Has it ever occurred to you that maybe I like it that way? I'm grown up, Nan, and I can choose. I choose to be in a cloud instead of in the gutter." Nan shook her head. There was a clattering sound, the hatches were thrown open, and daylight came in. The ocean air smelled better than the awful smell of sickness on that crowded, dark deck.

"Where are we?" called someone to the sailors above.

"Outside Boulogne. We went aground at the entrance to the harbor. You should see those French grandees all waiting on the dock." Nan and I scrambled up onto the slanting deck with all the rest, but I would not be parted from my box and my folded easel that was all tied with twine even though they told us no baggage. But then I looked over the side at the very tiny rope ladder that swayed and wiggled, and the very small boat bobbing up and down at the bottom of it, and I was frightened of climbing down even without my things, just by myself. I think I must have looked very dismayed because a nice man with an earring who was a sailor laughed at me and asked what was in my boxes, my jewelry? And I said more important than that, it was my paints and my easel that I couldn't get another of, and I needed them for my living and would have to be a beggar if they were lost. And so he climbed down the rope himself with my box and his friend took my easel. They also helped me and Nan, although I did cling on in the middle of the ladder and couldn't move even though people were talking to me from the deck and also from the little boat and saying I should let go and keep moving or I would be there until doomsday. I think I hate ocean voyages.

We were all wet, and the sky being all gray and cold did not help any. It was also very confusing and people were shouting, and the grandees were making speeches of welcome, and people seemed to have forgotten everyone else, particularly people of no account like ourselves. So while they were taking the horses off and making them swim behind the boats Nan and I went to find a place to get warm. We found a tavern with a sign of a giant eating several whole sheep in his huge mouth, where they were all speaking French, it being in France and all. But it was a problem, with all that strange language just rattling by my head, managing to get a place by the fire. Besides, all these horrible foreign sailors just crowded around and said things that were not in my French lessons.

"I thought you knew French," said Nan, after she slapped some man who tried to put his hand in my bosom.

"I do know French. The right kind. This is the wrong kind. Besides, it's much too fast."

"In short, we're trapped in a foreign country where we can't even make them understand we want to buy a meal, not sell our favors. What on earth are we going to do?" I had never seen Nan so rattled.

"*We* are going to order something to drink," I said, and, speaking in my very best court French, I said we had just come from England and we were servants of the princess and we would have food and drink. I am not sure it came out right, because everyone laughed, and some man puffed himself out and pretended he was a lady with a long train, and some other people shouted to the proprietor using my exact same words and also my accent, which I gather was humorous to them, and a big striped cat came and lay on my feet. In short, it was the Goat and Jug all over again, except that we were inside, which is always a mistake. Then some woman in a foreign headdress came and whacked them all with her broom and said more things I did not understand, and her husband came and asked if we had money, which I did understand, and soon all things were settled.

"So you see, Nan, I *do* know French, after all," I said, as we settled in to some very good hippocras and also a chicken and some bread.

"Not enough, that is plain to see. Whatever will become of us here?" she asked, looking around unhappily at the crowded, low-ceilinged room with its floor of pounded dirt. Around us were crowded sailors of all nations, drinking and playing dice. In a corner, a woman sat on a man's lap, and several drunks were singing, each one something different. But there was a big, warm fire, and being dry again was a great encouragement.

"Why, I'll paint old ladies young, and young ladies beautiful, and all men with fiery glances, and we'll save our money and go home again," I answered.

"You can't do that," said Nan. "Wolsey wouldn't have you back if you left the princess, and she's going to be queen, and then queen mother, and we are going to be surrounded by all these foreigners *forever.*"

"It will all work out, Nan, you'll see," I said. "We're going to live in a palace and wear silk every day."

"A *French* palace," Nan growled.

It took several days for the princess's wedding train to be reassembled, and while we waited for news of the ships, I did several small sketches of ladies in the great house where the princess and her suite were staying. While the gilded carts, and horses, and pavilions, and gowns were being made ready for the journey to Abbeville, where she was to marry the King of France, the terrible word came to us that the *Lübeck* had been lost. Of five hundred soldiers and sailors aboard, only a hundred had been saved, they said, washed onto the rocks with the loose wreckage of the ship. Everyone rejoiced that the ship was not one that carried the wedding plate. But my heart sank and my hands shook when I heard the news, and in hopes that it was some other ship, I sought out the officer who had brought the message and found him putting his borrowed horse in the stable. He was hollow eyed and unshaven, a ghost in the festive atmosphere, where livery-clad grooms were gilding the hooves of white palfreys, and whistling stable boys jostled past carrying jingling, newly shined harness.

"You are the man from the lost ship?" I asked, and at the sound of my voice, he turned from the stall.

"I am," he said slowly.

"It . . . it wasn't the *Lübeck,* was it?"

"The *Jesus of Lübeck,* yes," he said.

"I . . . I need news. Of a man . . . and a boy." His face was grim and silent.

"There were six boys on the *Lübeck.* None came ashore."

"Not . . . not a cabin boy. A boy in a russet jerkin and gray hose. Brown hair. Just fourteen."

"Your son?"

"No, my 'prentice. He . . . he ground my colors."

"Him I don't know. Was he on the roll?"

"Maybe . . . maybe not."

"Well, then, perhaps there's a chance he's alive. They've brought the living into Calais, where many lie sick. You might send for word. Did you say your colors? Then you must be the paintrix I heard of."

"Then you spoke with my boy? You must have seen him then . . . before."

"No, it was Wolsey's man. Ashburn, or something like that. He kept staring at the *Great Harry,* before we lost sight of her. He told me there was a woman on board that was a painter, bound for France. He said he was doomed, whether he lived or died. It made him as brave as a madman when the storm hit." The hollow-eyed man looked at me, then shook his head. "Funny. You don't look like a temptress. He asked me if I'd ever had a fatal attraction. I told him I wouldn't think of it." Master Ashton. Then he must have felt it, too. The white-hot silver in the veins, the pounding heart. The sin was in us both.

"Then he was saved, too?"

"Him? No. They say he was on the upper gun-deck, when one of the serpentines broke loose. I heard he was crushed, mistress, and swept overboard. Him and the others. Gone. So many gone. Their breastplates pulled them down. Two brothers I had on that ship. I keep thinking—" He shook his head, then turned toward the stable door.

"But Master Ashton wasn't in armor, I'm sure." I wanted to see him, to speak to him. How could he be gone? That strong life that mocked fatal bolts and deadly poison, taken by a common accident? I could see him as clear as clear in my mind, the torches sputtering above him, the lapping waves of the night harbor sounding beneath his voice. But already his features had begun to fade. Why hadn't I ever made a drawing of him?

"Why me? Why was I, a sinner, the greatest sinner of us, spared? Why my poor Jemmy taken?" The hollow-eyed man was fast going away into his own thoughts.

"Couldn't you see them swimming?"

"Swimming? No sailor can swim. It's bad luck to have a swimmer on board. Why was I spared? Have you an answer, mistress? Does anyone have an answer?"

"God has the answers. It is His will." I answered without thinking, a numb answer from a heart too frozen for anything but mindless speech.

"God! What good are His answers when He never says them? Those are no answers at all. God is silent! Why is our sin so great that God must be silent?" As I fled from the man I could feel tears running down my face, and at night his morbid questions haunted me. If only I had not paid Tom's way; if only I hadn't been so selfish, so willful, and so proud of my cleverness. I'd brought him to his death. And Robert Ashton. How strange, how stupid. Our lives had only touched, and then he was gone. Is it possible that all over the world there are people who might care for each other, but they never meet? Or if they meet, they say hard things instead of kind ones, and so never discover what was actually meant to be? What a cruel punishment, the cruelest of all, to know in the last moments of his life what could have been. Oh, where does all this wasted might-have-been love go, when it is vanished and thrown away? Is it all saved up somewhere, all the tears for something that, but for an accident, you might never even have known was lost? Stop this, Susanna. You will drive yourself mad.

Then I saw him in my mind, trying to send Tom home. I should have listened. He was right. He had the foreknowledge that is given to the doomed. He had tried to save Tom. He had tried to tell me things, prophetic warnings. He knew. He had always known. The image of Master Ashton, like some sorrowful, disapproving night spirit, seemed to hover in the blackness beneath the ceiling. My heart felt raked and battered with grief.

The Seventh Portrait

Lucas Hornebolte. Charles Brandon, Duke of Suffolk. *Ca. 1520.*
2 × 3½". Gouache on vellum. Hinged gold case on chain.

The earliest-known portrait of Charles Brandon, first Duke of Suffolk, celebrated courtier and boon companion of Henry VIII. Thickset, dark bearded, and ruggedly handsome, Charles Brandon first rose from a comparatively obscure background to prominence through military prowess and a series of dubious, financially advantageous marriages. This portrait is set in a closed frame on a fine gold chain, doubtless as part of a woman's toilette.

—*Exhibition catalog. Bayerische Staatsgemäldesammlungen*

Now I have already told you how I came to paint this portrait with a very fiery glance as the Duke of Suffolk said he wanted, but I did not say that later on he ordered a copy of it made in secret. I marked the copy in a hidden place because I was sure it was for a lady and because of a curiosity inspired by wickedness I wanted to know it from the first one if I ever saw it again. That is why I have put this portrait here in my story because it was much later that I came across the portrait's copy, all set in a gold case on a chain, and in very different circumstances than I had ever even dreamed of. As it has turned out, I have been beholden to the duke on several occasions, both for the custom he has given me and also for things he did for himself, in which my portrait was involved and which worked to my advantage, as you will see later on.

SIXTEEN

"You say she is beautiful? The picture did not lie?" The rain was rattling at the narrow, Gothic windows of the Hôtel de la Gruthuse, the king's residence in Abbeville, some fifty miles from the harbor at Boulogne. There he had promised to meet his new queen in splendor. Hundreds of troops, high officials, influential churchmen, and the greatest noble families in the land had overrun the little town. Behind them came an army of cooks, servants, musicians, banner painters, and carpenters to create the pavilions, feasts, and balls for her reception. Now they swarmed in and out of the halls, kitchens, and cellars of the great house. In addition, a good two score courtiers waited on the king, even at this informal moment.

"Your Majesty, she is as beautiful as an angel," said the Cardinal d'Amboise, leaning forward slightly toward the king, who sat in a great cushioned chair, his gouty foot propped up on a stool before him. "Monsieur de Vendôme was with me to greet her at the dock. He will bear me out."

"A paradise," said the Duc de Vendôme. "Words cannot do justice to her beauty."

"Yes, yes, a miracle of beauty," murmured the courtiers, most of whom hadn't even seen her.

"And to think such a creature was produced by the English," said the king. "Those … merchants. Did you know, Monsieur d'Amboise, that the English ambassador demanded to see the jewels with which I would endow my queen and then asked to have them all sent to England? No, no. I told him I intend to give her only one at a time, once we are wed, and to be paid for each one in many kisses." The king's eyes glittered in anticipation, and a wolfish smile crossed his ravaged face.

"Most right, Majesty. And what a joyful payment that will be."

"I cannot wait. I must see her."

"That cannot be, Majesty; until the official reception here even a royal groom must not see his bride."

"Am I not king? I will arrange something . . . unofficial. Accidental. A hunting party. I will surprise her en route. Send a message to Monsieur d'Angoulême, who has gone to meet her at Étaples, that I and my hunting party will meet her, by purest coincidence, at the Anders Forest. Have him ride ahead and arrange it." Within minutes, a fast courier left the stables with the word that the king would be wearing cloth of gold on crimson when he went hunting, so that Mary would be dressed in the identical colors as she traveled, for custom decreed that the King and Queen of France must always wear the same colors when appearing in public.

The last of the golden leaves still clung to the high, arching trees of the forest as the princess's party made its way along the muddy, rutted road. Ahead of her rode more than a hundred men: nobles and ambassadors, uniformed squires, heralds, macers, trumpeters. Behind her the row of heavy, gilded carts carrying her huge train of ladies, maids, and immense wardrobe labored through the mud, each pulled by six great horses, harnessed one before the other. In the rear, following the carts, were the two hundred men of her military escort, minus the troops lost in the wreckage of the *Lübeck*. At the sound of the king's hunting horns in the distance, the procession halted in a wide meadow, already brown and dappled with impending winter. At a distance, through the trees, they could see the bright uniforms of mounted French guardsmen. As the two hundred guards of the king's hunting escort poured into the clearing, they parted, to allow the cluster of nobles and churchmen surrounding the king to advance toward the English party. Then English and French nobles alike drew aside to allow the "accidental" meeting. The princess, young and fresh, reined in her white palfrey, pretending surprise. She was wearing cloth of gold, and a crimson hat settled rakishly over one eye. Her cream-and-rose English complexion, her slender figure and glittering youth elicited mutters of admiration from the French nobles who rode beside the king.

"But her hair—it's red," whispered one of the French nobles. Red hair was a sign to the French of unbridled sexual appetite and haughtiness.

"Oh, not at all. It's golden," was the reply of a more tactful courtier.

"Perhaps a reddish gold," added another. There was a snickering sound behind him.

"The king will have his work cut out for him."

Above the clatter and creak of harness and the pawing of horses, voices in English could be heard in grudging admiration of the wealth and trappings of the French king. Shrewd eyes on both sides assessed the state of health of the elderly bridegroom.

"Look at him there, that old man, licking his lips and gulping his spittle," the Italian ambassador whispered cattily to his companion. "If the French king lives to smell the flowers of spring, you may give yourself five hundred years."

The king, mounted on a Spanish war horse trapped in checkered black and cloth of gold, rode forward to her, and she doffed her pert little hat to him. He smiled and paused. She motioned a footman to help her dismount, that she might pay him formal homage, but he waved his hand to stop her. Bright eyed and shrewd, the young bride looked at the dark, hungry eyes of Louis XII and realized that he was hers. The great king was won. She had only to hold him. Smiling, and remaining mounted, she blew him a kiss. The king pushed his great horse forward to her, threw his arms around her neck, and kissed her there in front of the mounted company. No one could hear what he said, but she smiled and nodded, and he, in his turn, spoke and smiled. Then he turned to go, giving a signal to his guards to stay with the princess. The "accident" was over. The king raised one gloved hand, and at the signal, Francis of Angoulême rode his big chestnut stallion to the side of the princess's white palfrey. At the moment of ceremony, only rank and court precedence had influenced the king's choice of a companion for his new queen. And so in a moment, with the heedlessness of a child playing with fire, the old king set the most practiced seducer in the court to accompany his young bride for the rest of the journey. Gathering his old nobles to him, he turned his horse back in the direction he had come. As the sound of horns proclaimed the departure of the king and his escort, Francis turned to Mary.

"I am afraid the trip will be long and dull," she said, glancing up through her lashes. At last, a Frenchman who was not short. A

Frenchman of rank, and of an age to appreciate her properly, even if his nose was too long and his eyes a bit narrow and foxy. Compliments are always better when they come from someone young and visibly charmed. Perhaps the court of the old king would not be as dull as she imagined.

"In the presence of such beauty, no journey could ever be dull," answered Francis, but his faun's smile and knowing eyes gave the routine gallantry a secret edge. How lovely, how infinitely desirable, he thought. Look at how she threw that kiss, look at how she speaks to me. Englishwomen. Wild, mannerless, without morals. A practiced temptress. And red-haired. A prey to ungovernable lust. As soon as the wedding is over, she will be wanting a lover, he thought. I know the type. Francis thrilled to the danger of the chase, the quiet bribery of maids, the warning whistle of a guard at the window, the vanishing down secret passages, the stolen pleasure in another man's bed. A triumph to conquer another man's wife. An even greater triumph when she is a queen.

The Eighth Portrait

The Triumphal Entry of Mary Tudor into Abbeville. The Master of the Angel Triptych. *Oil on wood. 7 X 10". Brussels, Palais des Beaux-Arts.*

This badly scarred, unfinished panel is chiefly of historical interest. It depicts the typical elaborate procession with which the rulers of the Renaissance entered the cities that lay along a route of travel. Here, Mary Tudor, the younger sister of Henry VIII of England, meets her future husband, King Louis XII of France, their marriage sealing a diplomatic alliance between England and France. The unfinished figures at the left edge of the painting show the characteristic warm, rosy underpainting identified with the Master of the Angel Triptych, which gives his finished figures much of their charm. X-ray examination of the scars across the face of the painting seems to confirm that the painting was somehow damaged in the Master's workshop itself, and therefore was left incomplete.

—*G. Manning.* The Pageantry of the Renaissance

I always intended to finish this panel, but since it was in oils, all I could do was sketch it out and then it had to wait until I had my own studio, and then after what happened to the queen there was nobody who wanted to pay for it so it just sat there awhile and I kept putting off finishing it for the sake of other commissions and groceries which are necessary to any artist, no matter what anyone says. Then after the terrible thing that happened in my studio it was one of the pieces I could rescue so I kept it for a souvenir and show it to you here so you can see the grandeur of the Queen of France's entourage even in an unfinished state. The other part I will tell you later, but I don't have a picture of that.

SEVENTEEN

"I tell you, it is we who go first, following the queen in the wedding procession." I could hear the sound of stamping and clattering. If they were throwing things, I didn't want to go in. That is the problem with serving people of great estate. You don't get to choose. And if it were me, I'd choose not to get hit by some flying boot, and instead I'd take my runny nose and fever to bed. Just my luck to get thrust by an errand into the middle of a quarrel.

"And I say no flute players go first; it is the trumpeters. Have we not gone before her in the procession entering the city?" Trumpeters have big lungs. I sneezed in my sleeve again and put my hands over my ears. Then I took a deep breath and stepped into the musicians' dorter, which was in ordinary times a wine cellar. Knowing musicians, the proprietors of the house had taken out the casks, however.

The princess and her large following had been given a house separated from the big, ugly old Hôtel de la Gruthuse by only a garden. But it was very crowded, for besides the guests of rank she had brought from England seventy-five lords and gentlemen, fifty household officials including her secretary, chamberlain, treasurer, almoner, and physician, and more than forty ladies and maids as companions as well as Lady Guildford, who had been her governess since she was small and was now her chief Lady of Honor. That is not to count all the running footmen, stable boys, servants, a jester, and me. So you can imagine everyone was always stepping on everyone, especially trying to prove how close they were to the queen and quarreling over who went first.

"No, no, no!" cried a slender priest. "The singing priests and boys follow first in the procession behind the queen and her pages, then the instruments, then the trumpets, who double back to stand at either side of the hall beside the dais. Oh! What are you doing here?"

"Tell her not to sneeze in here. She'll poison the air."

"Mother Guildford wants a flute player to accompany Mistress Boleyn on the lute, while the queen is being readied for the banquet." Genteelly, I wiped my nose with my sleeve again.

"And a singer?" the clerk's voice was plaintive.

"Mistress Boleyn and Mistress Grey sing very nicely already, thank you. And Lady Guildford will have no more men than needful in the queen's chamber." Then there was considerable quarreling and grumbling about what a dragon Mother Guildford was and finally they picked out one of their number. Hurriedly, he put on his livery coat, then followed me up the winding stairs and passages to the state chambers.

In the midst of all this hubbub, jockeying, and jealousy, I passed in and out of the chambers of great ladies with hardly any notice, carrying my paint case where I willed, and Lady Guildford favored me because I took her likeness once in England and made her look most distinguished instead of full of wrinkles. And when there were games and music on a rainy afternoon, I was there, too, for amusement, taking sketches of gowns and faces. For to calm my heart after losing poor Tom and Master Ashton, I had begun the drawings for a little panel of the queen's triumphal entry into Abbeville, and all the ladies liked to comment on the progress of the work and ask that their complexions be made pale and their jewels large. There was something about painting all that splendor, and a world better than it is, that took some of the ache away. It was an elegant little wood panel I was working on, not bigger in size than three hands' breadth, and our princess, now styled the Queen of France, sat in her litter at the center of it, as bright as the rising sun.

So except for the flute player and one very old footman, it was a quiet ladies' time that afternoon, while the maids of honor combed out the queen's hair and laced her into her big gown for the reception banquet and ball being given in her honor by the Duke and Duchess of Angoulême. Two ladies opened her coffer of jewels, and two more brushed her cloak and shoes. Even so, there were many who just waited to be of assistance, or sang good English songs in harmony to the sound of the lute and flute. The music echoed strangely in this ornate foreign chamber. In the corner, I was working on a sketch of Mistress Boleyn at the lute to be sent to her father. Quietly supervising it all, Mother Guildford glanced up every so often with her eagle's eye from her embroidery tambour.

Suddenly there was a crash and the door was thrown open. Everyone turned and stared. We could all hear the sound of men speaking French and laughing beyond the open door. A pale-looking footman barely had time to announce the Duke of Angoulême before several very drunk men tried to push their way into the room. The tall one in the damask gown and crimson hose I recognized from the ceremonies. Duke Francis, swaggering with drink, his gown thrown back to show his slashed doublet and embroidered codpiece. Beside him was a dark-haired man I had seen before, and behind that man two more who looked familiar. Mother Guildford set down her tambour and hastened to the door, blocking it.

"Her Majesty receives no one at this hour. She is not yet dressed to receive a gentleman of your rank, monsieur," the old lady announced firmly.

"Nonsense, she is my honored mother." The duke swayed as he spoke. "I have come to pay homage to her. See, Bonnivet? I was right about the color of her hair. As red as can be. Either you are blind, or you have lied from gallantry." The queen's long hair was flowing over her shoulders, not yet confined beneath its headdress. I could see that her eyes were shocked, as if she saw something new and menacing in the man that Mother Guildford was keeping from her chamber.

"Step aside, woman, my lord of Angoulême wishes to greet his guest of honor, with the affection due a relative," the man called Bonnivet said.

"The Queen of France sees no one today before the banquet," announced Lady Guildford. The queen's ladies took advantage of the delay to hurry her into an antechamber out of sight of the duke and his companions. I could see the duke's eyes narrow. He was not used to being crossed, I could tell, especially by women. French are that way, you know. Touchy. Especially about things like that. They're always pulling out their swords because someone stepped on their shadow or insulted the way their moustache grows or something. I could see him deciding not to make a scandal by pushing past an old lady who would probably scream and make a terrible stir, but I could also see him being very insulted that he didn't get his own way, even if he *was* drunk.

"The old woman gives herself airs," he growled as he turned away. "I'll see to *her.*" The sound of malcontented grumbling followed them as they swaggered away.

"So, you see, Nan, it was really a terrible scandal. And I think that the duke did it just to see if he could catch a glimpse of her undressed." I was huddled up in bed at last, wrapped up against the cold, and coughing as loudly as the last trump. Everyone was off at the banquet, and since it was in the annex of the king's hôtel, we could hear the shouting and music from the hall and the scurrying of cooks and lackeys just by opening the shutters on our little attic window.

"Oh, if you'd heard what I heard from the boy who turns the spit—see what I've brought? They hardly even missed it, they had so much. Besides, they never even noticed me in the bustle. Everything's going on out there. They've even lighted some big bonfire on the other side of town. Everyone's celebrating." She took a napkin off the dish and revealed several slices of ham, all spicy and hot, to go with the loaf of bread and flask of French wine she'd gotten.

"Oh, you are clever, Nan. How would I manage without you? That looks very good. I think I'll live."

"I think you will, too, God be thanked, but not the way you've been rushing about. You don't want that cough to settle in your chest. I'll make a poultice tonight. Now, about that boy, let me tell you. *He* says he got it from the cook, who speaks French even better than you do, who got it from a liveryman in the duke's household. That man has a *terrible* appetite, just terrible. When he's in Paris, he never attends to business, just roisters at houses of ill fame with his friends—that Bonnivet, and Fleurange, and all of those that he grew up with, all of them old hands at troublemaking. They ride through the streets looking for likely women, then follow them home and demand them from their husbands or fathers—or deceive them, or bribe them, or take them by force. They just don't hear the word *no*. And women of the court—oh! You can't even count his conquests, and him only twenty. His sister and his mother, they just look the other way. And his sister, that Duchess of Alençon. She gathers men and women together to debate things no proper person discusses. And do you know what's worse? They say she's writing a book."

"A book? And her not a nun? Why, that's a scandal, Nan."

"The scandal's worse than that. They say it will be a dirty book, Mistress Susanna, a book of racy stories that she's been collecting about love affairs at court."

"Oh, my. Cut me another piece of that ham. Then I do believe that what I thought is right. That man wants an affair with our princess. After she's married, she'd better keep her door locked."

"He won't get past Mother Guildford, that's for sure. I wouldn't care if he were the king himself, he'd get nowhere with *me*, and he'll get nowhere with *her*. He doesn't understand Englishwomen. When we are looking after our own, we are made of iron."

"I'm afraid I'm feeling made of slime just now, Nan. Pass me that cup. Even wine tastes odd with this horrible cold."

"Well, you're to be pardoned this time," said Nan, and her face softened with the sad memory. "It's hard here, and I loved that boy, too."

"It's not just him, you know that, Nan." Nan stiffened with indignation.

"The man defamed you, Susanna. Stealing a kiss doesn't make it right again. He never apologized, never at all. And after all you did for him! If I could wish a man back from the dead, I would wish it for him, though as far as I'm concerned I'm much happier never seeing him again. But he should come back to make good to you, so you can see him plain, and not keep mooning over him as if he were some martyr and dead saint. That's what I would wish! For him to stand here, as rude as ever, so you could be rid of him for once and for all!"

"I've tried to put away my thoughts on him, Nan. I can't help it, I keep thinking on him. I want to tell him he was wrong. I wasn't making my way in the world like these bad French ladies. I do honest work. Well, sort of honest," I added as an afterthought, thinking about all those Adams and Eves. Well, whatever it looked like, it wasn't as bad as telling everyone's secrets in a book of racy stories. But maybe I was wicked, for thinking over and over again about that kiss, instead of offering prayers and pious meditations to God about sin. Why had I suddenly begun to yearn for sin so much and me not even married, when being wedded to Master Dallet had made me yearn only for virtue? Ah, God, Robert Ashton was dead and rotten at the bottom of the ocean. Was it a judgment on me for my wickedness? My thoughts had strayed so far from those recommended for the virtuous widow in Chapter the Ninth of *The Good Wyfe's Booke of Manners*, that I had grown ashamed to open it up. And my heart kept hurting, or maybe it was my chest, from coughing.

The next morning, preparations began at dawn for the wedding, and I managed to get a perch in a crowded window with a view of the garden to see the procession. There was a light wind, and it brought cinders onto the sill, where one of them caught the back of my hand. It was a tiny, blackened fragment of floating paper, with a letter, in even deeper black, still visible on it.

"What's this?" I sniffled. "They're burning books?" I felt all feverish, and the garden seemed to sway in the gray, early-morning light. A potboy squashed in beside me answered.

"Oh, it must be from the great fire last night. Half the town, they say, burned on the other side of the river. I heard the Italian ambassador complaining he was nearly killed." Oh, I thought, now I'm going deaf, too.

"I didn't know. I had a fever last night. I guess I didn't hear the fire bell."

"They didn't ring it. It would have spoiled the ball last night. They say they might have stopped it sooner if they'd had more men to pull down the walls." First the storm, then the fire, I thought. I've never heard of so many bad omens before a wedding. How can it turn out well?

"See there, the English knights. How many? One ... two ... I count twenty-six. Not bad. Ah, the queen looks much better dressed in the French fashion." The Frenchwoman on the other side of me was making her own personal assessment of English glory. Behind the heralds and macers followed the musicians with all their different instruments and the singing priests. Now the princess had stepped from the wide stone doorway, accompanied by two great lords, Norfolk and Dorset, who stood on either side of her. She paused a moment. Laden with jewels, almost dwarfed by her huge dress of cloth of gold and ermine, she looked small and lost. The cold wind ruffled her gown and set the embroidered silk banners in the procession flying. The gray light shone dully on the golden gown and glanced feebly from the heavy burden of jewels, making them look almost black. Music, praises, and the shouts of admirers filled the garden. Then the heavy, bearded old lords in their ponderous, jewel-encrusted gowns assisted her down the steps. Behind her followed thirteen of her favorite ladies, and each of them was escorted by two gentlemen, as well. Behind them, the procession seemed to go on endlessly. The brown, autumnal garden, passageway to the great hall in the Hôtel de la Gruthuse, was all blooming with moving color. I stayed in the window until the last page had vanished into the wedding hall. I suppose somehow I thought it was my duty to try to impress the scene, the costumes, on my mind for some unknown future purpose, but I found them blurring strangely. All the singing, and praises, and glitter, seemed oddly darkened, as if some evil shadow had floated over them. Maybe it's just the fever, I thought, as I made my way back to bed. The rain, which had broken briefly, began to pour down in sheets. In the distance, far beyond the gray towers of the Hôtel de la Gruthuse, I could hear the roll of thunder.

Claude of France, heiress of Brittany, eldest daughter of Anne of Brittany and the King of France, and Duchess of Angoulême, was in her dressing chamber, attended by several of her favorite ladies, a half dozen spotted, hairy lap dogs, the Duchess of Alençon, her sister-in-law, and Gaillarde the Fool, a fierce, dark-browed, sharp-tongued little woman no taller than a dwarf. Claude herself overshadowed the little woman by only an inch or two, limped badly, and was, in addition, immensely fat, her face puffy with some strange disorder, her eyelids swollen and her eyes squinting. An unfortunate luck of the blood, everyone knew. She resembled her mother, but some unhappy trick of breeding had pushed the French princess from the merely ugly to the abnormal. Sweet tempered and simpleminded, she was still far from her twentieth year. As if to compensate for the cruelty of nature, humanity had made accommodation. Alone in the court, she had no enemies. Her mind was incapable of perceiving that she was being used. To her, everyone was handsome, everyone was clever, everyone was virtuous. And because the courtiers enjoyed seeing themselves reflected so admirably in the mirror of her simplicity, they never disabused her of her notions.

"Oh," she said, looking down disconsolately at the embroidered crimson velvet gown she was wearing, "this gown sorrows me. Mother not dead a year, and the king has ordered that I put off mourning in honor of my stepmother. Even for my own wedding to my lord the duke, I wore black. How could he forget Mother so soon?"

"When a man catches sight of a redheaded woman, everything else flies out of his mind," said Gaillarde in her funny bass voice, and with a mincing walk, and head held high, she mimicked the new queen in that droll way she had. Marguerite, the Duchess of Alençon, burst out laughing. "He has told the court that three times last night he crossed the river, and could have done more if he wanted. An astonishment of nature! Blame the red hair." Gaillarde patted her own dark head in an imitation of primping. Now even Claude laughed. Then a puzzled look came over her face.

"Three times?" she said slowly. "But even my lord, who is so much younger . . ." She shook her head as if thinking deeply. "It must be because he is a king," she announced, as if she had solved a very complex puzzle.

"That's it!" announced Gaillarde, and Marguerite snorted. Her own mother, Louise of Savoy, had stayed away from the festivities in pure rage, pleading illness and the state of the roads. But Marguerite's husband had featured prominently in the ceremonies, and so she had smiled and smoldered while the old king celebrated his wedding to the woman who would displace her brother from the throne. How sure that foreign woman seemed of her beauty, how cold, how arrogant! And how the old king seemed to simper over her. Disgusting! And what a great train of followers she had brought with her, all clattering away in their alien tongue, rude, boastful, and ill-mannered!

"Things will be different now," said Marguerite, thinking to enroll Claude in her cause. "The English swarm everywhere. They will all

want favors and influence. To think that only yesterday they were attacking our cities."

"Yesterday? I thought yesterday was the wedding ... yes, certainly it
was yesterday. The foreigner brought a large suite so she could hear her
own language. Mother did that, you know. She could not be happy without hearing Breton about her. Of course, English is different. Breton
sounds comfortable, but that English! What an ugly-sounding language!
I'm sure they must be embarrassed to have such a language. Doubtless
they will try to learn French."

"Ha! They think they are speaking French!" announced Gaillarde.
"Hey, mounseer, move-o zzee cheval, je swee gentilhomme, goddam,
goddam!" She imitated the rolling, graceless, swaggering gait of an
English lord. The ladies all giggled. Gaillarde, encouraged, added a leer
to her performance, then pushed an imaginary hat over one eye and gave
a tug to the waist of an imaginary doublet as she pretended to be seeking out a likely lady. Claude looked puzzled, then, when she saw the
others laughing, she pretended to laugh herself, so as not to be left out.

"Oh, Madame, that's them exactly. They have no manners!" exclaimed one of her ladies.

"But some of the new queen's ladies have lovely manners," said
Claude. "That one that played so sweetly, Mademoiselle de Boline, for
example. She has been raised at the Regent's court and speaks almost
like one of us. And, oh! Madame d'Alençon, I must show you something—" Claude went to a large chest and rummaged among the
gloves and stockings she kept there. Then, triumphantly, she held a
sheet of paper aloft. "You see?" she said, "I can so find things after I
have put them away. Look at this." She brought the paper and spread it
out on her dressing table for Marguerite and her ladies to see. "This
one, here, beneath the angels, will be the queen my mother, and the
one on the other side will be the king in full armor, kneeling. And
there, in the center, at the hem of the Virgin, see that sweet little
winged baby? That is my brother, the Dauphin. Just so he looked before he died. She will paint them all just this size, and put little joints
between the frames to form a triptych that folds in on itself. See this?
It will all be no bigger than my hand." With a pleased look on her
face, she set her fat little palm beside the tallest drawing, a Virgin on a
cloud, with a winged angel peeping from a corner and a little cherub

entangled in the hem of her flowing robe. "I can take it with me every-where, and always think on the goodness of the Virgin, and the bless-ing of heaven."

"She?" said Marguerite. "Who is doing this for you?"

"Oh, the holy father, the English Archbishop Wulsei, has sent the cleverest, most pious widow to us, who paints these lovely tiny pictures to bring us closer to heaven. So you see? Not all English are bad. After all, we are all Christians."

"That we are," agreed Marguerite. "Pious, you say?"

"Oh, very pious. At first, I thought perhaps I might not wish her services. It is not respectable for a woman to go wherever she wishes, to travel without a husband. I had Mlle. de Boline question her in her own tongue, and she said she was a widow, whose hus-band left her nothing because he was murdered, poor thing, so she must make her own way. So then I thought, it will do no harm just to see what she can do. And she is so very respectable. She is never seen without a very fierce, dour old Englishwoman who protects her honor better than a mother. So I called her back, and had Mlle. de Boline question her again. And I found her conversation most edifying, for a person of low degree. She reads holy books every day and seems to know so very much about the life of the Holy Virgin. . . ."

"Reads books, you say?"

"Oh, very virtuous books. She told me of one, by a very devout man, that gives instructions to wives and widows. I think it should be made into French, to aid and comfort widows in their sorrow."

"English virtues into French, *hmm*," said Marguerite, and the odd-est little smile turned one corner of her mouth up. "I think I would like to see this prodigy. Send her to me when next she comes to you." It must be this one, she thought, looking again at the sketch. This is the one who painted the portrait de Longueville sent. Virtuous, in-deed. I'll have the real story, so I can tease de Longueville with it. I like the idea of the little devotional triptych. Perhaps I'll have one myself. Claude is too much of a simpleton to appreciate this work. A drawing of a monkey that was supposed to be her mother would please her.

A door opened far down a corridor, and she could hear scurrying footsteps traversing the long, tapestry-hung chambers into Claude's quarters. A maid of honor, young, out of breath, her headdress askew, was running toward her.

"Madame! Madame! There is news! Oh, what a scandal! The English queen is weeping in her chambers, and all her ladies are weeping, too!"

"What is this?" asked Marguerite, as Claude and her ladies turned toward the newcomer expectantly.

"Oh, Madame, the king has dismissed the English queen's entire suite. He says he will have only Frenchmen and women serve her."

"Do you know more? What has brought this about?"

"Oh, he is mightily incensed against that Madame Gil'for' who came with the queen. She puts on airs, and says who may see the queen and who may not. And she is always there, even when he would be merry with his queen, and he cannot be merry with her when someone he dislikes so much is always there. Oh, he says no man ever loved his wife so much, but he would rather be without her than have such a one as that Madame Gil'for' serving her. So now she is weeping, and he is lying down again, scarcely able to move with the gout."

Claude and her ladies had clustered around Marguerite and the attendant, all eager to hear the news. "Ah yes, the English, there were too many," said one.

"It was their airs. I myself have disliked that Mère Gil'for', she is a foul-tempered dragon."

"It is good they will be gone. They could help her carry on intrigues, and the king is too old to catch them."

"It is the honor of France...."

"Oh dear, oh dear!" cried Claude. "If they go away too soon, I shall not have my picture finished. I must go to my lord and beg that he intercede with the king. He must not send away the paintrix with the others. Or that charming little Nan de Boline. And Mademoiselle Bourchier, why, she is almost French. Surely, they are not displeasing to him like that haughty Madame Gil'for'."

But as usual, it was Gaillarde who had the last word. With the liberty allowed jesters, she plumped herself in the duchess's own chair, tipping her nose up arrogantly and assuming a broadly comic English accent. "I am sorry," she sniffed, "the queen is not receiving today. Who are you? The Pope? Oh, too bad, you'll just have to wait in the antechamber with the others. After all, I am Madame Gil'for', and a woman of great importance in Reechmon'. Oh? You have not heard of Reechmon'? Then that proves you are unworthy to know *me*." The ladies dissolved in laughter at this portrait of provincial snobbery, and Gaillarde clapped her stubby-fingered hands together, the bells on her red velvet dress quivering as she applauded herself.

The Ninth Portrait

Lady at the Virginals. *Silverpoint on prepared paper. 8 × 9". Anon. Early sixteenth century. J. Paul Getty Museum.*

Falsely identified in the upper-left-hand corner as a portrait of the young Anne Boleyn, this delightful drawing illustrates a typical evening in an upper-class household of the early Renaissance. Two good-looking couples in Italian dress are seated at a table, part-singing from a sheet of "table music," printed on all four sides for ease in sight reading. An older woman sits dozing over her embroidery, while two little dogs fight over a scrap beneath the table. Behind the virginals, a young man with foxy eyes and a long nose leans perilously close to the lady's bosom as he helps to turn the pages of music that sit before her on the instrument. The domestic charm and sly humor of this drawing, as well as the precise and slightly stiff draftsmanship, have led to its identification with the Flemish school.

—Exhibit catalog. Renaissance Drawings at the Getty

I made this picture at Mistress Anne's request to send to her father, but then because of things that happened it did not get sent and so I kept it with my other drawings for along time. Mistress Anne was brown-haired and slender, and most clever and interesting in conversation, as well as skilled in several kinds of music. She also had a sixth finger on one hand, which she usually hid in a fold in her skirt except when she was playing, but I did not draw that, because it would have annoyed her. I would never have thought her destined to be a queen, but that is how it turned out, although it is not part of my story. I always thought she was more likely to wed some rich country gentleman and spend her time telling him how to get on at court, which she was very good at. Perhaps that would have been a better idea.

EIGHTEEN

The Queen of France, her eyes red with weeping, sat in her chamber at Abbeville, dictating a letter to her secretary. It was a desperate letter, written in haste to her brother, the King of England. Around her sat a dozen of her ladies, pale with the disgrace of being sent home. In the outer chambers, in the kitchens, the storage rooms, the stables of the old stone house, men and women, stiff with shock, talked numbly to each other. How would they pay for the voyage home? What other household might employ them? Servants were aplenty in England. Musicians, cooks, stable hands might never find another place. The eight trumpeters clustered grimly in the courtyard, their voices bitter. How many lords were so great that they required trumpeters? From the height of the world, service to a queen, they had been tumbled into the abyss with the rest.

"I must pay them something . . ." the queen broke off in the middle of the letter. "How will they manage? They have served me honestly."

"You must ask the King of France to pay their passage home," said the secretary, looking up from his writing.

"Whatever you do, don't anger him," added one of her ladies. "Wait until he sends for you. Then be most kindly and gentle. If you are demanding, he will harden. Instead, beguile him. Then you must beg sweetly, prettily. . . ."

The hysterical girl paused, horrified. Was this what it meant to be a queen? To be a beggar surrounded by scheming foreigners? Why had no one told her? Why had she not understood?

"But I must have my Mother Guildford. Who will advise me if I have no one older and wiser near me? Oh, if only my lord of York were here. He is subtle, he would surely convince the king not to send away my good Mother Guildford." Her eyes were frantic. She felt she was stifling. Oh yes, the letter. She must tell the king, her brother. Mother Guildford had been taken ill with the news, and without her steady presence in the room, the girl-queen could already feel how lost and isolated she would be with her gone.

"You must write to my lord of York when you are done with this letter to the king. For while he will surely act from brotherly affection, my lord of York will advise him of some clever web of intrigue to get us back to you," advised one of her gentleman-ushers. Yes, it had to be. The Archbishop of York was shrewd and subtle. Wolsey would think of something terribly clever. He would advise her brother. They would make the King of France take back her servants.

"Begin again where we left off," she said to her secretary. Pausing, she breathed deeply to regain her control. "Tell him I am left alone, for on the morn after my marriage my chamberlain and all other men servants were discharged, and in like wise my mother Guildford with all my other women and maidens, except such as never had experience to give me counsel in my time of need, which is more to be feared than your grace thought at the time of my departing, as my mother Guildford will show you more plainly than I can write, to whom I beseech you to give credence . . ." Mother Guildford must tell King Henry the whole story in private, the part that could not be written, the part that would send him to her defense. He must hear that her physician had told her the King of France would most likely not live long enough to get her with child, that the heir apparent was pressing his unwanted attentions on her, that her honor was in danger, that all of England's grand dreams were on the verge of blowing away like smoke. Oh, yes, Mother Guildford must tell it all. She was abandoned here, in a court of intrigues too deep for her to fathom. Surely then, the King of England would somehow send Mother Guildford back to her again to tell her how to thread her way through the maze. He must.

That afternoon, the king sent for her. Pale, frightened, but determined, she took her lute to his sickbed. At the sight of her, so humble, so determined to be charming, the king's sunken eyes lit up, and the hint of a wolfish smile curved his pallid lips. *I am not yet too old to break this little filly to the bridle,* he thought.

"Play me some music of England," he said. "I would be merry today." First she played an air, then sang, in her pretty, light, girl's voice. *Charming,* thought the king. For hours she played. Spanish pavanes, English ballads, Italian airs. Sometimes the king listened with closed eyes, lying back on the pillows. Then he would sit up with a start, trying to conceal the signs of his growing weakness. She told him a riddle. He laughed. Delicious, he thought.

"My lord," she said, so sweetly that he thought she might be begging for some trifling toy, "might I ask one boon?" He nodded benignly. "Of all my servants, my dear old Mother Guildford has been my guide since infancy, could you not spare one . . ." Suddenly, the girl found herself looking at two hard, black stones, set in a fearful skull barely covered with an old man's parchmentlike skin.

"I will not hear that woman's name mentioned in my presence," said the King of France.

The queen broke off, frightened. She could hear her own heart beating, and her hands were clammy with the cold realization that she was no longer a petted princess, immune to the fearful dangers of court life. This man could do anything he wished with her. But beneath her fright, she could feel rage rising. Tudor rage, violent, passionate. Who was this old man that he thought he had a right to suck away her youth and joy? He was like some creature from the grave that needed to feast on the living to retain unnatural life.

"You will soon learn to be happy without her," said the king. "Besides, you should seek to please me in all things."

"My lord and king, that is my only desire," she said, bowing her head. Before this moment, she had seen only the king, the glory, the honor and wealth. Now she saw the man, and plainly. He is missing teeth, she thought, and his breath smells bad. His skin is old and putrid with disease. His body is corrupt and repulsive. I have been cheated. I have been sold. And it is my brother who did this. No, he will not send Mother Guildford back to me. He knew all along. He took the risk, but it is I who must pay. I will be destroyed here in France. For the first time in her short and spoiled life, the girl-queen knew true fear.

Two days later, a grand procession departed from Abbeville in the direction of Paris. Hundreds of French soldiers, mounted guardsmen, and nobles on heavy horses trapped out in gold and velvet led the vanguard. In their midst was the King of France, borne on a litter carried by two black mares, and the Queen of France, mounted, at his side.

Behind her rode those few of the English that were still in her suite, her almoner, her physician, her master of the horse, a half dozen ladies. Following them, her heavy gilded wagons, loaded with dowry plate, labored through the churned-up mud, and French stable boys, perched atop her spare heavy horses, led the long train of her white palfreys. Farther back, with the baggage train of mules, a few minor attendants, ushers, and grooms mingled with the army of French servants that followed the king wherever he went. Awestruck peasants pulled off their hats and knelt in the mud as the procession passed the wintering farms and little villages on the way. It was the sight of a lifetime: the King of France and his beautiful English princess on the way to Saint Denis and her coronation.

From Abbeville on the same day, a long, straggling parade of English departed in the opposite direction. Heavily bundled against the cold, clumps of nobles were followed by their pack mules. Behind them, beneath the steel gray sky, followed hundreds of servants, strung out along the muddy road on foot, carrying all they had on their backs. Ahead of them were Boulougne and the dangerous late-fall crossing of the Channel.

NINETEEN

"Why ever did they bury a lawyer so near the church? Someone's bound to hear us." The hour was just past midnight, and in the black sky, a half moon seemed to have entangled itself in the barren branches above the little country churchyard. Beyond them the gray stone of the square, Norman church tower shone dully in the moonlight.

"Trouble enough for us that he went and had himself buried in this village, master," said a burly man carrying a torch and a shovel.

"The damned wretch should have been buried in unconsecrated ground. It was his own fault he died. He shouldn't have crossed me, and that, I'd say, is suicidal, wouldn't you?" Crouch chuckled briefly at his own joke. "Well, he's in no position to refuse me anymore." Septimus Crouch smiled wolfishly as he took out his long, white, necromancer's wand. He gloried in the cold breeze that ruffled his dark, horned hair and brought to him the faint odor of decay. His nostrils flared, and his cold green eyes glittered with incipient madness. Tonight, the dead would talk, and at last the middle portion of the book of prophecies would be in his hands. Ludlow was a fool, to think he could elude him even in death. Crouch's assistants, who were his cook and his lackey, dipped their torches so that he could sprinkle the proper mixture of henbane, hemlock, opium, and mandrake into the fire. "Now," Crouch commanded, drawing his sword from beneath the long, black ritual gown he was wearing, "the circle." With the sword's point he described a counterclockwise circle in the dirt around the lawyer Ludlow's grave. The soggy ground, not yet sunken and hardened over the coffin, was quickly thrown back, and there was the sound of iron hitting wood.

"Berald, Beroald, Balbin, Gab, Gabor, Agaba, arise, arise, I charge and command thee," chanted Crouch, touching his long magic want to the coffin lid.

"I wouldn't bother with that if I were you," a sly, insinuating voice said. Swiftly, Crouch looked over his shoulder in the direction of the churchyard gate.

"Oh, I'm not there, I'm up here," said the voice. There was something about it that made even Crouch's flesh crawl. His assistants, hardened to their master's experiments, looked up in horror. A steamy sort of thing, like breath on a cold day, was swirling up above them, directly over the coffin.

"Avaunt, spirit, whatever you be," said Crouch, holding up the talisman that he wore around his neck.

"Avaunt, indeed, piffle," said the demon, and Crouch recognized the taunting voice from the mirror. Belphagor. In the shape of the grayish mist, shining in the moonlight, Crouch could see the form of an ugly creature with a long nose, little narrow eyes, bushy eyebrows, and scrawny arms with very long, ugly fingers. The figure was entirely naked. Analytically, Crouch noted a goat's tail and hairy legs like a goat's forming up in the mist. This is the most he's ever manifested himself, thought Crouch. He must have been feeding very plentifully somewhere. Has he goat hooves as well? But the long, skinny feet, with knobby toes, each knob growing a tuft of hair, were not at all like a goat's. And as the creature turned full face toward him, Crouch saw that he was equipped in a manner that far excelled any goat. Fascinating, thought Crouch, the demon master. A distant amusement stirred Crouch as he realized suddenly what kept bringing the demon to him. Why, he feeds on the emanation of my crimes, following me the way some starving cur follows a butcher with a string of sausages. That's how he's gained so much substance, compared to the previous times I've seen him. It explains why he keeps popping up, stirring my mind into some new rage. Carefully, Crouch, carefully, and you'll be able to lure him into your hand. After all, it's not as if I were dealing with a mind of the quality of Lucifer's.

"Lord Belphagor, what has led you to grace our humble essay at necromancy?" said Crouch, beaming on the swirling, misty thing, and bowing genteelly.

"You've done it wrong," said Belphagor. "You'll never raise his corpse that way."

"What do you mean? I've eaten dog's flesh for nine days, and I've worn a used winding sheet since the sun went down yesterday. I think I have everything in order. You're not speaking to an amateur, you know." Crouch's voice was arrogant and assured.

"You ate salt," answered Belphagor.

"I did not," said Crouch.

"Master," said the cook. Crouch whirled on him, cracking his wand across the burly man's shoulders.

"It's you. You salted something."

"Master, I didn't. But remember the bread you bought? Straight from the baker with never a thought. I told you you shouldn't."

"Ha!" said Belphagor. "I told you so. Never contradict a demon. Now, listen to me, Crouch. I've decided to reveal the hidden treasures of the earth to you in return for a few favors."

"My soul perhaps? Regrettably, I've already signed a contract for it to Lord Beelzebub, but I'm sure with a person of your stature in the infernal, an arrangement can be made...."

"Your soul's a joke, Crouch. I don't want a used soul in that condition. I do have some standards, you know. Now a nice virgin, or a pious widow, or maybe a new little priest, all fired up with virtue, those are good souls to have. Hardly used, all fresh. Yours is shopworn. No, I need something else. I hear you're an expert in antiquities. What do you know about genealogy?"

"I know a great deal. It's part of the study of antiquities, and a fit subject for study for any noble gentleman. Is it something you wished to take up, your lordship? I can only commend my own poor talents to your glorious self. How honored I would be to instruct you. I can trace the line of the Caesars straight into the great houses of modern times, with only two breaks. I know ancient seals, heraldry, the descent of kings...."

"Yes, this's what I want. Royal houses. What do you know about King Philip of France, from around, ah, let's see, your time, 1312. He's dead, isn't he?"

"Ah, you mean Philippe the Fair of the house of Capet. Yes, he is, regrettably, dead."

"Then that wretched feather ball was right," muttered the demon to himself.

"What's that you said, Lord Belphagor? How may I serve you further?" Crouch was an expert at sensing weakness, even in demons. Something has made him desperate for this knowledge, he thought. Tease out the cause. Gently, gently. Flatter him. Make yourself indispensable.

"I need to know his house. Who rules in France now?"

"The Valois rule. They are the cadet branch of the Capetians."

"Then they're still there. Ten thousand curses! I'll have a terrible job, finding them and rooting them all out," muttered Belphagor.

"Is Your Grace in need of expert assistance?"

"Not grace, you idiot," said the demon, swirling upward in a rage, "Your Damnedness, *if* you please." The two quaking assistants had dropped their torches, crouched down, and put their arms over their heads, but Septimus Crouch still stood upright, his green eyes as hard as diamonds, his mind calculating at full speed.

"Why, yes indeed, yes, yes, Your Damnedness." Touchy beggar, thought Crouch.

"*Much* better," said Belphagor, and the steamy stuff settled toward the ground and firmed up. Crouch's assistants had fainted. Puffing, Crouch knelt down and picked up a sputtering torch before it went out in the damp mud. Fascinated, he held it near the demon, the better to behold him. Belphagor folded his arms and smirked. "Seen enough? Now, let's get down to business. I need to travel on this earth among men. I had plans to get a body for it, but . . . someone spoiled them."

"Indeed. Had you planned a possession?"

"No, they're hard to keep. I was going to be born." The demon confides in me already, Crouch exulted. Get him to reveal more, and you shall own him at last, he said to himself.

"A pity, I do commiserate," said Crouch, looking touched. Belphagor cocked his smoky head to one side, inspecting him. As a demon of destruction, he always knew the right thing to say to cause the most trouble.

"You'd be more touched if you knew what you're looking for was not hidden by that dead man. Always look for a woman when you're looking for trouble. It will save you the bother of rummaging in that grave."

"Susanna Dallet, that lying little vixen!" Crouch exclaimed, almost dropping his torch in his excitement and rage. Belphagor swirled happily above him now.

"Do you want her?"

"I want her body—in pieces. I want the manuscript she hid from me. Who is she working for? Wolsey? I swear, she's Wolsey's agent. Has she sold it to him? Did Ashton get it from her?"

"She's off to France, on that fat churchman's orders," announced Belphagor.

"The Valois. Damn. The manuscript goes to them, to thwart the plan of the Priory. I can't expect a penny from the Valois." Crouch clenched his jaw and began to pace back and forth before the open grave.

"What is all this mumbling? What's on that bit of parchment?"

"The Secret that will unseat the Valois from their throne. It's the center of a conspiracy. Get hold of that paper, and you can sell it to half the monarchs in Europe. It will cause untold trouble. . . ."

"Trouble? Then I'm with you on this, you dear, malicious man. Trouble for the Valois. Listen, Crouch, I need a human assistant. Someone who knows how you creatures breed, so I won't make any mistakes." Belphagor's large eyebrows twitched, and his face grew greener in the torchlight. He dipped and hovered close to Crouch, peering at him as if nearsighted. "Besides," he went on, "you humans all look alike to me. Well, with the exception of someone like you, so excellently shaped, you understand, with such a lovely whiff of evil about you. It makes problems for me, you see. It's just a little task, but once it's done, I'll reveal the treasures of the earth to you. Oh yes, and power, too. Glory? Fame? The sexual services of your choice, in great abundance? You can have all that if you like. The whole thing—it's yours, once this is done. Agreed?"

"Why, of course. A brilliant idea, Lord Belphagor. I couldn't have thought of a better one myself." Unheard of, thought Crouch. The demon has drawn the net around himself. He is caught, Crouch exulted. At last, he thought, the demon has fallen into my trap. First I'll explore his weaknesses, obtain his confidence and learn his secrets, bit by bit. I'll use the mirror to spy out his hidden dealings. Then I will discover and usurp his magic powers. "Would you like a contract?" Crouch asked agreeably, masking his eagerness. "Signed in blood, or possibly some other fluid you might prefer?"

"Oh, don't bother, friend," said the demon cozily. "Between us damned, a word is all that is needed. We'll shake on it." The demon extended his smoky, translucent fingers, and Crouch offered his heavy, gloved palm. The demon's touch froze him through, and the hair stood straight up on his head. The next day in his barber's mirror he would note that it had turned entirely white. Small matter, he thought, I'll turn it back again when I have acquired the demon's powers. But now, with the demon's touch still lingering on his palm, he shuddered.

"Cold?" said the demon, apparently full of concern. "We'll finish up at your place over a good hot posset."

"I'm afraid first you'll have to wake my servants. You haven't killed them, have you?"

"Oh, you'll have to do that," said the demon. "They've only fainted. Just give them a shake."

"Can't you shake them?" Suddenly, Crouch regretted his familiarity. The demon seemed angered.

"Of course not, you ninny. That's what I needed the body for. The one that stupid woman and that feathery oaf, Hadriel, tricked me out of. I can't move things out of their natural order without a body. The most I can do is push things that are almost going to happen into happening. A leaf about to fall, a cloud about to rain, a loose brick that just might fall on someone's head, that sort of thing. I can foment arguments, gather the storm clouds, but only when they're already there." Belphagor oozed like a sickly vapor over the two unconscious servants, staring resentfully down at them. "Why do you think demons go about whispering in people's ears to do evil, anyway? If we could do it all ourselves, we wouldn't bother wearing ourselves out whispering." Crouch looked up, amazed. It had never occurred to him. It makes sense, he thought, as he looked at the irritated demon. "Those sluggards of yours are not about to wake up, unless you give them a good kick," announced Belphagor in a petulant voice. Obligingly, Crouch kicked them awake.

"I . . . I didn't realize you needed to, um, possess someone . . . ah, can you lift anything?" Astonishing, thought Crouch. He can't pick up a poniard and run me through.

"Don't you get any ideas, Crouch. There are a thousand accidents a day, just waiting to happen. They provide enough for me to do what I wish. I guide a horsefly to this horse, rather than another, the horse bolts, and a man is crushed. I have sunk ships. . . ." Belphagor paused, irritated at the top-heavy, clumsy vessel he had failed to capsize in the storm. But that wasn't his fault. His almost-solid form grew vaporous with remembered rage.

"Great Lord Belphagor, Your Damnedness, I would never for a moment fail to remember your mighty powers," said Crouch smoothly.

"Good," said Belphagor. "Now, I'll see you to your mule, and just float on behind you back to the City." Together, the naked demon and the diabolist knight walked to the tethered mules, as if they were the oldest of friends. Belphagor put one icy arm around Crouch's shoulder, waggling his bushy eyebrows as he spoke.

"Lord Belphagor, let me make a small suggestion," said Crouch, as he put his arm chummily around the demon, hardly flinching at the cold. "I do believe you could walk among men without notice, if you wore elegant enough clothes. It's the goat's tail that gives you away. But most people are so impressed with a handsome suit they never notice insubstantiality. And your codpiece would hardly be larger than some I've seen at court. We'll make an appointment with my tailor in the morning. I think you'd turn quite an elegant figure."

"Why, Crouch, my friend, what a splendid thought. What do you think of travel? I've a mind to visit Paris on business."

"Paris? I travel there often, my dear Belphagor. But the fashions are somewhat different there. You'll have to have another wardrobe made."

"Fashion? What is that, my dear Crouch? I told you, I need introduction to the affairs of men." Already, Belphagor began to dream of greater elegance and consequence in the infernal order. Lucifer had such splendid manners. Now, if he could only learn that smooth way of talking Crouch had. . . .

"Ah, fashion," said Crouch, sensing the demon's childish vanity. "The mastery of fashion is the first sign of a gentleman. That, and the art of carving. Yes, I'll be delighted to show you. In Paris, a man's gown must be longer, cut low to reveal the doublet across the chest, and the linen! Ah, the linen. You should have Spanish embroidery, the best."

"Done by nuns?"

"Of course, done by nuns. It will become you most excellently. . . ." Vanity, thought Crouch. With all the human sins he's sucked up, he's managed to drink in a hogshead of vanity—it's gone all through him. It all goes to show you should watch what you eat. And what a convenient handle to control a small mind. I have him.

At every word, Crouch's servants could feel their skins crawl. And yet—and yet they had to give credit to a man who could strike up a friendship with a supernatural monster without even seeming to turn a hair.

Three unknown knights in romantic disguise, their old-fashioned surcoats marked with red crosses in the manner of the crusaders, clattered through the muddy streets of Canterbury to the gates of the gray, Norman castle within the walls. Behind them, a horde of esquires, pack horses, and armed retainers numbering over a hundred proclaimed that these were hardly the wandering knights errant they pretended to be. These were England's champions, bound to answer a challenge to the wedding joust issued by the Dauphin of France, Francis of Angoulême. Entrusted as the king's lieutenant in these games of chivalry was his closest companion, Charles Brandon, Duke of Suffolk. Beside him rode Sir Edward Neville and Sir William Sidney, partners in the affair. But neither of them knew that Suffolk had been given another, secret, task to carry out, the negotiation of an offensive alliance between France and England against Ferdinand of Aragon.

Suffolk had not yet dismounted when a messenger, his horse lathered, clattered into the castle courtyard. Looking about him, he recognized Brandon, fabulous disguise and all, and rode toward him. "My Lord, news!" he cried, and Suffolk, turning his head, recognized a fellow courtier, who had preceded him to France.

"What is it, Sir Gerard?" he asked, pulling his horse to a standstill. Behind him, his mounted guardsmen, his retainers, his pavilion-laden packhorses, all stopped, crowding the gates of the courtyard so as to make them impassable.

"The King of France has dismissed all the English servants, ladies, and attendants sent into France, even Mother Guildford. They are making their way home with great hardship, and the queen is left alone, and very distressed."

Blood traveled up Suffolk's thick neck. He drew his beetling, dark brows together. The muscles in his massive jaw twitched with rage. "It is the Howards," he said. "The Howards and Norfolk. They have done this. They have influenced the French king to send away these attendants."

"Doubtless, my lord, doubtless. Norfolk, who accompanied the queen, agreed to the plan."

Then it is sure, thought Suffolk. He was never swift of thought, but once his slow brain had seized upon an idea, it worried it and tore it apart like a bulldog. The king wanted the alliance with France because Wolsey thought it was good. In this, Suffolk had risked all to stand with Wolsey. A nice little side payment from Wolsey had not hurt his conscience on this matter, either. Now, Wolsey had chosen the servants. If they were gone, Wolsey's influence with the queen was gone. But he knew Mary. She would grow frantic without her Mother Guildford to steady her. She would do wild things, imprudent things. She was a woman; no, worse than a woman, a girl without experience of the world, her head easily turned, her will easily deceived. She would misstep, she would alienate the king, she would undo the alliance, and with it Wolsey's and his own fortunes. Who knows? Grief might make her lose the child she had conceived. Or worse, without faithful attendants, some French enemy might drug her food, so she would miscarry, and with the child would go England's hopes. Yes, it had to be his enemies the Howards. They would ruin the alliance to ruin Wolsey and himself. Anything to gain the exclusive right to influence the king. A family of wolves they were; they were capable of anything that would advance their clan. He must abandon his heavy horses and ride full speed to the coast. He must get to France to negotiate the treaty before the Howards could stop him.

That night, Suffolk sat up by the light of a candle, writing his alarming news to the king in the unformed hand and outlandish spelling of a man who had spent less time with his tutor than in the lists. The next day he and his two companions rode alone at full speed to take a ship for France. With gray, hooded cloaks thrown over their curious disguises, they were the very picture of knights errant hastening to rescue their queen from her distress. And as far as Neville and Sidney knew, that was exactly the case.

"This Duc de Suffoke has landed at Calais, and my son has gone to meet him and invite him to the boar hunt before they arrange the tourney in Paris." Louise of Savoy's tone was meaningful. Her eyes were as bright and hard as a ferret's on the hunt, and her nostrils tight with the smell of conspiracy aborning. "The King of England sends him as ambassador with a purpose, an evil purpose, my daughter." At the news, Louise had at long last deemed it politic to recover from her "illness" and leave her country seat at Romorantin posthaste to come to Paris for the coronation. She had arrived the very day before, reclining in a litter, pale with rice powder, and stewing with pure rage. Now she had come to the very house in Saint Denis in which the uncrowned queen was staying, attended at the king's order by Claude, her son's wife, her own daughter, Marguerite, and her dear friend, the Baronne d'Aumont. Keen and fierce eyed, she had taken up the reins of the conspiracy for her son once again, drawing informants to her, counting her allies and her enemies. She must undo these rival conspiracies. Nothing must keep Francis from the throne. Her son would rule France, and she would rule her son.

"Suffoke? Which one is he, Mother? Not the old scheming one with the beard who left just after the wedding?"

"No, far worse. I have received a report from Longueville. He was the queen's lover in England. King Henri must have fears our king cannot sire the son he desires. The son that will steal our throne for the English. He sends this Suffoke to do the deed, disguised as England's 'champion' for the great tourney at the coronation. 'Champion,' ha! Champion stud, to keep our beloved Francis from his due." Louise leaned back against the pillows of the bed on which she was "resting," fully and immaculately clad in her black widow's gown. Schooled in the hard court of the old queen regent, her enemy, she was incapable of perceiving anything as coincidence. Were there such a thing, and it did not favor her son, she would stamp it out with the same ferocity with which she had foiled the dozens of other plots against him. She passed the back of her hand across her brow. "I suffer greatly, my daughter. You must help me in this."

Marguerite, standing by the bedside, looked alarmed. "The English ... they are unscrupulous. What a schemer that Wolsey is!" Louise sat sat up suddenly, ramrod straight, and her voice was fierce.

"Listen, my daughter. Neither you, nor Claude, nor the Baronne must leave the queen alone for an instant. Especially when that Suffoke finally arrives. He must be given no chance to make an English heir to the French throne." With strong fingers, she grasped her daughter's arm, pulling her closer, as she spoke with quiet ferocity. "Impress upon Claude that it is her duty, her duty to France, her duty to her own children, who will be disinherited by her innattention, her inability to be suspicious and watchful enough. Make sure she understands and does not blurt out the Secret in some weak moment to the wrong person. I rely on you. Not an instant alone, if you love your brother."

"Yes, Mother, not an instant alone," said the Duchesse d'Alençon, taking leave of her mother and returning to the great gallery where the queen, Claude, and her ladies were whiling away the time before their great midday dinner.

Braziers at each end of the gallery flickered and smoked, chasing the damp chill from the air. Rich arras, tapestries hung on frames a foot or so away from the walls, stopped the cold breath of the stone from entering the room. Even so, the heavy silks and brocades of the ladies were lined with fur, and their elaborate, jeweled headdresses and hoods served the double purpose of warmth as well as display. The queen was playing at cards with Lady Grey and the Baronne, while Mistress Nan Boleyn, so pleasing with her charming French and the supple manners she had learned at the Regent of the Netherlands' court, was explaining the game, an odd English one, to the French ladies who watched at the card table. Claude herself had requested that the girl stay, on the grounds that she "was so mannerly that she could hardly be called English."

Claude herself was not playing. Cards confused her in general, and new card games even more so. Besides, listening to foreign accents made her head hurt. She sat apart on a wide, cushioned bench, while a lady attendant read to her from a book of pious meditations. She was holding her face curiously still, and Marguerite instantly saw the reason. Seated on a stool in front of a stolid and curiously carved little easel with folding legs sat a young woman in widow's black, a black silk smock over her clothes, painting with the tiniest brushes imaginable. In spite of the importance of her errand, Marguerite found herself pausing. A brief smile played over her curved mouth, and the intelligent eyes above her long nose lit with instant recognition.

The little square of parchment pinned to the board, ready tinted with a pale flesh color and no bigger than a baby's palm, told the whole story at a glance. The paintrix's last strokes had finished the dim, reddish outlines of Claude's likeness. Now she took a clean brush from the trough at the bottom of the little drawing board and dipped it in the color that filled one of the mussel shells that lined the niches carved up each side of the board. With a fascinating precision, the artist began to lay on tiny strokes of color, so fine as to be almost invisible. One brush done, she put it in the narrow cup fastened to the side of the board, then took another. Delicate blue violet was mingled with the flesh tone, and shadows began to form on the tiny visage. A flick of black created Claude's dark eyebrows, the dark of the nostril, the shadow between the lips. Or was it black? So cleverly were the colors mixed that Marguerite could hardly divine the true tints. All she knew was that when they were laid on the drawing, the true color of a human face, scarcely bigger than a man's thumb, emerged. Marguerite inspected. Claude's homely visage, plump and squint eyed, peered back at her, the very image of life. And yet, somehow, the painter had caught her simplicity, her capacity for earnest devotion. Marguerite found herself touched, then marveling at the talent that had such capacity to arouse her sympathy. I would like my likeness taken, too, she thought. Something spiritual. Perhaps in prayer.

Now as the artist left he first work on the face to dry, she began to fill in blocks of color on the bosom of Claude's gown, and on her elaborate sleeves and headdress. There was no question in Marguerite's mind. It was the painter of the miniature, the woman of the ghost story, come over in the English queen's baggage. So, she didn't have a lover after all. She had painted the miniature herself and passed it off as a man's work to get the fee. How had she come to emerge from her disguise? Marguerite, the lover of stories, hesitated for a moment, wanting to call over one of the last English attendants as a translator to question the painter. No, she thought. Later. This business is too important.

"Madame, I must speak to you alone. Send away your lady reader." Claude, careful not to move her head from its pose, consented, and the lady folded her book and bowed gracefully before withdrawing. The artist continued to paint. Doubtless, she does not understand French, thought Marguerite. Even so, she lowered her voice. "My lady mother has arrived, and she has heard bad news. The rumor is about that the

English king has sent the queen's former lover, this Duc de Suffoke, to get her with child should the king fail. His position as ambassador is a pretense. The treaty with England is not his first task. Mother warns you that you must never, never, leave the queen alone, especially with that Suffoke, no matter what the pretense is, or you will have aided the disinheritance of your own children."

The painter continued to paint, as if heedless of the drama unfolding beside her. Claude's mouth moved to form the words "the disinheritance of your own children" as if she were figuring out a difficult problem in mathematics. Then, after a period of thought, she gasped. "You mean the English king has sent this man to commit such a great sin? Adultery? Dishonor? And she consents? Oh, what wicked English! They are capable of anything!"

Even at this outburst, the painter continued to paint, her eyes never leaving the tiny picture. She blocked in Claude's gold-toned velvet bodice in clear yellow ocher, ground with gum and mixed with sugar. Cleverly, she blended the shading color, made from ox gall ground with gum water, on her tiny mother-of-pearl palette, and then with a few swift, delicate strokes down the side of the shape, threw it into three-dimensional form. "Now you must not tell anyone of this but the Baronne d'Aumont," said Marguerite. "She alone is trustworthy. The queen must never know of our suspicions, or she will deceive us. Remember, this is for the sake of your children yet to be, and for your lord."

"I will always do everything for my lord's sake," said Claude, quite forgetting to hold her head steady. The artist was washing her tiny brushes in a bucket of water. How interesting, thought Marguerite, who was a great patron of artists and deeply fond of fine illuminations. The paints are water based. I thought perhaps they were oils, they are so richly colored, and that there was just too little of them to give off a smell. The artist began to pack her brushes. The box beside her was neatly laid out inside, with tiny compartments full of mysterious objects, little jars, and strange things wrapped up in paint-bedaubed linen. Claude waved her off with a gesture. "Tomorrow," she said, "at the same time. And bring the triptych with you, I want to see the progress."

As the artist bowed silently in assent and farewell, closed her box, folded her curious little easel, and left without a word, Marguerite regretted that she had not stopped to ask her about the ghost. And how like Claude, to insist on speaking French to a poor foreigner who obviously didn't understand a word. Then her breath stopped with a sudden thought.

"Madame Claude, dear sister, that is a very clever painter."

"Why yes, isn't she? She is making a devotional triptych for me, with Mother's portrait, and angels."

"But she doesn't speak French, does she? How does she know what you want?"

"Oh, she speaks lovely French," said Claude. "It's a bit slow, and has the oddest accent. Not altogether English. Sort of Flemish, too, I think. But I can understand her. I don't let her talk too much because accents give me a headache." Marguerite's heart froze. Everything. Revealed directly to a servant of the English. Quickly she called one of Claude's maids to her.

"Please, go find that paintrix right away. Take her to my chambers and have her wait for me there without seeing anyone. Tell her I will meet with her as soon as I can come away."

"Marguerite, my sister, is there something wrong?"

"Why, never, dear Claude. I am simply envious of your lovely portrait. I would have one made of myself, as well."

The Tenth Portrait

Charles II, Duc de Bourbon and Constable of France. *Ca. 1520. Oil on panel. 10″ × 11″. School of Clouet. Kunsthistorisches Museum, Vienna.*

This unusual portrait of the young Duc de Bourbon in half armor depicts the gifted military leader at the height of his power. Master of most of the heartland of France through his marriage to Suzanne de Bourbon, only child of the former queen regent of France, he maintained a household to rival that of the king himself. The watchful expression on Bourbon's swarthy, narrow-featured face and the arrogance reflected in his dark eyes seem to presage his later armed rebellion against the throne.

—*R. Briggs.* Wars of the French Renaissance

The Duc de Bourbon was one of those who are too great to bother with mere money, and I found out too late that even though he was very grand, he was always in debt. He still owes me for his portrait, which he condescended to take away with him after offering many criticisms which I suppose were to take the place of cash. He said he would not have his portrait in small because he was greater in blood than any of the great personages I had yet painted and so would have his image greater, too. But the truth is he wanted to be in fashion, and to be in fashion he needed to have his portrait taken by me and that irritated him because I was a woman, and women shouldn't be in fashion.

He was very touchy about things like that and also who stood on his shadow and who sat ahead of him at the table or walked before him through a door. Everything anyone said to him seemed to set him off, but luckily I just filled him with flattery while waiting for him to pay, which he never did, but at least I didn't say anything that caused me trouble. I painted him in his tournament breastplate and tawny velvet and silver after the great wedding tourney in celebration of our princess becoming Queen of France. This is where I discovered a special way of putting the highlights on velvet which I have made one of my secrets and which sets me in great demand these days among the gentry.

TWENTY

The day the queen's servants were sent away, I was busy packing my box and wondering how I could get it and Nan and myself to Boulougne with no money and also no horses and wagons, because they were all going on to Paris, when a French lackey came with a list and said I could stay.

"It must be that Madame Claude. She wants her angels finished," said Nan. But all the rest of the day, people looked at me with red eyes as if I had done something wrong and by the time we left two days later I was glad they were gone, because some woman who did laundry for Lady Guildford started the rumor that I was asked to stay because I was having an affair with a lackey of the Dauphin's and I wasn't really English anyway, and what could you expect from someone who spoke French and put on airs the way I did. I know it wasn't right to be angry, but I was, even though I read through the part about the Virgin's perfect patience several times in my book in order to calm my mind. But it all just convinced me that it was utterly hopeless trying to be like her even leaving aside the fact that my station in life was not as exalted as hers and also not so virginal. Then that reminded me of the terrible things Master Ashton imagined about me and the great Wolsey, and that made me think about how the poor man was on the bottom of the ocean and dead and gone after only one most extraordinary kiss, and Tom with him because of my pride. And then I thought that maybe he had thought me an immoral woman which is why he had kissed me without asking, and now he was dead and I couldn't explain, and that made me all mixed up and sad and angry at once.

But work hid away my troubles, and even while we were traveling with the court to Saint Denis, which is outside Paris, I worked on the sketch for Madame's angels in spite of not being able to start the painting until we quit traveling, because I had to get the wood for the panels and also you can't boil up rabbit-skin glue without a place of your own because it smells odd. It was funny about those angels; they all had Hadriel's face, though I gave them different hair. I did think about him, because after all, not everybody is given the chance to see a real angel. But I have come to the conclusion that they have their own ways and you can't count on them for everyday, though I wouldn't tell just anybody that. Still, it was all very inspirational and lingered on in the picture I was making for Madame Claude, who was very fond of little tiny things, especially illuminations, and looked to be a source of money because she was better about paying than many other of these great folk.

It was a lucky thing that although I was still short of money because nobody had paid yet, I had plenty of first-quality parchment, and I just cut away some more at that used stuff Master Dallet had gotten. The part with the writing was not good enough for portraits but I thought I'd try dissolving the ink with an invention of my own and then burnishing it fine and using a good thick base coat on it so that I'd have something for some ideas of my own that were burning in my head. Somehow many of my pictures involved very beautiful babies, because still inside me was the sadness that I had had no baby except a very ugly one that was luckily dead. But if I could not have them I could paint them, much as I once painted beautiful dresses with great fervor when I was a girl in my father's house. But in between my ideas were still many grievous thoughts about poor Tom who had followed me and died from my fault, and also Master Ashton, who told lies and thought wrong things and kissed women without permission, but still did not deserve to drown so horribly. Besides, I could imagine what they felt from having been on that lower gun deck and sure the water would come in when I crossed the Channel myself. Sometimes I had bad dreams about it.

By the time we had gotten to Saint Denis it was very clear that Nan was needing a new shawl and some stockings and also my shoes had worn out and started letting cold water in and I couldn't just wear clogs to a fine place like the court so I needed another pair. That meant money, so I quit dreaming about my own ideas and worked very hard and used up almost all my colors that I had brought with me finishing Madame Claude's picture, so I could ask her for an advance to have the frame made and maybe also get another commission. It all turned out excellently, because Madame Claude liked my angels very well, especially since they included her mother who was dead. After, when I showed her my paintings in small, she stared at them a very long time. Then her face got all twisted, and she looked into the air as if she were thinking very hard, and finally she spoke.

"Could you make my picture like that, for me to give to my lord? If he took it with him on his travels, he could remember my face, and that I await him at home." Poor, poor thing, even if she was a king's daughter. Did she think a picture alone could stop that husband of hers, Duke François, from following everything in skirts? "And ... and, could you make me pretty? A ... a little more slender in the waist? The queen sets the fashion now ... he, ah, they all talk about her slimness...."

"However, Venus was more generous and shapely, they say," I said, trying to be tactful. But the poor girl looked very puzzled and alarmed, and then said, "Venus? Wasn't she a pagan?" I changed the subject to the sturdiness of the ancient queens of France, none of whom were pagan, and she finally said with a sigh, "I do look just like Mother. It is the royal blood of Brittany. Besides, they tell me that the father of that English King Henri was an usurper, with only the most distant claim to the throne. That would explain it. Doubtful blood. Shallow people run after false things." The workings of Madame Claude's mind were all visible, like the workings of a great clock when you go inside the church tower to see them. They creaked and clattered a great deal, too, not unlike the clock. But one forgives the noise for the miracle that it works at all.

The reason we had to wait in Saint Denis is because that is where the coronation of our princess was to be, and the French never allow an uncrowned queen into Paris. So she couldn't live in the palace of Les Tournelles until after the coronation and her formal entry into the city, which is a great celebration in itself. So everyone just waited and whiled away the bitter weather indoors, while the French ladies, including the duchess Claude, all attended the queen, instructing her in French customs and court etiquette. It was there that I discovered that painters are supposed to have no ears, because there they were all gossiping and scheming as if I weren't even in the room. And they had everything female, just to keep them safe, even female dogs and a female jester, which goes to show you how French men think. So when they were by themselves, they just told stories that would make you blush, except for some old ladies who counted themselves holy because they like to hear terrible things about martyrs, no better than those monks I used to sell Adam and Eve pictures to. So of course I heard right away about how the Duke of Suffolk was coming to cheat in the tourney and what a "petite famille" he had and how our Archbishop of York or even our king had really sent him to get the queen with child because the old King of France couldn't get her pregnant. But I had to be quiet instead of defending the queen's honor by asking how the secrets of the wedding bed could get across the Channel that fast. Too much pertness can get an artist hanged, as Nan often reminds me. But the danger of having something wrong fly out of my mouth was lessened by the fact that it would have to be in French to be understood. Also even though it made me nervous to worry about doing something wrong in this alien court, it was not so worrisome as thinking I might see that man in black following me. It felt good to have left him far away in London.

But I knew I had heard too much the day I came to paint Madame Claude, and that Duchess Marguerite who was collecting dirty stories to write a book walked right in and started to tell her how "Mother" told her never to leave our Queen Mary alone. I wasn't sure who "Mother" was, because I was still new to things there, but she certainly seemed like a mastermind and nobody's friend. I thought I might ask later who "Mother" was, but I didn't have the chance, because I was hardly out of the room when a lady in waiting came pattering after me and told me the Duchess Marguerite wanted to see me for some great honor, and I should come and wait in the antechamber to her bedroom without talking to anybody because, of course, the honor was much too big to let anybody know about. Some honor, I said to myself, thinking about that hangman's noose, or maybe some dreadful French oubliette somewhere. And I can't even say good-bye to Nan, or she'll get the same honor. Then I thought, well, maybe this is what happens to people who think unkind thoughts about husbands and then take money for lewd Bible pictures from wicked monks. It all catches up with one.

But soon I heard quick strides and the rustle of a heavy dress, and the Duchess Marguerite motioned me into her chamber and shut the door. She was about my age, but tall and athletic, with one of those unbelievably big noses that the French think are aristocratic. The only one bigger is on her brother, that Duke François who I am sure got the king to dismiss Mistress Guildford just out of spite because she barred the door to him. The Duchesse Marguerite also had eyes and hair that matched, a light chestnut color, and the eyes looked very worried. Oh, good, I thought. Maybe she doesn't want "Mother" to know that she was so careless with the secret. That means she can't do anything obvious to keep me quiet. Her bedchamber was very nice, even if it was only borrowed. There was a huge, dark, wooden bedstead hung with tapestry curtains with her initials and the crest of her husband, or at least what I took to be that, all embroidered on them in gold. There were also some excellent tapestries on mythological subjects including the Judgment of Paris with Athena looking quite angry, though entirely unclad except for her helmet. That was more than the others were wearing, and I must say, it made my Adam and Eves look modest by comparison.

"I was quite taken by the tiny portraits you make. They are quite in the style of our own late Maître Fouquet. Where did you study this art? It is most unusual for a woman to make her way alone like this." She had seated herself on her bed to receive me, and first I knelt down to her even though they are not such a kneeling court as in England but you can't be too careful, especially if you are in trouble. Then when she told me to rise, I stood to hear her speak. I was very cautious in the way I answered.

"My lady, it was my father who taught me this art, which he created by combining his own secrets with the arts of the manuscript illuminators. He said it was good for a woman to learn a clean and decent trade, in case a cruel fate left her alone."

"Then you are alone? Quite alone?" Oh dear, this wasn't the right direction for the conversation to take. I remembered Ashton's warning about how crafty the French are, and I felt great danger, so I answered in a way that would let her know I was not a nobody who could just disappear without being noticed.

"Even though I was left a widow, I have had the good fortune to be able to rely on the generosity and concern of my former patron, the Archbishop Wolsey." The name did its magic. She put an elbow on the bolster, but her face didn't change. Her eyes were shrewd, and her thinking process stayed invisible, unlike poor Claude's squeaking, groaning clockworks.

"Tell me of the Archbishop Wolsey. Is he an old man, fond of good works? I have heard he is often sickly and would send him some token of my favor." Aha. She is a clever one, this lady, I thought. If I say something personal, she will know me for a gossip and then I'll really be in trouble.

"My lady, I am not privy to the archbishop's secrets, being too humble to have knowledge of the great." She smiled.

"You seem properly discreet," she said.

"My lady, I have always taken as my guide 'Silence in a woman is golden.'" I expected her to nod piously, the way other ladies do when you say things like that. But she tightened her mouth, and her eyes grew sour.

"Where did you learn this maxim?" she asked.

"My lady, from my study of a book of virtues given me by my mother. It is called *The Good Wyfe's Book of Manners*, all about how one should behave in every circumstance. It also has an excellent recipe for roasting a bream, but the one for suet pudding never comes out right." I thought I could see her mouth twitch under that long nose of hers. Somehow, she seemed too curious, and too humorous, to be a wicked, scheming lady as I had thought.

"And why does the recipe fail, if the book is so excellent?" she asked.

"Oh, I am sure I have not read it correctly. The man who wrote the book is so wise in everything, surely he could make suet pudding come out."

"Has he other recipes that give no satisfaction, or only that one?" she asked, suppressing a smile. I gave a great sigh.

"There is one for husbands who take their pleasure elsewhere. It says to emulate the lady who cared only for her husband's pleasure, and so sent her own linens to the bed of the poor woman with whom he slept, that he might have greater comfort."

"I have read that story," said the duchess. "It is written in France, too. The linens had her own initials embroidered on them, and when the husband saw them he was ashamed and returned to her. So, you actually tried that?"

"I couldn't, my lady. My husband had pawned the linens to buy her a bracelet." I could feel my face burning with remembered resentment. The duchess burst out laughing, though I really didn't think it was a laughing matter.

"But still, you would say that your experience doesn't invalidate the recipe?" she said.

"Why of course not. It was just that my husband must have read the book first. And since he knew the holy man who wrote it is always right, he understood that the only way to avoid having to come back was to get rid of the sheets," I explained. The duchess snorted, which was really rather rude of her.

"Tell me, Maîtresse Susanne, if I were your patron, would you keep silent about all that you heard from my mouth?"

"My lady, even if I did not have that high honor, I would do so. I do not repeat things that are too high for me to understand and also none of my business. And besides, even if I did, who would believe me? I'm already thought to be half a madwoman, for my painting." I sighed just at the thought of it.

The duchess laughed again, and said, "I think I am right about you. I have in mind several commissions, when we are in Paris. Tell me, have you a studio?"

Now I thought about trickery, and how the Devil cozens people with what they want most, but then I thought about the studio, and was cozened. Ashton's advice flew out of my mind, and besides, he was dead, and what did he know about painting anyway? And then I thought most righteously about how I could paint the queen much better if I had that studio, and it was clear this duchess had money of her own. So I gave the duchess the answer that pleased her and let her know I could be bought, and at a good cheap price, too.

"No, my lady. I am confined to the miniatures, which are water based, until I have a place of my own. But I am afraid I may never get what I need, in a strange city, perhaps with powerful guilds."

"Then you will need me, I think. I am an important patron of the arts in this country. No one will dare cross me if I favor you. I will see that you have your studio." I could see her studying my face, and I knew she had seen the look of gratitude in my eyes. Her face relaxed, and her smile was genuine. "It pleases me to sponsor a woman in a man's craft. In *The Book of the City of Ladies* all creation is sustained by women's art and virtue, which is most pleasing to God."

"There is a city all of ladies somewhere?"

"There is a book, but not a city," she responded, in the tone of a governess correcting her ignorant charge. "It was written to celebrate women's virtues, by Christine de Pizan, a poetess of renown in our country." What a country, I thought. No wonder it's so full of sin. Women write books all over the place. Still, I can't be picky. The vision of my studio warmed my heart. When would the queen have the power and influence to help me this way, isolated as she was, and thoughtless, too, about the requirements of the artist's craft? It wasn't as if she ever paid me a penny, even when she had it. Besides, every sou of her attendants' allowances must now come from the French king, who was very stingy and hadn't paid anything either. Then I remembered that Wolsey had never advanced anything on that fifteen-pound allowance, and the duchess's patronage, even if she was a bit too, well, *French* for me, looked better and better. I could hear the duchess's chuckle. How annoying. I am used to reading people's thoughts, but she does it, too.

"I would have you come and read that book to us, making it into French, that my ladies and I may debate upon its merits," she said. Debate a work of virtue? I was shocked. What is to be debated about virtue? I felt sucked into the sin of it. I could just imagine how those loose-living court ladies would talk. That was what I got for my wickedness. It had all started the day I first put my foot on that slippery slope, that first step away from being a truly good wife, when I used my husband's sins as an excuse to do what I pleased. Now I was adrift in an alien court full of schemers. Ashton was dead, and the queen didn't know I was alive, and everyone had forgotten whatever it was Wolsey had sent me for which he had never bothered to tell me about. All I knew was that he wanted portraits but had never told me whose, and he wanted to know what paintings the king had, which I hadn't seen yet anyway. I was in a way the queen's servant, except that she didn't pay me; I was paid by the duchess Claude, but not her servant; now I seemed almost to have a patroness, but only if I didn't get in trouble with her or the rest of them. And on top of it all, I was to be not only a paintrix, but a jester.

"Oh, don't imagine it," said Marguerite d'Alençon, picking the thought from my head. "Gaillarde can't read." She smiled that knowing little smile she had, the one I was to paint her with later on. Then she looked me up and down, in a much too speculative fashion. "Tell me," she said, "would you like to marry again? If your work pleases me, I will arrange your marriage to a respectable gentleman of my household." My eyes widened in horror.

"Oh, the sheets." She laughed. "Maîtresse Susanne, haven't you yet learned that all men are the same? If you are to live in France, you must become more philosophical. Virtue must be tried by reality, or it is only fantasy. That, or hypocrisy. Remember, come tomorrow, and bring your book." I left wondering at the strange French lady, who seemed odder than anyone I had ever known, except, perhaps, myself.

On the Left Bank of the Seine, forming part of the stonework and walls of the rambling old Hôtel de Cluny, and beneath the streets and the narrow, respectable houses and garden walls of the still-medieval city, lie the vast and subterranean ruins of the ancient Roman baths of the city, the Palais des Thermes. Here, entangled in a maze of secret tunnels, shrouded in perpetual blackness, are great arched halls and crumbling marble corridors, where the sound of trickling water can be heard, and the black waters of the tepidarium wait to drown the unwary explorer whose candle fails. Portions of the vaulted rooms have become the cellars of some of the old houses; here casks and crates are piled in homely array, and the light sifts in through grated vents in the ceiling. But to those who know the plan of the secret palace below, a web of decayed corridors hollowed out within the buried ruins connects the houses on the surface, all the way from the rue de la Harpe, beneath the Hôtel de Cluny, and the monastery of the Mathurins, to a hidden spot on the riverbank, via slime-encrusted Roman aqueducts which long ago lost contact with the waters. Here and there in the blackness and rubble of collapsed stone and low caves dug in the remains of buried corridors are burned-out candle ends, expired oil lamps, a shoe, a discarded leather jerkin of the previous century. But in this century, the secret of the tunnels has been lost to all but one secret brotherhood.

Deep underground, in the heart of this rotting mass of stone, there is a door to a tiny room beneath the tepidarium that is new, stout, and well oiled. Inside that room are brass-bound chests in which, wrapped in oiled silk against the mildew, there are genealogical tables, a work of prophecy and secrets, and the records of the coups, the attempted coups, the assassinations, and the plots of the Paris branch of the Priory of Sion. The room is a little scriptorium, with a high, narrow standing desk from the days of Jean le Bon, and a lamp rarely lighted. Beyond it, a narrow service corridor once used by the slaves of the bath leads up through the hypocaust to the vaulted remains of the calderium, where water still collects in an ancient tile pool through lost underground channels. Between the Roman columns of the calderium are modern torch brackets and resin-dipped torches that show signs of recently having been lit. There is a broad oak table with silver candelabra on it and venerable old chairs around it. At one end is a great, cushioned chair with arms, a veritable throne. Drops of water sound, as they fall, one by one, from the mouth of a lion's-head fountain on the far wall. The waters of the pool lap fitfully in the dark, then catch the glitter of a single candle approaching down a hidden staircase. The man in black has come to light the torches. The Helmsman has arrived in the street above, and has entered by a concealed doorway into the house of the eminently respectable doctor of theology, Maître Bellier. It is here the masters of the Priory will meet.

"Brethren of the Secret"—the Helmsman, tall and swarthy, his eyes burning and intense, leans forward in the thronelike armchair at the head of the table—"we have here a crisis." The orange glow of sputtering torches has filled the ancient vault, their smoke rising into the shadowy heights above. There is a smell of pine resin from the torches cutting through the scent of moldy water that hangs eternally in the room. "The astrologers have foretold a favorable conjunction this coming winter. Such signs will not be ours for another century. The king will not live into the new year. The time of the fall of dynasties is upon us. But the stars also indicate great danger for the Priory." There was a stir of worry among the company and a shaking of heads. "Six months ago, outsiders discovered our presence, and our Secret. Maître Bellier, here, informed us that a certain English gentleman had discovered our work of sacred prophecy. It had been, however, divided in three parts between three partners in treasure seeking, and he had only one. The other two parts had been sold before our brother in London had discovered the fact." Gasps of horror echoed in the watery chamber. At a signal from the Helmsman, Maître Bellier spoke.

"While in London, I made inquiries; this Sieur de Crouch had discovered the significance of the work and was determined to regain the remaining two portions. One partner murdered the other, and he murdered the remaining one, thinking to collect both missing portions of the manuscript. The central portion, however, eluded him. It was either in the hands of the widow of one of his partners or had been sold by her to one who would appreciate its full significance: the English archbishop Wolsey." The chill silence of fear fell over the little group at the table as they heard this narrative. The Helmsman spoke again:

"You will appreciate, my brothers, that there were three possibilities at this point: Wolsey had sent the Secret to Rome, Wolsey retained the Secret for himself, possibly to reveal it to our king in support of the new alliance he seeks, or that the Secret had somehow eluded him and this Sieur de Crouch would get hold of it at last, and attempt to use it to his own advantage with the French throne. Now, what says our brother who has returned from Rome?"

A young man in the black-and-white habit of a Dominican spoke quietly: "I may tell the Helmsman that no manuscript or message bearing the Secret came from England into Rome during the time that I was there. Secrets there were aplenty, but not the Secret. This Wolsey is an ambitious man, but for himself, not for the Church, which is in our favor. Ah, brothers, he was busy! What letters he sent to his agent, Sylvester Giglis! But not about us." Bellier raised an eyebrow, and, urged on, the Dominican, or Dominican in disguise, continued. "Wolsey's appointment as cardinal was blocked by the Cardinal of York, who was resident there. Then, oh how fortunately, Bainbridge was poisoned by Rinaldo of Modena, his chaplain. When questioned, he blamed Giglis, but Giglis claimed Rinaldo was only a poor madman, acting on his own. Then—how odd!—the madman killed himself, as madmen so often do. The pity of it, that so many lone madmen are driven to political assassinations and then commit suicide. . . ."

"Then we may conclude, brother, that Rome remains ignorant, and we are safe from the Inquisition?"

"That is correct, brother and Helmsman, at least in regard to this instance."

"And now, what news from London?" The Helmsman looked again at Bellier, bidding him to speak.

"Wolsey has a servant who found and escorted the widow, at his orders. He obtained her confidence. He went through her things. Wolsey then ordered the servant to cross the Channel and join the French court as part of the entourage of the English princess. I came to the natural conclusion."

"The king! He would betray us to the throne!" the whisper ran round the table.

"Twice we made the attempt to assassinate the servant before he could reach the French court. Each time, we were foiled by accident." There was a groan of disappointment. Even the Helmsman's jaw clenched, and his eyes narrowed with the beginning of rage.

"But then the Hand of God intervened in our cause, and the ship carrying him was lost. He is dead, and whatever messages he carried are lost forever."

"Excellent."

"However, there remains the last possibility. I had the house of the Sieur de Crouch watched. He searched, he searched frantically. He was in and out of Wolsey's house. He questioned his servants. He followed the widow. He even tried to commune with the dead to find the lost portion of the manuscript. Then, suddenly, all was calm. He, who loathes travel and discomfort, suddenly sent his servant to arrange passage across the Channel."

"He has it!"

"Yes, it must be!" The voices echoed in the stone vault.

"I took passage on the next ship. Thanks to our brothers at Calais, I arranged for the fastest horses, and have come here ahead of him. It is not the servant of Wolsey but the Sieur de Crouch who comes to the court to betray us to the Valois."

"Then you know what must be done."

"Exactly."

"The Secret must be recovered and his copy of the manuscript destroyed. No outsider who discovers what it contains must be suffered to live. That is the law of the Priory." The Helmsman rose, and the servant who had lit his way down through the tunnel rose from his haunches beside the pool and relit his candle for the ascent. Silently, the members of the secret brotherhood lit their candles from the great candelabra on the table, then rose and followed him. At last only Eustache, the man in black, remained. One by one he plunged each torch into the pool to extinguish it. With the last fierce hiss, the chamber was plunged again into darkness. Silently, the bobbing flame of a single candle vanished up the hidden stair.

They say that at the coronation, Dauphin François held the crown over the queen's head himself, to spare her the weight, and even though I didn't see it, I could imagine him taking the opportunity of casting many improper looks at her with his sharp little eyes the way I had seen him do before. Then once she was crowned, the queen had a triumphal entry in procession through the Porte Saint Denis, into the city of Paris itself, where Nan and I had already gone to see about the new studio space that one of Duchess Marguerite's lackeys had rented for us. It was really quite splendid, being the whole third floor of a narrow little house on the Pont au Change, right where the goldsmiths and money changers are—and also several dealers in jewelry, expensive curiosities, and manuscripts of olden times, and galleries for the sale of works of art previously owned by distinguished persons in temporarily impecunious circumstances. There is also a shoemaker who makes very elegant slippers, but they are too fine for me. It was also convenient for me, being not all that far from the Hôtel des Tournelles, the palace where the king stays when he is in Paris, or from the Louvre, the greatest of his city palaces. The floor of my new studio was only a little bit tilted, and there was a fine window to the north, which is the best kind of light, and two fireplaces. It was also furnished, though very simply with a commodious old cupboard, a bedstead big enough to fit a huge family, and a well-scarred worktable.

"The last man to have this was an engraver," said the landlady, looking at us suspiciously. "I thought the duchess's notary said a painter and his household were to move in." And not a woman of ill fame, masquerading as a widow, her eyes seemed to say.

"I am a painter, to persons of distinction only. Ordinarily, I live at court. This is to be my studio space. The duchess's notary assured me it was a suitable place for a respectable woman, but perhaps he did not notice that low establishment across the way. I am not sure my patroness would approve of my staying even a night opposite something called The Giant's Cask. In England, I would never have suffered such an indignity. I think, perhaps, it would spoil my reputation to stay here." The landlady's eyes traveled from my widow's black, to Nan with her severe expression and neat gown, and then to the lackey in the duchess's rich livery who was carrying my box. I could see the calculation in her eyes.

"I have never heard of such a thing," she said grumpily.

"In England, there are many respectable women engaged in trade—and simply dozens of lady painters. Perhaps you have lady weavers here in Paris?"

"But of course, how else can an honest man's widow live?"

"Well, then, it's just the same with lady painters in England. Only more genteel, of course, from the association with persons of rank." The fierce old Frenchwoman in the cap and apron shook her head wonderingly. "Disgusting ...," she muttered, "foreign ... still, the duchess herself ..."

"What did you tell that woman?" asked Nan, as we listened to the landlady's heavy steps thumping down the outside staircase.

"That there were dozens of lady painters of the highest rank in England," I answered.

"You are a terrible liar," said Nan, with a fierce frown. That was what Master Ashton used to say, and hearing it made me feel sad, but I didn't want to tell her.

"Oh, look out the window," I said, changing the subject. "There're three drunk fellows on horseback in front of the Giant's Cask. Oh ... there ... I thought so. One of them's fallen off." The man who had fallen off lay on his back in the mud. Suddenly he spied me and pointed upward. There was a lot of shouting in French as the other two looked up and pointed and howled things I couldn't make out.

"Merciful God, another tavern," said Nan. "And you a hopeless simpleton in spite of everything. Susanna, what you need is a man to look after you—a proper one, not a drunk or a philanderer—or sure as fate, you'll not be safe on this earth."

"Oh, nonsense, Nan. I had a man, and he didn't look after me at all, and now I'm just beginning to enjoy myself. Listen, I hear the cheering. It must be the queen's procession on the way to Les Tournelles." So of course we had to drop everything and rush away and crowd into the street to see the queen pass by on her litter, the Dauphin François riding beside her very cosily, with all her troops of French attendants, banner carriers, mounted guards, and trumpeters, riding to meet the king, who had skipped most of the festivities to go ahead of her and go to bed. It was a very grand and inspiring sight, and everybody there was talking about nothing but the great tourney between England and France, which would be grander than the queen's entry. Grander than anything ever seen before. It would be held in the queen's honor, and it was the Dauphin's idea.

"Nan, I just have to see that tournament."

"Nonsense. The only safe place for a woman will be in the stands, which are for ladies only. Besides, you aren't invited."

"I just have to. Everyone says it will be the most splendid display ever. I'll take an easel and tell everyone I'm commissioned to make a print of the celebration."

"That's another terrible lie. And who would believe it? No decent woman would be seen in such a fashion. You'll be attacked. Try to get a view from a window at Les Tournelles. What are all those towers good for, anyway? Besides, it will probably rain. What good will you be if you get sick again? This time it could be lung sickness. Just think, you could die because you can't stop being foolish. . . ." But the more Nan warned me, the more I wanted to see everything. And not all of it from far away in a window above the Parc des Tournelles.

"The very first thing one does in Paris, Lord Belphagor, is have one's money changed. Then off to the *cour des miracles* to hire a sly Frenchman or two for your body servants. We'll want eyes and ears in this city, and men who aren't afraid to use a knife in the dark." Crouch's tone was confidential, worldly. Belphagor looked at him impatiently.

"Look, Crouch, the imps can do what I want for me. I don't need crafty fellows in my service. I'd rather have a sweet, innocent soul or two. They're more trustworthy now and positively delicious afterward."

"Ah, but do your imps speak French? Even my faithful Watkin here does not have enough language to handle our more delicate errands."

"You speak French. You do my errands," said Belphagor bluntly, and since Crouch saw the steam issuing from his ears, he nodded and smiled a wan little smile.

"An excellent idea, Lord Belphagor. Let as few people in on our plans as possible," said the cunning demon-master. You fool, he whispered to himself. Soon I will have all your dark powers, and your imps to do my bidding. Already you've given too much away. How fortunate the mirror has told me I'll be the victor.

"You find this conspiracy for me, Crouch; I want to make common cause with this Helmsman in the destruction of the Valois."

"But the manuscript . . ."

"Writing. What's writing anyway? I don't need it."

"But I . . . you do, Lord Belphagor. You need to know their Secret. Then when they gain power you can betray them to their enemies." This demon's a child, thought Crouch. How easily one can distract him with a promise of trouble! It's like offering a baby candy. But wearying. This damned creature gets more spoiled by the minute. It's something about living in the city; it corrupts even demons. When will I be done with this tiresome thing? I'm beginning to see why the Templars locked him in that box.

"Well, then, get it too."

"We must find Mistress Dallet."

"What do you mean 'we?' I am a gentleman now; you will do my bidding, Crouch. You find. You get. Remember, treasures of the earth. Do you think I should wear both sword and dagger, or would it be considered extreme at the French court? Oh, yes, and find me a dancing master. I overheard a gentleman at Calais say you simply can't be received anywhere important unless you know the new steps."

Crouch ground his teeth. I've done the job too well, he thought. Still, it keeps him distracted, and I can use that to my advantage.

Bystanders heard nothing of this conversation. What they saw were two distinguished-looking foreign gentlemen, mounted on black mules, followed by a rogue of a lackey on an old spotted mare riding through the narrow, muddy streets of the Right Bank. One of the gentlemen was tall and heavy, with snow white hair rising like wisps of steam and a square-cut beard with just a touch of iron gray still among the white hairs. He had heavy, malicious eyebrows, lines in his face that bespoke a life of vice, and eyes of a glacial green. He was radiating a kind of servile charm toward the second gentleman, who was even more richly dressed than he. The second gentleman had a curiously insubstantial look to him. His face had been whitened with powder, through which an odd greenish tinge showed through. But his neck, which had not been powdered, seemed to vanish as if it were smoke. A rich chain sat against it as if it rode on air. But the defect soon vanished beneath the rich fur trim of a heavy velvet gown and was scarcely what one could call a fault on a gentleman of such obvious wealth and distinction.

Strangest of all, perhaps, were the two black mules laboring beneath their handsome tooled-leather harness. If anyone had given them closer attention, he would have noticed a faint glow of flame from their nostrils, almost hidden by their steamy breath. They were in fact two imps from hell, conjured up by Lord Belphagor when the party found that every riding animal save the spotted mare had been purchased by the visiting English and their servants who had arrived in force for the great tourney.

The insubstantial gentleman was craning his invisible neck at the sights, and his nose, the approximate size and shape of a medium cucumber, was sniffing up the foul stink of the streets as if it were perfume. "*Hmm.* The place has changed since I was here last. But there's that damned cathedral, still squatting like a toad at the center of it all. Ah, the old days—there's Les Tournelles ... they've added to it. Crouch, you were right. I spent entirely too long in that box. Never again. Ah! Freedom and excellent clothes. What could be better?" He looked speculatively at Crouch. How much longer did he need his advice? I've almost drained him dry, thought Belphagor. Then I can get rid of him. Perhaps I need a Frenchman, somebody clever-looking who can explain philosophy and genealogy, like that fellow over there in the gown who's talking. A priest would be good. Or maybe a student, all tender and innocent. I could eat him afterwards.

Maître Bellier, who had come out of a tavern still arguing a point of theology with several friends from the Sorbonne, felt the demon's stare and looked up. Crouch, that's him, he thought. What has happened to turn his hair so white? And that gross fellow he's with, all dressed in imitation of a gentleman. Some shopkeeper, some, ugh, I can't imagine, but certainly no one for a man of distinction to associate with. With an almost invisible gesture, he pointed out the pair to Eustache, who followed behind the little knot of theologians, just outside their conversation. Eustache blinked, then broke away to follow the unholy pair.

"Power, Lord Belphagor," said the wily Crouch, who knew exactly how to gauge the signs of fatigue in minds smaller than his own. "I will show you how to get it."

"I know how already. I'll just buy slaves with this money that you've got for me. Isn't that how it works here on earth?"

"Of course, Your Damnedness. Money buys everything. Don't you see how it bought the tailor and the ship captain?"

"It didn't buy mules."

"That's because they weren't there. But in general, there's not anything you can't get with money. Or any person, either. All humans have their price."

"Then what's wrong with my plan, Crouch?"

"Lord Belphagor, you must buy them one at a time. If you learn how to gather power, you can destroy thousands with a wave of your hand. Why use old-fashioned methods? Just as buying people is quicker than tempting them by whispering in their ears, power is quicker than buying out people one soul at a time. If you set it up right, you can have them all at one another's throats without all that tiresome flitting about you must have had to do. All you have to do is sit back and harvest them when they're ready."

"Oh, splendid, splendid. I didn't realize power over men could be obtained. With us in the other world, it just is as it has been, since the beginning of time. Power remains exactly the same as it began." Interesting, thought Belphagor. Power rearranges itself with these creatures. If I learned their secrets, perhaps I might raise my rank in the sphere of the infernal. "But these humans seem different in so many ways," he said aloud. "Tell me, have they invented a science of rebellion?" Crouch was delighted at Belphagor's speech. It was almost as if the old demon counted him as a fellow demon. His guard is slipping, thought Crouch.

"Trust me, your damnedness. I have only our own interests at heart. Through my help, you can gain supreme power here on earth."

Hmm. And in hell, too, perhaps, if I master these secrets, thought Belphagor. Suddenly, the demon glanced suspiciously at Crouch's bland, pale face. The green eyes were glowing with malice and ambition. "Trust you, Crouch, whatever for? You're a damned soul. They don't make them much more treacherous than you, even in hell. I'm not stupid, you know."

"Lord Belphagor, I respect a mind that is a subtle web of scheming. Like is drawn to like, you know. Trust me not because of my word of honor, which is indeed worthless, but because of my respect, which is worth far more than honor. I respect you as my master in deviousness and evil. Besides, I am necessary to you, just as you are to me. Why not trust me? Aha, here's the place. The Pont au Change. We'll soon have enough French money to carry out your plan, Lord Belphagor. Now watch out for these money changers; they clip the coins. And sometimes the gold is false."

"My nose smells true gold. No mortal can deceive Belphagor." Crouch was silent but smiled inwardly. He paused, surveying the street with an arrogant stare, and then stepped down on the mounting block before a tavern with a sign featuring a monstrous cask guarded by a sleeping giant. As the lackey held the spotted horse, the black imps in the form of mules grumbled softly to each other in a language that only they understood.

"After we have changed our money, you might deign to look at some of the wonderful shops of antique curiosities on this bridge, my lord," said Crouch, as they entered the low door of a money-changing establishment.

"I don't see why you like them. They certainly aren't antique to *me*," said Belphagor. "I'd rather stop in for a drink." As they vanished into the shop, a drunk came out of the Giant's Cask and stared at the two black mules, who were waiting without being held. Then, with inebriated curiosity, he peered closer at their nostrils. His eyes widened in horror, and he fled right back into the tavern.

The shop door opened again, and two contented figures emerged. "You see, my lord? It works every time."

"I still don't see why we have to change it at all. I thought you told me money was the universal solvent."

"It is, it is, Lord Belphagor, but each country has its own. I spoke in general terms."

"And this tourney everyone is so mad for. Why, that man simply couldn't stop going on about the foreign lords who'd come for it. Is it worth seeing? I'd hoped to visit an orgy or two, or perhaps some murders while we were in town on our business, but everyone seems to have given them up for the tourney."

"It is planned for five days, and with any luck, you'll have enough mayhem to please you, my lord. And then there're the banquets at night. Plenty of assignations and things going on in dark corners, I'll warrant. So you see, you will have both orgies and murders in the most respectable and ornamental form."

"Ah, I see, I see. Crouch, you are changing my idea of pleasure. Civilization, how splendid. Sin with artistry. I feel myself growing more refined daily. And to think, I once settled for simple things. I think I'll have some more new clothes made. The French style is more splendid than the English. What think you to an Italian brocade, embroidered with brilliants? I intend to cut a figure at this tourney. And ... oh, yes ..." He broke off and looked at the mules. "I'll be wanting something a little more impressive than mules. You boys will have to become chargers. Big ones. Nothing less than the best." The two mules looked at each other, their red eyes full of annoyance, and grumbled again in the strange language.

At the place where the Pont au Change joins the Right Bank, there is a very tasteful little gallery where just the right statue or tapestry may be purchased at a bargain, if you are lucky, and where a gentleman in need can get a very good price for a table clock or perhaps the family nef, or saltcellar, without waiting or dealing with distasteful people of the lower sort. But best of all are the paintings that can be found there. Just the thing to add elegance to an otherwise barren reception room or cabinet. Subjects worthy of public or private contemplation, religious, secular, mythological can be seen mounted on the walls all the way to the ceiling, though how the proprietor gets them down is a mystery, for she is a crippled hunchback, and very pale from illness, her hair gone quite translucent.

Still, the neighbors speculated that she might well have been married, if it were not for her deformity, for her face is very lovely. And the artists of Paris found something sympathetic there besides a ready buyer for speculative works otherwise unsaleable. Perhaps it was the sight of a new work in the Italian style, or the serene smile of an ivory Madonna on display in the corner, or the humorous, encouraging look in the dealer's face as she said, "Why, the brush strokes here on the hand are perfection itself! What do you mean, the count would not take it? He has missed owning a masterpiece." But whatever the mystery, a man could come in discouraged and leave full of inspiration. And sometimes a woman, too, for many of the illuminators of the city were the daughters and wives of the makers of rare books, and the woman in the shop also dealt in exquisite manuscripts and antique missals and books of hours.

"Ah!" said Hadriel, flinging off his old gray cloak and stretching out his wings. "Not a customer today! They must all be off trying to wangle an invitation to the tourney. The social event of all Paris! A little higher, my dears, and to the right." High up near the ceiling, a half dozen twittering little cherubs, their wings beating faster than a hummingbird's, were holding a heavy gilt picture frame with a stained canvas portrait of Saint Jerome in it. A seventh was pounding a big nail into the wall with a hammer. "Yes, that's it! Perfect!" cried Hadriel, clapping his hands with pleasure, and the little curly-headed creatures fluttered down and settled on the counter, putting away the hammer beneath it.

"I saw Uriel today. He was flying over the city in a storm cloud. What will you do if he catches you, Hadriel?" asked one of the cherubs.

"Why, I'm just doing my job. Can I help it if I've had an inspiration about doing it? And it's ever so much more efficient this way. Flying here, flying there, whispering in people's ears to inspire them, I tell you, it was a poor use of my time. This way, I just set up shop and they all come to me. Artists, would-be artists, everyone who loves beauty and craves wonder comes here, and I inspire them in great batches. Once I have the kinks worked out of my plan, I'll set you all up in branch offices, as the Italian bankers do. Oh, I tell you, I could have worn my wings off, just flying between Rome and Florence! And there were so many neglected. Why, I haven't had time for the Scythians in centuries. Same old horses. Same old panthers. What's the good of being the angel of art if you are confined to such a narrow, old-fashioned way of doing business?"

"They won't like it, you know, the archangels. They don't approve of changes. You'll get in trouble," announced another little cherub, his dark brown eyes serious.

"Oh, pooh! Where would the world be without new things? It's time those old fellows quit being so stiff! After all, I don't inspire the same old art all the time. Otherwise, these mortals would still be painting bison on the rocks. And now, just look!" Hadriel announced happily, gesturing around him. "I don't think I've had so much fun since I stopped at Mistress Susanna's house. Why, I've half a mind to take time off and go see that tourney myself. The way these Parisians carry on about it, it really ought to be worth seeing."

"Hadriel, you're playing too much. You know if they find out, they'll be angry with you. Suppose they tell the Father?"

"But isn't it fair to take a little time for yourself if you've saved so much by inventing a better way of doing business? Entirely fair," said Hadriel, answering his own question. Taking a comb from the pocket of his extraordinary robe, he peered into a mirror mounted on the wall for sale and combed his translucent curls down flat over his forehead. Then he turned his head this way and that to admire the effect.

"Hadriel, can we go, too?"

"Oh, yes, me too, me too!" cried the others.

"I thought you didn't approve of playing," said Hadriel.

"We don't."

"We'll be working."

"Yes, we're working for you. It's all your fault," the cherubs' high little voices twittered. They were neither girls nor boys, just as Hadriel was neither man nor woman, although humans, who think their own way of doing business is the only one in the world, were continually trying to assign a sex to them. The Father had made them first, then changed around his plans when he made humanity, although no one knew why. After all, He wasn't entirely satisfied with either model, as everyone who has ever given it thought knows. Hadriel himself thought perhaps He had been bored, but then, Hadriel always did have rather odd ideas. The archangels had spoken to him more than once about his problem, and Hadriel always promised to be good, but then he forgot. Then, all over the world, artists got into trouble. They painted bearded patriarchs in the nude, studied anatomy in secret, and dug up ancient pagan statues for copying. It gave everyone ideas, and the world started to change, and the archangels went hunting for Hadriel again, to impress upon him the awful damage his eccentricities could have in a world of simple, gullible souls.

"Why, that's so," answered Hadriel. "The blame's all mine. Shall we lay bets on the champion? No fair influencing the outcome. You have to promise."

"Agreed!"

"Let's go!"

"Vacation!" shouted the little angels, as they rose like a flock of birds right through the ceiling and out into the cloudy gray sky over the city.

The Eleventh Portrait

Francis, Duke of Angoulême as Dauphin of France. *Eighteenth-century engraving from a lost original.*

Francis is here depicted before old age had thickened his jowls and torso, and before growing the beard seen in all his mature portraits. Slender and handsome, connoisseur of arts and letters, he was already a spendthrift and a favorite of the ladies, the very model of a Renaissance courtier. The original portrait, a miniature described as set about with brilliants and engraved with a dolphin on the obverse of the case, vanished during the French Revolution.

—Lebrun. A History of the Kings of France

One of the first portraits I did for the Duchess Marguerite was a picture of her brother, on whom she doted most immoderately, even though he was wild and spoiled. After all, what would you expect from a man who had Madame Louise as a mother, who was the kind of lady who just had to run everything even if it was all for his own good? Besides, in my experience with the great ones, which grows more every year, they are all spoiled, so it is just a matter of what kind of spoiled. And if they appreciate fine art and write poetry and have an open purse like Duke Francis, why, then, it's just right. Far better than spending it all on horses and ornamented tournament armor. When you find ones like this, it is important to pamper them and tell them frequently how much higher their thoughts are than ordinary people's, and that refined appreciation is the mark of nobility of soul, and things like that. It keeps them from getting nasty and gets you invited back.

TWENTY-ONE

François d'Angoulême and his brother-in-law, the Duc d'Alençon, mounted on a pair of pacing palfreys, were riding the length of the wall of the Parc des Tournelles, inspecting the progress of the construction on the lists. Ahead of them, the row of little watchtowers, flat topped and gray, vanished among the trees at the end of the park. Behind them, on the dozens of similar ornamental towers of the great palace, the silk banners of the French king flapped dismally beneath a cloudy sky. The shrill cries of the tame peacocks that wandered in the park seemed to augur another storm.

"I don't like the looks of the sky," said d'Alençon, looking upward into the rolling gray clouds. He took off his right glove and held up his hand to feel for any stray drops of rain.

"The ladies will not so much as dampen their headdresses," said Francis with an expansive gesture. "Over here, above the stands, there will be a canopy of canvas, painted with rare designs." In the cold, carpenters swarmed over the stands, and there was the sound of hammering and sawing. "Then the lists will stand here, when completed. The English will have their pavilions there. . . ."

"That seems an ill-favored place."

"They would not appreciate better," said Duke Francis, dismissing the issue with a wave of his gloved hand.

"The Duc de Suffoke, they say, is a barbarian. Entirely untutored. And yet his king trusts him with the greatest affairs of state."

"I have made inquiries. He borrows his subtlety, such as it is, from the devious Archbishop Wolsey. I plan to disgrace him utterly on the field." Francis's tone was easy, confident.

"This may not be so easy. Have you met the man yet? He has arrived with Milord de Dorset, the other English champion. The Duc de Suffoke is built like a bull. What he lacks in brains, he has made up in brawn. The other English knights are buying French horses, but he is shipping in his own. He spares no expense in his attempt to defeat the finest of French chivalry." They had ridden to the far end of the lists by this time, looking at the green grass which would soon be nothing but churned up mud, mixed with blood. They turned, now, riding back toward the royal apartments. Beyond the stone walls that surrounded the park, they could see the flat towers of the Bastille looming against the gray sky, marking the boundary of the city walls.

"I do not think he will find that as easy as he thinks," said Francis, his eyes sly. "I have a plan. In the spirit of chivalry and friendship between our nations, I have asked both him and Dorset to be my aides in the sponsorship of this tourney."

"Aha," said d'Alençon, "that means if you are unable to take the field . . ."

"They will have to stand against all comers, even their own answerers to the French challenge."

"So, should the English do too well, which of course, they will not, then . . ."

"Then I retire and the English defeat the English."

D'Alençon's response was an appreciative chuckle. Then his face grew grave as he thought of something else. "Do you think," he said, "that there is anything to the rumor that is sweeping the court about the English champion's true purpose?"

"You mean that he is sent by the King of England to get an heir to the throne of France? In this, he will be defeated, too. My wife and your wife, my sister, are with her every hour of the day. She will never be alone, especially with him. Have you ever yet known my mother to be defeated in women's business?" Francis laughed. But even as he did, the image of that slender, red-headed, bright-eyed girl rose before his eyes. Too fine a wife for an old man, he thought. Unbidden desire rose in him, the desire for an unattainable woman. Hadn't old Louis the Twelfth himself put away his ugly, deformed wife, the daughter of a king, in favor of the previous king's wife, the heiress of Brittany? All things would be possible to him when he became king. He would have this woman. Now. Later. He willed it, Francis of Angoulême, heir of the house of Valois.

"What if it rains?" asked the Duc d'Alençon, looking about him at the field.

"I have planned a series of *indoor entertainments*," said Francis, his voice bland. Somehow, d'Alençon knew that feasting and dancing were not all that were meant.

Cold ocean fog rolled through the narrow streets of Calais, the English foothold on the Continent. It was early morning, but the sun was not visible through the grayness. Heavy horses, each ridden bareback by his groom, moved in a column like fabulous monsters through the gloom. Each animal worth a fortune, they were surrounded by armed soldiers, their fodder, tack and armor, blacksmiths, trainers and attendants following in a train of heavy wagons. The duke's horses, the finest in England, were being transported to the great tourney at Paris.

At the Sign of the Ship, a boy holding a bundle stood in the doorway. "Don't delay, or you'll have to run to catch up." The man leaning in the doorway coughed even making this brief speech. He was thin and gray faced from recent illness, and his eyes were set in dark hollows.

"Master Ashton, it's the chance of a lifetime. How can I ever thank you?"

"Learn the business, boy, and make a success of it. It's just your good fortune that I knew Master Denby, and that he needed a boy. Your experience with apothecary makes you valuable; it's not everyone who's quick enough to learn the art of horse physicking."

"But . . . but I shouldn't leave. How can I, when you're not well?"

"Go now, and don't look back. You've stayed long enough already with me here, and it wasn't always easy, I know. It's I who owe you, and not the other way around." The first of the covered carts was rumbling past, and the boy recognized the postillion on the wheelhorse, who waved to him and gestured to the back of the cart.

"Good-bye, then, and thank you." The boy ran and swung on the back of the cart, and hands inside pulled him up. Since they had been pulled from the floating wreckage of the *Lübeck*, a strange bond had developed between the two. Tom was no swimmer; it was Ashton who had pulled him to the rope-tangled remains of the foremast and tied him there. And Tom had stayed on when a lighter-headed creature might have fled the near-fatal illness and violent delirium that had come to Ashton from long exposure to the icy water. How curious fate is, thought Ashton. If Susanna had not defied me and smuggled him here, they'd be burying me. And if I hadn't been brooding over her and courting death on the deck, I would have gone down in the hold. And then, what Tom told me about her . . . suppose I have been wrong, a fool? He paused, aching inside. Well, for all he has been through, Tom deserved this chance, thought Ashton, and fortune has brought it to him. At least it has been kind to someone. He limped inside to sit by the fire and stare morbidly into it, refusing to break his fast, despite the temptations offered by the innkeeper's wife.

"You'll miss that boy, won't you?" she asked, wiping her hands on her apron. "I know I shall."

"You're a woman."

"Well of course I am. What else?"

"Then you can tell me about women. You'd know all about them, wouldn't you?"

"I should think I would," she agreed, taking the dirty mugs and wooden trenchers from the table. She carried them off to the kitchen, and Ashton stared gloomily into the fire again. When she returned to wipe the table, he said,

"Explain to me how you would judge this about women. If a man heard from a gentleman that a certain woman had done an evil deed, and then from another that he trusted that he knew of proof the woman had not done it, would you imagine that the woman was guilty or not?"

"It would depend on how evil the deed was, and what the secret interests of the gentlemen in question were."

"One is secretly in love with her, but doesn't know that I know."

"Then I wouldn't trust him."

"The other is a schemer, possibly a murderer. He posed as my friend."

"Well, I wouldn't trust him, either. Suppose this schemer fellow had tried to seduce her secretly, and she refused, and spreading an ugly rumor was his revenge?"

"That could be, too."

"Then there is only one way of finding out. You must ask the woman herself."

"She could be a liar, but if she is innocent ... I have been too cruel to deserve an answer."

"This is where I will speak to you as a woman, Master Ashton. You may have forfeited her friendship, but she will be glad if you are man enough to erase this stain on her honor."

"Oh ... I'm not speaking of myself ... just of a general case, that's all. . . ."

"Oh, and I'm not speaking of you either," she said, throwing her damp towel over one arm and taking the poker to stir up the embers of last night's fire. "I'm just speaking of general cases, too." She turned and looked at him. "Speaking as a woman, you're about the worst-looking general case I ever saw. If you like her that much, you'd better go apologize and make good if you've been spreading the story. I mean, as a general case, in the opinion of this general sort of female person."

Heavy rains had fallen, churning the lists into deep mud, and dowsing the bright pavilions and gaily painted stands of the tournament grounds. But at last, the sun had broken through the rolling November clouds once more, and the banners were unfurled and the stands filled with the very cream of the French court. In the place of honor, the king lay on a litter, his beautiful new queen beside him. The dead horses and dead knights from the previous days' encounters had been unceremoniously hauled away, for there were hundreds more where they came from, and dying brought no glory, only rapid disposal. It was a great pity, the muttering could be heard in the stands, that the English were ahead. It was especially the fault of Le Duc de Suffoke, who had run fifteen courses victoriously, shivering lances, unhorsing opponents, and littering the field with dead and wounded French contenders. It was almost unfair, he who was so uncouth in dinner conversation, and who was incapable of turning a verse in admiration of a lady, to collect so many victories against men of better family and higher chivalry. It must be cheat of some sort. An English cheat. And did you see how he bowed and scraped and preened himself before the queen, as if he were somehow upholding her honor, rather than undermining the glory of her new nation? And the queen applauded his victories. Everyone could tell by her eyes that she followed the victories of her countrymen with undue enthusiasm.

Invisible to mortal eyes, a half dozen little angels, fidgeting with impatience, sat on the canopy that sheltered the royalty of France.

"Where's Hadriel?" asked one of the little creatures, shaking his blond ringlets.

"Gone to mind the shop. Who are you betting on?" asked the dark-eyed one, smoothing the iridescent feathers on his tiny wings.

"This time the French. I'll wager three."

"Only three? I'll put five on the English."

"Five? That's a lot of good deeds for just one day, especially since Hadriel is always so busy, busy, busy! You'll never have the time."

"I'll have the time and more. It's you who will be busy, because *I* say the English will win."

"And *I* say the French. They are ever so angry. They have a plan. Just you wait."

"No cheating. Hadriel said so."

"Oh, *I'm* not cheating, but they are. Go see for yourself, then come back and tell me you put five on the English." The first little angel dangled his plump, pink feet over the canopy's edge, swinging them back and forth. Beneath them, the queen looked up and saw the most curious ruffling motion of the canopy's fringed edge. The wind's coming up, she thought. We might have to move the king indoors again. She thought she heard a fluttering but decided it must be the sound of the royal banners flapping above the canopy in the wind.

The dark-eyed cherub flew all around the French pavilions. Beneath him was a confusion of men and horses, litters, surgeons, armorers hammering out dents, squires polishing helms and breastplates, stable boys, masters of the horse, and pages running errands and carrying messages. He flew through the canvas wall into the silk-hung pavilion of the Dauphin and perched on a suit of armor standing all polished and ready in the corner. Francis, dressed in the heavy, quilted doublet he wore beneath his armor, was surrounded by his knights and esquires. Before him stood the hugest man ever seen in France, a veritable giant with a blondish brown beard and large, fierce features.

"Where on earth did you find him, my dear Bourbon?" said the Duc d'Alençon to a tall, dark, rather sour-faced young man, his padded doublet sweat stained from his jousting armor.

"I got him through a contact with the emperor," said the Duc de Bourbon, "and had him invited as an ambassador of goodwill."

"Goodwill, indeed," said d'Alençon with a laugh.

"Take a message to my dear friend, the Duke of Suffolk," Francis was saying. "The finger I hurt in the last encounter has not yet recovered. I am most grateful that he has agreed to stand in my place to accept the mystery challenger." There was a flurry, and a page in velvet livery hurried away to deliver the word to the duke. The French knights roared with laughter, and the immense champion chuckled deep in his vast chest.

"And now, we must have a French surcoat for you, my dear chevalier," said Francis. "And we have here a French helm, so that your German one will not give you away." As the squires armed the huge German, the French knights commented as if he were not even there.

"My God, he's a monster."

"It's fair. The English are too large. That is how they cheat. It gives an unfair advantage."

"He's twice the size of that ox, Suffolk. He's sure to bring us the victory."

"A German mystery challenger for France; there's a joke."

"Chevalier, you must know Suffolk's tricks. Remember the sword stroke from below—like this—that was how he tricked me."

"Are you sure you have it?" The French knights crowded around to coach their ringer.

"I have practiced the defense against this stroke only yesterday. Remember, I have been the emperor's champion," replied the immense knight. "The Englishman will surely fall."

In the corner, the little angel twittered with indignation. It seemed hardly fair, when he couldn't cheat himself, that the French were cheating so outrageously. With an annoyed sniff, he rose through the ceiling of the pavilion and fluttered off to the English pavilions. Here was the same jumble of horses, squires, armorers, and spectators all picking their way through the muddy grounds beyond the lists. The French messenger picked his way through the crowd past two women, one carrying a drawing board followed by another with a wooden case. Behind the two trailed an ancient lackey in the livery of the Duchesse d'Alençon, carrying a stool. *Aha,* thought the little creature flying above, that will be Mistress Susanna, the one who paints funny pictures.

"Mistress Susanna, Mistress Susanna, look ahead of you and go back the other way." Susanna looked up into the air and saw nothing. She rubbed her ear, wondering where the clear little child's voice had come from. Then she looked ahead of her and saw two men facing away from her, riding on immense black horses in the direction of the lists. The sight of one of them, a tall, broad, white-haired man in a green velvet gown, made her blood run cold. He was looking away from them. But to Susanna, even his back looked sinister.

"We need to leave," she said to the older woman carrying the case.

"At last you've seen sense," the older woman replied. The lackey, not understanding English, said nothing.

"No, I've seen something worse. Septimus Crouch. The murderer. He's here."

"Here? What on earth for? He must be following you."

"He must be," whispered Susanna, her face shocked. Panicked, she turned and began to run, and tripped on a tent peg, pitching into the mud. An armorer's assistant came to help her up, and at the sound of a woman speaking English in this foreign place, several other curious people offered their help, pulling at her elbows and rescuing her drawing board from the mud. Curious, the little dark-eyed creature fluttering above turned back to listen in on the commotion.

"Oh, a picture," the armorer's assistant said. "It's a sketch of our duke, triumphing over those French dandies. See here, you've done the engrailing on the tasses wrong. Come in and see the duke's own armor if you like, then you'll get it right." Susanna looked about her, confused, while Nan tried to wipe the mud off her skirts.

"Mistress Dallet, Mistress Dallet!" a boy's voice called. Susanna looked up at the sound of her name. The voice, cracking between high and low, sounded familiar.

"Do you know her?" someone asked.

"Why, it's Mistress Dallett. She is the most wonderful paintrix in the whole world," said the familiar voice. Susanna looked up amazed.

"Tom! Oh, Tom, you're not a ghost, are you? I dreamed of you drowned so many nights."

"I'm not a ghost; just ask anyone here. I—I meant to come looking for you, but they've kept me so busy."

"Tom, they told me you were lost with the *Lübeck* and Master Ashton." Susanna flung her arms around the angular, freckled boy, who blushed horribly.

"Say, mistress, I was almost drowned on the *Lübeck*, too," said a wag.

"And me!" cried another.

"How did you get here, Tom?"

"Master Ashton lashed me to a spar with his own belt. He saved me, Mistress Susanna."

"Then he died a hero, as they said."

"He didn't die, Mistress Susanna. He's getting well in Calais, with the others. The water was too cold and gave most of them that were pulled out the lung fever. He got me a place here with the horses. He's too sick to come now, and he says he's waiting for a letter from the archbishop." Susanna turned pale and put her hand to her heart. Her eyes were huge.

"Alive," she whispered. "He's alive."

"He says he keeps turning up, like the bad penny, much to everyone's annoyance."

"Then he's the same as ever...." Tom looked at her face and was suddenly angry and envious, all at once, even though he felt guilty for it, and for not being grateful enough. But in that moment he realized that Susanna's face had never looked like that for *him* and never would. Jealousy pricked him. He stuck his thumbs in his belt and cocked his head to one side.

"No, not the same. He's all thin and wore-out-looking. Limps, too." And not handsome anymore, even if I *am* plain, he thought with satisfaction, thinking of Ashton's sunken, dark-rimmed eyes and skeletal, gray face. "He got very sick with coughing and talked nonsense a lot. A lot. He's full of suspicions, you know. You wouldn't like what he said. He's not a true friend to you, for what he believed, even for all you've done for him. It's me who's been faithful to you, Mistress Susanna. It's me."

"Will he come, Tom? Do you think he'll come?"

"Hey, Tom, you rogue! You're needed to assist in compounding a poultice. The duke's best horse has gone lame, and he is beside himself." A tall stranger with a bridle thrown over one shoulder came to pull Tom away.

"I suppose," said Tom grudgingly, as he turned away from Susanna to follow the stranger. Above them, the little angel who had been hovering close to listen in was transfixed with a sudden look of joy, then sped away with a flash of iridescent wings.

Susanna watched Tom go with a pang of guilt. She had been cruel, without meaning to. She wanted to run after him and say she was sorry, but she knew that would make it worse. She couldn't hide from Tom what she felt, and it was not for him. Robert Ashton. He was alive. I'm bound to see him again, she said to herself. He'll come. It was all meant to be, after all. But then she thought: What if I was wrong? What if I felt nothing in him, and what I thought I felt in him was only in me? What if he steals kisses like that from all sorts of ladies and counts them all the same? What if I really don't like him when I see him again? What if he never comes? Her heart in a turmoil, she turned to trudge back through the mud to Les Tournelles, where she and Nan could wash out her dress. Suddenly, the tourney had lost all its charm for her.

"Nan, do you think we could go to Calais?"

"Nonsense, Susanna. You get giddier every day. Stick to your work, and what will happen, will happen."

The cherub spotted the French page at the entrance of the grandest of the pavilions and followed him in.

"What's this?" said the duke. "Duke Francis asks me to stand for him? Bigod, the man's a weakling. That finger is something only a lady would cry over." The knights around him laughed. But then Suffolk's face grew serious. His best horse had gone lame, and the one he had counted on as a spare seemed to have become ill from eating French grain. He needed a fresh horse, a good one. He was about to ask

Dorset, when a child's voice, as clear as clear, seemed to speak from a point just above his ear:

"Look outside, my lord, and take your purse with you." He felt something like a fly somewhere near his shoulder and tried to swat it off, but there was nothing there.

"Come outside a moment, my lord of Dorset; I have had an idea," said the Duke of Suffolk. Striding out of his pavilion, surrounded by his followers, he spied a pair of preposterous horsemen, so overmounted as to appear ridiculous. One of them was white haired, a man more suited to a sweet-going gennet than a warhorse. The other sat all crouched up, his stirrups too short, his reins dangling as if he had never ridden anything before. Yet his mount, a great, shining black stallion so spirited that he seemed to breathe fire, was as docile as a lamb. Perfect horses, shining blue-black, the biggest he had ever seen. Horses to take a real warrior to victory. Quickly, the duke said to one of his knights, "See there? Go and ask those knights if they will come here. I would buy one or both of those horses."

Septimus Crouch was gratified by the attention paid to him. Once dismounted, with the plentiful aid of several of the duke's retainers, he practically simpered.

"My lord, I cannot sell these horses, even for the honor of England. They do not belong to me, but to my companion, the most noble foreign prince Belfagor-o." Crouch had been quick to realize that a fellow like Suffolk would recognize any name claimed to be of a great English or French house. And he was desperately angling for the coveted invitations to the festivities that he had promised Belphagor he could easily obtain.

"Belfagor-o? What kind of name is that?" asked the man who had helped him from his horse.

"Oh—ah, Italian. Belfagoro is a mighty prince in his own state." Belphagor bowed his head slightly. The duke bowed his head equally slightly.

"What state is that?" asked Suffolk, who was very rigid about precedence.

"Oh, why, um, Tartarus. Yes, Tartarus. He is an archduke."

"Tartarus? I've never heard of the place."

"Oh, one of the smallest Italian states. In the ... ah, mountains, very isolated. The archduke is unvanquished in war, but he ... hum, concentrates his efforts these days on horse breeding." Belphagor was enjoying himself. There was a time when he would have sprouted up fifty feet high, spouting fire, just to terrify the man, but now that he was learning civilization, he delighted in the game of jockeying for precedence. What fun, for a being who must usually sift through walls, invisible, to be instead invited in by his victims, in full infernal form! Belphagor felt intoxicated with the new game.

In the meantime, the duke's master of the horse was inspecting the two mounts, who were being held by one of the duke's pages. Amazing creatures. Their hooves seemed made of solid steel, rather than horn, and there was no soft spot in the middle. A soft, hot, orangeish glow seemed to come from their nostrils, as if they were stoked by some internal furnace.

"Why should I help the English in the victory when I favor no side?" Belphagor asked the knight who had made the duke's offer.

"Because, Most Noble Lord Belfagoro, our lord the duke is undefeated in the lists. Now the French have used his own chivalry to betray him, they know his horses are done, and they expect the victory. So if you sell us these horses, you can place bets at very favorable odds in the French camp and then trick the trickers, collecting a large sum in addition." The imps grumbled to each other in their own language, and the boy holding them felt the hair going up on the back of his neck.

"Ah, I see. A double betrayal and wealth in the bargain. Agreed," said Belphagor, nodding agreeably. "But the horses can't be sold. They belong to themselves. However, I can rent you out their services for the length of the engagement. I would, however, expect handsome payment."

"A hundred pounds."

"Not good enough."

"And two seats in the stands."

"Where in the stands?"

"In the middle, with the ladies."

"No good," said Belphagor. "I'm not a lady."

"In front then, next to the princes of the blood."

"I suggest, Most Noble Lord Belfagoro, that you accept this offer, since you may enhance your esteem in the eyes of others by sitting next to the princes of the blood." Crouch, smooth and politic, stood by Belphagor's elbow.

Belphagor nodded affably at Crouch, whose face was a study in disdain. How curious, thought some of the onlookers. We have never seen an uglier lord. His trunk hose, what a huge cut, and his shoes, as big as boats. And what curious eyes, all sunken and red beneath beetling brows of never-before-seen hairiness! White powder like a clown and—is it possible? No neck at all. Still, a man who could own horses like that must be respected, no matter what his appearance, even if it is rather dim in places.

"Will you require an indemnity, if the horses are killed?"

"The horses will not be killed," said Belphagor, and the master of the horse silently nodded his head. Not those two hellhounds, he thought.

"Let me try them first," said the duke.

"Of course, Illustrious Duke," agreed Belphagor, and then he spoke softly to the two imps in their own language. "Go with this fellow. Don't give him any trouble. Give him the victory. I, Belphagor the Great, require it of you." The imps grumbled, but the nearest one allowed himself to be mounted by the silly mortal with almost no fuss at all. Then the duke put the horse through his paces: tight turns and figures, cantering on both leads, a stop from a full gallop. Pleased, he tried the more complex maneuvers that require the most perfect training; the piaffe, the levade, and the other movements used in parade and war.

"Perfect," he breathed. The immense black thing beneath him was not even damp with the exertion.

"My lord, your horse armor is not large enough for him," said the master of the horse.

"Don't worry about that," said Belphagor. "I told you they can't be killed."

The duke had a sudden shudder of superstitious awe. What on earth had he bargained for? What was the source of the mysterious inspiration he had had? What were the two big black things, anyway? Horses, just horses, he said to himself, shaking off the mood, and sure enough, there they were, contentedly taking a handful of grain from a stable boy's palm. This is for the honor of the king, my master, he said firmly to himself. He would not go creeping back to Henry the Eighth a failure. The negotiations for the secret treaty were going hard. The old king wanted money, he seemed devious and wary. With his gray-white face, his wheeze, his slow and deliberate language, he was stifling and frustrating to deal with. The tourney, on the other hand, was refreshing. Francis's trickery, to the degree that it had been explained to him, seemed easier to deal with than the old king's craft. It was straightforward and French. He, Charles Brandon, Duke of Suffolk, would conquer by force of arms. He would cover the French with humiliation. Just thinking of it, he breathed hard and clenched the muscles in his massive jaw. He didn't care what he was riding. They were damned good horses.

Above him the little cherub laughed aloud and clapped his tiny pink hands. The wicked trick was all the fault of the demon Belphagor. Hadriel couldn't blame him, even if he found out. He hadn't broken the rules at all. "Three for five," he shouted happily, as he shot away from the duke's pavilion as swiftly as an arrow.

"Bandage it heavier," said Duke Francis. "I can't be seen watching unless the bandage is visible from the stands." His surgeon obligingly added another wrapping of white linen and a dark silk sling.

"There, my lord. You must be careful to hold it thus, to avoid engorging it with blood and attracting ill humors."

"Exactly," agreed Francis. "In this moment I would avoid ill humors." He laughed. A boy held his white palfrey outside. With great content he mounted and ambled to the lists. There carnage was being done in foot combat. Damn, he thought, the slain are all French. We must do something about that. Even behind the barrier all the way across the field, he could feel the eyes of the ladies on him. One waved her handkerchief. He just knew that they were saying, "What a hero. Why, even wounded, he would not fail to appear to direct the queen's tourney. What a fine figure of a man." There was his sister. There was his mother. There was his ugly little wife. There was his king, and the English princess who had become queen. God, look at that ape, Suffolk, ride up at full gallop, stop so fast he splattered mud in every direction, and then bow until his plumes brushed the saddle! And his horse was unarmed. He must be very sure he would unseat his oppo-

nent without a struggle. This time, Suffolk, you will get what's coming
to you.

There was a great cheer from the stands. The French challenger,
astride a mighty gray stallion from Francis's own stable, came and
made his bow. Seated, the German's immense size was not easy to dis-
cern. Wait until he dismounts to finish off Suffolk, thought Francis.
Then they will see something. But the two knights had closed their
helms and were rattling down the field directly at each other. There
was a crash as both lances landed square on the mark, and a terrible
squealing of horses as the gray went down. But the huge man in the
French surcoat had kicked aside the stirrup, and as the gray struggled
to rise, then sank again, he managed to dismount. Well done, thought
Francis, who had seen many a man killed beneath a falling horse, unable to disentangle himself from the high, embracing jousting saddle.

Suffolk had thrown aside his shattered lance. So far, the match was
his. There was a roar from the French in the stands as the challenger
stood. Suffolk looked as he dismounted to face him on foot and saw
the reason. The man was a giant. That's no Frenchman, thought Suffolk, as they advanced on each other with drawn swords. He could feel
his rage rising. It was as if, through the slits in his helm, he could only
see the world washed in red. Rage drove him; he could hardly feel the
blows that passed his guard. He was too furious to use the stroke from
below for which his opponent had prepared so assiduously. Shouting
his battle cry, he smashed past his opponent's parries, landing blow after blow. The man stumbled and fell. "Stop!" came the cry, and he saw
that blood was gushing from his opponent's helm. Then the man was
surrounded by French esquires, and he could hear Francis shouting in
the background, "Get him off the field before they open his helm."

No Frenchman, thought Suffolk as he stepped past the dying gray
stallion and saluted his queen, giving the victory to her and to England. He could see her face was flushed with excitement. Ah, good, he
thought. She will give a good report of me to my king, her brother. A
faint flutter of regret passed briefly through his triumphant heart.
There was a time when he had thought he might approach her, but
now she was as far above him as the sun in heaven. But I shall have her
favor, he thought. He looked again at her admiring eyes. Yes, definitely,
her favor. It made the triumph double.

TWENTY-TWO

Now that I was in Paris, I made a plan to improve myself by trying to see the important works of art that were in the king's palaces and in the churches of the city, and make copies where I could of the work most excellently made. But it was not always easy because women aren't allowed everywhere and Nan said my plan of sneaking into the priory of Saint Magloire dressed as a man was a bad idea and she wouldn't allow it at all, and besides, she would tell on me, which wasn't fair. But the palace of Les Tournelles is a school for any artist lucky enough to be in the city of Paris, for there are valuable paintings in nearly every room. In the chapel among the rare carvings and statues are ancient devotional works by now-anonymous masters, gilded and without depth, in the antique style. Then there are the paintings of hunts and mythological scenes and the portraits of long-dead kings that hang in the long galleries.

The good word of Marguerite, the Duchesse d'Alençon, got me access to many of the rooms that might otherwise be closed to me, and also to her private collection, which included a book of portrait drawings of her friends, mostly made in the atelier of the master Jean Clouet, who had the biggest portrait studio in Paris, and with his many assistants and apprentices was busy all the time. Luckily for me he did not know the secrets of painting in small, which I kept for myself. It was easier because I was a woman and people thought it was some kind of instinct or magic, and not from hard studying.

Not only did I learn much from studying all these different paintings and drawings, but some of them cheered me up because they were really awful, even if they were famous. That made up for the ones that made me despair of ever equaling them, like some of the new ones from Italy. Besides, it turned out that the king did not have a Leonardo. That was just talk. He had a copy of a Virgin with angels, but I could tell from the composition that this Italian painter was a real master and probably had seen angels himself because one of them looked rather a lot like Hadriel.

Also, I had not forgotten Archbishop Wolsey's command to send him a list of what the King of France had on display, so I was making the list but was not very far on it yet. True, Wolsey had never paid me any part of that fifteen pounds a year he had promised, but that is the artist's lot. At least he had given me plenty of business, especially by sending me into France, and some of those people had paid me, and since I was thrifty, I still had money in my purse. Besides, the names of my high clients were useful in getting materials on credit, which is especially hard for a woman. That is how it is with those who serve the great. First you have to borrow to get the materials to deliver what they want, and then everyone is in debt to everyone else and waiting for payment, which may or may not come someday when the great lord or lady remembers it. But now I was better off than before because I had free meals with the English servants of the queen as well as a studio with the rent paid ahead by the Duchess Marguerite and the prospect of a handsome fee from the Duchess Claude when her angels were done.

So it was that I was busy in the long gallery just after Saint Nicholas Day looking at a painting of King Charles the Seventh's mistress as the Holy Virgin in a scandalous state of undress done by that Maître Jean Fouquet they all spoke so highly of. It was when I was thinking that if he'd known more about female anatomy, he wouldn't have painted her right breast in the shape of a large cannonball practically on her shoulder, that I heard footsteps behind me in the gallery. Nan was dozing out of pure boredom on a bench, with her mending almost sliding off her lap, and a couple of ugly cats had come to rub their heads on my skirts as if I could give them something to eat, which I couldn't. I had my magnifying glass in my hand to look at the brush strokes on the draperies, and my attention was very concentrated, so I didn't look around.

"Not as undressed as *The Temptation of Eve* and not as pink, either," said a voice behind me. Outside, the rain was rattling on the lead roofs, pouring down the steep towers in sheets. The long gallery was cold and stank of urine. I turned and saw Robert Ashton standing there, in a damp gray cloak, as thin and pale as a ghost.

"Master Ashton! They told me you were dead, and then I saw Tom, and he said you had lived. But . . . but I thought you'd gone back to England."

"They told me I'd find you here." Ashton came closer, and I could see that he limped. He looked wan and frail, and his eyes were sunken in dark circles. He could have been a ghost, except that he made my heart jump. I wanted him to embrace me again; I wanted to put my arms around him, but there was something in him that said I couldn't. And oh, he was thin. I felt the strangest urge coming over me. The urge to feed him. Joints and cheese and heavy English ale and thick pottage laden with parsnips and onions and carrots came all unbidden to my mind. I was never much of a cook, but I could feel it all rising inside me. He needed feeding up.

"Tom is a good boy. He stayed with me, when I . . . he stayed. We talked. You were right. There was a man who did murder, and he is one that I knew and whose word I trusted. I trust him no more. Did you know that Tom was in love with you?" That odd gesture again, the stiffened shoulder, the nervous unrolling of one hand with the other.

"Always. But I didn't lead him on. I knew he'd grow out of it and find someone more suitable." Ashton paused, as if thinking.

"While I was . . . lying ill . . . they gave me up, you know . . . while I was at Calais, one thing haunted me. There is something I must hear from you alone. Then I'll go and not bother you again. How did . . . how did your husband pass from this life?" What was wrong with him? He looked as if he had some disease of the soul. Why come so far, to ask a thing like that once more, a thing he already knew? Had I just imagined the magic of that night before we left Dover? Was it just some wistful dream hatched of solitude and disappointment?

"Master Dallet was murdered in bed with another man's wife. Why do you want to bring up old things that cause me pain?"

"I need to know . . . how the husband knew to return home at that very instant."

"You mean that Captain Pickering? That I never knew myself until later. Someone sent him a letter. I found out from Sir Septimus Crouch that it was a man called Ludlow—a dreadful carrion crow of a lawyer who wanted to get his hands on something my husband had and wouldn't give him."

"Ludlow. And Crouch. Jesus! It fits. It all fits. You didn't rejoice when he died?"

"Rejoice? My God, you think that? What do you imagine me to be? A ghoul? He left me without a penny, and I found the man his funeral money. Ask anyone! He was buried like a gentleman, even if he did live like a whoremaster. *I* did it! I paid his debts with my parents' wedding bed, which they died on! What do you imagine I did? Carouse in some tavern with all the money he left me? Every penny, every gift, went to his mistress! *She* had a fine big son who looked like him, and *I* had a dead baby! Ask Nan what he left me! Nothing! Less than nothing! Everything I have, every debt was paid, with the arts my father taught me. He took everything and left me with nothing. And I was married in church with God's blessing! Where was God's blessing then?" I burst into tears, and he stepped back, aghast.

What with all this shouting in English, Nan woke up with a start, and her mending dropped on the floor. The cats went and hid in the gallery fireplace, which was piled with wood, but unlit. Ashton's face had turned sheet white, and his jaw dropped.

"Your father taught you?"

"Of course. He was a great master. How do you think I learned? Out of the air? Do you take me for a freak? Master Dallet only married me to find out my father's secrets when he wouldn't sell them. Once he had become great with my father's wisdom, he left Nan and me to starve."

"Wrong. I was wrong on every count," I could hear him mutter to himself, as he shook his head. He seemed torn between fleeing and speaking. I suddenly realized that whatever it was he believed about me, it was far worse than being Wolsey's doxy, which in itself was insulting enough.

"What was it you heard? Who told you?" He hesitated a long time before he answered.

"Sir Septimus Crouch. He . . . he said . . . you'd sent the letter." He hung his head down. I was cold all the way to my heart.

"That monster," I whispered. "That lying monster."

I remembered him now, all disheveled and crazy. I remembered Crouch, standing by his side, so confidential and cozy. I thought of his fits and starts, his silences, the way he watched me when I was in company. He must have been in love then, maybe always, as much as Tom. But what kind of love is it that hurries to believe the worst? Bad love. He looked at my face. "I'm sorry," he said. "I'm not your minder any more, so I've no right to speak. I'll go now. I'll write to Wolsey about you. I've been put on another task anyway...." Stiff and pale, he turned and limped away.

"Master Ashton, you stop now!" said Nan, barring his way. "You should be ashamed."

"I am." I could hear his voice respond, even though it was low.

"And proud, too. Too proud to see what you've done to my darling. Turn around and look at her face, you selfish man." He looked over his shoulder, but I couldn't see him very well, on account of the blurriness caused by the tears. It was so stupid standing there in that cold, urine-soaked gallery, and sobbing so; the rain was crying down out of the cold, gray sky, and my face was all wet and my heart broken open in a hundred places and dripping away all my joy. It all matched, me and nature, which is not original. As a work of art, it should have been better composed.

"You've made too much of a mess to walk away without a word. You haven't the right," Nan said firmly. He stopped. "Oh, I always knew you were no good for her. Do you think I didn't try to keep you apart? But since you're here, I expect you to make good on what you've done. You go back. You go back now and make it right with her, or I swear, my ghost will haunt you until the end of your days."

"I can't," he said.

"You mean, you can't make it right with *you*," said Nan. "But you owe it to her to make it right with her. You apologize, and beg forgiveness, as Our Lord says you must do, before you just dance off into a cloud of self-pity and start preening yourself for being such a tragical, lonely figure." He looked shocked and horrified.

"You know I'm right, don't you! Let me say this. I may be old, Master Ashton, but I am not stupid. Speak now, before you lose your chance forever." The gallery seemed very long at that moment. The uneven sound of his boots as he limped the length of it seemed to echo unnaturally in the silence. Outside, the rain gusted against the stone wall and roared like waterfalls from the mouths of the gargoyle rainspouts.

"Mistress ... Dallet. I believed ... what no man of honor ... should believe of a woman ... I ... I beg your forgiveness," he said.

"I never would have done such a thing. You were wicked to believe it...." I rubbed my knuckles in my eyes, but they just wouldn't quit being wet.

"Susanna, you have not forgiven. You must." Nan's voice was firm. Just as when I was ten years old, and my brother, Felix, spoiled my drawing of the Virgin, just because it was better than his. I didn't forgive for a whole week. But then he grew ill, and after I forgave him, he died, and things were never the same. I should have forgiven sooner, even though I didn't want to. I looked at Master Ashton's pale face. He didn't like apologizing either. He would rather make excuses for himself. So would I. He could die. We all could die. Life is no good with a hard heart.

"Master Ashton, you are ... forgiven. I forgive you."

"I *truly* forgive you," prompted Nan. I could see a little spark of something, something faded but humorous, in Master Ashton's hazel eyes. The gray light from the window picked up a hidden chestnut tint in his dark brown curls. He's one, too, I thought suddenly.

"Did she have to do this often, when she was small?" he asked.

"Of course," said Nan.

"So did I," he said in a small voice.

"Two of a kind," said Nan. "It's the hair."

"My hair is *not* red, Nan, only a little gingery."

"And mine is really brown. A dark brown, almost black, if you look at it right. Not red a bit," said Robert Ashton. I couldn't help smiling. I touched his curls.

"Your hair's caught fire, then," I said.

"And how long has yours been smoldering?" he asked, running a finger along one of those little bits I can never get to stay under my headdress.

"Since birth, Master Ashton, since birth," announced Nan.

"Do you always have to be right, Nan?" I asked.

"Always. Who is older and wiser?"

"You," said Robert Ashton and I together, and Nan nodded happily.

"Mistress Dallet, may I have your permission to pay you court? I am only a younger son, without prospects. I inherited ten pounds and a horse when my father died, but the horse died and the money is spent. I rise no further in the archbishop's service because Brian Tuke blocks my way. Say yes or say now that you scorn me, and let me go. I will feel none the worse for it. I have been scorned by ambitious women before, and I am hardened."

"Master Ashton, I have only the work of my hands as my dowry, and should any man take my work from me, then he shall have no marriage portion at all. Consider that, before you pay me your addresses, if they be honorable. And remember that for all your wicked imaginings I am a reputable widow, and will accept no dishonorable propositions."

"Then I fear we are well matched, in fortune as well as hair."

"In hair? Never," said I. "But as for fortune, I have never bothered much about that. God makes our fortunes."

"Then you are different from all the women in the world, for which difference I am grateful," he said.

"Then I take it you still plan to address your suit to me?"

"I do, for as long as it takes to convince you that I am not a hateful villain and a gossip. I rue the day I ever let that odious Septimus Crouch twist my mind with his venomous calumnies."

"Crouch? He is the vilest monster I've ever known. I saw him do a murder and walk away as if he'd been to a supper party. He killed the lawyer Ludlow, and all for some book that could hardly be worth it. I supposed it was fate. Ludlow took the baby's cradle, you know, and it was accursed because the baby died in it. And now I've found that Crouch is here, too. I've had a terrible time, hiding from him."

"Here? Susanna, does he know where you are?"

"He might know I'm here, but he hasn't found me yet. He goes about with some horrible Italian fellow, these days."

"Signor Belfagoro. I know. He is a hero to the English. And even the French court him now. I dare say nothing about him; they can find no words high enough to praise the two of them. And yet I am sure that they are up to no good." He shook his head slowly, and his eyes were serious.

"Do they have anything to do with why you are here?"

"I don't think so, but I would be happy if it were so."

"Why happy?"

"Because it would solve a mystery. There is someone—or perhaps many someones—linked in a conspiracy to destroy the alliance. They believe that the failure will cause the House of Valois to fall and they will achieve supreme power. I have been asked to find out who is involved with this secret organization, and who leads them. I stayed overlong in Calais, thinking I might find a clue among the captains there. But no, in spite of his name, he is no sailor."

"I'm glad. I've had enough of sailors, especially captains."

"But in all your travels among the great, keep your ears open for me, for the archbishop, and for England. Somewhere, most probably at court, there is a man of power who calls himself the Helmsman."

The great Salle Pavé at Les Tournelles was hung with rare tapestries and silk banners ornamented with Tudor roses and King Louis's boar. The light from hundreds of candles glittered on the green-and-yellow designs in the celebrated faience floor. Musicians played from the gallery, and the glistening tiles swarmed with dancers of both sexes as Suffolk, the victor, led the queen herself in the first figure of the dance. Those who felt themselves too old, or too infirm from their recent battles to dance, contented themselves with clustering by the walls, gossiping while they admired the grace of the ladies and the elegant figures cut by the men.

On the dais, the king sat on a high, cushioned seat beside a similar one still warm from the impression of the queen's young body. How she had wanted to dance! First her finger had tapped on the arm of the seat, then her toe had tapped as well, and he could hear her breath coming in time to the music. But the old king's joints hurt too much to carry him out on the floor, and he was beginning to regret the young queen's giddiness, her animal spirits, her enthusiasms. Perhaps he should have married the older sister, after all. Someone steadier, soberer, less inclined to dance. He had given her another jewel the night before, the night after Suffolk's triumph over the giant challenger, but she had not seemed as delighted as usual. She did not turn pink, or clap her hands, and her kiss of thanks seemed cool and obligatory.

Now she had danced with d'Alençon, with Dorset, and was cavorting with Suffolk. The Dauphin, however, was a model of rectitude, the king mused. He was maturing, beginning to understand his duties.

There he was, bringing a cup to his duchess. Claude, how like her mother she looked, thought the king. Suppose she could only produce living daughters, like her mother? The house of Valois was at risk. Civil war might ensue. Disaster. He must, he must get a son with this new wife. "Monsieur," he said, gesturing to Francis to join him, "the queen dances too much with the English duke. Escort her back to me." As he watched the queen squirm among the cushions on her chair, barely able to suppress the petulant look on her face, he realized more than ever that quiet evenings such as pleased him would not suit her. He must keep her busy, he must keep her amused, he must show himself to be still-young and gallant at heart. Was he not king? Had he not been victor in greater tournaments in his day? He would show them; he would show them all that he was still young. He would attract her eyes to him and only him.

Francis glanced sideways with his narrow, sly eyes at his lord and king, then at the fidgeting girl beside him. His eyes sought out her creamy profile, then the bulge where her bodice compressed two white, delicious breasts upward. Cleverly, he concealed his thirst for the delights he imagined beneath her gown. The old king's face was gray, jealous, determined. You are not fit for her, he thought. I will be the victor. Beneath his long nose, the corners of his mouth turned upward as he imagined the sweetness of his victory, the look on her face . . .

Across the great hall, Crouch, who was now an honored guest of the English, was pointing out to the foreign Archduke Belfagoro of Tartarus, the famous horse breeder, the various great persons who were in the room, and doing his best to explain French royal genealogy to him. "Now, the House of Valois is the cadet branch of the Capetians, who include King Philip the Fair, and the throne has come to this, the cadet branch of the Valois, through the failure of King Charles the Eighth to have a son. That is why this king, Louis the Twelfth, is a generation older, being the son of the late king's great-granduncle, the Duc d'Orléans. He, too, has had no living son."

"*Ugh*, branches, cousins, cadets, what a tangle! But you say this king has no son? Why then, looking at him, all pale and old like that, I shall soon be free," muttered Belphagor. Crouch, who, though wide, was taller than Belphagor, looked down at him and smirked. How little you know, he thought. Belphagor, surveying the roomful of branches, cousins, and cadets, said, "So, Crouch, tell me more of King Charles's father, the illustrious Louis the Eleventh. Now there was a fellow I would have enjoyed knowing! Murder, rapine, torture! Now, how was it that he maintained his power?"

"The Spider King shut himself in Plessis-les-Tours, surrounded by a Scottish guard loyal only to him . . ."

"Now who is that fellow over there—the tall, thin, dark-haired one, who stands by himself? I like the look on his face. Arrogant. Treacherous. He seems like the sort of fellow I'd get along with."

"That is the most noble Charles de Bourbon, a great warrior and hero, who has just married the heiress to most of the lands in central France."

"Has he a claim to the throne?"

"Only a most distant and dubious one. But his possession of the heiress, a direct desendant of the Valois through the female line, will give any son born to him a mighty claim . . ."

"Ah, perfect, perfect," said Belphagor, rubbing his hands as he gazed possessively at the dark man with the smoldering, rebellious glance. "If this king dies without sons, I can set the country at civil war."

"But any contender you support would meet with powerful opposition from the king's cousin, the offspring of the Angoulêmes, who is not only the closest male heir but married to the king's eldest daughter and named Dauphin, unless the current queen has a son."

"Oh, I can hardly keep track! You mean that big, long-nosed fellow over there that you pointed out to me? The one with the ugly little wife, who spends his time dancing and cavorting with other women to show off before others?"

"The very one, Your Damnedness." Belphagor looked across the room at Francis and then squinted to try to retain the memory. Crouch, who stood close by the demon's ear, so that they might not be overheard, said softly, "There are many possibilities here, Lord Belphagor. You must be sure to control the man you use to unseat the Valois. Then his power will be your power. The best way to make him strong is to set his followers at odds with one another, then he holds the balance, and you hold him. The art of power is a science too rarely studied, my lord. Rely only on me, and I shall guide you through the maze." Belphagor gave Crouch a suspicious glance.

"Introduce me to that Bourbon fellow; I like the way his eyes shift. He seems a surly, ambitious sort, suitable to be my king." Maybe I need a new tutor, the demon was thinking. Someone with a superior social position. Crouch is beginning to bore me. He clings too much. He wants to know too much. He meddles with my imps and spends too much time looking in that silly brass cup of his.

"My lord, it will be difficult now; he has joined the dance."

"Oh, a pox on all this disgusting festivity! I'll just have to see him later. Come, Crouch, these creatures swarm all over the place like maggots. No, I'm fond of maggots. Like . . . like . . ."

"Rabbits, perhaps, Lord Belphagor?" suggested Crouch, his pale eyes shining with malicious amusement.

"Yes, rabbits. Furry. Brown eyed. Disgusting."

Across the festive hall, clustered around stubby little Claude, who did not dance, were a group of ladies, who for one reason or another preferred the restful indoor sport of gossip to the more active one of dancing. The frail, crippled little Duchesse de Bourbon, the greatest heiress in France, was there with her redoubtable mother, Anne de Beaujeau, once Regent of France, who would have been queen in her own right if women had been allowed to inherit the throne.

"I say that little filly the King of England has sent the old fool will jog him straight to hell," pronounced the old lady.

"But she is most gracious. Did you not remark at the banquet how she asked for a portion of the dessert to be sent to the Princess Renée in her nursery?" Claude had forgotten again that Mary was the enemy and had slipped back into her old habits of finding good about others. The ladies intensified their efforts, not only to satisfy themselves, but to reinforce Claude's too easily forgotten resentment.

"Did you see how your husband danced with her?"

"Yes, they were talking. I could see her blush."

"He only offers her courtesy; it is the king's order. He told me so, and I have heard the king himself ask it."

"Then you are as innocent as a lamb."

"A lamb going to the slaughter."

"He speaks to her in private. Did you see him show off at the tournament in her honor? It was not before you that he bowed, but her."

"But ... but he sponsored the tournament, it was the proper thing...."

"But *she*, she is a filthy thing. Redheaded, you know."

"Yes, that gross English duke was her lover. She has sent for him."

"She will make the king an heir. He is incapable, you know. The whole court has heard it. An English heir for the throne of France. What they failed in by force, they will get by trickery. There's no fool like an old fool, I say."

"He won't see the spring, I'm telling you. Look how pale he is, that old man, all dressed in satin, as if he were some twenty-year-old. If he doesn't have a nap, he becomes ill."

"Then you'd better beware if your husband becomes king, my dear Lady Claude. It wouldn't be the first time a King of France has put away a wife to take one he liked better."

"Remember Jeanne de France. You'd better hurry and have a baby, then he can't put you away in a nunnery like that poor queen."

"Stop, stop! It can't be true. My lord is good to me. He will love me in time; I am sure. Besides, it is I who hold the province of Brittany from my mother. He would never sever Brittany from France."

"Your marriage has given him Brittany. He'll hire lawyers, just you see. They'll find a loophole to let him keep your inheritance without keeping you. You had better learn to look after your own interests better, Madame Claude, or you will spend the rest of your life looking out of an iron grille."

"Never trust lawyers where a man's right to property is pitted against a woman's. I've had bitter experience of lawsuits," announced the old lady who had once been Regent of France. Across the room she spied her son-in-law, Charles de Bourbon. Perfect, she thought. A powerful captain, bitter, proud, resentful. Through my daughter, I will raise him to the supreme power, and he will avenge me. It is my line that will rule France, not the line of that miserable little woman, Louise of Savoy. "Yes, lawsuits," she said. "Beware when a man sees lawyers. He will—oh, here come two of those English ladies. They should be forbidden to speak together in that ugly tongue! Ah, my dear Mademoiselle Grey and Mademoiselle Bourchier, do come sit here with us. We were just discussing the new alliance...."

"Politics are too deep for us, Madame de Beaujeau. We are speaking of the new Italian fashion, with the waist of the bodice set higher...."

"Yes, with the sleeves gathered up, so, right here above the elbow, and then again puffed below and gathered together.... Do you think it lacks dignity? A full sleeve makes the wrist and hand look more dainty, it does seem."

"Yes, two things most beautiful, small hands and small feet."

"That was three things," replied Madame de Beaujeau, repeating the ancient formula for beauty in a woman. "A small mouth is included." She pursed up her own mouth, which was surrounded by little wrinkles that proclaimed the expression to be a habitual one. Everyone knew that a small mouth in a woman signified small other things, which were greatly to be desired in any lady. Anne de Beaujeau's eyes, bright and beady like an ancient bird's, shifted about the room, as if to signify that the newcomers were not worth giving her whole attention to. She cast a brief look at the dais, where Suffolk had come to address the queen in that ghastly alien language. The queen laughed in response. "A woman must be careful not to laugh too much," said the old lady. "It stretches the mouth." Her voice was disdainful. But the two ladies had not seen their queen, who was behind them, so the barb missed them entirely.

The Twelfth Portrait

Portrait of an Unknown Man. *After Holbein. Mid-sixteenth century.* *7 × 8". Charcoal on gray paper. Heightened with red and white chalk. Staatliche Museum Preussischer Kulturbesitz, Berlin.*

Remarkable for its draftmanship, this portrait depicts a clean-shaven young man in his late twenties, from his plain dress a member of the merchant or middle classes. His frank, amused stare makes it clear that he considered posing for his portrait something of a joke, and the unknown artist has faithfully recorded his attitude. The unfastened collar and stray curls that straggle across his forehead suggest he was caught in some inadvertent moment, possibly after exercise or some exertion. Attractive and direct, the portrait suggests the common humanity that unites us across the centuries.

—*Johnson.* The History of the English Portrait

"Now murrey is a hard color for painting in small; it must be made just right, you see, and it is so very expensive. It's best made with a lake from Venice, but this lake here is from Antwerp, and it will do nearly as well." Master Ashton set down the big sack of plaster he had carried home for me and took up the little packet I had just purchased from the shelf where I had put it, inspected it, and put it back again. Then he looked so curiously about my studio, I thought he might be staring at a foreign country.

"It's different than before. All those French gentlemen looking down their noses."

"You mean, you're missing my Adam and Eves, after all."

"The smell. That can't be your glue boiling. It's got pepper in it."

"Oxtail soup. I had a notion you'd be over."

"How did you know, when I only ran into you by accident, trying to carry that big sack? And where's Nan, anyway?"

"Off arguing with the butcher and the grocer about their bills, and trying to get more credit. But I really couldn't wait for the lake, and if you're going out to get one thing, you might as well get others, too."

"I've never seen a woman run through so much money that was not for clothing."

"I just knew it. You *were* following me! Don't you trust me yet? I'm buying paints, not seeing lovers. I haven't got any lovers. Just one suitor, who follows me to see what I'm doing and then pretends to bump into me when the packages get too high." He looked crushed, or at least pretended to.

"It really *was* an accident, at first. I thought you'd turn and see me, but no, your nose was in the air the whole time. Too snobbish for an honest woman, I said to myself. Then I saw you were by yourself, and I thought I'd best make sure you'd get home safely. . . ."

"And you thought I just might have a little supper waiting here?

And possibly Nan wouldn't be home yet? Wrong thinkers would see it as not respectable." He looked embarrassed and changed the subject.

"What did you buy the rock candy for? Surely that's not for painting." I got two bowls from the shelf and ladled soup into them.

"These colors here I grind only with gum arabic water, but the black lakes are better grinded with a bit of sugar candy in the gum." I set the bowls on the table and went to hunt for two spoons. Silently, he took a wine bottle from inside his doublet where he had been carrying it and extended it to me.

"What's this?" I asked. "I thought it was an accident, our meeting."

"It *was* an accident, I told you. But ... I *had* thought of coming over ..." I looked at his face and laughed. He turned red. How funny we are, I thought, the way we dance about each other, each afraid of being hurt by the other. He moved onto a safer subject again.

"And all this plaster—what did you get it for?" he said, gesturing to the sack with the toe of his boot.

"I use it fine and slaked for gesso—that is the white ground on that panel, there, that I made yesterday. Also, thickened, it makes molds, like you see on the shelf." I found a cup for the wine and set it with the bottle on the table.

"Your father taught you all this?" he asked, sitting down.

"Of course. Wisdom like this does not come out of the air, Master Ashton. My father was a great man, a great painter in small and in large. He traveled all over the earth in search of these secrets." I cut some slices of a loaf of bread left over from the morning. As I ate, I watched him eat. He looked healthier, filling out again, and his color was better. I couldn't help taking a proprietary interest, since I had fed him quite a few meals lately—always by accident, somehow, but never before without Nan. Suddenly he looked up.

"You're fattening me up, aren't you?"

"Me? Never!" Caught. I could feel my face turning red.

"You have that look in your eye. The look of a housewife inspecting a rooster penned up with a full feed dish. Am I less bony? Are my feathers shiny enough now? When do I go into the soup?"

"Robert Ashton! What do you take me for? I'm not making soup!"

"Well, actually, you did already. Oxtail this time. And it's very good," he said, looking at me, his eyes speculative and humorous. I looked away quickly and pretended to be slicing more bread. Now he could see that I was embarrassed, so he changed the subject back to art again to spare me.

"The hands cast in plaster, why them?" asked Master Ashton, gesturing with a soup spoon toward the arms, hands, and feet, all casts of mine and Nan's, hanging from hooks on the wall.

"To see the shadowings and the way the light falls on them, when I am painting a full figure. It spares the sitter." I poured more wine into the cup and drank off several gulps much too fast.

"Did you love him? Your father, I mean?" I could feel the wine working on me. He picked up the cup and drank.

"Of course. Didn't you love yours? He gave me everything; he gave me . . . myself." I took the cup from him and finished up the last of it.

"Yourself?"

"I couldn't be myself without drawing, you see. I love the smell of paint, and the quietness, and the images I see in my mind." Master Ashton looked at me curiously, a new way, as if he saw something he hadn't expected. The last wintry glow of the sun was spilling through the little circles of glass set in the tall, narrow window of the studio. It caught for a moment on the bright colors of the paintings, lingered in a long streak across the wooden plank floor, and rested at last on Robert Ashton's battered old leather doublet and pensive features. I loved that light, and the faint golden shine it gave to whatever it touched. And as it touched Robert Ashton, I knew that I loved him, too. All in that moment, I knew that my heart would break without him, that my body ached for the touch of him, and that my eyes rejoiced only in the sight of him. But a little piece of my heart cried, "Hold back!" It was cautious, because it could sense he was being cautious, and I was afraid of being foolish and hurt a second time.

"I am envious," he said. "I don't love my trade as much as you love yours. Perhaps it's because I see nothing from it at the day's end. All I do is fetch and carry for others."

"But they are very grand others." I looked at his hands. They were just right, very strong, with good long bones and veins that showed on their backs. "Master Ashton, would you grant me another favor? It is not so laborious as helping me bring back the plaster." He looked surprised. "I have no cast of men's hands. Would you let me take one of yours? You will have the gratification of seeing your hands on every saint and lord that I paint from now on."

"Is this all you are interested in me for? A pair of hands?"

"They are very nice hands," I said, reaching across the table to capture one of them, then taking it up in mine. "See the veins here?" I traced the pattern with my finger, looking down as I could feel his eyes battering on me. His breath was coming hard.

"Good God," he whispered, "you ask more than is human of me." But the touch of his hand, the sound of his voice had broken something in my mind, a little lock, something tight and careful. All in an instant, it was smashed beyond repair.

"Robert..." He grabbed my hands across the table. The wine bottle, now empty, crashed over. "Robert ..." I stood, and he rose, embracing me across the narrow table. Pewter bowls and spoons tumbled to the floor as the little table overturned. There was the crash of glass.

"Susanna," he whispered. "Save me. I never meant this for you, but I can't ... I have wanted you forever ..."

But I was a lost soul. Hinder him? Remind him of duty? I couldn't. My heart was battering at my chest, waves of heat were moving over me, smothering me; his kisses were explosions that lit my mind with unquenchable fire. What was this thing that he did, that I had never dreamed of, never felt before? Not Master Dallet's obligatory, boring proddings in the dark. This was transformation, shining, liquid like quicksilver, in the full glow of northern daylight. His face was transfigured; his sweat dripped onto me, mingling with mine, his scent enveloped me like a blanket. Ah, God, I was a widow. How had I not known everything? How had I not known this? There we were fully clothed among the fallen dishes and broken glass, before the fire where the soup kettle boiled dry, but we could have been in heaven or in hell, and never noticed.

At last, limp and ruined, I came to myself. "Oh, God, Robert, what have we done?" I whispered. I looked at his face. Tears stood in his eyes.

"Forgive me," he said. "Forgive me for loving you so much. We must marry. I'll marry you. I'll make it right. I can't live without you. Swear, swear, you'll marry me and forgive me, Susanna."

"Marry? Robert, marriage? You will be ruined. You'll be put out of your place for marrying without permission. The archbishop will never forgive you. We'll starve. Oh, what are we to do?" I began to cry and shake.

"You regret it that much? You won't have me? What have I done?" he cried.

"N-no. It's—it's that I love you, God forgive me, my body lusts for you, Robert, even now. And I've sinned, and can't regret it. What does that make me?"

"I'll wipe the stain away. We'll marry. I'll win the archbishop's permission. I know I can't marry without his consent, but I'll win his approval. I'll make a great success and then approach him subtly. He'll think it was his own idea that it's all for the best—you'll see." I smiled at him as I sniffled and began to pick up the dishes.

"You, subtle? Oh, Robert, when have you ever been subtle, even now?" But the afterglow was in me. I would have done anything for him. Anything. Jumped out the window. Married without his master's consent, and walked barefoot begging after him. But I could hear him beginning to plan, then I could hear him calculating. As my love became wider, broader than comprehension, I could feel him trying to push his love into a box. The box of "career saved, marry anyway, get a nice wedding gift from the archbishop." Have it all. Sacrifice nothing. I could feel my love bleeding. But as it bled, it grew, even there.

"I must find the Helmsman," he said. "Only that will do. Everyone told him it was impossible; that's why he sent me. Tuke had a hand in it, I'm sure. He wanted to ruin me, but I won't be ruined. They say the Helmsman's in the south; I'll go and find him, and when I send the news of my success, I'll ask permission to marry. It's always best to approach the archbishop in a mellow mood. That's how to win him over. And Crouch is in this, I swear. What's he doing here, oozing around and currying favor everywhere? God, I hate him now. He's come, you know, and works in company with some false Italian charlatan passing himself off as a gentleman. It's the secret paper they're after. I swear, I'll have the paper for the archbishop. I'll tell him I have it and hold it from him until he gives his consent. Susanna, I swear here and now I'll marry you when I have made a success of things. It won't take long at all. Everything will work out."

"Oh, Robert, Robert, can't true love win out? Tell me all these plans are as nothing compared to our love."

"But, Susanna, my darling," he said in a soft voice, "can't you see I'm doing all this because I love you?"

Again, icy rain was falling in sheets from the leaden sky. The English ambassadors had returned, the court had left Paris for Saint-Germain-en-Laye. It was the season of Advent, with the great feast of the Nativity of Our Lord only two weeks away. That powerful courtier, the Duc de Bourbon had packed away his wife and mother-in-law and horses with the court, remaining alone in Paris on the "legal business" that seemed to eat up so much of his time and leave him so embittered that even the most suspicious soul knew that his "legal business" could not be an excuse to visit a mistress. Bourbon had removed himself from Les Tournelles to the house of one of his lawyers, one Maître Bellier, the better to deal with this mysterious business. Men came and went, bearing messages. And the great vaulted chamber beneath the ground resonated with the sound of men's voices arguing, as the torches burned low, night after night.

"I tell you, I have seen him in the past week. He has been everywhere. He provided the English duke with horses when his cause was lost."

"There is no doubt he has come to deliver the manuscript, then."

"But to whom? The Valois? Or has he another plan?"

"And yet he claimed it had been divided in three, and he possessed only two parts."

"A lie. Unless the third part is here, in other hands."

"Impossible."

"This means he uses the manuscript to conspire for his own power."

"No. I believe he has come to betray us to the king. The complete book reveals our secret and our aim of destroying the Valois to restore the Merovingians to the throne. We must act now, or we will be executed for treason."

"No, if we move early, before the conjunction of Jupiter, all is lost.

Our forces are not gathered, and the day is not ripe, according to the prophecy. Consider this, the king is too weak, too busy with his new bride to deal with the manuscript. No, Monsieur Crouch plays a waiting game. Why else would he travel about the city like a tourist, purchasing a few antiquities, ingratiating himself, introducing that foreign prince he travels with as an Italian? Protected by the English, he whiles away the time, waiting for the king to die so he can deal with Francis. A new and vigorous king could exterminate us."

"Then he must never deal with Francis."

"We cannot move early. The time is not ripe."

"It is easy. All we have to do is prevent Francis from taking the supreme power. The English queen must have a son and be made regent to protect him until he comes of age. Francis cannot then ascend the throne. But she will be unable to rule without assistance. The Helmsman can insinuate himself into her good graces, become her advisor. It will not be easy. The kingdom will be thrown into turmoil, with Francis opposing the Helmsman. But in this time of divided power, the emperor can gather his forces and bring them to our assistance."

"Impossible. The king can sire no more children. That I have had from his closest advisors."

"But the king has given out that he can."

"The king fades daily. When he is dead, the queen will be forced into mourning, confined to her chambers until they can discover whether or not she will give birth to a posthumous heir. We will take control of her there. We will smuggle a newborn child into the chamber, proclaim that an heir has been born, and make her regent, in our power."

"What if she refuses to claim a child smuggled in to her?"

"She will not dare. She will seem the author of the conspiracy. She will be ruined. Better to be queen regent, under our control, than imprisoned for life by Duke Francis."

"Since Crouch delays as part of his strategy, why not simply assassinate him before he can make his move?"

"We do not know how many are in his conspiracy. Perhaps the English dukes, perhaps others who are pledged to act for him should he disappear. Certainly, that Prince Belfagoro is one of them. We would have to assassinate them both, and the English dukes as well."

"Did I hear someone mention my name?" There was a puff of smoke, a whiff of brimstone, and Belphagor stood at the head of the table, at the left hand of the Duc de Bourbon, who shrank back in sudden horror. The torches in the iron sconces flickered in an invisible wind, then sprang up brighter, as if fed by some infernal force. The unpleasant stench of sulfur began to filter into the ancient chamber. The black waters in the calderium splashed, agitated, as a thin, yellowish vapor spread over them. One of the conspirators began to cough. Maître Bellier took a large handkerchief from his sleeve and put it to his face.

"Oh, I beg you, do not be disturbed. No, no, keep your seats, gentlemen. There is nothing I love better than a conspiracy, except perhaps a mass murder. And one often leads to the other, doesn't it?" But the Duc de Bourbon, who was as polished as he was hotheaded, had regained his suavity.

"My dear Sieur ... ah, Belfagoro, to what do we owe this honor? And from whence have you arrived so suddenly? Surely, we will do all that is in our poor power to be of assistance."

"Monsieur de Bourbon, you may call me by my true name. I am Prince Belphagor, Lord of the Underworld, Ruler of Demons, and Commander of Legions of Imps, come to assist you in your cause."

Maître Bellier and the others looked horrified. "But—but our cause, it is a sacred trust," the old theologian said.

"It is ordained by God Himself. ..."

"The true blood ..."

"Someone has cursed us with this visit of the Tempter. Who could have done it? It is the others, the fallen ones."

"The Splitting of the Oak. The Templars. Avaunt, demon."

"Avaunt yourself, you silly old man. Don't avaunt me, or you might make me angry. Our cause is the same. I heard you want to get rid of the Valois. So do I. I don't care what house you put in power afterwards. Just so there're no Valois."

"Why are you against the Valois?"

"A little disagreement with King Philippe."

"I told you it was the Templars. They have set this devil loose."

"So what if I've know a few Templars in my time? I've been sitting in this room with you for quite a while. I gather you are a conspiracy against the ruling house of France. No, no—don't bother to leave; I have no intention of betraying you or your delicious little meeting place here. I have a personal grudge against the king and his heirs. I wish to make common cause with you. Now, the idea of a false heir, that is excellent. A scheme with many brilliant facets."

Belphagor made himself comfortable, sitting on the table, crossing his legs over the edge. He looked quite the gentleman. A velvet hat with an egret plume affixed by a great jewel was tilted rakishly on his head. He had a ring on every finger and a great pearl as an eardrop. His doublet was heavy crimson velvet, reembroidered in gold and silver, and his immense boots were Morocco leather as soft as silk. His voice, contrary to his natural uncouth instincts, was suave and modulated. Crouch had done his work well. Belphagor, though somewhat incorporeal in spots, and giving off an unmistakable aura of evil, seemed every inch a creature of their own set. Never, thought Belphagor, have I had such an attentive and cooperative audience. No troublesome magic circles, no protective amulets. I've moved right in with them. How splendid; I can make an agreement and they won't think to bind me to it with some dismal little grimoire oath. Then I can betray them at my leisure. For a moment, he gritted his pointed, demonic teeth, remembering the chicken. When I'm free, he thought, I'll avenge myself. Then he remembered that the demon masters were probably all dead by now, and that irritated him further. It must have made a bit of sulfurous smoke boil out of his ears, because it clearly unsettled the men at the table.

"Lord Belphagor, how may we be of service to you?" Bourbon was speaking. Splendid. *They* wanted to be of service to *him*.

"This little group of yours, you are truly dedicated to removing the descendants of King Philip from the throne of France?"

"But of course."

"For centuries, we have been dedicated to restoring the True Blood to the throne."

"True Blood? And just who may that be?" The conspirators looked at one another.

"The Merovingians, the true rulers of France, who are destined by the prophetic text to create a great, well, um, Christian empire in all the known world, including the lands of the pagan Saracens." But despite the slip, Belphagor did not spout fire; he simply replied in the mildest of tones.

"Oh, Christian? Why, excellent. Some of my best friends are priests. And monks. What splended, overripe souls some of those monks have." The conspirators breathed a sigh of relief. Belphagor noticed it. He had lulled them, the better to deceive. What fun conspiracies were! He could hardly believe he had ever been so simple. Now that he had risen to dealing with these more elegant circles, he was beginning to become embarrassed that a mortal like Crouch could know the secret of his uncouth origins. As soon as I find another convenient mortal, I simply *must* get rid of him, thought Belphagor. Why should anyone ever know I was not a demon of the highest fashion?

"So, gentlemen, I plan to assist you in your endeavors. If I ensure the death of the king within the next month, I wish to make sure that you will play your part and interrupt the succession with the false heir. What do you say to a contract?" Mortals loved contracts. It was a bit of a problem that he couldn't read, but Crouch had taught him to write a fiery *B* that glowed with unearthly light. It was a nice touch, he had assured the old demon. He watched the commotion about the table. Some of the old gentlemen seemed shocked. One of them began to protest that a sacred cause cherished for centuries should not be tarnished by compromising with evil. Then there was a muttering about deals with the Devil in a good cause being basically moral, and the protesting old man was quieted. I must remember this argument for next time, thought Belphagor. I imagine it will be quite useful for convincing others.

"Who signs for you?" asked the demon.

"I do," said Bourbon. "I am the Helmsman."

TWENTY-THREE

When all the jousting was done, the Duke of Suffolk went home, the king went to bed, and winter set in for good, with frost and the first snow. The tourney had been set for five days but lasted nearly a month, what with all the delays for bad weather. The feasting and entertainments in between had left all the courtiers exhausted, and also the cooks and musicians and banner painters and servants who picked up and swept and polished and brought in enough loads of wood to fuel hell itself.

Before the English left, Tom came to see me in my studio, where I was finishing up Madame's angels and also laying out a number of dead-babies-in-heaven pictures, because several ladies who saw the drawing for the angels said it would be a great comfort to have pictures like that. I knew what they meant, so I would sit with them and they would cry and tell me how their babies looked and I would draw until they said, "That's right," then take that baby home to put wings on it and some clouds until it was all lovely again. A Holy Virgin or special saints cost extra. It was a big change from Adam and Eves, but the same kind of idea, making people happy, though in a more respectable way. Also it took fewer materials, because these were small so the ladies could carry them around and weep, but getting fine enough little wooden cases and panels and folding frames was a big problem until I found Maître Julius the *tabletier* who was really Flemish like my father and so we came to an understanding.

"It's warm in here," said Tom. He looked bonier than ever because he'd been growing again. "But it smells. Are you boiling rabbit skins again?"

"I've got some panels from Maître Julius. I'm doing angels these days. That and the portraits."

"I could be finishing up that glue and gessoing those panels for

you," he said. "You have so much custom, you'll be needing help now."
He looked about him. The studio was bare and cluttered all at once. I
still didn't have proper shelves, but I had a chest and a cabinet. My
mirror that I use for looking at things backward was propped on top
of it. There were a couple of little panels, half finished, propped up
drying, a sketch laid out on the table for copying, and several that
looked not quite right pinned to the walls for me to look at and think
about. I saw Tom's eye fix on a drawing of Robert Ashton on my
worktable. Nothing special, just charcoal with a bit of red and white
chalk, but I'd drawn him with his shirt open and his dark hair tumbled
about his ears, and when Tom saw it a look of bitterness passed briefly
across his face.

"I guess I will be getting someone if this keeps up. But I'm thinking that you plan on going home. I think I did too good a job when I
bribed them to take you with the horses." He looked down at his feet,
embarrassed.

"I'm learning about physicking horses. It's a good trade, and they
like me, for all that I learned about compounding remedies from Master Ailwin. Besides, the language here tangles my tongue."

"You'll be safer in the household of a great man."

"He's the king's own Master of the Horse, and a great hero,"
said Tom.

"I know," I answered.

"And besides, it's hopeless!" Tom burst out. "Mistress Susanna,
you are so beautiful and good, and as far above me as the stars! What is
the use?"

"I'm much too old for you, Tom," I answered. "But I care for you
like an elder sister."

"That Master Ashton, for all he saved me, is not good enough for
you. At least I told him so. Not good enough at all. He doesn't deserve
to love you, not as I do. I saw you first. . . ." He turned on his heel.

"Wait, Tom, wait!"

"Don't think to embrace me again. It's only a cruelty," he said.

"No, no. I won't hold you here. But I want you to take a letter I've
written to Mistress Hull and Cat. I was wondering how to send it." I
had a sudden excellent idea. "And I've something else. A gift for them.
Tell them I think on them often and to keep my things yet a bit longer.

I am doing well painting angels for French ladies." I hunted in the chest in the corner and found my portrait of Cat. "This," I said. "Keep it next to you; don't let it get damp."

"But . . . but you need it, to show your work."

"I have others now."

He opened the case. "I always thought you made the hair too yellow," he said. But I could see the picture was working on his mind. He glanced sideways at me, then back again at Cat's pretty face, barely out of babyhood. Not so different from his own. A boy with a trade, the servant of a great man—she'd be impressed. She'd wait for him to become a master, and while she waited she'd say pridefully to all the neighborhood gossips, "My Tom, the duke's man, they can't do without him." I saw him seeing all of that as he stared at the little portrait, and Cat's impatient blue eyes. He shut the case and looked up at me again. "That fellow Crouch is staying, you know. He's all the rage, along with that ugly Italian, since they assisted the duke in the tourney. He says he has business here, but I told Master Ashton that I thought he was following you, trying to find you alone. Be careful when you attend the court. You've been clever to keep your studio hidden, but you need to attend the court to take the likenesses. And at court . . . at court you are exposed. Be sure to keep a lackey with you there. Nan's not enough. We saw him murder once. I . . . I feel like a traitor, leaving you like this."

"It's better that you go. But we can be friends always. I regard you kindly." His eyes looked resentful.

"I always knew it was hopeless," he said, as he left, barely managing to nod farewell.

After that I thought about how it is that women don't even have to lead men on, they just follow anyway, and what a problem it could be, only luckily Tom had turned out to have very gallant manners, unlike some of these Frenchmen who just try to push a person into a corner, like that Bonnivet, Dauphin Francis's friend, who I saw just grab some serving maid and vanish into a dark corridor even while he was paying court to another lady and also proclaiming that he carried the pure white banner of adoration for that clever Duchess Marguerite, who was already married and not to him.

That afternoon, I went all bundled up to Les Tournelles to see the Duchess Claude and take her the angels, which were all finished and very handsomely mounted in a little three-part case that hinged on itself made by Master Julius and all gilded by me with gold leaf that I had gotten on credit. I had worked very hard to get it done because of needing the money. Even with all those new commissions I had, nobody had thought to pay me anything on account, and even when the work was done I couldn't count on money coming, because in general ladies are the worst payers of all. If it weren't for Duchess Marguerite, I would be in very bad trouble indeed, I mused. Then I thought of my experiments in dissolving the ink on that old but extremely fine parchment and decided that people who didn't pay in advance would get their angel pictures on the used part with an extra-heavy base coat so the last of the stains from the writing didn't show through. After all, portraits require clear, unused parchment, but with the angel pictures I could put heavy drapes or dark lines over the parts that show through, and people who aren't good payers deserve that. But it was very hard, because I had expected a little something from the Duchess Marguerite before she left and now I didn't have much hope of her for the next several months because once the feasting was done, she had left town with her mother, just as so many other of the great families had done once there was nothing more to do in Paris.

When I was shown in to see the Duchess Claude, she was sitting with the queen and several other ladies both English and French and Mistress Nan Boleyn was playing the psaltery with some new music that she had propped up in front of her. Duchess Claude and the queen were embroidering a monstrous great cope, and the queen was looking very irritated. I had heard all about this cope, which was for the Pope, and that old Queen Anne had died before it was finished and it was her chief regret in leaving this earth that it was not done. So nothing would do but that royal hands would finish it, which meant that Queen Marie as she was now called had to stitch away even though she hated embroidering. Also Claude was helping and she didn't think much of Claude, either, for being all squashed-up-looking and squint-eyed and not very clever. But Claude said it was all right for her to work on it because she was Queen Anne's daughter, and Queen Marie was glad someone else had sacred-enough hands to touch it because she wanted it done and gone. When you are in the business of painting angels, you hear a lot.

So Queen Marie was very happy to put down the cope and look at Madame Claude's angels, and Madame Claude wept and said it looked so very like her dear dead mother, and wasn't the portrait of the king so very like, dear Stepmother? Queen Marie looked very pouty faced, but she agreed, yes, the likeness was just miraculous and changed the subject by asking if I was English. And then I explained that I had come over with her but she had probably been too busy to notice, and she said, "Oh, yes, that's right, Archbishop Wolsey said something." Then I explained that I was to make commemorative miniature portraits of her and the king which Wolsey wanted to have set in gold and diamonds and present to King Henry, her brother, and she cheered up considerably.

"Oh, then you are the person who paints the clever tiny portraits. Did you—ah, I have heard that you once painted the Duke of Suffolk." Then I knew that he must have had that portrait painted to give to her, which sounded pretty suspicious. Besides, her face lit up when she spoke his name.

"Yes, Your Majesty, I painted him fresh from the tilt yard. He said to paint his gaze fiery."

"That sounds very like him. But . . . have I not heard of you before? I heard that . . . let me see . . . Longueville told the story . . . about a ghost and a picture. Do you remember it?" I could feel my face getting all hot when luckily Duchess Claude broke in, and said,

"Oh, yes, my, I heard that story. It was so very touching. About devotion beyond the grave. Do you believe that the ghosts of the blessed can return? I believe that my mother still comes to her bedchamber. I felt a presence, and a cold wind."

Queen Marie looked cross at anyone who could take a draft for a ghost, and the other ladies all chimed in with ghost stories and they all forgot about me, which was very fortunate. I would have left then, but I was waiting to hear about my payment. It was at that time that Duke Francis was announced, and he came in with Bonnivet and Fleurange and his other friends. He stalked in looking like a thundercloud, and bowed over his wife's hand and wished her farewell because they were going to Blois for some errand or other. When he saw the queen, he gave such a look to her, as if she were some scheming betrayer, that she was shocked, and then he bade his "mother" (that is, the queen) farewell so very coldly that I was shocked, considering how much he had been hanging about her lately. But Claude never noticed anything and was very touched by his courteous farewell to her and talked about it for long after he had left.

"Oh, you are still here," she said after a while, noticing me waiting. "I have no money here, but I'll have the steward of my household make your payment. I like your work even better than the prayer book I had completed in Paris last spring, so I will pay you the same." She called one of her waiting footmen and while I inwardly rejoiced, he took me off to get my money, which was most sorely needed. Her steward, who was a knight, never did business but had a clerk who had set up near the kitchens with others of her household officers who traveled with them. There was a lot of clattering and the smell of things roasting and cooks shouting coming from inside the kitchens, and every so often somebody rushed in or out as if on an important errand. But while I was sitting on a bench waiting outside the steward's clerk's little door, I could hear them talking about how mad Duke Francis was.

"I tell you, he was in a fury."

"I'm not surprised. I heard even the queen's good French gentleman of the chamber, who could not be more loyal to us, said things must be taken in hand. He told Madame Louise yesterday that Monsieur d'Angoulême was likely to sire the heir who would displace him, if he kept up his mooning about that ambitious Englishwoman. There was no holding him, the great fool. What man wants a woman so much he would displace his own inheritance? But his *mother*, ah, she's the only one who can make him see sense."

"Thank God for Madame Louise, or that scheming English hussy would make herself queen regent."

"Yes indeed. Thank God for her. There is a woman who thinks like a man and lays plans like a general. When would I ever have dreamed a woman's conspiracy would save France? But that is how things stand at this moment. The monarchy hangs by a thread, and everything is in her hands."

"Softer. There's another English outside."

"The 'widow'? I hear she was Archbishop Wolsey's mistress, and he discarded her by sending her here."

I was very annoyed. I made some loud clattering sounds outside just to remind them I was there, and they called me in as if they hadn't said anything at all.

"You have kept back a *livre* from my fee," I said, emptying out the purse and counting it right in front of them.

"Oh, ah, it's customary. For goodwill. It is a fee you owe to the steward's office."

"Well, I'm afraid it's customary to pay that *livre* to foreign painters. It's for silence. It's an old English custom." They looked at each other and shrugged their shoulders.

"I think not," said the steward.

"Oh, I think so. Poor Duchess Claude. She is so honorable, she would hate to know her very own steward is a rogue. How many other illuminators and tapestry makers and merchants do you think might speak for me if there were an inquiry?"

"Pay the foreign shrew," said the footman.

"Damned English. The sooner they leave, the better," I heard the steward say as I left to find Nan so I could go home.

"Nan," I said to her as we trudged through the slush on our way to the Pont au Change, "that Les Tournelles is just a hotbed of enemies of the queen. They'd do anything to disgrace her and prove all their dirty gossip is right."

"It's none of your business, Mistress Susanna. Great people must look after themselves, and small people must get out of their way. You keep yourself to yourself, and don't go listening around corners anymore. But I'm glad you made that nasty fellow cough up your fee."

The king's physicians were arguing at his bedside in Latin, holding a glass retort filled with the royal urine to the light from the window as they debated. On either side of the bed, his gentleman attendants stood in clusters in front of the arras, trying to follow those fragments of the language that they could comprehend.

"They've said another dose of purgatives; I'm sure that's what it was."

"It's the urine. I think they said he'd passed a stone."

"The stone. A man recovers from the stone."

"I thought they said bleeding."

"They've tried bleeding."

The long-robed physicians nodded at each other learnedly and spoke of the overbalancing of humors and the value of a compound of mercury often used in such cases.

The king, the center of all this interest, lay in the ending throes of a gout attack. The covers over his feet and legs had been put on a frame to keep them from contacting his twisted lower limbs, but all night long he had writhed and tossed, shaking with chills and fever. The physicians had tried applications of heat, then applications of cold. At last repeated bleedings, the applications of certain holy medals, and doses of opium seem to have brought the attack under control.

"Tell me, Duprat, has my wife inquired of my health?"

"Only the orders of the physicians barred her from your room, Your Majesty."

"My affairs ... I am better now. Bring me my foreign correspondence."

"Your Majesty," said the shocked voice of the chief physician, "you must have absolute bed rest to recover. Do you hear? Absolute. Only the lightest food. And then, when you are up, regular hours, rest, no feasting. It is the great effort, the late hours of these last months, the travel ..."

The king struggled to sit up. Immediately, two of his gentlemen assisted him, propping up his head with additional pillows. There seemed to be an evil smell about the bed. Sulfur, perhaps, or a bit of brimstone, but the gentlemen took it for the smell of illness, or perhaps medicine.

Sitting on the head of the king's bed, Belphagor, his old smoky self, too transparent now to be seen at all, leaned his head attentively toward the king, taking in the whole scene.

"Rest, Your Majesty. You must rest to get well," said the first physician.

"Get away from the foulness and the smokiness of the city air. You must travel to Saint-Germain and rest," said his assistant.

"Ask about the queen," whispered Belphagor.

"My wife, how did she spend the night?"

"In prayer, Your Majesty. She worked on Queen Anne's cope all the afternoon with your daughter, Claude, and in the evening went to the chapel to offer prayers for your recovery."

"They lie," whispered Belphagor. "She tapped her foot impatiently and yearned for dancing and music. Do you remember how bored she acted the last time you gave her one of the crown jewels? That kiss was hardly a peck. She has eyes only for jousting champions. You must show yourself young or she will take a lover." Belphagor's voice was cynical and insinuating. The king started.

"Never!" he said, into the air.

"What was that, Your Majesty?" asked Duprat, but behind him the physicians began to mumble in Latin again about dementia. The last sign.

"Duprat, I wish to plan a grand feast, to thank the burgesses of Paris. And after that . . ."

"Your Majesty! Your health!" said the physician.

"Nonsense. Who is the best judge of my health but me? I'll have entertainment. I am still young. A day or two in bed is all I need. Send for the queen."

"Never let them see you are weak," came Belphagor's sly whisper. "They will try to steal the throne. Feasts, parties, dancing. Live like a king! Confound your enemies! Captivate the queen anew!"

"Why should I live, if I cannot live like a king?" said Louis the Twelfth. "I want feasts, parties, dancing! In the spring, I shall go to Blois, and hunt again. I am renewed!"

Belphagor, finer than a vapor, passed through the tiny circles of frosty glass in the window, well pleased at the damage he had wrought. The plan for the regency was afoot.

Originally, Belphagor had thought to flit right home to the house in the Ile de la Cité that Crouch had rented for him, but he was simply too tempted on the way by the excellent possibilities he saw. He sent a runaway horse through a group of bundled-up children who had been playing ball in the street, then he dazzled the eyes of an elderly merchant with the reflection off a gilded saint's statue in a niche, so that he did not notice the cutpurse who relieved him of his money with a single stroke of a sharp knife. Then he tripped an old lady carrying a basket of clean laundry and floated like a cloud of malice into a bakery, where he caused all the bread to fail to rise. By now he had quite forgotten to go home, but the bells of a church tower recalled the hour to him, and he whisked to his own house, where his new servant, a very promising young student of theology from the Sorbonne, awaited him. It was such a tempting little soul, all fresh and unused, and full of holy aspirations, that he simply couldn't resist. Slowly, slowly, that's how to do it, he had told himself, and so he'd begun by buying the starving fellow a dinner. Then he'd offered him a job—just a few harmless tasks. Reading aloud, running errands. The gratitude in the hollow, hungry eyes pleased Belphagor. If I get this tasty little priestling trained right, he thought, I can finally get rid of that Crouch. Between this little bookworm and those sly fellows in the cellar over there across the river, I can get anything I need to know. Besides, I know enough about being a gentleman already.

At the door, he was met by his imps, who were now in human form, dressed in the handsome Moorish regalia he had acquired for them. The house, an old, turreted place on a corner, had a cozy, homey smell to it: sulfurous. It looks quite elegant with those imps at the door, thought Belphagor. I think I should always maintain a town residence from now on.

"Has Crouch come back yet?" he addressed the first Moor in impish language, and the creature responded in the squealing, grumbling sounds with which it customarily spoke:

"No, he's been off at the public baths all afternoon, being stroked by female humans and eating pies."

"Wastrel. Is Nicholas here yet?"

"He's been waiting this half hour in your study, Lord Belphagor. He's been eating pies, too."

"Has it done him any good yet?"

"No, he's as thin as ever. Humans are ridiculous; no matter how they try, they are stuck with whatever shape they come in."

But Lord Belphagor, dressed in a heavy, fur-lined, brocade gown in the French style, a handsome silk shirt and velvet trunk hose, his splendid flat-brimmed velvet hat trimmed with an diamond and an egret feather, had passed through his great hall, where an array of meat pies and cheeses and a large decanter of wine had been laid out on the table. Belphagor inspected them. Wine half gone. Good. Inside his study, Nicholas, his skinny cheeks distended and still munching, was sitting in Belphagor's big barrel-backed chair and toasting himself by the fire while reading.

"Oh, Lord Belfagoro!" he said, jumping up so suddenly that the crumbs fell from his lap in a shower. "I was just reading ahead. This is a very interesting manuscript."

"Don't bother, my boy. Just give me back my chair. Mighty interesting, isn't it? In my opinion, the man's a genius. Took no end of trouble to get hold of this manuscript copy from one of his friends. They said it would be the book to change the world. Pity I can't read. But you—ah, yes, you've opened the world of learning to me, a poor old gentleman. How grateful I am!" Nicholas's eyes slid sideways, but Belphagor didn't notice, he was so pleased with his new gifts of devious speech. "Now, let's just start where we had left off, dear boy. . . ."

"Here we are: 'The Way to Govern Cities or Dominions That, Previous to Being Occupied, Lived under Their Own Laws.' "

"Yes, that's it. Read on. I am learning all the time." Nicholas read on in a clear, slow, voice:

" 'And whoever becomes the ruler of a free city and does not destroy it, can expect to be destroyed by it, for it can always find motive for rebellion in the name of liberty and of its ancient usages, which are forgotten neither by lapse of time nor by benefits received. . . .' "

"Ah, clever. Yes, clever. One must know when to destroy and when to keep, and what benefits may be expected by each course. That Machiavelli fellow is brilliant. How much I am learning from him! Yes, yes. 'The unarmed prophet fails.' What do you think of that, Nicholas?"

"Our Lord Jesus Christ was unarmed," said the theology student. A puff of steam came out of Belphagor's ears, but he maintained his calm facade.

"And he came to a bad end," said the demon. "Painful. Sad. No grandchildren to charm in his old age. It's nothing a man would seek out. Now, wealth . . ."

"All over the earth his church converts the heathen, so the unarmed prophet . . ."

"That was then, and this is now," said Belphagor hastily, for argument wearied him.

"But if something is truth, shouldn't it be so for all times, not just one?"

"You're tiring my mind, young man. Read on."

But scarcely had Nicholas gotten to the chapter on controlling new dominions acquired by the power of others or by fortune, than one of the imps knocked on the study door.

"Lord Belphagor, it is the Duc de Bourbon who wishes to have an audience with you," said the Moor in impish language. But Belphagor's brain was still operating in French.

"Ah, the Helmsman! Show him in, show him in! That's enough for today, Nicholas. My servant will give you your payment for the week. He speaks no French, but just show him your open palm, and he'll understand."

The Duc de Bourbon gave the scrawny young man in the student's gown an arrogant stare as he strode into Belphagor's study, and Nicholas felt as if he were slinking out like some stray cat. But outside, he paused. The table was still full, and the wine only half drunk. The two Moors were chatting to each other in the oddest, grumbling tones, as if they hadn't noticed him. Nicholas paused, reversed his hood like a huge satchel, and began to tuck away the extra pies into it. Then he paused. Voices were coming from the study, and Nicholas, who was very curious about Belphagor, who wasn't like any Italian he had ever known, paused. Belphagor, who never noticed whether doors were open or closed because he was accustomed to passing through them, had left the study door open.

"The plot progresses, my lord of Bourbon. I visited Les Tournelles today, and I assure you, after what I have done, the king will die shortly. How goes the plan for the substitution?" Nicholas's blood ran cold. A regicidal plot. Oh, Lord, he had already heard too much. He was frozen to the spot. Suddenly, the cheeses didn't look as tasty anymore.

"It goes well. The society has undertaken to bribe one of the stewards, who will purchase an infant from the orphanage. Even if all are arrested, my role will never be discovered."

"Well then, the fall of the Valois is assured."

"It is that I wish to speak to you about. That is why I meet you here, without them, and not in the hidden chambers. The Priory wishes to return the True Blood to the throne. The closest descendants of the Merovingians are the Houses of Lorraine and Guise."

"So?"

"Why Lorraine? Why Guise? Why shouldn't I, Charles de Bourbon, become king? Why should the Helmsman serve others? I was not born to serve. With your help, Lord Belphagor . . ."

"Oh, delightful! The betrayers betrayed! I love a double deception. . . ." Belphagor's hoarse voice rose to a high-pitched squeak of pleasure.

"Now, this is how it must go. When they create the false heir, I want to be made co-regent with the English queen. I will control the military. Then, I will seize power with your help. The false heir will meet with a little 'accident.' But through my wife, I have a direct right to the throne. My son will inherit my crown, by right of blood and by right of power. I am as close to the throne now as was Henry Tudor, who has created the new English dynasty. Bourbon must rule. . . ."

Nicholas paused over the pies, then swept them all into his hood and reversed it again, where it bulged like a peddlar's pack. Whatever his politics, Belphagor's pies were excellent. Then he stood behind the two imps, clearing his throat to get their attention, with his palm outstretched. They didn't notice. He coughed gently. Still, they didn't notice. Afraid to reveal his presence in the outer room by more noise, he tugged on the sweeping satin sleeve of one of them, who turned around with such a fiery eye that the poor student was suddenly terrified. The imp chuckled, then reached into a big purse and dropped Nicholas's payment into his hand. Nicholas's eyes grew huge. Instead of ten sous of copper, the imp had dropped livres of gold into his hand, as if he didn't understand the difference. Well, I certainly won't tell him, thought Nicholas, as he fled from the mysterious house and into the snowy street.

Outside, he shuddered. I feel filthy, the thought. And I'm in trouble, too. I'd better quit now. I'll change my room. But could he find me through the university? And all this gold. I could get anything I dreamed of. Books. The thought came to him of a beautifully illuminated missal he had yearned for in a shop he had stopped by once, but couldn't afford to patronize. He could buy it now. Maybe it would make him feel better. Dirty money isn't dirty if it's put to virtuous use, he reasoned to himself as he rushed off in the direction of the Pont au Change.

"No customers," said Hadriel. "The snow has made it such a slow day." Hadriel fluffed his wings and lounged back on the counter, putting the *hautbois* again to his mouth and blowing a lovely, flowing melody. Two little cherubs were perched on the stairs that went to the loft above, accompanying the melody on the rebec and dulcimer, while another hung in the air on swift, iridescent wings, beating time on a tambourine. "Not bad, not bad, human music," said Hadriel, taking the instrument from his lips, while the little angel with the tambourine lit at the top of the stairs. "One does get tired of the seraphs singing. And always the same words, too. Besides, they're such snobs! Just because they have six wings each . . ."

"Hadriel, there's someone coming to the door," announced one of the little creatures.

"Probably Gabriel, to give you such a talking to," said the little blond one.

"No, it's a student. The one who liked the missal. I do believe he's coming to buy it. I hear the clink of money in his pocket. And do look at his hood! He's been stealing pies!" In the twinkling of an eye, the musical instruments were hidden, and Hadriel threw on his old gray cape over his tightly folded wings. The door opened and the snow blew in behind Nicholas in a gust, then melted in tiny drops on the floor.

"I wanted to know if you still had the missal," he said to the proprietress, "the old one with the calfskin binding from Master Gregoire's workshop."

"Oh, I believe I do," said Hadriel. "It was just waiting for the right person to buy it. And you're a divinity student, right? You must have gotten lucky, finding so much money at once. And all those pies, too." Nicholas blushed.

"They . . . they were given to me. Would you like one?" he said, his voice hopeful.

"Oh, me, I don't bother with eating, usually," said Hadriel, waving a pale hand.

Something about the proprietress's face seemed so sweet and kindly, as if it were waiting for him to tell the truth, that the whole story seemed to just tumble out of Nicholas's insides.

"This money was given to me by mistake by a foreigner who didn't know copper from gold," he said, "and I thought it must be for a purpose, and that I was meant to have the missal, but now I see I am unworthy to own it. I've betrayed the lord who hired me, whose servant paid me, and taken all his extra pies in the bargain, even though I think he meant me to have them because he said to eat all I want of them."

"A curious lord," said Hadriel. "Especially with servants who don't know copper from gold."

"Oh, he's more than curious. And those servants! Black as pitch, and frightening as the Devil. They have red eyes, wear strange clothes, and the language they talk I swear sounds like nothing I've ever heard. Like growling and grumbling, it is, not like words."

"*Hmm.* Sounds like imps," said Hadriel, half to himself.

"I always thought he was odd. His house smells like sulfur, though it's always cozy warm, and half the time I can't afford a fire, so I'm grateful to be there. He's so very polite to me, for all that he's a great lord and dresses so fine, and says he regards me as a son. How could I have done it? Signor Belfagoro trusted me, and now, and now ..." Nicholas's bony face looked tormented.

Hadriel's whole expression was one of delight. His smile shed radiance throughout the room. Nicholas was taken aback. How could she smile so at his confession?

"Signor Belfagoro? So now he's Italian and dressed in the latest fashion? What a splendid joke. What is he up to in his too cozy but somewhat smelly house, with his pair of imps?"

"He says he's improving himself. He hired me to read to him."

"Read? What does an illiterate old buffoon like that want read to him?"

"First I read him some Italian book he had, which tells the latest fashions in fine manners. Then he took to carrying a fork to use at banquets. Now I'm reading him some other Italian fellow called Machiavelli, who writes about how to take power and conquer your enemies." Hadriel laughed out loud, and the sound was like a thousand silver chimes.

"So now, of course, he will try to take power and conquer his enemies. That old Belphagor always was transparent." For the first time in
weeks, ever since he had met Belphagor in a tavern, Nicholas felt safe.
This was the right place. Madame Hadriel was the right person, so
self-confident, so charming, even if she was deformed. She must have
powerful connections, to mock Signor Belfagoro so. She might have
ideas to help him. He would divulge his terrible secret to her.

"I . . . I haven't said the worst. Today . . . a great lord, a powerful
lord, the greatest lord in France, save for the Dauphin, came in secret
to Signor Belfagoro."

"*Humph.* I imagine he wants to be king, right?" Nicholas breathed a
sigh of relief.

"How did you know?" he said. "I fear for my life now, if he ever
even guesses that I overheard them . . ."

"Oh, I think I'd fear more for my soul, if I were you. Have you any
idea of who Belphagor is?"

"Belphagor?"

"And you, a student of theology? What have you studied?"

"Well, um, I've studied the Gospels, and the Old Testament,
though only in translation. And the Church fathers, Augustine, and . . ."

"Haven't you studied Evil?"

"But, but, Evil's bad. I want to be good. Someday I'll be a priest
and make my old mother happy."

"Oh, my dear, dear little Nicholas. By not knowing the face of
Evil, you've fallen directly into it. Did you not know that Belphagor is
one of the princes of the underworld? And here you've been cozily
closeted with him for weeks, reading him Machiavelli."

"Then . . . then I should throw away his money, shouldn't I?"

"Oh, no. You've tricked him out of it fair and square, so it's yours.
The problem is, what will happen to you next time you meet?"
Nicholas began to shake. Cold chills ran up and down him. "Help
me," he said in a tiny voice, full of fear. "Please help, Madame—"

"Oh, just call me Hadriel," said Hadriel. "I think I know what you
need, and it's not a missal. Luckily, I have one here. If you do the job
right, I'll give you the missal. Now, let me show this to you, and we'll
have a little chat. I'd like to know all about that plot he's hatching, and

anything else he's been up to lately. And I need to show you this...."
From under the counter, Hadriel took an ugly little book bound in
crumbling black leather. It was a grimoire. Nicholas's teeth were chattering. Hadriel put an arm around him just as if he were an old friend,
calming him with a touch while he said ever so sweetly, "Now, let's leaf
through this thing. See here? This one's specifically for Belphagor.
Now consider what a splendid priest you'd make if you not only knew
the Good, but had conquered Evil...." Above them, invisible and unheard, the little brown-eyed cherub laughed and clapped his hands. "A
trick!" he cried. "Five to three on Hadriel!" "No takers!" shrieked the
other little angels, tumbling and diving together in the air the way por-
poises play under the water.

"It's colder here in Paris," said Robert Ashton, pulling his heavy, gray
wool cloak about him. "That's the only virtue of being in the south
this season." A private crier passed us in the street, shouting the virtues
of someone's wines, competing with the noisy vendors in the used-
clothing stalls that lined one side of the street. "Buttons, buttons! Fine
buttons!" "Come here, monsieur, and buy that charming lady a rabbit-
fur muff, hardly used!" Master Ashton had returned, crushed that he
had found no answers, only riddles in the south, and then began to lay
plans anew. He'd try this, he'd try that. We walked so close, me on his
arm, basking in each other's radiance, that no one could mistake us for
anything but lovers.

Still, something was wrong. That speck in my heart. I yearned for
it to be mended by Robert saying, "Blast the Helmsman, blast Wolsey,
I am too madly in love with you to wait a moment longer. We'll be
married by the priest on the corner and tell all the souls in two kingdoms they'll just have to accept it." I know it wasn't practical. I know
he was struggling for my own good. I tried to see things the way he saw
things. But still I wanted it. I wanted him to love me that much, that
he could forget anything else, especially propriety. Hadn't I forgotten
propriety for him? What was wrong? Had he second thoughts that I
wasn't worthy of marriage after all? Maybe all these strange feelings
were because of that cold schemer and deceiver Rowland Dallet who

had said he loved me but didn't offer marriage until he knew the terms of the dowry. But still I loved Robert Ashton; I loved him even so much that I could love him with that one thing missing, with that tiny piece of icy fear in my heart.

"I'm not cold a bit, thanks to the wonderful dinner you bought me," I said to him. "And the music was something splendid. Who'd think they were only apprentices there? They could be masters, as far as I could tell."

"I'm beginning to hate this chase. Muddy roads, when there were any at all, the worst horses in the world for hire, and corrupt innkeepers. The south can keep its weather, for all I care. It has nothing else."

"Oh, listen, Robert! It's the bird market! Let's see." We followed the sound of chirping, twittering, and whirring wings around the corner. There were the bird catchers and their boys with cages full of blackbirds, larks, and birds of every description whose names I did not even know. An old woman with pigeons cried out, "Pigeons! Nice and plump!" "No, no, try my starlings! Very fine in a pie!" "Songbirds, songbirds!"

"Surely, those don't sing," said Master Ashton, stopping before an old man with a cageful of finches. "And they're too tiny to eat as well. What are they for?"

"For sellin'," said the man, as if that settled everything.

"Look, Robert, they're for themselves. They're so tiny and yet perfectly colored, with every feather just so. I could fit three of them in my hand. They remind me of my paintings. What do they eat?"

"Don't know. Ain't fed 'em. I just catches 'em."

"Millet, I imagine," said Master Ashton.

"I was thinking bread crumbs. How do you know what birds eat?"

"Oh, when I was very small, I put out crumbs for the birds on my windowsill in winter. I thought if I trained them with food every day, I could get them to eat from my hand. I know what birds like."

"Did you succeed?"

"Oh, no. My older brother waited until they were tame and then put lime on the sill and caught them and killed them all. My mother served them up for dinner. It's not a kindness, feeding birds. It's better to let them be."

"Oh," I said, in sympathy, but I couldn't take my eyes off the tiny, perfect birds, who were painted with God's strokes smaller than small, in speckles and soft shaded gray and brown and faded sweet yellow that was almost greenish. "Look, those two like each other. They are sitting together on the perch."

"I see that," he said, and before I could protest, he was negotiating a price for the birds, all six of them, and the cage, too.

"Then you don't want me to kill 'em for you?"

"No, alive. With the cage."

"Robert Ashton, how did you know I wanted those birds?" I asked, as we walked down the narrow streets toward the Pont au Change together, I holding one of his arms and he holding that big, tall wicker cage with the little birds peeping and fluttering about in it, with his other hand.

"I know things," he said. "I know, for example, that any woman of sense would have hinted and begged for an ivory comb, or a little silver mirror to wear at her belt, or perhaps even a necklace."

"I like the birds better. See their little black eyes? Look, that one is blinking. They remind me that working in small is not unworthy."

"God works excellently well in small," he said. He was not looking at the birds, though; but down on the top of my head. "I'm glad you like the birds best." Why did it make me happy just to be walking with him? It frightened me to be happy that way. I didn't think it was for me. Don't let it be taken away, my heart whispered.

"Were there more birds in the south?"

"Oh, many more. They fly there for the winter. And farther, to Africa, where it is warm always. But I found them in plenty in the south. And answers there, although not enough. I found an old monk who told me there is a secret walled up in the fortress of Montségur. That I doubt, since many people have searched the ruins for treasure since the Cathar heretics were destroyed there. But the Secret, or supposed Secret, is tied to some sort of ancient cult of fanatics dedicated to placing the Merovingians on the throne. Why, I cannot imagine. The Merovingians were the most useless kings in the world. The 'do-nothing' kings they were called, and the country is well rid of them."

The tenements on either side of us had given way to grander

dwellings, the town houses of wealthy merchants and the small nobility. Dark, carved doors topped with gargoyles, high, ornamented windows, and steep towers ornamented these stone houses. Servants ran in
and out at the side doors, and here and there, real Swiss guards, heavily
armed, were posted.

"At any rate, I hate to have to return and tell the archbishop his
conspiracy is a collection of lunatics. The Merovingians will never return, no matter what their book of prophecy predicts. He won't be impressed with an answer like that." Robert Ashton sighed. "And I so
wanted a quick success. I wanted a success for you."

The little frozen thing in my heart hurt again. You were too easy, it
whispered. Now he's tiring of you and starting to lie. Then I looked at
his face, so troubled, and I wanted to take my brushes and paint away
the trouble. A strange thought struck me there, like a pinprick soon
gone. Suppose he thought I couldn't truly love him if he were not a success? Was that it? He was afraid my love would go away if he were not
favored, not wealthy? But then I thought, How could he not see, not feel
how great my love is for him, how much I'd sacrifice? No, it can't be.

He looked again at me, and his face softened, then wrinkled up
with worry as he resumed speaking. "Now, if I had the book, he might
like that, even if it were useless. At least it would be a curiosity, something he might be inclined to reward me for."

"Book of prophecy? Like the one Crouch did murder for?"

"The very one. I can't imagine any book that would contain a secret great enough to return the Merovingians. Crouch has wasted his
effort, unless he has made a plan to blackmail this group, using the
book. Lunatics or not, they could all be executed for treason if their
plans were made known to the king. Either that, or Crouch has become
as lunatic as they are. Merovingians, indeed. They've had their day."

Two strange servants in Moorish garb were opening the courtyard
gate of one of the town houses. As they pushed the gate inward, there
was the sound of horses in the court. Someone was preparing to leave;
someone who might see us.

"My God, Crouch's house," Ashton whispered. "How can we have
walked this way? I must have been blind. Let's go the other way." As he
pulled me around the corner, I thought I saw something. "I just wish I

knew where they met," Robert was saying. "It's as if the earth had opened and swallowed them up. . . ."

"Look, Robert, look!" I whispered, pulling on his sleeve. Someone was vanishing down a side alley behind the town house.

"He's been watching the house," Robert whispered back to me. "Pray God he hasn't seen us."

It was the man in black.

The season of Christmas had come but not yet gone. It was the first day of the new year. Snow was sifting through the gray air. It buried the filthy alleys of Paris in white, it caught on the gargoyles of the cathedral and drifted into the brownish gray river that moved sluggishly between icy banks. It blew across the narrow houses on the Pont au Change, keeping everyone sane indoors, and hid the pointed towers of the Palace of Les Tournelles from view. Inside Les Tournelles, the king lay dying.

"What is it he said?" buzzed the crowd of courtiers waiting outside the death chamber as the queen was escorted out, white faced.

"He said, 'I give you the best present yet, my death,' " said someone.

"Imagine!"

"At last we'll be rid of that filthy Englishwoman."

"Not if she's pregnant."

"Do you think she is pregnant?"

"The Dauphin's wife is with child, they say."

"The queen is pregnant, have you heard?"

"Oh, here comes the Dauphin."

"Look how solemn he is."

"What will the king say?"

"Suppose the king gets well, then what?"

Inside the chamber, the king, gray faced and feeble, scarcely moved on his great bed. A violent fit of vomiting had overtaken him, bringing him so low that all hope of recovery had been given up. The priests had administered the last rites, but still the physicians labored. Now the physicians parted, allowing Francis to the dying man's bedside. Tall and robust, the long-nosed prince knelt to hear the dying man's words.

The king struggled to get up; two of his gentlemen in waiting lifted him up, and the king embraced Francis. "I am dying," whispered the king. "I leave behind me two young daughters, a wife; I confide them to your affection."

"Your Majesty, there is hope yet. Your physicians assure me that recovery is near."

"Nonsense, nonsense. I know that I am dying." The king's breath was slow, his voice weak. Francis, still embracing him, laid him back gently on his pillows. "We commend our subjects to your care," whispered Louis the Twelfth. Francis could feel the fever eating up the old man's bones. Relief and ambition mingled with shock at the speed with which the hour had come at last, with a certain horror at the ugliness with which death came even to kings. For long hours, Francis sat at the head of the king's bed, listening to the death rattle, his mind torn with new thoughts. Before it had seemed easy, the idea of being king. Now, suddenly, he found himself wondering how he could be as competent, as beloved by the people, as the old man who lay dying beside him. Time passed slowly as he sat, as the attendants lit the candles, as the candles burned down. By eleven o'clock at night, the king, his head cradled in Francis's arms, breathed his last.

"Fleurange, it is over," said Francis, stiff and exhausted, as he left the death chamber after midnight. "Send for my mother and sister." That morning, even as the king's body was being disemboweled, embalmed, and laid out in robes of state, a messenger left Paris at full speed for Romorantin. By the time the king's body was in its coffin, being carried in procession through black-draped streets to the Cathedral of Nôtre Dame, Louise of Savoy and her daughter were on the road.

"Now, you see how easy it is? The molds came off perfectly. That's how your hands look in reverse. Then we just use the molds to cast your hands in plaster." Just to look overlong at Master Ashton's handsome, wide-boned hands sent my mind off down the path of evil thoughts. Like a drunken person, I wanted more, more, and there was no satisfaction. Secretly, thinking of the hands, I wished I had a mold of his whole body, lying like a glorious plaster god, in the corner of my studio. Everything all there, for me touch and feel and lust after when he was gone.... All my feeding had filled him back out, and he was perfect. The way the wide, heavy bones of his chest melted into the muscles at the flank, the hint of bone at the pelvis and the heavy roll of muscle across the hip above the joint, which flowed to the lower belly, and then ... well, you can see my mind was full of the most lascivious wickedness day and night, and I just couldn't hate it the way I ought to. Of course, I kept it all inside so no one would know, but I think Nan knew, even though I had been ever so careful. She was pretending to be busy knitting and looking at my birds, which were thriving very excellently.

When Robert Ashton had come this day to get his hands cast, I saw he had washed his face all shiny and combed his hair almost flat with water and goose grease, which was a miracle although one I did not care for, because I liked him better plain and curly headed, and not in the fashion. It *was* flattering, though, to see that he still wanted me to think well of him, and went to all that trouble to dress up, even after he had obtained what all men want. And he had brought me a sack of millet for a present and looked at my birds a proper long while. The truly interested look on his face as he watched them hop made me think the right things might well be inside of him, unlike my fearful suspicions that he might only be good on the outside and full of deception on the inside, like that whited sepulchre you hear about in church that looks nice but is really just full of ugly dead things. Besides, Master Dallet would never have brought millet for my birds.

"They look very odd to me, these molds. But real, too. Can you paint the cast, or must it always be white?"

"Oh, it can be painted, but you have to seal it first, because the material is porous. That's how cheap saints are made for churches. The most realistic casts are tinted wax, though. The transparency looks just like human flesh."

"I can't imagine why anyone would want that."

"Oh, wax effigies for funerals, false relics, holy incorruptible corpses, that sort of thing."

"That's done?" he asked, with the oddest smile.

"Oh, a good artificer has to know how to make many things. The relic trade is a lucrative one—even better than making weeping statues."

"Susanna, you have some of the most profoundly sinful knowledge of any honest person I know. No wonder you are tempted into deception." He poured some water into the basin to wash off his hands.

"I suppose I can't help it. When I was little, I once watched my father make several excellent Veronica's handkerchiefs. A little red lead, tempered with a bit of umber, if I recall right. The color of old blood must be matched perfectly. The linen has to be aged, too."

"That's dreadful."

"Master Ashton, have you ever counted how many Veronica's handkerchiefs there are in the world? My father was not the only one. The only thing he wouldn't do was shrouds. Too big, and no money in them. The full figure, you understand. The monks don't pay proportionally."

"I made a pilgrimage to a holy shroud once. Now I am ashamed to think I wept."

"You shouldn't be. It's good to weep for the Passion of Our Lord. The shroud just helped you to do it, that's all."

"Susanna, you never cease to surprise me."

"Admit you're pleased I'm not boring. Do you like the soap? I made it myself from my *Good Wyfe's Book of Manners.*"

"*Hmm.* It is a bit, ah, *strong,* I think. But . . . effective. Very effective."

"You see? That is a wonderful book. It is not often one can have a book that touches on moral and useful questions all at one time."

"I wish I had a book that touched on one question."

"The secret? Don't tell me you are beginning to believe all that nonsense."

"It's not that I believe it, but that others do. What secret would make them undertake such risks? I have taken to following that Crouch around town, and I am certain he's up to something. For one thing, he's searching for this place, I think. I'm always careful when I come here, and you should be, too. Take a different route each time."

"I do, Robert. And I look behind me, too."

"Then there's something else that's going on. Men come and meet at the house he shares with that Italian, they exchange code words to enter, and I have seen the servants of some of the greatest notables in the kingdom holding their horses in the courtyard."

"Does Crouch know you follow him?"

"At first I thought not, but lately, he goes roundabout. I follow, he ducks into an alley. I stop. He hurries out by the same way he went in. He knows."

"Well, be careful you don't get too close. He has a long, sharp knife."

"All this for a treaty. It seems a waste."

"Oh, I don't think so. The archbishop is a shrewd man. I think he wans to know how strong the conspiracy is so he can judge which side to join."

"Susanna! That's unspeakable! Abandon our obligations, our sacred pledges, our princess?"

"Oh, I'm sorry. It was just a thought. I meant nothing by it."

"That's just as well. I fear that your natural bent for deception may overgrow itself. That way lies the fear of imaginary conspiracies, eccentricity, and the lunatic asylum. There are enough of that sort of people in the world already."

TWENTY-FOUR

It seems that once upon a time a Queen of France bore a son after the death of the king and therefore ever after the French have been afraid the same thing would happen. So immediately when the king died, they took the queen off to an old palace on the other side of the river called the Hôtel de Cluny, which has many narrow winding rooms and shut her up in the dark in bed just to make sure if there was or was not a baby coming, like that queen from long ago. I know because I got to see her there and she was very glad about it because they didn't let her see any English but instead that Louise of Savoy who runs everything had the Countess of Nevers who is very sharp nosed and unpleasant watched the chamber day and night. The queen was required to wear white in mourning and so they called her the "White Queen" instead of her having a name like a Christian person. That is how the French are.

The only person who was really sad about the king's dying was poor Claude, who looked over and over again at the picture I had made of her father and mother and the Virgin and angels and cried and cried. And then she sent for me because she'd had another one of her ideas.

"I have been selfish in my sorrow," she said, "and now I know that it is only blessed to console others." Now that she was to be queen, there were all sorts of petitioners and flatterers outside her door, and I practically had to step over them with the help of the lackey that she had sent to fetch me. She received me in her chamber, alone but for two maids of honor. In the corner was a prie-dieu with my little picture set out on top for her to contemplate. Her poor squinty eyes were all red rimmed, and I felt sorry for her because she was the only person not using this waiting time for plotting about how to get more influence when Francis was crowned. "There is one who is more sorrowful than I. I hear the White Queen has called for her English doctor, but they won't let him go. They never open the curtains. Oh, she has so clearly grown sick with grief, and they do nothing to console her. I, at least, have my picture. But I must sacrifice. I want you to take it to her to aid her in her prayers and make me another one just like it."

"That is generous indeed, Majesty. But will they let me in?"

"I have asked the Duchess Marguerite to ask her mother, who is the one who gives permission to enter the White Queen's chamber. She said she knew you and gave permission herself. 'Tell her to take her gallery of little portraits. The White Queen is bored.' Bored! Oh, poor Madame d'Alençon; she understands so little of loss." Claude's own liverymen took me across the river to the Hôtel de Cluny and through the wandering maze of narrow old rooms to the White Queen's chamber, which they save just for putting queens in so it doesn't usually get much use. At the door, Louise of Savoy's guards looked through the coffer I had brought with me just to make sure there wasn't a marriage contract with the King of Persia hiding in there, or maybe a live baby, or something else conspiratorial that the new king-to-be, or worse, his mother, didn't approve of.

Inside, big heavy curtains were pulled over the windows. There were very good tapestries, but you could hardly see them in the dark. There were candles flickering in iron sconces on the walls, and at the White Queen's bed table, another candle, and pen and ink and a half-finished letter. I went and curtseyed very low to her where she was sitting up in bed, all dressed in a white gown with white embroidery, and said I had been sent by Queen Claude to console her in her grief so the old lady sitting in the corner wouldn't become alarmed.

"Oh, don't bother. That's not the Countess of Nevers. It's her waiting gentlewoman, and she's asleep." The White Queen spoke in English, as if it were a great relief. "I don't know what possessed Claude to send you, or how you got in, but I thought I'd go crazy without someone to speak to me in English! They've sent my English ladies away. I've been screaming with the toothache, and they won't even send my doctor! All I do is sit here in the dark and write letters! And I'm not even allowed to get any back! They've trapped me here! I want to go home!" At this declaration, the old lady snorted and her eyes flickered open. I answered in French.

"Queen Claude, knowing you to be consumed with grief, has sent her greatest treasure to you, her picture of her father and mother with the angels, as consolation." The old lady's head nodded again, and she began to snore.

"Oh, that poor, silly thing. Let's see it, then. Have you brought anything else to amuse me? Pictures? Stories? They've left me with nothing but a book of prayers. I'm losing my mind with boredom in here. I need my doctor. I'm ill. I need my ladies. I need to open the curtains. Oh, that's Claude's picture? *Hmph.* That picture of the king looks very like. As for Anne of Brittany, how did you know to paint her like that?"

"The Queen showed me another portrait, then had me change it to be more beautiful."

"Yes, that sounds like her. I can't keep this thing. Maybe if you tell her that knowing how much it means to her, I'll borrow it only until you can make me another one, then they'll send you back. Do you think that would work? I need to speak English, or I'll scream."

"I think they might be satisfied to hear of you screaming."

"You know, you're right. You have sense. I'll tell her that while I hate to have anything disturb me in my grief, you are very discreet and quiet, and contemplating drawings of my beloved spouse will still the ache in my heart."

"It sounds as if you know how to deal with them."

"Ah, God, I'm learning. They've sent a horrid French physician with two midwives to poke and prod me. And never an English lady! This is purgatory. What will I do if Francis decides to send me to Blois? To keep me prisoner so he can make money from my remarriage? I hear he quarrels with my brother over who has the right to give me in marriage. Either one of them could decide to send me to the ends of the earth! Has my brother forgotten his promise that I might choose my own remarriage? I may never see home again!" She burst into tears, which was really a great intimacy for one so lowly as myself, but she was very desperate and even queens have to take what they can get, sometimes.

"Refuse to marry, Majesty. A woman has the right to turn down a proposal."

"That is what the archbishop has written me. My lord of York—he is my last remaining friend. I am bereft—even my brother abandons me!"

"The archbishop is very wise. He gives good advice."

"Ah, that's right. You have been in his service. But what will I do if I am held prisoner, my ladies sent away? Won't I have to say yes?"

"They won't dare treat you too ill. The scandal would be too great."

"But I must go home, I must. Yesterday Francis came to me and pressed his suit. Oh, how shameful, how odious! I, a queen, to hear such things! Just to get rid of him I told him I was secretly betrothed to another. Imagine! That horrible mountain of French vanity! I would rather leave this earth than yield to his suits! I have written to my brother to save me from him. What can I do? And then an old serving woman came to renew the candles and whispered to me that I should accept what came, for others thought of my good. Two nights by eventide and I should rule France. A conspiracy! Maybe more! Who knows where it will end? What if I don't want to rule France? I can't think of anything horrider!" Then she cried so hard I was afraid her mind would break, because after all it was a lot to bear for a girl only eighteen who would rather be dancing. This woke up the old lady for good, and she came over to inspect. But luckily the picture of the king was open on the bed and I explained that the mere sight of it had sent the White Queen prostrate with renewed grief. But the old lady didn't seem very convinced. Then a serving woman came in with food on a tray, and I had to leave.

"Well, what news from the White Queen's chamber?" inquired Duchess Marguerite, who had asked me to come to her after I had taken Claude's angels to the White Queen. Bearing in mind that everything I said to her would go straight to her brother Francis, and to their mother, that crafty Louise, I didn't say everything.

"She is very bored and sad there in the dark, and cries and cries and writes letters."

"Has she confided a pregnancy to you?"

"No, not at all. Though I am not the sort of person she would confide such matters to, I am sure."

"Oh, someone who speaks English, a woman, you never can tell." That Marguerite was certainly clever. I guess I was another test, like the doctors. "There is a rumor out that she has padded herself up with linens to look pregnant, you know."

"Oh, I didn't. She doesn't look padded at all. Just a little fatter around the chin, from having nothing to do all day but lie in bed and eat."

"It is as I thought. *Some people* are too suspicious. They see conspiracies everywhere." Some people. That must mean her mother, who was probably much better at conspiracies than the White Queen.

"Well, um, what if there were a conspiracy, one that she loathed and despised and had nothing to do with, yet had nowhere to turn?"

"I would say she needed someone in whom to confide, so that all could be dealt with in secret, to preserve her reputation."

"Then I would say eventide in two nights' time, if you would promise your help and spare her good name."

"She wants you back, you know."

"Really?" I said.

"Yes, we've already gotten a letter from her. It's an excuse, of course, but I don't see why not. What about just before eventide, in two nights' time? You will do her service, and me too." My heart started pattering. I must have looked pale.

"I'm not good at this sort of thing. I'd rather paint."

"Oh, you won't be alone. You see, we have already had hints that something might happen, but we didn't know when. Now that we do, I just want you to be there and tell me all that is said, afterwards." My mouth started to open, but nothing came out. "Oh, come, come, now. A story I can hear anywhere, but your imitation of voices is the drollest I've heard. I assure you, they'll never reach her. Our family must preserve its good name."

"I am most grateful for your patronage, and am your loyal servant in all things." In response, Marguerite smiled knowingly.

The Hôtel de Cluny is walled, a haven from the ocean of poverty that surrounds it, but those very walls conceal the secret of their own penetration. The ancient Roman palace that forms their base has made the walls above a honeycomb of secret avenues that lead into the cellars of the Hôtel. Not all these are negotiable: aqueducts filled with mud, collapsed corridors filled with a rubble of ancient brick and stone. But the Priory of Sion holds the secrets to these depths just as it holds the greater Secret. Hidden ways have been cleared beneath this section of the city; unlit candles are placed at intervals in niches along the ancient corridors, and at a widening of a tunnel that leads upward to a cellar door between two buildings in an alley, an old oil lamp with a deep reservoir is kept perpetually lit by the man in black. These are not the only secret ways beneath Paris: from the Hôtel Saint-Pol similar tunnels lead to the Bastille and Vincennes; the kings of France have been no less careful to preserve their exit than the Priory.

Now the Priory's secret avenues were readied to carry the destruction of the Valois. Everyone was at their stations: the torches in the underground chamber were lit, the lanterns for the ascent sat flickering on the great meeting table. And in the lowest cellar of the Hôtel de Cluny, a stout woman leaned on the handle of an immense warming pan, glancing furtively, every so often, at the door of a storage cupboard set in the stonework.

Outside, in the snowy alley between two shabby old tenements, two men stamped and shivered in the early winter dusk.

"Where is she?" whispered one. "Madame de Nevers leaves in the quarter hour, and Maître B—"

"*Shh.* The 'Fox.' "

"The Fox is due with The Egg at any moment."

"*Hssst.* That's him." But it was not Maître Bellier, the arch-conspirator. A heavily cloaked woman, poor and deformed, clutching a tightly swaddled baby, came limping through the snow from the street. A shabby hood shaded her head almost down to her eyes; her face was white with some fatal illness.

"True Blood," whispered the woman, giving the password.

"Forever," repeated the conspirators, giving the countersign.

"The Fox has sent me. This is The Egg," whispered the woman. The baby in her arms was very still.

"Is it alive?" asked one man, lifting the blanket that covered the infant's face. He found himself peering into a pair of lively brown eyes, far too clever and knowing for a newborn baby. "Ah, nice and healthy. It's a boy?"

"Of course," whispered the woman feebly. "My own dear newborn son, who has cost me my life in giving birth." *Hmm.* That explains how pale she is, thought the conspirators.

"The blessings of heaven will be upon you. Your son will live better than you can ever imagine. You may rest content that he will be well looked after. As well looked after as a king, in fact."

"Oh, a thousand blessings, you fine gentlemen." The woman paused to wipe away a tear. "Farewell, my son, be good, and don't make a sound." Silently, she turned away, her face pink with suppressed laughter, and limped histrionically down the alley back into the street. Poor woman, she was hunchbacked, too.

The two men vanished down the cellar opening, made a turn, and just where the light failed, found candles waiting to be lit at the feeble flame of an oil lamp. There the modern tunnel joined a square tile-paved segment of Roman waterway, which seemed to descend forever into the bowels of the earth. Hunched over, clutching the silent, bundled up baby, they made their way down the slimy, dripping path to an opening cut in the wall behind the lion fountain in the chamber below.

"True Blood," they whispered.

"Forever," came the answer, and gloved hands reached for the bundle while they clambered down the last step behind the lion's head.

"It's sleeping," said a man, not anxious to rouse the infant. He put his head to its chest. "It breathes well."

"A sound boy, purchased this morning. And very like the late king in looks, they say." The whispering echoed in the chamber over the melancholic *plink, plink,* of the single drops from the lion's mouth into the pool. Torchlight shimmered across the black waters. Silently, the two shortest conspirators took their lanterns from the table and entered the marble-framed door beneath an eagle with outstretched wings. They turned, and soon the passage became narrower, following the line of an ancient arcade filled with rubble, whose collapsing arched roof of brick formed the ceiling of the tunnel. They bent double, cradling the precious burden. At one spot they were so near the surface that a cold wind pierced the tunnel, and an old woman staring at the icy garden beneath her window thought she had seen a ghost when the glow from their light passed the narrow space in the subterranean arcade roof that had been pried open by the roots of fruit trees. They turned again, and the tunnel became larger and danker, smelling of old earth. Here it ended, obstructed by a stout wooden door. The first man scratched lightly on the door. "True Blood," he whispered.

"Forever," came the answering whisper of a woman's voice. The door was opened, and they stood in a vaulted stone cellar filled with kegs. A man held a torch over the sleeping bundle.

"It's very quiet. Is it alive?"

"Oh, very lively. It's sleeping." The baby made the oddest hiccuping sound as it slept beneath its blanket. It was almost like laughter, except that newborn babies don't laugh.

"Yes, I hear it now. Here, hold the pan. Yes, it just fits." The stout woman was holding an immense warming pan, meant to hold hot coals to take the chill off the sheets. A deep kettle with an iron lid on a long, wooden handle, it was the only container big enough to hold a child that would not be searched. Every evening it had been carried to the bedchamber, full of hot coals. No guard would risk searing his hand to inspect it. The conspirators popped the sleeping baby inside it and put the lid on. There it was, enclosed in iron, the child who would change their futures and the future of France. How much depended on it! Soon France would have a new heir, and a new queen regent. Francis would be pushed away from the throne. The Priory and its leader would control the government and destroy Francis, the last of the Valois, as soon as it was politic.

Awed by the significance of the moment, the two men watched the torch bob and vanish up the stairway into the service corridors of the Hôtel de Cluny, then they slipped silently back into the depths to report to the Helmsman.

It was already dusk when I arrived with my escort in the stone-walled courtyard of the Hôtel de Cluny. A footman met me at the entrance and carried my box, showing me the way through all those winding little rooms to the White Queen's chamber. Outside, several guards were lounging just as if they expected nothing. Madame de Nevers had just left for the evening, and a maid came to turn down the bed and warm the sheets.

"Stop," said the guards as I came to the door. "We need to see what's in there first." I set my box on the floor. "And you, too," they said to the stout woman with the warming pan.

"Just hot coals," said the woman. "You'll burn your fingers if you touch the lid."

"We'll risk it," said a guard, and I heard a lazy chuckle from behind me. It was the Sieur de Périgord, who was acting for Madame Louise. The woman looked suddenly nervous.

"You'll be sorry," she said. But a guard had put his hand on the pan. "Stone cold," he said, as he opened the lid.

It was then that something very strange happened, which is still rather hard for me to describe. There was a fluttering sound as if a dove or a live duck had suddenly been released from the pan, and a child's voice cried, "Surprise!" and started to chirp like a bird, only considerably more melodious. The guards fell back from the pan, which dropped on the floor with a 'clang!' while the lid rolled clattering away. The poor woman who'd brought it fell on the floor in a faint. "Oh, I'm a lovely, lovely, baby!" sang the little voice, and we looked up to see a sort of a little winged creature with dark curls and lively, dancing, brown eyes fluttering beneath the high, vaulted stone ceiling like an oversized moth, or a very large sparrow that's come in the chimney by mistake. In that moment, an idea flashed into my mind. Hadriel's behind this, I thought. This is his sense of humor. How ever did he discover this conspiracy? It must have been the poorest-kept secret in all of Paris.

One of the soldiers crossed himself. The Sieur de Périgord, who is very dignified, called out, "Stay! Who or what are you? Identify yourself." I could hear someone muttering a prayer. By this time, a lady's head had popped out of the White Queen's door.

"Oh, my dear God, a conspiracy!" she cried. "What on earth is that?" Behind her, a redheaded figure in a crumpled white gown stood, trying to peer out.

"The queen is out of bed. Get back, get back, no excitement now!" cried someone, and the woman at the door turned to give a hard stare at the girl in white behind her.

"Did you have that thing brought?" asked the old lady who was her keeper for the night. Above us, the little winged thing danced joyfully in the air. I noticed that the stout lady who had brought the warming pan had revived. In the new confusion, she managed to evade the guards and disappear.

"Send for a wild duck in a warming pan? I hardly think so," I heard the White Queen say with a sniff before the door slammed.

"What a splendid, splendid trick!" the little thing in the air sang. "Tell the Helmsman to look more closely at the next baby he buys! He shall never be king! Hadriel has said it!" With a flash of iridescent wings, the creature vanished straight through the solid stone of the ceiling.

"What was that? Was it talking?"

"A kind of chirping."

"It must have been a bird. Yes, a big bird."

Hadriel. He was right here in Paris, and he hadn't even come to say hello. Now was that fair, when I had been painting so hard, and was so in need of inspiration? Irresponsible, that's what it was, just plain irresponsible. Playing tricks like that and fooling around. He was probably drinking, that's what. But how was I going to tell the duchess what happened without seeming out of my mind?

Evidently, everyone else had had the same thought. They were busy fixing their story right now.

"They tried to smuggle a baby in a warming pan."

"Yes, a baby."

"But when the woman was discovered, she fled before anyone could catch her."

"Very fast. Probably a boy in disguise, she was so fast."

"Yes, a boy, dressed in woman's clothes."

"She took the baby."

"Yes, just snatched it away."

"She made a diversion."

"Yes, a live bird flew in the chimney."

"There's no chimney here."

"It flew in the chimney in the antechamber, then came in here when the boy came with the warming pan."

". . . and so, you see, something large and winged was put in the pan, instead of the baby that the conspirators had obviously thought they'd put in there, and it just flew out, and someone shouted 'A trick! Next time let the Helmsman look more closely at the baby he buys!' so everyone thinks that it had to be a baby that was there once." I had gone to the Palais, where Francis had moved after the king died in Les Tournelles, so it couldn't be used anymore. The duchess, seated in her big padded chair by the fire, nodded and smiled at my story. Several of her ladies were there, too, the same ones she liked to debate about Virtue and Perfect Love and such things with.

"It ends well at least. Someone has a sense of humor. Someone who knows the conspirators and is on our side. That is very discreet."

"If you ask me, that conspiracy was hatched by men."

"And what do you mean by that?" she asked.

"Well, only a man could count so poorly where babies are concerned. No *woman* would try to palm off a baby on someone less than four months since the wedding day." The ladies laughed until tears ran down their faces, and then wiped their eyes on their silken, fur-lined sleeves.

"That's what I told Mother," said Duchess Marguerite. "Oh, she was so angry when she heard the rumors! 'I swear, I'll have them all hanged!' she cried, but I just said, 'Let them hatch their plot and smuggle anything they like in. What sane woman would accept an infant who would testify only to the fact that she was not pure on her wedding day?' "

"Now there is nothing to mar the coronation of the king, your brother," said one of her ladies agreeably.

"At least nothing of that sort," said Marguerite. "The Helmsman. I wonder who that is and why on earth he'd try such a ridiculous scheme?"

On the Left Bank, not far from the Hôtel de Cluny, a perpetually scrawny student of theology was most curiously occupied in his icy little garret room. On the floor, he had inscribed about him a circle with his dinner knife, surrounded by words in Hebrew and Latin copied from the grimoire he now held in his hand. A smoking bowl of evil herbs, rue, mandrake, and hellebore root, sat on the floor before him. Outside the circle a little lead coffer, no broader than a man's palm, lay open. Slowly and carefully, so that he wouldn't make a mistake, Nicholas was reading aloud:

"By the Seal of Basdathea, by the name Primematatum which Moses uttered and the earth opened and swallowed up Corah, Dathan and Abiram, answer all my demands and perform all that I desire.

Come now, O demon Belphagor, peaceably and in fair form, without delay."

"You beastly little nit, what do you think you are doing?" Belphagor, in a half doublet marked with tailor's chalk, appeared outside the circle. "I was at my tailor's having a new suit of clothes made for the coronation. Now send me back and I won't punish you."

"You can't punish me anyway. This book says so." With a start, Belphagor noticed the grimoire in Nicholas's hand.

"Throw that thing out. Didn't you learn in school it's bad to try things you haven't studied? You could get into big trouble."

"I'm already in big trouble, as far as I can see. You said you wanted someone to read to you to improve your level of civiliation, but all I've read so far is pornography and Machiavelli, and now my soul's in danger."

"Throw away that book, dear Nicholas, and I'll take you out to supper and all's forgotten, all right? The book doesn't work anyway."

"It works well enough, because here you are. I don't know if I'd call what you are 'in fair form,' though. *Hmph.* That nose. Those big feet of yours. Hardly fair at all."

"Nicholas, Nicholas. Think a moment. Stick with me, and you'll have all the riches of the earth. Just throw away the book, and step out here and we'll shake on it. Agreed?"

"Step out of the circle? It specifically says not to, right here on page thirty-two."

"Damned bookworm! Who said you should read page thirty-two?"

"I always read the whole thing before I try something new. I read all of Machiavelli, too, even if you didn't sit long enough to let me finish. He says if men are bad, you are not bound to keep good faith with them. And you're bad. Tell me, what's worse than a demon? You deceived me. So that shows I don't have to keep good faith with you. Lord Belfagoro from Italy, indeed!"

Belphagor shot forth a jet of sulfurous fire from his nostrils, but it dissipated harmlessly at the edge of the magic circle.

"You crawling, cretinous idiot! You spineless, maggot-ridden heap of worm food. Die, you miserable mound of human garbage! Die!"

"Worthless talk, Belphagor. I have the grimoire, and my soul, too. Now, into the little box there."

"Never."

" 'O worthless spirit, who art wicked and disobedient, by the Names of Adonai, Sebaoth, Adonai, Amioram, Adonai, King of Kings, commands thee ...' " Nicholas read. Even though his knees trembled, his voice was firm. He thought of his old mother and all the sacrifices she'd made for his studies. I can't be a preacher if I can't box this demon, he thought, and he read the rest of the demon-catching spell loud and clear. "Pull the lid shut after you," he said, as Belphagor collapsed into a column of greenish, stinking smoke and shrank into the box. Carefully, Nicholas touched the box with the rod he had prepared according to the grimoire's instructions. " 'Seal, O seal, until the crack of doom, let no mortal words undo thee, by the dreadful Day of Judgment, by the Sea of Glass which is before the face of the Divine Majesty, by the Four Beasts before the Throne, having eyes before and behind, by the Fire which is about the Throne, by the Holy Angels of heaven and the Mighty Wisdom of God....' " The little box was jiggling and vibrating with the rage of the demon inside it. Gingerly, Nicholas stepped out of the circle.

"Nice job, Nicholas," said Hadriel's cheerful voice. The angel appeared sitting cross-legged on Nicholas's unmade bed, and suddenly Nicholas wished he were a better housekeeper, though he had been terribly busy getting all the evil herbs and studying in the last few days. "You know, even we angels can't do that. Humanity does have some advantages."

"I should hope so," said Nicholas, somewhat miffed. "I mean, we do have immortal souls and such."

"Which, if you forget, had to be redeemed," said Hadriel.

"I can't argue with an angel," growled Nicholas.

"But you'd *try*, wouldn't you. Humans!" Hadriel laughed, and the silvery chiming sound made Nicholas forget his grumpiness and the horrible lump of fear that had been sitting in his stomach for days, and came back even now as he looked at the little box, and heard the squeaking, raging sounds coming from inside it.

"What do I do with *that?*" he asked.

"Why, take it with you and it will make your reputation! Just think of the inspirational sermons you can give! How many theologians are so mighty in thought that they have boxed a demon?"

"Well, I had help ..." said Nicholas, looking at the toes of his worn-out shoes.

"Don't you all? But not so many of you take time to give thanks."

"Thank you. I do thank you, from the bottom of my heart."

"Ha! Thanks at last! Lovely, lovely." Hadriel laughed as he threw open the garret shutters, and, with the powerful sound of wings, flew into the heavy, snow-laden winter sky.

"Wait! Come back! I have more things to ask ..." called Nicholas out the window, but all he saw was a vanishing flash of iridescence in the grayness over the tall, pointed towers and high slate roofs of Paris.

TWENTY-FIVE

In the long, stone hall of Belphagor's rented mansion, the conspirators awaited word of the success of their operation. Signor Belfagoro himself, in an expansive moment, had invited them for a bit of a celebration, and in deference to their demonic partner, they had agreed to meet aboveground. The house, after all, was guarded by infernal forces. What could be more secure than that? Some of the conspirators sat at the great oak table and ate nervously from the supply of little cakes and dried fruits that Septimus Crouch had laid out for them. Others poured wine from the silver flagon on the sideboard. In a special place of honor, on a linen-covered stand almost like an altar, stood the curious goblet-mirror on its little pedestal, winking in the candlelight. The wonderful thing had been consulted by everyone who had crossed the threshold, from Signor Belfagoro himself to the sinister Duc de Bourbon, who had come furtively, at night, to spy out the moving figures on its face. With shining fidelity, the golden surface had reflected back to them the ever-more-fantastic desires of their own minds. Only Nicholas, who had taken it for a rather inadequate and overpriced cup, had left it alone.

Maître Bellier, tall and dignified, paced back and forth, irritated by the demon's absence and fearing some new plot. The Priory, reduced to commerce with a demon! And one of such low rank, such crudeness. And treacherous, too. One need only to look at him to see that. It was Crouch, that infernal, ambitious, betraying Crouch who had entangled them with this wretched Belphagor. How could the Helmsman be so blind? The mission protected for centuries, sold away in a moment by brethren dazzled by infernal promises and the shining image of their desire fulfilled in a demonic mirror. Where did it come from? What created the images it contained? Suppose the mirror was as treacherous as the demon? What could it end in but disaster?

"Monsieur Crouch, your, ah, partner Signor Belfagoro has not returned yet?"

Crouch, presiding at the head of the table, leaned back in Belphagor's great chair, a faint, superior smile on his lips, his pale eyes crackling with triumph. Nicholas and Belphagor had vanished at the same
time, leaving him in command of the infernal household, of the immortal imps of diabolical powers, of the strange treasures of the earth
heaped in the cellar. All. At first, Crouch had moved with caution, barely
believing his good luck. Surely Belphagor would be back, as petulant and
treacherous as ever. Then he had attended a mass at which he heard that
the sensation of the university was a poor student who had passed his
oral examinations in triumph by carrying to them a demon imprisoned
in a box. Nicholas, thought Crouch, and now I am master.

"Oh, Prince Belphagor?" Crouch said smoothly, "he has been
called back on important business by the Prince of Darkness. I do expect him back shortly, but you know how it is with demons—they just
can't keep track of time. Eons, you know, are a moment to them. And
he tends to get distracted with the pressures of business. But I assure
you, he has left me as his deputy. Any rewards you might offer him
may be offered to me instead and I will, uh, relay them to him." Ah,
you fools, thought Crouch. The mirror has shown that I will soon take
this conspiracy for my own.

Maître Bellier, his eyes dubious, looked down his long nose at the
gentleman who sat beside him with such visibly greedy, triumphant
eyes. Crouch smiled back at him condescendingly. He glanced at the
table. The candles were burning low, and the food needed renewing.
The air was thick with nervousness and anticipation. Crouch waved an
indolent hand at the imps. He was a lord now, a lord of hell, and
would let them all know it.

"You there, more fruit-o and wine-o, quick, quick!" Crouch was
one of those who believed that he could speak any foreign language,
even impish, by simply adding vowel syllables to the end of English
words. It was a habit that infuriated the imps, who had for some weeks
suppressed a powerful urge to disembowel him. They hesitated;
Crouch fixed them with a commanding stare. They squealed and
grumbled to each other and vanished toward the kitchen.

It is fortunate for the world in general that imps are so abominably lazy that they rarely use their unusual powers unless forced to by the lords of the underworld. These imps resented every shape change, every little personal service, each domestic duty that was required of them. Only Belphagor held them in check, and every day, as they swept out the place, emptied the slop jars, made the beds, and cooked up the gargantuan repasts that Crouch required to keep body and soul together, they got angrier and angrier. Now little flamelets showed almost continually at their ears and nostrils, and their grumbling sounds were almost constant. As Belphagor had gone out the door on his ill-fated trip to the tailor's, he had told them, "You boys listen to Crouch while I'm gone." That, and the icy glare of Crouch's compelling, pale eyes, grown nearly equal to the demon's in pure evil, held them to their duty. They, like the others, were under the impression that Belphagor would return.

There was a rattle at the front door, and one of the imps went from the kitchen to open it. A tall, dark, young aristocrat with smoldering eyes was shown in.

"The Helmsman, the Helmsman is here at last." One man ran to help him off with his cloak and shake the dampness off it in front of the fire. Another showed him a seat. A third poured him the last of the wine.

Crouch's pale eyes took in the scene with a certain distant malignance. Why should the Helmsman be treated like a God? Why shouldn't he be Helmsman? Didn't he rule the very imps of hell? It was time for Crouch to rule this conspiracy. Wait, wait, an inner voice counseled. You will be greater than he.

"There is no report as yet," Maître Bellier told him, leaning discreetly near his ear. Bourbon looked up at him, his eyes arrogant.

"No report? It is well past the hour. Did all go as planned?"

"I procured the boy from the Hôpital de la Trinité only this morning. Fine, healthy, and the very image of the king. He was delivered to the secret entrance as the sun set this evening." Damn, thought Crouch, I still haven't found their secret meeting place. If I am to take control of them, I need to discover their hiding place. How that Bellier sets himself up! Who is he? Not even a knight.

"Then something has delayed them. We shall be hearing soon." There was a sort of scratching at the front door, and again, the imps opened it. The disheveled man who entered stared, awestruck, at the two great, fiery creatures.

"Th—those," he said, pointing a finger. "They've got flames coming out of their nostrils."

"Well, of course," said Crouch, smoothly. "What did you expect? We're not amateurs at conspiracy, you know. When you joined us, you obtained the aid of the infernal." Trembling, the man knelt at the feet of the seated Duc de Bourbon.

"My lord, we are ruined," he said in a frightened voice. "The pan was opened. The infant was stopped at the door."

"Impossible! Are you certain?" asked the duke, glancing at the mirror on its stand.

"Yes, my lord, we have failed."

"Who has been caught?" inquired the duke in a voice accustomed to command.

"No one, my lord."

"No one? How could this be?"

"I assure you, no one. There is no accusation. Someone substituted a large, live bird for the infant. It flew out with great fluttering, and now everyone is laughing."

"Laughing? Laughing at me? I'll show them laughing. Where is the woman who carried the pan?"

"She vanished and cannot be found."

"Then it was she. She did it. They bribed her. Or she grew cowardly, like a woman. Yes, it makes sense. Never admit a woman to a conspiracy."

"Clearly, my lord, she betrayed us to the other side," said Maître Bellier.

"Yes, and in such a clever way that the White Queen could not be implicated, no matter what anyone said."

"Then she betrayed us not to the Valois, but to the White Queen's people. Someone coordinated this. Which of them could it have been? That damned English doctor? Who has been admitted to the White Queen's chamber?"

"Not him, my lord, he has been forbidden entrance. He and all the other English, even her ladies."

"Then I must seek among the French, surely the Countess of Nevers . . ."

"Wait, my lord. There was one. Sent by Queen Claude. A widow who does religious paintings of consolation. I have heard she is English, though some say she is Flemish from her accent."

"Susanna Dallet . . . damn her! That woman is always in the middle of everything," said Crouch.

"What name did you say?" asked the Duc de Bourbon.

"Mistress Susanna Dallet, paintrix, from the City of London. She has thwarted me at every turn. Maître Bellier, she is the possessor of the third portion of the manuscript you so desired." Crouch's eyes were glittering with the rising insanity of absolute rage.

"She has the third portion? Then that explains everything. The allegorical code in the pictures of Adam and Eve. It was not the lover, but she herself who read it, and she has deciphered the Secret, and is toying with us. The Priory of Sion is betrayed. Betrayed by a woman." The mutter of shocked voices filled the room.

"The secret of fifteen centuries."

"The Sacred Blood—destroyed. Treachery. We will be burned alive. She must be eliminated." The unnaturally calm voice of Bourbon penetrated the babble.

"But she is surrounded by friends at court. An assassination would never be secret."

"There are other means."

"My lord of Bourbon, I have tracked the creature to her den. She has a workplace, where she is alone, except for a maidservant, who goes out with her. I have already bribed the landlady to search it most subtly, but she found nothing."

"But surely she does not do this alone. What man uses this vicious and clever woman as his agent?"

"There is only one mind diabolical enough, masterful enough, in all these two kingdoms. Let us make sure." All heads turned toward the source of truth, the mirror of the ancients that had guided them to this moment. Crouch stepped before it, passing his hands over it and muttering the words of the spell. Those closest to him could see movement on the glittering surface, figures like reflections, but not of this place. Crouch bent his head closer, peering at the flickering shapes, then drew back with an exclamation. "Him! Again him! It is as I suspected. Archbishop Wolsey, the evil, plotting monster. She is in his pay. I see it here. He has trained her and used her."

"The archbishop—yes." The waiting men nodded at one another in agreement.

"And his agent, Ashton, has conveniently returned from the dead to guide her. He has been seen with her. Diabolical, this woman."

"And how do you know she is a woman? Strip her, I say, and you will find no woman, but a male agent of the scheming archbishop."

"That treacherous Wolsey. The treaty. Yes, it all fits. The prince of the Church supports the prince of the Valois. He wants to keep the Merovingians from returning."

"And keep the Secret from emerging. He has discovered the Secret and knows it would destroy the Church."

"Then we can count on his silence. He will protect the Church at all costs. Our Secret is safe with him." The Helmsman's cool calculation broke through the babble.

"But is it safe with her?"

"Safe with a woman? Never. As long as the manuscript remains, and she knows where it is, we are menaced with discovery."

"Then we are agreed," said Bourbon. "We must force the woman to reveal the hiding place of the manuscript, and then silence her."

"Agreed," said Crouch.

"It should not be difficult," said the Helmsman.

King Francis the First was seated in his audience chamber surrounded by his old friends, his gentlemen in waiting, all in the process of being elevated to new honors in consequence of their closeness to him. Bonnivet would become Admiral of France, Bourbon would be Constable of France, his sister, Marguerite, given a county, her husband governorship of Normandy, and his mother the title of Duchess, two counties, and the hidden power behind the throne. All day, Francis had been receiving embassies from the rulers of Europe, congratulating him on his accession, seeking favors and the renewal of treaties. But

Francis's mind was busy with other thoughts, thoughts of a redheaded woman sealed in a room in the Hôtel de Cluny. She had rejected him. She had mocked his ardor. He was king, now, and could do what he liked with her. Kings could do anything they pleased, couldn't they? At first, he had contemplated setting aside his ugly wife and taking her instead. But his mother had caught him in an unwary moment and lectured him until his ears rang. No wife, no Brittany. Don't be a fool.

He thought about how rude the White Queen had been, even through her cautious words, and how little she appeared to appreciate his well-turned legs, and said to himself, she's not worth it, the dirty thing. She's not worth half a kingdom. Then he pondered how amusing it would be to make her his mistress, and then palm her off on some other European prince once he was done with her. But once again, Mother had turned up, with a story of a conspiracy to produce a false heir to unseat her glorious Caesar. Mother had been livid with indignation. This time you were lucky, she said; the fools couldn't count nine months. Next time they might be cleverer. Francis knew all about false heirs. He had inherited several foreign ones from old Louis the Twelfth, all eating their heads off on French pensions, as foreign-policy insurance, just in case. Two were English, and Francis considered they had as much of a claim as the father of that Henry, his rival who now ruled England. No, he'd never have peace until he got rid of the White Queen—preferably in such a way that nobody would ever come and bother him about her again.

"The ambassador of the King of England, the Duke of Suffolk!" Francis looked up to see that damned, hulking brute stalking down the hall. You could dress the man up in silk and furs all you wanted, he thought, but he still looks like an ox.

"Your Grace," said Suffolk, addressing Francis as if he were still duke. This low-born oaf, as insulting as ever, thought Francis. The English must still imagine that that woman might produce an heir. Without paying attention, Francis listened to Suffolk repeat his formal congratulations. What do I care about your English treaty? he thought. I think I'll have my captains raid your shipping. The English king needs to be reminded I am powerful. But for now, I need to get rid of that beastly little White Queen and the plots that surround her. Suddenly, a splendid thought came to him. An inspiration, really. His foxy little eyes twinkled with the joke of it, and a half smile crept up beneath his extraordinarily long nose.

"My lord of Suffolk," said King Francis, "I hear you have come thither into this kingdom to marry the White Queen, your master's sister."

Charles Brandon, Duke of Suffolk, his king's right hand, hero of war and tournament, paled sheet white.

"I don't like it, Susanna; there's something wrong with the whole thing." We were on our way across the Petit Pont to the Hôtel de Cluny at the White Queen's summons. Robert's hat was pulled down low, and his long gray cloak was muffled around him, concealing the shortsword and dagger that he wore at his belt. In his doublet he had hidden a narrow little misericord, just in case. I had my hood up and was wearing a pair of Mistress Hull's lumpier mittens that she had given me before she had become inspired by Hadriel and gotten fashionable. The wind bit through my cloak, which was becoming a bit threadbare, and I was scheming how to get a new one. The notion of a nice little commission from the White Queen was just right.

"It's her seal, and a servant in the old king's livery delivered it."

"But the wording—it seems unlikely that she would write so. And why in French, when she could write to you in English?" Robert had gotten all jumpy lately and was sure everything was a plot. I would just tell him, what have painters got to do with plots, but he insisted on going with me if things didn't look right to him. So far, he'd cooled his heels outside the new queen's apartments, and also the Duchess Marguerite's, but that didn't stop him from being suspicious.

"Why would she write in other than the language of the court? Robert, I am glad of your company, but I am sure it just must be those angels she wanted. She's finally gotten around to ordering them at last—and every other painter in Paris is doing coronation portraits, or banners for the parade route, or coats of arms for the canopies. Coronations—why, they're even better business than funerals! Have I told you that the Duchess Marguerite has commissioned a dozen miniatures of her brother? I'm thinking I may take on an apprentice after all." As we pressed on down the street toward the Church of the Mathurins, he didn't do more than answer *"umph"* and look about him suspiciously. Here were some students hurrying toward warmth and someone from out of town, mounted on a horse in a shaggy winter coat.

"You're not jealous, are you? I was thinking of taking on a girl, not a boy."

"There's something wrong. It smells wrong to me. Someone's following us. Duck into this archway here, and he'll think we've gone around the corner, and when he follows us, we'll see who it is." In a flash, he'd pulled me in by the elbow, and I waited quietly and peered out, just to prove him wrong. A man driving a mule loaded with firewood passed by, and I was just about to step out when I saw him. A tall, cloaked figure glided from a shadowy doorway. I pressed myself back into the arch, and we saw him step purposefully past us and begin to round the corner toward the Hôtel de Cluny. There was no question who it was. A heavy black hood was pulled over his head, but the familiar square-cut beard and malicious pale green eyes, two glaciers set in pallid mounds of skin, made my blood freeze. It was Septimus Crouch. What was it he knew? Why was he following us? Maybe Robert was right about the message, after all.

He paused at the corner and, not seeing us, began to retrace his steps. With Robert pulling my elbow, we fled down the narrow corridor behind the archway. A high wooden gate barred our way. We thought we heard footsteps behind us. The gate wasn't locked. We pulled open the gate and closed it behind us. We were in the tiny patch of winter garden within the walls of the monastery of the Mathurins.

"Oh, Lord, Robert, we can't be in here."

"We can't be out of here, either." We heard him fumbling at the gate. "Surely, he must know I'm armed. Is there someone with him?" As if in answer, we heard another set of footsteps approaching the gate, and the sound of hurried conversation. "That cellar door, there. They'll think we've gone through the church," Robert whispered. Crouch had another man with him. Maybe more. Robert could be cut to pieces if he confronted them. I looked at the cellar door. I looked again at the gate. I hate cellars; they are full of rats and spiders and disgusting damp darkness. If it weren't for Robert, I'd have never thought of it. But quick as a wink we were on the narrow stony stairs behind the little door while we heard Crouch and whoever it was stamping around outside.

"They came this way; I'm sure of it," Crouch said. "You go search the church—*aha!* Look at this little door. Just the sort of place a rat like Ashton would scramble into." We fled down the stairs just as the first crack of light from the opening door illuminated the gray stone around us. Crouch paused, and we could hear the slither of steel as he drew his long Italian rapier. As Robert pulled me deeper into the dark corridor, my heart began to pound. We came to a locked grating and felt a soft pulse of air.

"It's the cellar. Damn, it's locked. They've protected their wine too well," he whispered as he felt about. "But here—the tunnel goes on. It's narrower; we'll have to crawl."

"N-no, Robert, I can't go there."

"You have to. Go ahead of me. Crouch has a rapier and a long reach. He'll skewer you if you're behind me. We need to stay far ahead of him. If we turn back, he'll outreach the length of my sword and leave us here like a pair of dead rats. See here, they wouldn't have made it if it didn't go somewhere. It probably has an entrance in the church." Softly, softly, muffled with his cloak, he drew his misericord. "With luck, he'll give up," he whispered, very softly, in my ear. Then I could hear a little click of his teeth and knew he was holding it in his mouth, so he could crawl better.

My heart full of horror, I crawled into the narrow stone way. It was flat, paved with what felt like wide, smooth stones, and a trickle of damp from some unknown source was running down the center. I heard rattling at the gate behind us.

"Curses," I heard Crouch's voice mutter. "They must have gotten in here. I'll have to give up." But his speech sounded suspiciously loud and forced. Behind me, Robert seemed to breathe easier. But I thought I could still hear the soft shuffle, shuffle sound of a man on his hands and knees behind us. It was all a ruse, the little speech, to make us think he'd left so we'd go back. As long as he's crawling, and we're crawling faster, he can't hurt us, I thought. There's no room. But the thought wasn't consoling. We couldn't go back. That's what he was hoping we'd do. We'd go back and he'd cut our throats; I just knew it. A man like Septimus Crouch doesn't follow people for no reason, especially when they have received a message that might be a forgery after all. My brain was seething with desperate questions, the kind you think of when you are in a place you hate and wish you were home and are afraid you might die in the place you are. Like, why did the man hate me so much he wouldn't back out and give up? I couldn't ask Robert to back up; the man hated him, too. He'd run Robert through and fill the narrow way with Robert's body and leave me trapped behind him to die there. No one would ever know he'd done it, and they'd never find us. That must be his plan. How stupid we were not to have faced him on the street. But there had been two of them up there—maybe even more. Who could have stopped them from killing us? Still we pitched downward in the dark, and I thought I could feel strange slithering things on my ankles, which made me shudder.

The corridor leveled off, then turned slightly and sloped downhill again. I felt a strange sort of cold breath on my cheek and, even in the blackness, knew it meant there was another, wider corridor on my right side. But far away down the trickling damp stones of our own, low, way, I could make out a flicker of light. I nearly cried out with relief to see it. A cellar! One with a cellerer, counting his casks! I could imagine him there, all homely, with his big apron, humming to himself. Oh, God, I'll never think badly of cellars again! Oh, my dress, it's ruined! The mittens, they're no loss, but I really liked this dress. My best wool, the one Cat and Mistress Hull and Nan and I made, with all the nice little tucks and touches here and there. How can I be seen, even in a cellar, with such a woeful dress? Now Robert saw the light, and urged me on by poking me on the ankle with one hand.

At last I came to the opening, scrambled out, and stepped down beside something like a dripping fountain without even thinking, hurrying for fear Robert would be trapped behind me. He dropped out behind me with a thump, and I saw we were in the strangest room I had ever seen. Entirely underground, it had no natural source of light, and yet it must have had once, for among the strange, high shadows made by candlelight up under the vault, I saw windows that were entirely filled in with a rubble of dirt and stone. There was an ugly smell of damp and decay, of old water that hid ugly secrets in its depths.

An eerie *plink, plink, plink* sound went on monotonously as single drops of water made their way from our corridor down into the wall fountain from behind which we'd climbed, and dropped into a square pond that filled the center of the room. On the far side of the water was a long table on which stood a large silver candelabrum filled with flickering candles that cast strange, pale patterns of light up among the shadows through the strange, colonnaded brick room. A servant with a candle was lighting the first of a row of torches that stood in iron brackets along the walls, between the ancient pillars that supported the roof. It caught with a *whoosh*, and orange light danced across the surface of the black waters of the pool. With a start, I recognized the man in black. And then I heard a measured, cultivated voice address us in French:

"Why, Suzanne Dolet, what a pleasant surprise. We were expecting you later, in the company of our Helmsman. But you have come here ahead of our appointed time and brought company as well. This, I assume, is Robert Ashton, no longer dead?" Behind me, I could feel Robert freeze with surprise at this speech. But I knew the man in the doctor's gown who spoke. I had last met him in London. It was Maître Bellier.

"Where are we?" I asked him, foolishly mistaking him for a friend and relieved to see him in this strange place. The man in black paused beneath the second torch, turning toward us, the candle in his hand, to hear his master's answer.

"Where? Somewhere beneath the gardens of the Hôtel de Cluny, I imagine. It is of no concern. Eustache, please go at once and inform the Helmsman that the guests he awaited have preceded him here." On the far side of the pool, beyond the table, was a marble-framed doorway with an eagle on the top of it. Beyond it into the dark stretched the rocky walls of a tunnel.

I could hear Robert roar, "No!" and heard him draw his sword to pursue Eustache, who dropped his candle and drew his knife. But Bellier was armed, too, and from beneath his gown drew his own shortsword, rushing to save his servant. Without stopping to think, I ran after him around the far side of the pool, grabbing up the candelabrum from the table to batter at the man in black. Candles rolled every which way and guttered out on the floor, as the man in black tried to ward off the fiery blows. At that very moment, I heard a clatter and glanced back. Ashton and Bellier had frozen in surprise. A third person had emerged from the tunnel, rapier drawn. Septimus Crouch had joined us. The orange light crackled across his malignant face.

"You, here? You are not of the brotherhood!" gasped Bellier.

"So, at last, I've found your little place. I thought when the Helmsman acted, they might lead me to it, but I never imagined how."

"This is forbidden!" cried Bellier. Crouch laughed at him. Robert, sword drawn, stood at the opposite edge of the pond from me, beneath the unlit torches, midway between Crouch and Bellier, uncertain as to which way to go.

"My dear sir, let us first cut Ashton's throat and argue later about propriety," announced Crouch, in that cool, unpleasant way he had. I looked at my Robert trapped between them, and, in a flash of inspiration, heaved the single lit torch that stood above me out of its bracket and into the pool, plunging the whole room into pitch darkness. There was the sound of feet, and I knew that the man in black had vanished out the marble-framed door. From the opposite side of the pool there came a clattering and banging of swords engaging in the dark, and I heard Robert cry, "Ah, I'm hit!" Swiftly, so that they could not locate me by the sound of my footsteps, I tried to crawl around the pool toward him, feeling my way with one hand on the edge. My hand met another hand, feeling in the opposite direction. Robert's. I'd know it in the dark, so often had I run my hands over the cast of it. Behind him, there was the sound of metal crashing against stone. A finger, not mine, found my lips in the dark, and crossed them. The sign of silence. How badly was he hurt? He could feel my thoughts. The hand took my hand and put it across his lips. I could feel him smile. I could feel him mouth, "I'm fine" without any sound. A trick. He'd set them on each other in the dark. But almost as soon as he touched me, the clattering stopped, and I could hear the heavy breathing of someone hunting for us in the dark.

My visual memory is perfect. Once I've seen something, I don't forget it, and in the first flash of sight, the plan of this room had been impressed on my brain. I felt for the corner of the pool, then pulled Robert toward the hole behind the lion fountain. And none too soon,

either. There was a flickering of lanterns in the marble-framed doorway, and the room was lit again by feeble light.

"What's this?" inquired a commanding voice, and from where we
were hiding, we could see the Constable de Bourbon, holding a lantern,
surrounded by several armed men and led by the man in black.

"They're gone," said Bellier, looking wildly about him in the sudden light. His gown was slashed and his flat hat with the earflaps was
floating dolefully in the pool.

"The Dolet woman and the man?"

"And Sir Septimus Crouch, the English servant of that unspeakable
demon you made partnership with. I warned you, and now he has
wormed his way into the heart of our deepest secrets." Bourbon, arrogant and dark, looked at Bellier with a stare that would paralyze a snake.

"It's the Helmsman," whispered Ashton, curled up as tightly as an
unborn baby with me, there in the tunnel. "Astonishing. Bourbon is
the Helmsman."

"Brother Bellier, will you and your servant kindly remove the chest
with our record books? Brothers, go at once and seal the entrances to
our tunnels. Our meeting place has been discovered; it must be abandoned at once. It is the law. And those who violate our secrets must
die. We will seal them in for all eternity. It is just." Even before he had
finished giving his commands, the armed men had gone by the way
they had come, and we had begun crawling up the tunnel as fast we
could, in hopes of beating them to the entrance.

The thoughts I had going up were even more unpleasant than the
thoughts I had had going down. What if the way they'd come was
short, and this way long? Then we'd meet a sealed entrance and die in
the dark. My heart kept swelling up with horror and slowing me down.
Robert kept poking me from behind to go faster, but it was darker and
more horrible, with no light at the end to see by. We passed the broad
opening, now on our left. "Robert," I whispered, "let's go this way; it's
bigger."

"No, the other way, it's not far, and we know where we are." We
crawled for what seemed an eternity, and I was sure I would meet a
snake or some horrible slithery thing, and I felt tears coming down my
face and Mistress Hull's very strong but ugly mittens tearing apart on

my hands, worn straight through by all that crawling. But then I could go no farther.

"Go on, go on," Robert whispered in the dark.

"I can't—a big rock—something—they must have rolled it."

"Oh, damn, we're not even at the grating yet. No one will even hear us."

"Back down, Robert, and we'll try the other way." But I knew if they'd gotten this far, there was no hope. I could feel Robert back away, then hear him sigh, and the faint whisper of a prayer. *If I get out of this, God, I'll never go into a cellar again. No stone corridors, no halls I can't see the end of. I don't care if I have to live in a tent.* Then I started praying, too, but in my mind, so that Robert wouldn't know how terrified I was. We reached the broader way, and Robert disappeared into it, pulling at my skirts to make sure I knew where it was. Now we could stand up, but to my horror, I heard the patter and squeak of rats and felt their furry bodies brush against my ankles.

"Rats, a good sign," Robert muttered. "They've got to get in somewhere."

"Somewhere tiny," I said. "Have you seen how little a hole a rat can get through?" I was shaking all over. I hate rats, too. And rats in the dark? That must be what they have in purgatory.

There was a bit of cool breeze, and we saw a tiny hole in the upper part of the tunnel, a web of heavy roots, and the edges of broken, displaced bricks. "There's your rat hole," I said. "Not big enough for us." We pressed on.

"Look, light," whispered Robert, and around a curve in the tunnel we saw a little niche in the wall, with a lamp with a deep oil well and floating wick, whose tiny flame glittered and shone in the dark like the answer to a prayer. Around it, stubs of candles were stuck onto the niche by their own wax. "It must be how they went in and out," he said. We lit candles from the lamp, and could see the rest of the length of the tunnel. Sealed, too. We pressed against the heavy oak door. Not a crack, not a hope. We felt the edges, and the points of nails, poking through here and there, told the story. They had nailed it shut. I just sat there, all curled up, and cried, while Robert held me.

"Don't cry, don't cry," he said, his voice full of despair. "I'll get you out of here, I swear." Hadriel, Hadriel, I wept silently, where are you now, you careless thing? I'm needing more than the idea for a new kind of painting. You've got me into this; it's all your fault for urging on my wicked ideas about leaving my proper place in life. Now look at how I've ended up! I wouldn't be here if it weren't for you. Open this hole and let me out, I shouted in my mind.

"That's a good idea," said Robert. "Worth a try. Anything's worth a try."

"What idea?" I asked.

"The one you said. We'll try to open up the rat hole."

"I didn't say anything," I said.

"Of course you did. I heard it plainly." He urged me up, and with the aid of the candles, we found the place much more quickly. Now as we looked about us with the light, we saw that we were not actually in a tunnel but a half tunnel roofed with a low, crumbling arch of brick and mortar that looked like part of a ceiling. The floor was compacted rubble. Farther on, the tunnel was dug through some sort of earth and in places lined with stone or brick, as if it were following the line of old walls, and then crossing them.

"These are buildings," I said. "Buildings beneath the earth."

"Of course they are," he answered. "You can see the top side of them in places where they poke through. Ruined walls in the gardens, parts of other buildings. Maybe even cellars. People never bothered to clear away the walls; they just built more on top of them. But I had no idea there was so *much* of this place. The palace of a very great king— outbuildings, baths. These fellows in the Priory must have hollowed them out." He passed me his knife, then took his misericord and began to chip at the mortar of the bricks nearest the hole. I took off the remains of my mittens and did the same, my hands freezing with the cold. We worked and worked. Each loose brick was a triumph, each root-entangled stone a disaster. Gradually the little patch of sky we could see through the hole blazed red, then purple, then turned black. I was hungry, I was tired, and I thought the tears would freeze my face. Robert labored on, his jaw clenched, his expression grim.

"You're smaller," he said, when the hole in the decayed brickwork had grown sufficiently. "I'll put you on my shoulders and you must cut away the roots above the bricks." So I hacked and chopped with his knife until he could push me up and through the hole. I lay on the frozen ground above, breathing deeply of real air and and weeping with relief. Then Robert's own head popped up and through the hole and I grabbed the back of his leather doublet and pulled as he struggled up and out of the pit beneath the tangled roots of a wintering apple tree, like some midnight mole. We were in a walled garden. Above the walls stretched the night sky, spotted with winter stars.

"Take me home, Robert," I wept. "I want to go home. I've had enough of grand things. I want to be home in the House of the Standing Cat again."

It was well past midnight by the time we got to the tall old house on the Pont au Change. I was frozen through and glad to see when I looked up at the fourth floor windows that there was a light in our room. "Look up there, Robert. Nan's there. She's waiting for us." Nan might even have supper kept warm for us, and it would be warm and cozy, and she'd exclaim over me and tell me how worried she'd been and everything would feel all right again. Inside, we found that the landlady wasn't there to give us a candle to light our way up the stairs, but by now we were very practiced in climbing in the dark. With our hands on the walls, we went right up as neatly as a pair of owls. There was a bit of a glow, as if from rushlights, coming from beneath the studio door, but when I got to the door it wouldn't open, even though I pulled the latch and pushed on it.

"Robert, help me push. The door is stuck shut. Nan, have you latched it? Come and open the door," I called, knocking softly, so as not to wake the other tenants in the building. We leaned on the door, and gradually it moved just a little bit, as if something were stuck behind it. There was something dark and slippery on the floor, coming from beneath the door. Then all of a sudden, it felt as if whatever was blocking the door had moved, because it opened wide from my pushing, and something snatched me inside and blocked the door behind me. I could see the ruddy light of several rushlights propped about my workroom that there was a big, dark puddle on the floor seeping out under the door, and also behind the door a hand nearly as white as my plaster ones, but coming from a sleeve attached to a dress all soaked in blood and unrecognizable. The body lay on its face, its headdress torn off and grayish hair mixed with dark all tangled where there was still part of the head for it to be attached to. There were apron strings, still tied neatly at the back of the waist, but red, red. Jumbled brains lay on the floor, as if something had been eating at them. Nan. Oh, Jesus, Nan, all mangled and dead. Waiting faithfully for us, she had met this horrible end.

"Blood," I said, all shocked, and I could feel coldness coming over me.

"Why yes indeed, it is blood," said a voice from the shadows. I knew at once who was in the room with me. I saw boots, I saw a heavy cloak, and I saw a white, puffy face with lines, all standing in the shadow by the fireplace, which was empty with the ashes scattered. All through the room, I could hear a steady drip, drip, drip. My skins of oil were slashed, my colors scattered everywhere, and the brushes I had made all tramped into the mess of oil and turpentine and dye powders on the floor. Drawings torn and crumpled, lay all about as if scattered in pure rage, and I could see my half-finished panel of the queen at Abbeville slashed across from pure malice. Plaster limbs lay shattered on the floor, as if a great slaughter had taken place. My chest of treasures was upended, my books lying open on the floor among tumbled cloth and Nan's half-done knitting. Behind the evil figure, in the half light at the window, the wicker cage still hung, the birds inside silent, huddled together in fluffy little balls, with their feathers puffed out.

"Septimus Crouch. How did you get here?" demanded Robert, from behind me.

"You're surprised to see me? No more than I am to see you," replied Septimus Crouch. "You seem to have taken the long way back. A pity you weren't entombed. I had hoped for it. No, Ashton, don't even think to touch that sword. Hey there," he said, suddenly speaking into the dark of the room. "You; yes, you. Take the sword-o from him. No, not the hand, you fool, the *sword*, that thing-o there at his side. You hold the hands, so he can't move. I want to talk to them first, before you take them apart."

All in a flash, I saw the most terrifying shapeless thing, only vaguely human, detach itself from the shadows. It was a full head taller than any man living, and flames came from its nostrils. Crouch fixed it with the gaze of his evil eyes, and I could see the white all around the rims of them. Then I saw it flash and change, moving like a lightning strike, and then I could see Robert struggling in its coils, as if in the grasp of a giant serpent. Then I heard an eerie chattering and grumbling sound answering it from the corner and realized there were two of them in the room. I could hear the *huff, huff* of the second one's breath, just like the bellows of a blacksmith's furnace, and see the glow. It was standing in the corner diagonal from us and opposite Crouch, waiting impatiently. I could feel its irritation, rolling off in waves, like a strong scent. I was so terrified, I couldn't decide whether to try to flee or to throw up.

"I suggest you not struggle," said Sir Septimus to Robert Ashton. "They have been very impatient lately. And it's their first trip out of the house since ... ah, well, under *my* command. Green, green, but they'll get used to it. That foolish old woman tried to hit one of them with her lantern, and just look what happened, before I could even order them to stop." I looked down at Nan, too frozen with terror even to weep, and around at the devastation of my work, and at Robert, coiled up so tightly in the black thing that all I could see was the flash of the whites of his eyes.

"You monster," I said.

"Monster? My dear Mistress Dallet, I assure you, I am far beyond being a mere a monster," Crouch purred. "The very imps of hell are at my command. I am become Evil Incarnate."

"Why? Why me? Look at all this. You've ruined everything."

"Oh, I haven't ruined *everything*. At least, not yet," said Septimus Crouch. "You still walk and talk. So does Ashton. You had best tell me where you have hidden it while you have yet the power."

"I don't know what you mean. Don't you dare touch me," I said.

"You still keep your mask, you sly, scheming little vixen? The poor innocent with the vicious depths. How deviously you plan, how ingeniously you conceal yourself. What you have not realized is that you cannot deceive *me*. The mystic mirror has shown me what you really are—your plots, your diabolical cabals." His eyes seemed to glow with some strange, knowing malice. So penetrating was his look, I began to wonder if there weren't *something* I was scheming about, just because he was so sure of it. I felt the dirtier for his looking at me. "And as for touching you," he went on, "I wouldn't dream of it. See these delightful, if somewhat uncouth beings here? One of them is barely restrained by my word from strangling the appalling little turncoat, Ashton. Just look, he's turning quite purple, or at least that part that I can see." Horrified, I could see that Robert was slowly being crushed alive.

"No, no. Not dead yet, you fool," said Crouch imperiously to the thing. "You wait until I, Septimus Crouch, have ordered it." Again, the fierce stare and commanding power flowed from his eyes. The thing made a sort of belching, squealing noise and loosened itself a bit, and the top of Robert's face turned from purple to crimson. The other black thing seemed to writhe in a sort of suppressed eagerness, making the same curious, impatient noise in response to the first creature's irritation. Their noise made the birds in the cage nervous. They smoothed their feathers and stared out with their little eyes, tipping their heads to see better. "This other one, the woman, is reserved for you," Crouch gestured to the thing in the shadows with a condescending wave. The glow of red showed at its nostrils. With all the spilled paint and turpentine in the room, I suddenly wondered that these things hadn't set it on fire with the sparks from their breath. "I shall have it pull you apart joint by joint until you tell—or, no, I see your face. Perhaps Ashton should be pulled apart first, while you look on."

Keep him talking, my mind said. I could feel something strange rolling off the hellish things, and my hair stood on end the way it does before a thunderstorm. Talking, yes, talking. Anything.

"B-but how, how did you get here even faster than we did? It's impossible," I said. Crouch smirked. There was a long, silent pause. Behind him, one of the birds hopped from the perch. Its feet made a scratching sound as it walked on the cage bottom.

"The large entrance, had either of you been intelligent enough to consider it, was obviously much shorter than the small one by which we came," Crouch gloated, his malicious eyes on my face. He turned to Robert, still buried in the monster's coils. "Yes, Ashton, more intelligent. Education, my years with antiquities, they mean something. I recognized our own way into the chamber as an ancient aqueduct. Roman, without a doubt. Did you notice the terra-cotta tiles? How little you see. But the great entrance beneath the eagle was fine and wide; I knew at once it was the path by which I should remove myself. I was not surprised to see it ended in Bellier's house in the rue de la Harpe.

An old servant stood in my way; he stands no more. How easy to elude the fools of the Priory. And once above the surface, I summoned my hell servants, here, and had them carry me here before the Helmsman could find this place." He paused again to inspect me, where I stood, paralyzed with terror, but my mind working like a windmill. He strode in front of the huge, wavering black thing, which seemed to tower to the ceiling like a column of smoke. "How dreadful you look, Mistress Dallet. Did you dig out with your fingernails? It certainly looks like it. With the application of superior intelligence and the service of these two abominations, here, I have not so much as disarranged a hair." The dark thing behind Crouch made that strange squealing noise again, and the other one twitched and uncoiled partway, in order to squeal back. It was a horrible sound, worse than fingernails on slate. It made my whole body shudder. I could see Robert's whole face now, still half strangled—looking, his eyes wide with horror as he watched the scene in front of him. Crouch turned, fixing his evil glare on the thing, and it was quiet.

"But why come here? Why destroy ... everything?" My Nan, my life's work, all, all. Though I knew I had to, I could barely speak. My voice came out all scratchy, and my body felt first hot, then cold.

"You've hidden it well," said Crouch. "It *was* convenient of you to come back to tell me where it is."

"What is *it?*"

"The book, the book, you abysmal, covetous, devious little nit. Did you think you could hide it from me forever? It is the last thing I need before I claim my throne—here, and in the infernal." Crouch's eyes seemed to swell as he spoke, and I could see whites all around the tops of them. He was totally insane.

"Th-the book?" I stammered stupidly.

"The book your treacherous husband gave you to hide."

"I—I don't have it ..."

"I think you may remember soon." Stepping carefully, so that both creatures were in his line of vision, he lifted a finger at the second fiery-breathed creature, then fixed it with his eye. "Here there, you, beast, grab that woman-o by the arms. And don't go breaking her carelessly the way you did the other. I'm tired of your slovenliness." He flicked his gaze at the thing that held Robert. "And you, I want you to begin dismembering that dismal wretch you're holding, slowly, now, while she's watching." Robert gave a horrible cry as the thing holding him began to uncoil from him and change its shape.

"No!" I screamed, as the second shape, squealing and grumbling, began to move. My voice frightened the birds in the window behind Crouch. They began to flutter about the cage, crying shrilly. The frantic movement and sudden sound distracted Crouch, who turned to see what it was, leaving the moving creatures both behind his back. His fierce glare removed from them, they paused, huffing glowing red, and silently began to change their shapes. I could feel my eyes open wide in amazement. The empty thing was moving in the wrong direction—away from me toward Crouch's exposed back. He heard the rustle as it passed over the crumpled papers on the floor and whirled back to face the creatures.

"You there," said Crouch, as he saw the dark, flaming thing unwrap from Robert, letting him drop to the floor in a limp heap, "don't you get anything right? Move! Grab that woman-o, I say. And that man. I want you to pluck off his arms, then hers." His face was arrogant, his eyes bulging and lunatic. He pointed his hands at the thing near Robert, and his white beard quivered as he spoke. But the things were on either side of him. He could not look at one without taking his eyes off the other.

The things were stock-still, towering there in the center of the room, their flaming breath heaving, as if deciding what to do. They looked at him with their fierce little red eyes. My skin crawled with horror, the blood stopped in my veins, and I was utterly, utterly still. All I could hear in the room was breathing—the soft *huff, huff* of human breath, and the deep, *whoosh, whoosh* sound that the fiery-breathed creatures made.

Then the first one began to ooze, silently, slowly, toward him. When Crouch fixed it with his eye, the other moved behind him. He backed up. They moved sideways. They're playing with him, the sudden thought came to me. Crouch flicked his gaze from one monstrous creature to the other. Glancing arrogantly up and down the first one, he looked disgusted, and then clapped his hands at the creatures. "Hey, hey, you damned beast-os, do what I say-o, quick, quick. Who is master here?"

Then I heard the most terrible, deep gurgling, creaking kind of sound come from way inside the black things. It seemed to be a word. "Belphagor," they said.

After that it was very confusing, because I could see those two big repulsive things must move toward Crouch bit by bit with the flames shooting much farther out of their nostrils and also their ears, as if they were enjoying Crouch backing and frantically shouting orders at them. Then they became sort of shapeless, oozy blobs, and Crouch stopped screaming orders and just screamed the unearthly screams of someone who is being disemboweled alive.

But then the screaming stopped short and there was just the a crunching, slurping sound as those two things huddled like smoky mounds over what was left of Septimus Crouch. Behind the things at the window, the birds sat on the perch, stretching their necks and peering with their curious little eyes at the movement beneath their cage. Robert was lying like a limp rag on the floor, groaning softly. I ran to him and tried to grab him up, but he shook his head, and we huddled still and silent against the wall, our eyes wide with horror, as the two shapeless blobs tore apart the remains of Septimus Crouch and bits of him started disappearing inside them, so I think they were eating him. The curious grumbling and squealing of their conversation had an eerie tone of pleasure and satisfaction to it, and then I was sure they were eating him because I could see them pass each other gory bits and bones the way you would offer a dinner partner a pheasant's wing or some other nice part of a dish, to make the evening more agreeable. After not much of him was left but his clothes, they sort of mopped up the blood puddle he had left the way you would sop up gravy with bread, except they used his cloak, and ate that too.

Robert was shuddering all over and muttering almost inaudibly over and over again, "Dear God, God in heaven, God, God," but I hadn't a word left in me. We could hear a sort of contented humming sound coming out of the imps as they spat out a couple of the smaller bones. We made ourselves very small against the wall, as far as we could from the door, just so they might leave without noticing us, but they just pressed themselves through the far wall when they were done and flew away, leaving a bad smell behind them.

"Are your bones broken?" I whispered, still fearful they might hear us, even though they were gone.

"I don't think so," said Robert, lying still and feeling his limbs. "But, God, I hurt." He pulled his shirt up, and I helped him undo his points so we could see what the thing had done. The dark stains of bruises were spreading on his belly, up his ribs, down his arms. "Close," he said. "Close. I thought it would strangle me. But every time Crouch spoke, it loosened up. I don't think it liked him. Except, perhaps, as dinner."

"Robert—Nan, my Nan is dead."

"We need to get out of here before the Helmsman comes."

"No, Robert, Nan. She must have a Christian burial."

"No, we must flee. Crouch is gone, and who would ever believe us? The Helmsman will accuse you of the murder, Susanna."

"Of my own Nan? Never. Who would ever believe it?"

"It doesn't matter what people believe. The Helmsman is the greatest lord in France, and what he says is what everyone will believe. Then he'll have you, and all within the law. We'll have to hide you and get you out of the country as soon as possible. If only . . . a diplomatic mission . . . only the king's orders could supersede his . . ."

"I won't leave Nan."

"You have to."

"She would never leave me. She died for me. Just look at her poor, cold hand there, just . . ." But as I looked closely for the first time at the horrifying hand, I saw something flash briefly in the flickering rushlight. A hair-thin gold band on the corpse's finger. "Robert, is that a wedding ring I see there?"

"Oh . . . yes, you're right. A ring, a very narrow ring. But Nan was a widow, wasn't she?"

"Nan never wore a ring, Robert. She wasn't married . . . no, that can't be Nan's hand. Robert, can you turn over that body and look at the face for me? I . . . I can't bear it." Robert groaned again as he stood, stepped around the ghastly dark puddle of blood, and turned over the corpse with his foot.

"Susanna, it's your landlady. And look, there's money in the blood beneath her. That's how Crouch got in here. She took the money to let him in." Warm relief rushed through me, and I started to cry. "Nan must still be out looking for you. No, no, don't cry now. The worst is surely over. I'll find Nan for you." Robert drew me up and embraced me, patting my head, my face. "See here, I'll take you to my place and we'll clean up. Then I'll find Nan. I imagine she went to the White Queen's servants to inquire for you and then couldn't come back in the dark. She's safe, she's well. It's you who must be out of here before the Helmsman comes looking for you."

"I can't go without Nan."

"I'll hide you while I find her, Susanna. Before the Helmsman thinks to follow her to find you." I sat down before the ashy hearth of my own fireplace and put my head in my hands. "Don't you understand, Susanna? We have acquired the most powerful enemy in France, save for the king himself. The Connétable de Bourbon commands a great force; he makes his own law. He can do anything to destroy us."

"The Duc de Bourbon. How can I hope to get away from a man like that? How can we get away?"

"It's not as bad as you think, Susanna. It will take him awhile to discover we weren't sealed up successfully, and then he'll have to hunt for us. The problem, the problem ..." He began to pace. "... how to hide two people as obvious as you and Nan while I make the arrangements to get us out of the country. *Hmm.* A diplomatic mission ... the king's orders supersede ... it could be done.... I'd have to borrow money; maybe Suffolk will back us ... while the king supports the treaty, no one will dare touch those in Suffolk's train ... still, Bourbon will surely try to have you arrested on false charges ... how to throw them off the scent?"

"Everything I've worked for—spoiled. What did I do to deserve all this, Robert?" I looked at the mess on the floor where Septimus Crouch used to be. I was a failure, a stupid failure, and all I'd done with my life was nearly cost other people theirs. I started to poke through the rubble to see what could be rescued. Oh, God, that expensive lapis, all draining between the floorboards. Slashed canvas, ruined master drawings, tramped into the sticky mess. At least I found my master drawing for the new commission intact, and there was my little traveling box of painting and drawing things, all in good order in an overlooked corner.

"You? Nothing, Susanna. But they think you have the middle portion of that book they've been hiding." It was almost dawn outside now, and Master Ashford looked all about the shadowy ruins of my studio. He picked up my books. "Your books, at least, aren't ruined. See here?" He handed them to me. "And your birds. Look at them there. They were too frightened to chirp." He took the cage from the hook and made a little chirruping sound at them. They looked at him with their tiny black eyes and smoothed out their wonderfully small feathers and began to hop about the perches as he brought the cage to me. I looked at them very carefully and counted them, just to make sure they were still all there. Still six. One of them made a peeping sound. How strange, they didn't even seem to know they'd saved us. Robert Ashton was walking the length of the room, inspecting the rubble. He kicked at a stack of paper and sketches in a corner beneath the table. "What's this?" he said.

"Just paper and some old parchment I've been reworking," I said, and then suddenly a new thought came so fast that I gasped. "Robert, pick up that raggedy pile of loose vellum there—the sheets that are all cut up."

"The ones that look as if moths have been at them?"

"That pile with all the first pages painted over, and the ink dissolved," I said. He picked up the mass of cut and mangled parchment and eyed it disdainfully.

"What is it?" he asked.

"Robert, it used to be written on in some other language like Latin," I said. "I took off the binding at the edge, and I've been cutting away at it ever since I've had it, but there are still some pages readable. I—I thought Master Dallet had salvaged the parchment for reworking."

"Reworking?" The first pinkish gray light of dawn was beginning to glow through the window. Now I was poking about in the half light, looking for things to rescue. I found my little round framed picture of Hadriel, all done on one of those reused pages, which I'd cleverly made almost like new for my own painting. It was unharmed, facedown in a corner. I blew the ashes and colored dust off it.

"Well, feel it," I said. "Just like silk. It's the best unborn calfskin vellum. It's good for centuries. . . ."

"Susanna, I can't believe it. You should have thrown it out the minute you found it." Oh, here were my master drawings for portraits, and Master Dallet's, too, only speckled in a few places, and still quite usable. They had fallen on my sketch for Madame Claude's angels, which was entirely spoiled. My heart kept grieving in the wreckage, for each little thing that I touched or turned over. Gone, gone. I took two old, spotty paint cloths and gathered up what I could, burnishing tools, knives, unspoiled brushes, with the drawings.

"Throw it out? I had pictures to paint, and unborn parchment, you have no idea how expensive it is. I mean, especially when people won't give you an advance...."

He just shook his head. "It's all smeared and painted over. What's that?"

"I was trying to find ways of getting rid of the writing."

"If I weren't so sick to my stomach, I'd laugh," he said. Then I made two big bundles of what I could and piled what I had saved of my work together and tucked it under my arm, and Robert took my birds in one hand and my case in the other, and we shut the door on the mess that had been my studio with many strange thoughts. But the saddest thought of all that I had was that maybe it was fate because women aren't meant to paint, just as everybody says.

We went first to Master Ashton's rooms in the Three Monkeys, and he had his man make a fire in the big iron brazier to take the chill off, and then sent him for food and drink while we changed and cleaned up. Then he sat down to try to read that cut-up, painted-over pile of parchment, while I sat down in my shift and took needle and thread to mend my dress that I always liked so well but now would never feel the same about. I mean, after something horrible has happened when you're wearing something, it doesn't seem lucky anymore. It seemed beyond the reach of even that powerful soap from my book to clean away the awful feelings that seemed embedded in the wool. "I think I want a new dress," I said, as he nodded without listening and went on reading.

"This is the book, all right. You've taken all the margins off, Susanna. It must be half the size it was, not counting all the holes you've made. That's why he didn't recognize it. It was the wrong size." He was munching on a half loaf of bread from the basket of food that his man had brought back.

"Well, they were the best parts. Why wouldn't I?"

"Look at this—here's a bit I can read. The Latin's bad. Let's see. 'The sacred blood concealed . . . the mystery of the ages . . .' Not much help. I'll try this one, it looks less spotted. Susanna, I still can't believe you did this. Well, I'll be . . . so *that's* the secret of the ages."

"You've found it? I hope it was worth all the trouble it's caused."

"Susanna, it's not a treasure that's sealed up in the so-called fortress of redemption, it's a genealogy. A genealogy of the Merovingians. They claim it's the Holy Grail and contains the blood of the King of Kings."

"I thought the Holy Grail was a cup. Where's the rest of that sausage that Will brought? Ah, yes, a cup. When will Will get back with Nan? There's no danger, is there?"

"Soon, soon, I'm sure," he said distractedly, as he kept on reading. "There's no problem getting her—it's just a matter of making sure she doesn't try to go back to the studio. God knows, there'll be a hue and cry once they find that body." He brushed some crumbs he had let drop from the page, and without really noticing it, picked up the cup and went on reading and drinking at once. "Let's see. *Hmm.* You certainly mangled this bit. Ah, here. Well, well. This genealogy, it seems, is the only true record of the descent of the Merovingians from some royal house in Provence descended from the House of David . . . My God! What heresy! No wonder they've been in hiding so long!" He was so shocked, he put down the cup from which he'd been drinking.

"What is it?"

"They claim that the Merovingians are descended from Our Lord Jesus Christ, who was a true earthly king and evaded crucifixion by a tricky substitution of a criminal at the last minute . . . For that alone, these people could be burned alive by the Inquisition. What on earth makes them cling to this idea? You'd think they'd just be quiet and avoid trouble. Ah, yes, here's the text again."

"He wasn't crucified? How could that be? Then he wouldn't be resurrected, and the Church . . ."

"That's the idea. The Church is founded on a lie. One that it must conceal at all costs."

"Well, I'd think so. They have a lot of treasures at stake. No wonder those Priory people were so secretive. The Church would do anything to root them out. Maybe it is, even now, searching for them."

"Desperate men, Susanna. Desperate men. They'd stop at nothing. *Hmm.* According to this, Jesus went into exile."

"Exile? Where?"

"Well, well. Provence. Not a bad place, what do you think? Convenient, too. And He had descendants, founding a divine race of kings in the South of France ..." My dress was as fixed as it would be. I brushed off as much dirt as I could, then spread the damp spots near the brazier, to dry quicker.

"Why there, Robert? Why not in the Holy Land somewhere? It doesn't make much sense to me."

"Ah, here we are, this is the important part. The genealogy connects the House of David through Jesus Christ to the first Merovingian kings. Ha! No wonder they want to be rid of the Valois! It says here the divine blood is destined to conquer both the Christian and heathen worlds at some time in the future, bringing a permanent reign of peace and happiness on earth, because the Merovingians are descended from God himself." To strengthen himself while thinking about the strange story, Robert resumed eating. In between the steady *munch, munch,* he went on talking. "I wonder if this secret had some influence on the Cathars who held that fortress. How strange. How very strange."

"And just whom did Jesus marry?" I asked, because to a woman, those are always the important questions.

"Mary Magdalene."

"Of course. She was supposed to have settled in Provence, too. I'm glad she didn't stay single."

"Susanna, you are being flippant. This is a terrifying secret, a dangerous secret."

"Robert, it's a totally ridiculous secret. Either Our Lord was crucified and rose again, which proves his divinity and makes it impossible that he sired the Merovingians, or he was just another earthly king who produced a useless line of descendants, which makes him not the Son of God at all. And if they're not descended from the Son of God, then all this big prediction of their permanent reign can't come true. They've got it all mixed up. You can't have it both ways, you know."

"Susanna, you're right. What makes you so shrewd about this?"

"You mean, when I'm so silly about everything else? Think about it, Robert: I know a lot about false relics. This is just another one of them."

Robert shook his head slowly. "What fools. What lunacy. And yet they continue to conspire, century after century."

"It probably makes them happy," I said, thinking of Master Ailwin and his True Religionists.

"The Roman emperors used to claim descent from the gods ..."

"... to impress the gullible. It makes sense. And none of it was worth ruining my studio."

"Your studio!" said Robert with a sudden start, as if recalling himself from some dream. "Susanna, you need to be hidden. This place of mine is the first place Bourbon's men will look for you when they discover we're not at the studio."

"I've thought it through," I said, looking at my bundles of salvaged drawings, panels, and tools, where they sat mournfully in the middle of Robert's floor. The birds, awake from the sound and the light in the brazier, hopped up and down in the cage that sat on the floor near the fire. There wasn't much left from all my adventures here in the royal court. Crouch had even slashed up my clothes. There was nothing but what I stood up in. "I'm going to the Duchesse d'Alençon. The Duchess Marguerite will hide me."

"You can't do that. She is a dear friend and supporter of Bourbon. She and her mother advance his cause every day."

"You think like a man, Robert. I will tell her that he tried to seduce me, and I spurned his advances, and now he seeks vengeance. She knows what they are, those courtiers. She has protected humble women of virtue even against her brother."

"The Duchess Marguerite ... who would have thought it?" he mused. Then he sprang into action. "I'll find Will and bring your woman to you at Les Tournelles. That leaves you time to try to get an audience with the duchess by this afternoon. Blame Crouch for everything. His disappearance will look suspicious. Yes, the Duchess Marguerite. She is our only hope."

"Here," said the Duchess of Alençon, "you mustn't cry so. You just need to hide awhile until his eye wanders elsewhere." The long shadows of afternoon were spreading over the Parc des Tournelles outside, and a feeble breeze, laden with the cool of coming evening, had entered through the open window to stir the hangings on the walls. She was sitting at the table in her cabinet, writing. Then her own eye looked up and lit on my ruined dress. It ran over my shabby little pile of belongings, my bird cage, and my little case. Slowly, she shook her head with wonderment at the wickedness of men. "Take this letter to my dear friend, the Abbess of Sainte-Honorine. I say here that it is an affair of honor and you are an honest woman with great skill at the brush. You and your servant will be welcome there as long as you like, and I'm sure they'll find projects for you to earn your keep. As I recall, they've an altarpiece that needs repainting, and some of your angels would look very good in the sanctuary." I wiped my eyes.

"How will I get there?" I asked.

"I'll have two horses from my husband's stable and send my own lackeys as an escort. Imagine! Destroying your studio in vengeance for your scorning him! A woman's virtue, oh, it's so hard to keep these days. One is pressured from every side. . . ." I looked at her with new eyes. Who was it who was pressuring her? Suddenly I was grateful to him, whoever he was, for he made my lie believable, whereas the truth would have made me look like the greatest liar in the world.

"I . . . I'd like to leave right away."

"Oh, you *must* leave before evening. A man of great rank, such as you describe, would think nothing of forcing himself into your bed." She poured sand across the letter to dry it, then sealed it with a bit of candle wax and handed it to me. "Here. And don't forget to have the abbess send me my miniatures when they are done."

"I will not, madame, and God bless you," I said, curtseying profoundly and then backing out of her cabinet in the greatest respect.

That night Nan and I, my case loaded behind us, and I still clutching my birdcage in one hand, rode double on the frozen road to the north, behind the Duchess of Alençon's armed servants. Tense and terrified, I listened for the sound of following hoofbeats but heard only silence, the rustling of barren branches, and the ringing of our own horses' steel shoes on the iron-hard earth beneath the pale, winter half-moon. In the dark, I worried endlessly. How would Robert

Ashton save me from Bourbon's lackeys and take me home? What would happen if the Duchesse Marguerite told my story at a dinner party, and Bourbon heard, and guessed where I was? Would I have to live in a convent forever, just when it seemed that I might be happy with Robert Ashton? Suppose something terrible happened to him and he never found me? At last, all I did was pray. Home, dear God, I want to go home.

"You have to marry me, you have to! Take me away! Take me home! Didn't you once send me tokens of your affection? Your portrait, which I wore in my bosom until the day of my marriage? Did you not swear eternal devotion and fealty? Now prove it! Prove all those words you have said to me!" The White Queen's face was red and swollen as she wept and clung to the Duke of Suffolk's gown. They were alone in the darkened chamber; the king had granted him a solitary audience and sent away the French women. Yet even that had not set the alarm bell ringing in Suffolk's thick head. But even he had sensed some of the elements of the dilemma, though it was a strain to hold more than one idea at a time in his brain. At first, he had feared King Henry. A man who elopes with his sovereign's sister must properly pay with his head. Then, he had feared King Francis. The man hated him. He could destroy the purpose of his embassy, at the very least, and then he would be in King Henry's disfavor anyway. But on the other hand, Francis could do anything. He certainly wouldn't be the first absolute ruler to imprison or destroy an ambassador he didn't care for. But how could he get out of marrying Mary Tudor without offending King Francis? He didn't like the way Francis smiled at him, as if he had it all figured out already.

But all this was before he confronted the whirlwind of passion contained in the White Queen's chamber. Queen Mary, crazy with long confinement, had flung herself on him, her long red-gold hair flowing loose, her white gown crumpled and tearstained. And she was every bit as willful and stubborn as her brother. As a hurricane of words stormed about him, he tried to retreat but found the door barred. She was very lovely—he had once thought it would be very pleasant with her. But his head? He couldn't.

"Oh, what kind of a knight are you? Aren't you sworn to protect widows? Protect me! Marry me, or I will think you the falsest creature in the whole world. I will tell my brother, I will tell everyone. Charles Brandon, false knight and betrayer! Why do you delay? Don't you love me? Are you afraid of my brother?" Numbly, Suffolk nodded. "Then know this, my brother promised me I should wed as I wished, after I was queen in France, and I shall remind him of this promise."

"But . . . but, I would do you every service, but . . ."

"Oh, disgrace! You have broken my heart!" cried the girl-queen, flinging herself on the bed and weeping passionately, in great, gusty sobs.

Suffolk sat down on the bed beside the convulsing body and tried to stroke her, to calm her. Women. Incomprehensible, mindless, too many humors. She might die of all this sobbing, and then where would he be?

"I . . . I have always admired you," he said, tentatively. The wild sobbing continued. "You are the sister of my sovereign, my lady, and I would do . . ."

"Marry me," came the muffled demand from the pillow.

"I will marry you, my lady. I pledge you my troth, here and now." One swollen, tearstained eye turned up from the pillow.

"Really?" she said.

"In truth, and most honorably, I do beg you to marry me." Anything, anything to stop that infernal weeping.

"Take me from this horrible place," she said.

"That I promise," he answered, relieved.

Outside, Francis and several of his courtiers were waiting.

"Well?" asked the king. "What said the White Queen to your suit?"

"She has accepted, Your Grace." Francis winced internally at the hidden insult. Once again, the Duke of Suffolk had not addressed him as king. Was he acting under orders from the English king? The man never quit. Suffolk deserved everything that was in store for him. His king would behead him for treason, and the White Queen would be so thoroughly disgraced by marrying beneath her that she could no longer become the center of plots against his throne. Any current or future pregnancy would be laid at the door of this petty English duke.

All that, and he would take her out of the country as soon as possible. Perfect.

"Congratulations, my dear chevalier," said Francis. "I have already summoned the priest to my chapel. I myself will serve as a witness."

Only later did Charles Brandon begin to comprehend the true outline of Francis's plot against him. Disgrace, ruin, death, all encompassed with a woman. How French. He sat, pale faced, in the apartments given him and his new wife by the French king.

"My lord, you must not sit like that, staring at nothing," said Queen Mary, who had decided to retain her title, despite marrying a duke.

"We are ruined," said her new husband.

"I think not," said Mary, firmly. "But you must give up my dowry to my brother. He thinks a great deal of money." Brandon, the man who had married before, for dowry money, did not catch the irony in her voice.

"I will write to my brother and remind him of his promise at the waterside." The duke was silent, still brooding. "I will write to Archbishop Wolsey, and he will smooth my brother's mind," said his wife. The duke looked up at her. How could she not understand what would become of him?

"But first, you must write the news to my brother, before he hears of it from elsewhere. The man must write first. I can only write after you have told him." She took out paper and ink and laid them on the writing desk. "I'll leave if you want," she said.

"It will take time," he said, beginning to feel his hands sweat. What could he say? How would he start? The duke was no writer. Alone in the room, he crumpled start after start and threw them away before the lackey came in to light the candles. Perspiration was pouring down his forehead, and he could barely grasp the pen in his big, sweaty hands. I'll write Wolsey first, he thought, and he'll mend what can be mended. How to explain? It was easier to Wolsey: "The queen would never let me be at rest til I granted her to be married," he wrote. "And so to be plain with you, I have married her heartily, and have lain with her, insomuch I fear me lest she be with child." Ah, that made it easier, he thought. But what shall I tell the king? How can I make him understand? At last the pen scratched across the page, offering this as his only explanation for the tangle: "I newar sawe woman soo wyepe." Spelling was never the duke's strong point.

Archbishop Wolsey sat close to the fire in his paneled cabinet in York House. Outside was a fog so thick that no man could see his hand before his face. The chill was everywhere.

"Master Warren, add to the letter I have written to my lord of Suffolk that never have I known man in such mortal danger. He must not return to England until the king's wrath has faded. Ah, the fool, the fool." Wolsey sighed heavily. His policy was in ruins. The Queen of France was returning in disgrace, and it would take all his wiles to make sure she was not soon a widow for the second time. Francis, who cared little for the treaty, would be king. Already, French ship captains were seizing English ships, and Francis had not hindered them. What would come next? England could not face war with France without allies. Must Wolsey's king endure the infinite pricking insults of the new French king?

Ah, but here was Tuke at the door with a new mountain of correspondence. Something about Tuke's face irritated him. Ever since Ashton had left, the man seemed to be expanding like a toad. The pleasant pliability had become more weasel-like. I need to set him down, thought Wolsey. I think I shall favor Master Warren for a while. Ah, would that it were so easy to set down King Francis the First. Silently, he opened once again a little wooden case and looked at the face of his adversary. Young, but sly and foxy beyond his years. Arrogant. Lascivious. Willful. A fierce and devious enemy, with a smiling, glittering surface. The portrait said it all.

"Another letter from the Queen of France, Your Grace, and one in cipher from Master Ashton. There is also another little packet."

"At last. What has he been doing over there, anyway? I've had nothing for over a month, since he sent me some rubbish about a conspiracy in the south of France and this portrait of King Francis. Useless dithering. Master Tuke, I'll want the letter decoded at once." Tuke snapped a finger at the code clerk, who bowed to hide the anger in his eyes, then sat to decipher the letter. While he labored with code wheel and candle flame, Tuke, still as smooth as silk, showered Wolsey with flattering, amusing remarks. With rising irritation, Warren heard Wolsey's responses. My lord of York was clearly charmed. Who works, and who flatters? thought Warren, gouging the paper with his pen, so that the quill split and splattered, and he had to sharpen another.

As the decoding proceeded, Wolsey undid the oiled silk and, with a pleasurable anticipation, opened another of the familiar little wooden cases. At least Mistress Dallet serves me well, he thought. Staring up at him were a pair of resentful dark eyes, implanted like smoldering brands in a narrow, arrogant face. Ambition, betrayal, and war were written there. And to think, thought Wolsey, he was probably delighted to sit for this, never realizing he was betraying every secret. Splendid, splendid. Who was this? Ah, the Duke of Bourbon. Constable of France. A bold commander. Definitely a man to be watched.

"Your Grace, your letter here," said Tuke at last, with a deft movement handing the archbishop the product of the code clerk's labors.

"Fascinating, fascinating. There was a failed conspiracy to take the throne, led by the Duc de Bourbon." Well, well. As one mind-compartment in the archbishop's brain began to work over the idea of this new conspiracy, another began simultaneously to calculate about the writer of the letter. So Ashton has joined forces with the paintrix? He couldn't have made it clearer if he'd written it. Ha, this must be his latest method of trying to worm his way around Tuke. Suppose he wishes to consolidate his position by marrying her? I imagine I might allow it—after all, it will keep her in my service. I'll make him promise me that she continue to paint. Ah, how delightfully that will offend him! Should I cut her wages after she is wed? Perhaps I'll raise his by the amount I lower hers. After all, they shouldn't starve. I think I'll begin by opposing the wedding. I'll denounce it, just to see the look on his face. Yet even as this mind-compartment generated a certain enjoyment, the first one was still churning with the news in the letter.

"Bourbon's role in this has not been discovered, and he continues to ingratiate himself with King Francis daily. The conspirators—ha, they are fools. Next time, Bourbon will choose a more powerful group of allies." Bourbon, calculated this mind-compartment in Wolsey's brain, heir to half the territory of France, with some slight claim to the throne. If Francis were wise, he would behead him instantly on some false charge. In statecraft, Francis is still young, thought Wolsey. Then he leaned back in his great oak chair and thought, tapping his fingers on the wooden arm of the chair, Yes, yes. Bourbon. Interesting. I think I might wait until he shows overt signs of discontent, then contact him. Let's see. An alliance with the emperor and Bourbon against Francis. It could be done, Wolsey thought. Bourbon would split France in half, and Francis would come begging for the old alliance again. And I, I could choose . . .

"Your Grace," said Tuke, interrupting Wolsey's musings. Quietly, the archbishop filed it in yet another mind-compartment, under "Alliances, Treacherous," which was not far from "Cardinalate, Progress On," and "Hampton Court, Rebuilding of Waterworks Of."

"Ah, yes, Tuke, the latest letter from the Queen of France. How *shall* we disentangle her?" he asked.

"Ah, Madame la Duchesse was right. This is lovely work," said the abbess. She was seated at the great desk in her plain, whitewashed cabinet. Marguerite d'Alençon's letter was open in front of her, and she was looking through what remained of my sketches and little paintings. Nuns came in and out on errands, and also the head of her gardening staff, who was a man, and the nuns' confessor, who was an old priest with so little gray hair left that he didn't need a tonsure. Nan and I sat together, waiting to see what else she'd say. "It is a great enterprise, a convent of this size. I am sorry I have not been able to give your story uninterrupted attention. Ah! What is this angel? He is the loveliest thing you have brought."

"Madame, that is the angel Hadriel."

"Hadriel? I have heard of Gabriel, Uriel, Raphael, and Michael, but never a Hadriel."

"He appeared to me in a dream once. I drew him as I saw him."

"You are fortunate, to be able to draw out your dreams. Did he give you a message?" She sounded very professional. I guess abbesses know a lot about people with visions and dreams.

"Well, actually, he did, but I never understood what he meant. So I just drew his picture and kept on as I was." The abbess smiled.

"Usually people amend their lives when they are given such a dream. Just what was it he said?"

"He said if I could catch the rainbow with my hands, I could keep it. But I've never done it because it's obviously impossible, and all it's done is rain ever since I came here into France except for when it's snowing, and I've never even seen one bit of rainbow. It was all just nonsense. But nice nonsense, I guess. Maybe if I'd been a better person, I might have been granted a dream I could understand."

"Oh, what a strange message! What did you do after that?"

"Well, my husband was killed, and so I made my living painting."

"*Hmmm,*" said the abbess, as she tapped one finger on her desk and looked into the air. "I'm thinking of your interpretation. It's not easy. I will ask for guidance. Visions and dreams, they always have meaning. You are meant to do something, and obviously you haven't done it, or you wouldn't be in all this trouble. Well, I am asking Sister Claire here to show you and your companion two beds in our dormitory. Are you good at gilding? We have manuscript illuminators and copyists here in great plenty, but Sister Agatha, who did our gilding, passed on not so long ago, leaving the regilding of the altarpiece only half done."

The next few days were very peaceful and regular. There were prayers and singing every two hours which is soothing to the mind and makes a person forget evil pale green eyes shining insanely in the dark and also shapeless black things that eat people, at least for a little while. The birds had to live in the kitchen because the rules said no animals even though everyone was hiding cats and little dogs just about everywhere and besides it was warmer there. Nan was so very worried about me, and also so prying, that at last I cried and cried and told her about Crouch's end due to the horrible black things from hell that he summoned up.

Nan promised to keep it a secret, but then it worked on her mind so much that she had to tell the abbess all about the great wickedness of the lord who pursued me and how he studied evil arts to work his wicked way and had black things from hell for his servants, all in strictest secrecy. Then she took to helping in the laundry because she said it would take all the washing in the world to wash out the very thought of those black things, and soon she was remembering that she saw them herself, just as she so often saw the Devil and other menacing Signs that proved the end of the world was coming. After that, everybody was asking her about the fiery black devils that were sent by a wicked practitioner of sorcery all because I wouldn't give him my virtue. And of course Nan told them all in strictest secrecy, and they were very scandalized but I was so happy to have my Nan back again that I just couldn't resent her for telling my secret over and over and being so happy making a sensation among all those holy ladies.

As for me, there were many things to mend such as a very pretty little Madonna who had gotten rained on by accident from a leak in the ceiling and also some old pictures of abbesses that were not well done and the paint had come off. I think they must have kept them in some cellar where the damp got them, they looked that bad. I also worked on those miniatures for the duchess, and so you see hiding was really very pleasant except for the worry that bad people would come, because I was very tired of bad people altogether. I decided that if I were an old woman, this would be the best way to spend my time, but just now I was too young, because the thought of Robert Ashton was always in my mind and that showed I did not have the makings of a nun.

The afternoon had brought out the sun, where it sparkled on the frosty branches and frozen puddles in the road, but still, men's and horses' breath showed like steam. Across the rolling, frozen landscape, two riders on little, winter-coated horses made their way, leading behind them a packhorse with a packsaddle only half laden. Robert Ashton and his man, heavily bundled against the cold, paused at the crossroad. Two narrow tracks, rutted, pawed up, half-frozen mud, crossed the winter-bare fields and seemed to meander nowhere. Which one was right? Beyond the crossroad, a track led to an ice-choked stream, and a little village of shapeless thatched huts, smoke escaping from their roof peaks.

"Down there," said Ashton. "They'll know the way." A barefoot, sooty-faced woman answered their knock.

"The convent?" she said. "It's easy. Follow the road to the north, the one marked with fresh hoofprints. There's a dozen armed men ahead of you, and if you hurry, you can catch up. It's no good travelin' alone like you are, these days." She watched as the two men glanced at each other in alarm. "If you be wantin' to avoid them, take the other road," she said.

"Did they say who they were?" asked Robert Ashton.

"Soldiers from the Connétable de Bourbon. But *they* paid me," she said. Ashton leaned over in the saddle and pressed a couple of sous into her hand.

"How far is it from here?"

"Oh, three or four hours' ride—that is, if your horse don't slip on this ice and break a leg." The riders returned to the road and, despite the risk of ice, pushed their horses to a trot.

"Pilgrims, eh?" said the captain. "Why pilgrims in this season?"

"A vow to my mother on her deathbed," said Robert Ashton. "I've never seen the place. Almost got lost looking for it. I hope they've a good guest house. I don't want to ride on in this cold."

"You'd best ride back with us, when we've made the arrest. There are robbers on this road, even in this season."

"An arrest?" Ashton made his voice sound merely curious.

"A criminal. A murderess, who has taken sanctuary. Who'd believe it, eh? Women are getting as bad as men these days."

"It's the times," said Ashton, shaking his head sympathetically. Ahead of them, on a low rise of ground, were the convent buildings, plain whitewashed stone, almost barnlike in their simplicity, huddled together around a church with a tall, unornamented steeple. At a distance from the other buildings, but still inside the abbey walls, could be seen the pointed, slate roof of the kitchen building, smoke boiling from its chimneys. The great gates were barred from within. While his men waited, the captain rode to the gate and shouted. There was no answer. With a gauntleted hand, he lifted the iron knocker and battered it against the door. Still no answer. After he had repeated the process several times, a little wooden shutter behind a tiny grille beside the gate opened, and half a woman's face appeared.

"We are from the Connétable de Bourbon, with orders for an arrest. Is one Suzanne Dolet, a painter, hiding within?"

"We have here a woman who claims the right of sanctuary. You must wait forty days before Suzanne Dolet must leave." A murmur of threats came from the armed soldiers, with coarse suggestions of what they might do if crossed.

"What is this nonsense?" replied the captain to the face in the grille. "Let us in now. You are ordered to do so."

"It is not our custom to admit armed men to our holy precincts," said the face, firmly.

"You had best consider changing that custom, or we shall set fire to the gate and enter anyway."

"Let me consult with the abbess," said the face, and the little shutter banged shut. While the horses stamped and moved about in the cold, the armed men waited, the captain cursing all the while. Ashton's mind was teeming with ideas. If he could only get in ahead of them . . .

But his hopes were dashed when the face reappeared at the grille.

"Monsieur Captain," a different half-face said, "we would be delighted to open our gates immediately to you, but we must warn you that there is plague inside our community." The captain shuddered and several of the soldiers crossed themselves. But still the captain persisted.

"Where is Suzanne Dolet?"

"Alas, Monsieur Captain, she is one of several who have received the last rites. They are lying in our poor little infirmary, awaiting the inevitable meeting with the eternal."

"I cannot leave on your word alone. How do I know you are not deceiving me?"

"There is no doubt that by morning she will be dead. Do not disturb the dying, monsieur. Even your orders do not require that you risk infecting yourself. In the morning, those who have perished will be laid before the high altar for the funeral service. Come then, satisfy your eyes for the sake of your master and your orders, and leave before you risk death. That is our abbess's suggestion. She says also that she regrets not offering you the hospitality of our guest house, but under the circumstances, you might prefer billeting your troops in the village below the abbey."

Ashton hid his face from the others as they turned away from the gate. Dying! After all this, after all his plans, his ingenuity. And he was not even there to say a word of comfort to her, to hear her last breath, to breathe the infection and die with her. What bitterness, what evil was in the world. God Himself was evil, to taunt a man so by showing him love and then snatching it away. What was the good of anything? The plague. Evil, monstrous disease. He could not even touch her corpse. He thought of her, looking at the little birds in the bird market, evicting the glue pot from its place of honor in her fireplace to make him dinner, of her little, short-fingered hands moving with precise delicacy over one of her tiny paintings. Then, in spite of himself, he thought of her rollicking, vulgar Eves. There was no other such woman in the world, he thought. I found her, through a miracle, and now I have lost her.

I was hard at work on that Madonna under the rain leak when there was a great sound of scurrying sandals with the abbess came in all hurrying, followed by several of her nuns.

"There are armed men at the gate, Maîtresse Suzanne, armed men who have come for you. They say they will not go without you. Our gates are not strong enough to keep them out. If I hide you here, they threaten to tear the convent apart. I have no choice but to give you up."

"Give me up? Who are these men, that they can defy the king's own sister?"

"Soldiers of the Connétable de Bourbon, the greatest warlord in France. They claim they have orders for your arrest. I have no desire to let them in, and I would obey the dear duchess in all things, but I dare not keep them out any longer."

"My arrest? But I've done nothing."

"You know that, I know that, but we must let the judges decide."

"But . . . but, tell them to wait."

"I have done that already. They say they will wait until the crack of doom, and not so much as a mouse will get out of here. I fear that they are planning to break sanctuary. God knows what will happen once they are inside. You must give yourself up. I would keep you if I could, but they know you are here, and I have no choice." There is nothing like mortal fear to speed the mind. Mine was working very desperately, trying to escape those wicked soldiers outside.

"Wait, tell them I am deathly ill."

"What good will that do?"

"Tell them it is pestilence, and is catching."

"They'll hardly believe me unless I produce a body." That is where an idea came to me and I smiled, and the abbess looked at me very curiously.

"Oh, but you can produce a body," I said. "God has just in this moment showed me a very excellent idea. An inspiration, really. You can make the captain happy, you can make the Duchesse d'Alençon happy, and you can make God happy by doing the right thing. It's all come to me. But we'll need a night."

"A night? I think I can delay them that much. But what do you mean, an idea?"

"Well," I answered, "I'll need some help, and a very large beeswax candle, and plaster . . ."

"For what would you use these things?"

"For deception, Holy Mother. For taking a life mask and a model of my hands. Can you keep them from touching the body?"

"Of a plague victim? I believe so." I could see that the abbess, for the first time, had begun to smile. I could tell it pleased her, not to give me up. She could deceive the seducer and have a wonderful story to tell the duchess next time she visited. We both knew how Duchess Marguerite loved a good story—why, it would probably be worth a very substantial donation. We looked each other in the eye, the abbess and I, and we understood each other perfectly.

"Good, start right away," she said, because she was a woman accustomed to command.

We worked most of the night, waiting until morning for new light to finish up the coloring. First I changed my clothes for a novice's habit and we stuffed my old ones with straw. The plaster molds of my face and my crossed hands had come out absolutely perfectly the first time.

"Where did you learn this?" asked the abbess as she watched us work in the evening before the light failed.

"Painters cast molds all the time—of limbs, of things they need to draw. You can't get the shadows right otherwise, and who stays still long enough to model an elbow?"

"*Hmm.* Makes sense. I can see that it's not simple, the new art. Though I do prefer the old. All the faces looking alike, and just hands, feet, and draperies. And halos. I find a good halo inspirational. This fashion for nudity in art is most unseemly. And as for that little bit of glowing stuff that passes for a halo these days, well, it just isn't much."

"Oh, I agree completely," I said, as I tinted the melted wax and poured it into the molds.

"What's the color you're using? People are pink."

"Live people. Dead ones are bluish gray. I'll paint on some livid sores when we're done. I don't want to look too pretty on my bier." The abbess laughed.

"Most people don't get the choice," she said.

In the morning they tolled the death knell and opened all the windows of the church and the door, too, so that those outside the gates could hear all the chanting. I was just finishing up some very terrifying-looking open sores when the abbess came in to inspect.

"Magnificent," she said. "But where did you get the hair?"

"See here?" I said, lifting up a corner of my coif. "It's mine." There was nothing left on my head but a mass of gingery curls cut very close like a boy's, but then there is really nothing I wouldn't sacrifice for verisimilitude in a case like this. I'd even cut out little hairs like eyelashes and planted them in the wax.

"Just look at all the colors you've used," said the abbess. "Even more than a live face, I imagine."

"Oh, no. You'd be surprised how many colors it takes to make a human face. You have to start with underpainting, then lay other colors on top, to throw the face from flat into round."

"Why do they always start the saints out in green?"

"That's terre verte. You have to start with a midtone, then build up and down from that. For the miniatures, I begin with a mix of ceruse and red lead, sometimes with a bit of massicot. Then I build all the way to pale yellow or the whitest pink for highlights, and shade back with a mix of blue. Black makes muddy shadows."

"You've used almost all your colors even before you begin the gowns," she observed.

"Oh, yes, all the colors are in the human face." The abbess looked very strange.

"All the colors are in the rainbow," she said.

"That's true. I guess you might say there's a rainbow in each human face. The tones are just different, depending on the person," I answered, painting some gory ooze down my wax hands. "And then, of course, none of them are as bright as rainbow colors," I added, thinking.

"Maîtresse Suzanne, I understand what the angel was telling you," said the abbess, all of a sudden. I looked up from my work at her. What a time to be worrying about dreams! Soldiers were about to batter down her gate, and we were risking everything in a very dangerous deception that could lead to everything getting burned down and maybe some of us being killed if they discovered it. But religious people, they're odd. "The angel told you to do just what you are doing. Paint. Paint humanity."

I just stood and looked at her. Here I was painting up my own corpse to deceive assassins and I'd only finished half my commission for the duchess and Master Ashton had probably been killed and there was no living way I could get home again. If that's a blessing, I'd hate to know what a curse is. "Well, maybe you're right," I said, just to be agreeable. "Now look, I'd say you can let them in."

The abbess directed her nuns to lay the "body" on the bier before the high altar. I was very pleased with my work because it did look like me and especially ghastly, and no one who loved his life would come anywhere near it. Then the abbess opened the gates and escorted the captain of those troops in herself and made him take off his helmet in the church. I hid up in the loft because an artist always likes to see the impression her work makes, and I was very proud of the job I'd done and in only one night and part of a day, too.

"We, of course, have no fear of death, for it is but a gateway to the other world, but you might not wish to come any closer," she said, in a pious whisper. The guard looked as if he did not want to stay.

"Plague, you say?"

"Yesterday morning she laid down her brush, here in this very church. See that little Madonna? Now it will never be repaired. And the face half done. What a pity. She cried out, 'Oh, God, what pain' and we saw she was perishing of fever. Plague—it takes a soul so quickly. If you fall ill in the morning, you must write your will before evening ..." The guards had backed out the door, but the abbess persisted in following them, telling them how if they caught a disease in a blessed place like this it would probably take a million years off their stay in purgatory, so they should count themselves lucky.

They left my body set up just in case the soldiers should come back, and after the morning meal, I went back just to admire it and found the abbess walking about it, chin in hand, thinking and talking to herself.

"A pity," she was saying. "An incorruptible body, so nicely made. A martyr to chastity, taken by God to protect her heavenly crown from a seducer. What a waste. A shrine, now, something cool, like a crypt below ground level with a grille, where it wouldn't melt ..." but I hesitated to come and greet her and disturb her holy thoughts, so I stayed in the shadows of the side chapel. It was then that I saw a dark, bundled figure of a man in prayer beneath that poor little half-repaired Madonna where we had left my brushes and paints artistically scattered to make a better impression. Could it be Robert Ashton? I heard the man groan and then start weeping, and I was sure it was him. My heart wanted to run right to him, but then I thought a person must be cautious and make sure before embracing the wrong person. Also a very tiny wicked thought came to me as well. You see, not many people can find out what people really think of them when they are dead, and I was very gratified to see that Master Ashton cared so much about me. It all had to do with that speckle in my heart that was sharp and cold like ice, and even though it had done much shrinking in all that we had been through together, it was not yet altogether gone, and did so prick when I heard him calculating his advantage. And seeing just how sorry he was about my being dead really seemed to be the final proof that he was not a deceiver like other men, but really loved me for myself. So you see how tempted I was just to wait a little bit and see what else he would do before flinging my arms around him to make a happy ending.

"Too late! Gone! Like that! Oh, monstrous!" he cried. "Cruel God, take me with her!" He rose suddenly and approached the high altar, where the abbess, still thinking holy thoughts, appeared to be in prayer. "I must touch her," he cried. "I wasn't here to console her in death, now I will hold her icy hand and pledge my eternal troth!" I had never suspected that Robert Ashton had such a dramatic, poetic side, that is, being a privy secretary and rather rational at most times.

"Stop, stop! It's certain death!" cried the abbess, fearful that our deception would be revealed.

"How can you understand, Reverend Mother? I waited too long, and now I can never prove to her that I loved her above all things. What coldness! What bitterness! Had I not feared my patron's wrath, we would have died as man and wife. How small, how cowardly I was in the face of her great love. I swear before you now I will kiss her cold lips for the last time, and we will be wedded in death," cried Master Ashton in a frenzy, pushing past the shocked abbess. I tiptoed up closer, to see everything, because it was truly the most sadly beautiful poetical scene and beyond anything I could have imagined. My heart felt absolutely warm with love for him. What excellent, devoted passion! Tears even started coming, it was so tragical to see him there falling on my lovely work of art.

Slowly, his lips approached the bluish ones. He had shut his eyes. He pressed his warm ones to the cold ones...

"What the ...!" he cried, as he opened his eyes suddenly and pulled back his head as if he had kissed a snake. "What *is* this thing?" he said, poking my straw body with a finger while he stared at the wax head.

"Robert, Robert, don't blame the abbess. It was my idea," I called out, for I was still almost halfway the length of the nave behind him. He whirled around toward the sound of my voice. His face was still tear streaked, but now it was red, too.

"I should have known," he said.

"Robert, it was a deception. I had to fool the guards and get them to go away. I didn't intend to deceive you. ..."

"But you just couldn't resist, could you?"

I came out of the shadows and into a ray of sunlight that came down all colored through a stained-glass window. He looked very good but awfully disturbed, and I suppose I should have been ashamed not to have told him right away, but I was very glad to know he loved me so highly as to join me in death, which may be excessively melodramatic, but a good sign always. "Oh, Robert, who couldn't love a man who would follow her to the tomb?"

"At least you know I'm not false," he said, still embarrassed and angry. "But . . . but, you are considerably better not blue."

"I did a good job, didn't I?"

"Good enough. When will you quit deceiving people?"

"I can't help it, Robert. It just comes over me. It's natural. You know that's the way I am. I mean, I was in so much trouble. The connétable de Bourbon. That's not a small enemy, you know."

"I know," he said, and his face grew soft.

"But you know my heart's honest," I said, hoping he would forgive me this small sin and consider instead how badly I had been betrayed before and see it was a natural sort of thing to do when a person wants to make very, very sure that she is loved.

"That I do know," he said. He looked first from me, then at my excellently made corpse, then back again. Then he sighed, then he smiled, then he laughed. He laughed until he doubled over and the tears came out of his eyes, and the abbess said, "*shh!*," and then he said, "Susanna, have you any idea of how relieved I am? Here I thought I would die of a loathsome disease and join you in the grave. My life had become an empty shell without you. Now here you are, and I will live, and I'm not sure why, except that's the way you are. You know it, I know it. You have led me such a dance since the day I first saw you." Again, he shook his head, as if he couldn't believe what he was seeing. He really was very attractive and just quirky enough to please me, with his funny mind, which gave birds instead of a silver mirror. "If I had any sense," he was saying, not understanding how I was looking at him, "I'd want to change you. How fortunate for me that it's impossible! There was a time I thought you'd scorn to marry, to leave your high patrons in France, and all that is grand and glittering. And what living could I give you if the archbishop cast me out for my contumaciousness? And you, I thought you'd be counting every shilling from the match in advance, just as every other woman in the world would. What woman loves a man without a place? Why didn't I understand . . . you are not like any other woman?" He looked at me so tenderly, I thought I might weep, but I didn't, and instead, I felt as if my heart had doubled, tripled, inside my chest.

"Ah, God," he said, shaking his head, "it was the pride in me that feared your refusal. But now, if I asked . . ."

"Then ask, Robert, and see what I say."

"Susanna, will you marry me? Now? Here? No matter what the future?"

"Yes I will, Robert, with the most loving heart in the world." We had spoken in English, but the abbess broke into our conversation in French.

"I take it he has made a proposal. Is it decent or indecent?"

"Decent, Holy Mother. Is there a priest who can marry us here?" asked Robert Ashton. "I have passage with the servants of the Duke and Duchess of Suffolk and want to take Mistress Susanna home with me as my wife. We must hurry if we are to catch them before they leave Paris."

"Duke and Duchess? Robert, whom did the Duke marry?" I asked.

"He married the White Queen in secret, and it's only now public."

"The princess? I always thought she had eyes for him. How did it happen?"

"Redheaded women, Susanna. They always get their own way."

"I am *not* redheaded, Master Ashton. It's only a little gingery tint. But if we are married, Robert, will you let me paint?"

"See what I mean? I'd never take it from you, Susanna. It means too much to you. But you must swear: no more false corpses, no more posthumous paintings, no more naked Adam and Eves."

"I swear, Robert." It was easy to swear. I never do the same thing twice, anyway. Besides, this time I was going to follow the virtues in my Good Wyfe's book much more closely and also try the recipe for bream again. Robert once mentioned liking bream, and besides, it was Lent.

The Thirteenth Portrait

Infant with Finches. *Artist unknown. Flemish, ca. 1500. 30 × 21".* *Silverpoint, heightened with red and black chalk. The Hermitage Museum, Saint Petersburg.*

   With a liveliness more characteristic of the depiction of putti in the Italian works of the period, the unknown artist has presented us with a real baby, propped up in a laundry basket in the shade, attempting to grasp the finches which perch on a branch just above its reach. Note particularly the delicacy of the work around the face and hands, and the Italianate influence on the treatment of the folds of the infant's gown and blankets. Despite the informality of the pose and expression, so different from the portrayals of aristocratic children of the period, this is clearly intended as a portrait, possibly of the artist's own child.

                              —*Michaels, P.* Flemish Drawings of the Renaissance

The little silver bell on the door of the gallery on the Pont au Change rang, but the visitors stepped right through the door. There was a flurry and a twittering, and the curly-headed cherubs abandoned their dice on the counter and vanished through the ceiling.

"So, Hadriel, we've found you at last. Look at you here! Just what do you think you are doing?" Uriel's voice was deep and fierce. Behind him stood Michael the Archangel with his fiery sword.

"Do put that sword away, Michael. You'll set fire to some of my *objets d'art*," said Hadriel, thoroughly unrepentant.

"We have informed the Father that you have abandoned your duty. I wouldn't be surprised if he demotes you for this, Hadriel."

"It was all an inspiration. It just came over me, you understand. I imagine you haven't had any inspirations in simply ages, or you'd be considerably more understanding. Look here, see all these lovely things that have been created? I do my job ten times as fast with my new method. I've covered this whole city with a web of inspiration, and next month I'm opening up several branch operations. What do you think of Amsterdam?"

"We think you are a troublemaker, Hadriel. You've set the whole world on its ear again. And where do we find you? *Keeping a shop.* It's lowly, that's what. It tarnishes our reputation."

"Is that all you care about? I'd say an angel ought to do what has to be done. You're even more snobbish than the seraphim. I've never been afraid to get my hands dirty, like *some* I know. Why, I've even boxed Belphagor, and what thanks do I get?"

The two archangels conferred briefly. "Boxed Belphagor? How did you do that?" Hadriel seated himself on his counter, kicking his bare feet and examining his fingernails.

"Don't you wish you knew," he said.

"Hadriel, you lack respect."

"Oh, I have lots of respect. I have respect for my job. I have respect for being an angel. I have respect for the Father, too. How do you know this wasn't all His idea, anyway? After all, He knows everything, before and after time, alpha and omega, the whole lot." Michael scratched his head in bewilderment.

"Nevertheless, you're coming with us," Uriel said firmly. "And bring those cherubs of yours with you. I'm sure we'll have the whole story from *them*. Hadriel, we expected better of you." Together, the three of them rose through the ceiling and were soon flying over the walls of the city, the cherubs, now silent, fluttering about them like a flock of chastened sparrows. Beyond them, the clouds spread to the horizon over the undulating French landscape. Here and there, on forest and field, a light spring rain fell. Where the clouds broke, patches of blue spattered across the sky. One of the cherubs pulled on Hadriel's gown. He looked down. There on a narrow road far from the city, two horses carrying double toiled along in the mud, followed by a packhorse laden with baggage topped off by an odd wooden box and a birdcage. Riding behind the man in front was a woman enveloped in a heavy cloak and hood. Neither were enough to disguise the fact that she was dressed in a novice's gray gown.

"Look," said Hadriel. "It's Mistress Susanna." Uriel looked disgusted.

"So now you are acquainted with nuns who elope," he said.

"Oh, not really. She's all right. It's just another of her deceptions."

"Hadriel, you had something to do with this, didn't you?" said Michael, in a tone of growing suspicion.

"*Not* his job," said Uriel.

"Oh, no. Really, it was," said Hadriel. "Look, just wait a minute, will you? I promised Mistress Susanna a rainbow."

"One minute and one only," said Michael. Hadriel blew and fussed and rearranged the clouds so that the sun shone through the falling rain. A great rainbow sprang across the sky, wider than a mountain, its half arc disappearing into the clouds above. Inside it and opposite it sprang up two little rainbows, full arcs with feet that rested on the rolling countryside. From the angels' vantage point, it seemed that the riders were toiling along through a bath of color where the smallest rainbow touched the ground. Around them, dappled sunlight made the first bits of green life shine as they pushed their way up through the winter-dead meadows.

"*Hmph*. You do make a good rainbow, Hadriel," said Michael. "*That*, I'll grant you."

"But as usual, you've overdone," sniffed Uriel as they vanished away into eternity.